The Perfect Knigh

The Perfect Knight

Book 20 in the Anarchy Series
By
Griff Hosker

'Samuel, it seems does not make mistakes. He is the perfect knight'
The Warlord- Earl Marshal

The Perfect Knight

Published by Sword Books Ltd 2021

Copyright ©Griff Hosker First Edition

The author has asserted their moral right under the Copyright, Designs and Patents Act, 1988, to be identified as the author of this work.
All Rights reserved. No part of this publication may be reproduced, copied, stored in a retrieval system, or transmitted, in any form or by any means, without the prior written consent of the copyright holder, nor be otherwise circulated in any form of binding or cover other than that in which it is published and without a similar condition being imposed on the subsequent purchaser.
A CIP catalogue record for this title is available from the British Library.
Thanks to Design for Writers for the cover and logo.

The Perfect Knight

Dedicated to Teresa, my mother in law who died the day after her 100th birthday. She was a strong lady who lived life on her terms, dying in her own bed and her own home. There were five generations alive when she died and that is a testament to a great lady She would have given Matilda and Eleanor a run for their money. Sleep well, Teresa.

Contents

The Perfect Knight 1
Prologue 7
Chapter 1 10
Chapter 2 24
Chapter 3 34
Chapter 4 53
Chapter 5 65
Chapter 6 79
Chapter 7 93
Chapter 8 107
Chapter 9 125
Chapter 10 141
Chapter 11 153
Chapter 12 166
Chapter 13 182
Chapter 14 193
Chapter 15 200
Chapter 16 209
Chapter 17 226
Chapter 18 237
Chapter 19 250
Chapter 20 262
Chapter 21 273
Epilogue 286
Glossary 287
Background to the novel 289
Other books by Griff Hosker 291

The Perfect Knight

**The Anarchy Series
England 1120-1180**

English Knight
Knight of the Empress
Northern Knight
Baron of the North
Earl
King Henry's Champion
The King is Dead
Warlord of the North
Enemy at the Gate
Fallen Crown
Warlord's War
Kingmaker
Henry II
Crusader
The Welsh Marches
Irish War
Poisonous Plots
The Princes' Revolt
Earl Marshal
The Perfect Knight

The Perfect Knight

Historical characters

King Henry II- King of England
Henry the Younger- heir to the throne of England and eldest son of King Henry
Richard, Duke of Aquitaine, son of King Henry
Geoffrey, Duke of Brittany, son of King Henry
John Lackland, Lord Lieutenant of Ireland and the youngest son of King Henry
King Philip Augustus- King of France
Alys of Vexin- the half-sister of King Philip of France
Frederick Barbarossa- Emperor of the Holy Roman Empire
Guy de Lusignan- King of Jerusalem
King Tancred of Sicily
Duke Leopold of Austria
Conrad of Montferrat- Claimant to the crown of Jerusalem

   Isaac Dukas Comnenus- Ruler of Cyprus

The Perfect Knight

Prologue

When my father, the Earl of Cleveland, and I travelled back to Stockton to bury grandfather, my father enjoyed something which had always been denied his father, the Warlord, Earl Marshal of England, peace. The Scots, thanks to my grandfather, had been cowed and William the Lion now paid homage to King Henry of England. That is not to say that there were no disputes and conflict, there were. Henry the Younger and his brother Richard Duke of Aquitaine fought each other with both words and, at times, the swords of their oathsworn. There was little brotherly love between the sons of King Henry. Queen Eleanor and her daughter Joan were now held at her husband's pleasure in England and could no longer side with her sons. With Prince Geoffrey now Duke of Normandy all the conflict which took place was across the Mare Anglicum. We were not called upon. That does not mean we had an easy life, but it was relatively peaceful along the border. There were still occasional raids, not from Scottish lords or their armies, but men who wished to take our cattle and sheep. Sometimes they also took our women and so we were vigilant.

Many of the men we had formerly led to battle now gave up the sword. Most had fought for as long as they did out of loyalty to my grandfather. Others seemed just to fade away. Masood, my father's scout whom he had brought from the Holy Land was one who did not seem to enjoy peace, or perhaps our cold climate finally took him. I know not the reason, but he died a bare two years after we buried the Warlord. It was a peaceful death in his sleep, but my father and I mourned him for he had been as faithful a warrior as

The Perfect Knight

any. When Aelric and Roger of Bath gave up their bow and swords my father chose not to go to war any longer. He would still ride to deal with incursions, but he would not travel to serve the king any longer. That would now be my inherited responsibility. I did not mind for it was my duty and my father had done enough for England and the Plantagenets.

    William was still my squire but soon he would have his spurs. My father had decided that when he hung up his own sword. He knew that the strength of the valley lay in its knights and the men they led and he wished us to have a good number of knights. I had already picked out my next one, Jack, son of John of Oxbridge was just twelve, but he had shown an interest in all things martial. He was my page and helped William. It was in the nature of things that nothing stayed the same for long. Thomas, my son, was desperate to be my squire and when William was knighted then I would take him on and he could serve as a page. My wife and I had tried for another child, but we had as yet failed. It was the only blight on an otherwise perfect world. We lived, happily, in our valley and were immune from the plotting and deceit in the rest of the kingdom.

The Perfect Knight

Chapter 1

Stockton 1180

I am Sir Samuel of Stockton, the grandson of the Earl Marshal who saved England and the son of Sir William of Stockton, the Earl of Cleveland. My father did not outlive my mother for long. He was not yet sixty, but I think that war had taken its toll on him and when mother died of the wasting disease the heart seemed to go from him and he wasted away before my eyes. My father's old housekeeper, Alice, blamed the Scots for his death. I suppose, in a way she was right. Two years earlier we had chased cattle thieves north and my father had fallen from his horse. He had broken ribs and had been unconscious for two days. It may have been the cause although the doctors pronounced him well. Had I been in Stockton then it would have been my eyes that saw the deterioration, but I only learned of the rapid decline when I returned from the tournament I had attended in York. I only went because the other knights of the valley were taking part and my father insisted. Hindsight is a wonderful thing, and it was only when he began to become ill that I really regretted my decision. He was still alive when the raiders next came but, as fate would have it, the knights from my valley were at another tournament in York.

The messenger had come from Fissebourne not long after dawn to tell us of Scottish raiders who had attacked some farms close to the small manor. John of Fissebourne had been the lord of the manor but he had taken the cross and gone to Jerusalem. There was a reeve and but a handful of men to protect the farmers. They had been slain. Of course, my father, despite my mother's worsening condition, was ready to ride after the raiders. I dissuaded him and as we had recently knighted William, my former squire, I said that I would lead the men of the valley. So it was that I did not see him shrink from within. I told him what I intended and he nodded, dully. The life was oozing from him, not as on a battlefield, but drop by drop and day by day. It was a sight I did not enjoy. My mother was already at death's door and I was willing God to take her for the pain she endured each day as whatever worm it was, ate at her had taken the life from her already. My father sat by her bed and held her hand. It was a sad sight to see. I could do nothing. The doctor had given up on my mother and almost given up hope for my father. He merely nodded when I told him what I was about.

Richard of Hartburn, Roger of Norton, and Ralph of Thornaby would have come, of course, but they were in York. I felt that this was something I needed to lead and sending to fetch them would have taken time and time was something we did not have. A few raiders would not need a large force of men to teach them a lesson. The raiders who headed south were, in the main, men taking a chance. Most were little better than brigands and bandits. Perhaps they had known that the knights of the valley were away and took a chance. They would be taught that even one knight, so long as he had the Warlord's blood in his veins was someone to be feared. I had learned much when I had been forced to command at the Tower of London. My grandfather had been laid low and I had to lead the men to defend the king's home, but this was different. Hitherto, when we had chased raiders and robbers, I had followed my father. The other knights would have offered me advice, kindly meant, but I needed to be my own man. My grandfather had thought well of me and told me that one day I would be Earl of Cleveland. He had even told me I was a perfect knight. I was not but the accolade from the Warlord meant more than any approbation from the king!

I acted instantly and that was mainly because I had to. With only the now knighted Sir William in the castle and not wishing to denude the castle of every defender I took those

The Perfect Knight

who were already mounted and ready for the morning patrols. I would leave quickly without gathering supplies. Speed was of the essence. I acceded to Thomas' request to accompany us and Jack son of John, my squire, was also keen to go. I told Thomas that he would have to earn his place. He was a big boy for his age and could ride a full-sized horse. He would act as my horse holder. That relieved Jack of a major duty. I had ten men at arms and ten mounted archers who had been designated as the daily patrol. There were more archers, but they were afoot, and speed was what we needed. William and his squire, Geoffrey, son of Roger of Bath, had yet to gather retainers and so it was a small band we led north and west as we sought the trail of the Scottish raiders. My two captains were Aelric's son, Richard and Gerard of Chester who had come to us from the Countess of Chester, Maud. She had been a good friend of the Warlord and my father had accepted the man at arms immediately. That there was both a story and a secret behind Gerard's move was clear, why else would he leave the service of such a great lady, but the close-mouthed Gerard did not say what it was, and I never discovered it. We trusted the Countess and Gerard had proved such an asset that we had promoted him within a month of his arrival.

    Only we two knights were mailed. Our men at arms wore padded gambesons and carried the shorter kite shield which had replaced the long one used by the Warlord when he had returned from the east. We had long spears which were almost as long as a lance while our helmets were the ones with a nasal but we each had a good metal coif which protected our jaws and cheeks. More often than not we rode with just an arming cap covered by our coif. The archers wore a leather brigandine, but it was covered in a short surcoat with the same livery as the shields and surcoats of my men at arms. Their hose was a contrasting colour. It was my sister, Ruth, who had suggested the design. The gryphon upon shield, surcoat and banner was a weapon that inspired fear in our enemies. The sight of it often turned defeat into victory, or that had been the case when the Warlord led us. Their strength lay in their war bows and sheaths of arrows.

Each archer carried two on his horse. One held the bodkins which were used against armour but on this expedition, they would use their war arrows. The Scots would not be wearing mail. Each archer had a short sword as well as an axe for when we camped, they would make a palisade to keep us safe. I doubted we would need such a camp. We would be riding in our land and farmers offered us rooms if they had them or barns if they did not. I was not a precious knight who needed cosseting. Only Sir William and I rode coursers, the warhorses especially bred to fight. The men we led rode hackneys or palfreys. They were serviceable animals and would be more than adequate against the Scots.

Eleanor fussed and fretted as she prepared Thomas for his first taste of war. It would not be a real war but each time a man drew a weapon he risked death. We had still to have another child and that made the parting worse. Thomas was our only one and she knew, better than any, how dangerous was such a ride into the unknown.

"I will bring him back. You take care of yourself. We shall not be long."

She nodded, "And I have your father to watch. His spirits are low. Your sister and I will try to make up for your absence."

"The returned animals and the defeated bandits will make him more cheerful."

The rider who had brought the news, Peter, was refreshed enough to lead us back straightaway. It had taken him less than an hour and a half to bring the news. A speedy ride might catch the Scots close to home. It was a short eleven-mile ride to Fissebourne, and we rode hard, reaching it in under two hours. It was not long after noon when we reached the tiny manor.

Edward of Fissebourne was the reeve and when we arrived, he was supervising the repair to the damage done by the raiders. They had fired buildings and while the fires had been doused work had to start sooner rather than later to keep out the worst of the northern weather. I turned to Richard, "Have the scouts find which way they went. The rest, water your mounts." My men obeyed.

Edward had his head bound as well as his hand. He bowed, "My lord, they struck before dawn when we were all abed. Had they arrived during the day they would not have found it so easy." He took a cloth and dabbed away some blood that trickled from his head wound. "It was a large warband and they attacked all the farms in the manor at the same time." He pointed to the barn, "We were held there while they gathered the animals. By the time dawn came all the warband was gathered with their captured animals. It was only when they left that I was able to send Peter to you."

I had dismounted and Thomas was holding the reins of my horse, Storm Bringer. "They left one horse?"

He stopped dabbing the blood and said, "Aye, now how did they miss that?" It made no sense to either of us. A horse was valuable, especially to bandits and leaving one made both of us suspicious.

I had already worked out that if they left one horse then it was deliberate, and we were intended to follow. I put my arm around the reeve, "Were any men lost?"

He shook his head, "We had wounds, of course, for we resisted but we had no time to organise a defence."

"Then all is well for we can recover animals. Dead men are harder to replace, especially good men like you."

"There is neither lord nor garrison and we do our best but...."

"I will speak to my father and we will send men to man the tower." The defence for the manor was not a castle, King Henry had been reluctant to allow a new castle to be built. During the civil war between his mother and Stephen many lords had thrown up castles and they had proved to be a thorn in the side of the Warlord and the King. The tower was there as a simple refuge in times of invasion. Raids could only be prevented by vigilance. That vigilance should have come from the Palatinate of Durham through which land the Scots had to have come. Was there collusion?

Richard son of Aelric, my captain of archers, rode in, "My lord, they have headed east by north towards Crook."

As I mounted, I nodded for it made sense. The land north of the Wear was farmed but there were no castles. Durham

The Perfect Knight

lay to the east and it was the Bishop who should have ensured that no raiders came. As we followed Richard I wondered if we would catch them. They had more than a four hour lead, but they were driving cattle and sheep. They would have known there might be pursuit, the Valley of the Tees had been a graveyard for many a Scot since the time of the Warlord. I had to assume that they had planned for that. To the south of us lay the castle of the Bishop of Durham at Auckland and to the north lay his fortress of Durham. They had used the narrow corridor between the two.

As I rode, I spoke my thoughts to William knowing that our squires and my page were listening. It was how I had learned. "Wolsingham is too large a place for them to use as is Stanhope to the west. They will head further north."

William nodded, "It is wild and empty, wooded land there."

My former squire was right, "And by the time we reach it then it could well be night."

Thomas was every inquisitive and still asked the constant questions he had when he had been but five, "Then we will have lost them?"

I laughed, "They might think so, but night gives us a chance to end this quickly. They will light fires and we have noses. The smell will reach us even if they mask the light. We have ears. Cows low and cannot be silenced. Our horses also have a keen sense of smell and if they detect cows then they will let us know. No, Thomas, we have a better chance of finding them, but we will have ridden a hard thirty or more miles. When we near the high ground, if we are still on their trail, we shall walk our mounts."

There was silence for a while, and I looked sideways at Sir William who grinned back at me. He knew Thomas well and there would be another question. "But how do we know that they have taken this road? They could be anywhere."

Jack son of John was a bright youth and had inherited many of his father's traits, "Look at the ground, Tom. What do you see?"

"Why the road of course!"

"And upon it?"

The Perfect Knight

Realisation dawned when he saw the pellets left by the sheep and the larger patches of cow dung. "Their spoor!"

I patted Thomas on the shoulder, "This is not the first time we have done this. Had the Scots used the fields then we would have followed the trail they left there but it is a slower way for them to travel. This way they drive the livestock up the road and the walls and hedges keep the animals penned as they walk. That is why we need to be wary for they will expect pursuit and unless they are complete fools then they will plan for it. We can expect an ambush."

I turned to Sir William, "And that is what I cannot understand, William. Why risk the wrath of my father and our knights? It is more than thirty miles to the Tyne and almost another thirty to the Tweed." I rubbed the back of my neck. Something did not feel right about this. We should have been safe in the valley, protected as we were by the knights and men of the Palatinate but a Scottish warband had managed to penetrate, seemingly without being seen, to raid in the undefended land around Fissebourne. They had left a horse for us to be summoned. Had they known that there were just three knights left in the valley and one of them an invalid? I would have to use all the experience I had gained following my grandfather or this could end in defeat for the Warlord's gryphon banner! I looked down at Thomas. More to the point I was risking the last heir of Sir Alfred of Cleveland!

The light was fading as we followed the trail of animal dung as it left the road to take a trail up into the trees and rocks to the northwest of Stanhope. They had not passed through the settlement, but they had been seen. A farmer told us that there had been at least fifty men with the flocks and herds they had gathered. I could have used my father's authority to command the men of Stanhope to follow us and double our numbers but that was not my way. Instead, I commanded them to keep a night watch in case the Scots tried to evade us that way.

I raised my hand to lead us from the cobbled yard of the farm when Gerard of Chester turned in his saddle, "My lord, the hackneys and palfreys we ride are almost done in. If we continue to ride, then many will be broken. We should rest."

Sir William and my other men looked to me. Was this a challenge to my authority from the dour Cheshire man? I did not think so and he was right. Our two coursers were better kept but we dared not lose horses here. I turned to the farmer, "You know this land better than we. Where do you think that the Scots will rest for rest they must?" I saw the fear in his eyes. His farm was to the north of Stanhope and the Scots were always more of a threat to him than to Stockton. "Come, for no matter what you tell us they will know that we stopped here. If you tell us, then we have a chance of ridding the Palatinate of these barbarians."

He nodded and pointed, "There is a burn which flows into Stanhope Burn. We call it Lodvir's Burn. The trail follows the east side of the water and about three miles from here it flattens out and there is a ridge of stones across it which makes for a wider patch of water. They can water their animals there and it is flat enough to camp. It also overlooks the trail which leads from here."

I put my hand on his shoulder, "Thank you. We shall leave my horses here with you in your yard." He nodded, "And my son, Thomas."

As I had expected Thomas reacted, "No, father! I shall come with you! I am your page!"

I saw my men smile at his defiance, but I shook my head, "This farmer may know his livestock but you, Thomas, know coursers. Sir William and I need our horses to be looked after." I turned back to the farmer, "Can you give my son a bed for the night?"

"My wife and I would be honoured, my lord."

"Hopefully, Thomas, we shall be back some time tomorrow. If we fail tonight and they escape, then we shall need our horses. Another good reason is that night work is the time for knives and you are not ready for that, are you?" I looked my son in the eyes and even though he was young he knew the truth in my words. He nodded. I turned to my men as I unfastened my cowled cloak. "We will not need spears

The Perfect Knight

nor cloaks. Take off your surcoats for we need to be invisible. Eat and drink for we have work to do this night."

I dismounted and handed my cloak to Thomas. I also took off my helmet. I would rely upon my coif and arming cap to protect my head. I had my sword and a long dagger as well as my flat-topped kite shield. I used the long strap to hang my shield over my back. Jack handed me a small lump of salted pork and an ale skin. I was not hungry, but I knew that I should eat something, and, after eating the meat, I washed the salty taste from my mouth with the ale. Without being summoned Richard son of Aelric and Gerard of Chester joined Sir William and me. "Richard, you and your archers shall be the scouts. We have three miles to travel over rough ground and it will be dark."

He nodded, "Aye, my lord, but that suits my men. We have no mail to jangle." My captain of archers had been named after the greatest archer, Sir Dick who had served my grandfather. He was too humble to accept the diminutive as he did not think he was worthy enough.

It was a warning for Sir William and me. The men led by Gerard also had metal but not as much as the two of us. I nodded. "When you find the Scots then you wait for us."

Gerard asked, "You have a plan, my lord?"

"The Scots have deliberately led us here and left enough clues for us to follow. What they cannot know is how close we are. We rode our horses hard, as you pointed out to me. They may well expect us to be further south." I looked at Gerard, "When you fought the Welsh, would you have fought afoot?"

He smiled, "We might but not the knights. You are right, Sir Samuel, the Scots will expect us to come at them on horseback and will have defences prepared. They will think to see us in daylight." He nodded at the farmer who was helping Thomas to move the horses into his barn, "Yon farmer said that this place was well known, and the Scots would have chosen it well. They will be vigilant this night but the longer it goes without the sound of horses the more comfortable will they become. At dawn, they will make it a fortress."

The Perfect Knight

I nodded, "That is my reasoning too. I want, when we reach their camp, their sentries eliminating. That is your task, Richard."

"Aye, lord."

"I know night does not suit archers, but I want you and your archers to get around the north side of their camp. Your task is to attack from that side when we attack from the south and east. You will stop them bolting and cut off any chance they have of a retreat back home."

He nodded and then asked, "How do you know they will be to the east of the water?"

"The farmer said that the trail went along the east side of the stream. They will have defences prepared on both sides but, until dawn, they will not be manned. They too will be tired and why man defences which are not needed?" Darkness had almost fallen and soon we would have to follow the trail in the darkness. "Let us leave now. The three miles might take two hours. That will be time enough for them to eat and then believe that we are not coming until the morrow."

Richard and his archers had now taken their bows from their cases and, slinging them over their backs they headed off. Without our surcoats, we were just dark shadows. The only danger came from the mail Sir William and I wore. If the moon came out it might mark us. I made sure we were at the back. It was not cowardice but common sense. This was only the second time I had led my men to war and was the first time we had gone afoot. It was a learning experience for us all. We had to trust that Richard had a good man at the fore and that each of us would not go too fast and stumble into the man ahead. It was a shapeless and shadowy world through which we tramped, and we had to study the ground before placing our feet. As we were also climbing up the burn valley it sapped the strength from our legs. My father would not have managed this walk even before his fall. After his return from France and the death of my grandfather, he had not warred as much, and the inactivity had taken its toll. It was why the other knights of the valley were at tournaments whenever they could. It was a way to hone

The Perfect Knight

skills. Whichever archer led kept stopping and I guessed it was to listen for the Scots. At one such stop, I heard the lowing of cattle and sniffed woodsmoke. We were getting closer.

The smell of the woodsmoke and cooking mutton was overpowering when I was finally stopped by the man at arms, Edgar, before me. There was a hum of conversation from our left but it was too far away for us to hear words. I moved up the trail followed by Sir William and our squires. My men had their swords drawn and their shields were pulled around. When I reached the archers, they had all strung their bows and slung them over their backs. Their arrow cases lay in an orderly pile to the side. Richard had drawn his dagger, as had the rest of his archers and I nodded to send them on their way. The plans had been made at the farm outside Stanhope and there was no need to repeat any of them. I swung my shield around and drew my sword. I pointed to the right and Gerard of Chester led off four men. Sir William led off his four men to the left. That left me with two men: Martyn and Henry as well as my squire. I headed through the woods. We were following the path taken by my archers. I had heard nothing but when I spied the body with the slit throat, I knew that my archers had done their work. I had to assume that all the guards were on the trail side and that, as there had been no noise that they remained undetected. They would now be making their way to the north to cut off the chance of escape.

I could now hear individual words but as some of the men spoke Gaelic, I did not know their meaning. The fires they had lit illuminated the camp and as I could not see animals then I had to assume they were penned close to the water. I could see some of the Scots beneath blankets and it was logical to suppose that they had finished their meal. It was as a Scot shouted, "Relief guards!" That I knew there would be armed men coming out to replace the sentries we had killed. That was not part of my planning and it decreased the chances of success. My grandfather had taught me to deal with any adversity and I now did so. I did not falter but kept walking. The Scot who advanced towards me had his head

The Perfect Knight

down, watching his footing, and the first he knew of danger was when my sword was rammed up into his chest and out of his back. He sighed as he slid from my blade to the ground. Not all of my men were as lucky as I had been and when I had advanced to within five paces of the edge of the camp, I heard a shout from my right as our attack was discovered. The effect was amazing. Every Scot jumped to his feet and, drawing a weapon, they all advanced towards the sound of the Scotsman who had died noisily. It meant Sir William and his men were able to race into the camp, as were my men and me, unseen. The Scots might have been armed but they did not know whence came their enemies and ten of the Scots fell to either blades or arrows before the rest realised where we were. An attack in the night, if you are a defender, is a frightening thing for you know not the number of your enemies whereas an attacker normally does. The ten bodies and their death cries made the others turn to allow Gerard and his men to slay three men and for the arrows of Richard and his archers to strike another three. If their plan had been to ambush us the next day, it had gone dreadfully awry.

Their leader shouted, "Kill the bastards!" and they turned to face us.

We were not facing cowards, but they were, compared with us, lightly armed and armoured. The archers we had brought were able to send arrows from the safety of the trees towards targets well-lit by fires. At a range of fewer than thirty paces, it was harder to miss than to hit. I think some of them realised that and threw themselves at us so that they could avoid the deadly arrows. Certainly, the leader, who held a two-handed sword, chose to race at me screaming unintelligible curses in Gaelic. He swung his sword around his head, and it would have been easy to be mesmerized by it. The secret of fighting such a weapon was to deal with it for what it was, a deadly blade that could be avoided if a man kept his head. If he did not then he would lose it! His speed towards me worked in my favour for it meant I had the chance to close with him as he swung the sword around to hack me in two and the closer I was to him then the less

The Perfect Knight

force he would have when he struck. My speed was such that I was able to punch with my shield at his head and whilst the edge of his sword closest to the hilt hit the edge of my shield it did little harm. There was little edge to the weapon there. My sword thrust was not the best I had ever made and that was because I was keen to close with him. Even so, I saw blood on the blade where it had torn through his leather brigandine and the padding which lay beneath. Grandfather had impressed upon me the need for a keenly sharpened weapon.

The man was a fighter and as we were the same height, he tried to drive his knee between my legs to force me back. I moved my shield around and he kneed the boss in the centre. It hurt him! I brought the hilt of my sword up for we were too close to each other for a real swing with either weapon. The hilt tore a jagged line across his face and nose. It would make his eyes water.

"Norman bastard!"

Grandfather had taught me that insults were a waste of time and energy. I pulled back my left arm and punched the boss into his already damaged nose and was rewarded this time when he reeled. He was too much of a fighter to risk allowing the combat to continue. I had wanted him as a prisoner but that was not to be and so I swung my sword at his throat. The tip of my blade caught on bone and when the blood spurted and his eyes went dead, then I knew that we had won. His fall was the signal for the Scots to turn and flee. They had seen three of their exits closed off and they took the only one left to them: the burn and the water. The cattle and sheep made alarming noises as the Scots took to their heels. Richard and my archers hit some as they fled but none fell. We had defeated the Scots and recovered the livestock and, I daresay, some of the treasure that had been taken but I felt cheated. I had wanted to know why they had risked coming so far south and whose idea it was to lure us into a trap. Had we not been so speedy on the ride north then it might have worked.

"Pile the bodies together after you have taken their weapons and any treasure. The treasure will belong to the people of Fissebourne. I would have all of it returned to them. When the bodies are collected pile wood upon them and burn them."

It was not a pleasant night. The smell of burning hair and flesh is never acceptable but I did not wish the folk of Stanhope to have a plague of vermin feasting on the dead!

Chapter 2

Poor Thomas was beside himself as it took until noon to drive the animals down the track and I could see from his face that he feared we had found trouble. We were better warriors than farmers. The farmer who had watched our horses had a fallow field for the animals. He was not being altruistic; they would fertilise it for him free of charge and until the animals were collected, he would have free milk.

"Richard, take your men to Fissebourne and escort the reeve and some of his people back here to fetch their animals and treasure. Sir William, you and Gerard wait here. I will take Jack and Thomas to Durham. I need to inform the Bishop of what has happened in his lands."

"Will you be safe, Sir Samuel?"

I laughed, "If not, Gerard, then it is time I gave up being a knight and joined a monastery. I will be fine. Come, Thomas, I am sure Jack is desperate to tell you of the fight!"

I knew he was for Jack had slain his first man. While I had been fighting the leader of the brigands, he had watched my back and when a Scot had tried to ram me in the side with his spear, Jack had first hacked the shaft in two and then had the wit to swing his sword at the chest of the Scot. The warrior died but it took him two hours to do so. I only listened with half an ear for my mind was filled with both questions and speculation. In his dying the man had rambled but something he had said had piqued my curiosity. He had cursed the Frenchman. As none of my men was remotely French either in dress or language, I had to wonder who he meant.

The Perfect Knight

We headed south and east to the great fortress that was Durham riding through increasingly fertile, tilled land. The Palatinate was rich and the Bishop, Hugh de Puiset was a most powerful man. Some said second only to the king. He had been the Prince Bishop of Durham for a long time. He was older than my father. For some reason, my father had never liked him and was dismissive of him. I could never fathom the reason and when I asked my father, I received a stony silence. Even more telling was that my grandfather had little time for the man and that surprised me. I had no views on the bishop for I had not had any dealings with him. I knew that I had to report the raid, but did I have the authority to question Bishop de Puiset? I doubted that and yet I needed to know how the Scots had penetrated so far south without being either seen or stopped.

Since King Henry had made his eldest son Henry a king in waiting, there had been tensions and plots aplenty in the kingdom. King Henry the Elder, as some now termed him, had tried to assuage all his sons but it had just fuelled the disagreements between them. Richard thought that Aquitaine was not enough for his ambition while Geoffrey felt being the Duke of Brittany meant he would be treated with more honour. John just waited and plotted. The one who should have been the most content, King Henry the Younger, was far from it and wished his younger brothers to swear fealty to him. The result was that many young knights had sided with one or the other brothers and that normally placed them against the king. My father had told me that King Henry the Elder was a clever man and the setting of brother against brother might be his plan to ensure that they did not combine again and try to usurp him. If that was true, then I was certain that he had failed. He had set the kingdom on the road to civil war and my grandfather had been adamant that another anarchy should be avoided at all costs. I always kept my grandfather's words and philosophy with me. I would support the rightful king against all enemies, domestic and foreign.

It was late afternoon when we crossed the river at the stone gatehouse over the Wear. Our livery and the gonfanon

The Perfect Knight

carried proudly by Thomas, gained us a rapid admission to the town, and we wound our way up to the second gatehouse at the castle and the mighty cathedral where lay the bones of St Oswald. We were greeted by the constable, Guy de Mornay. I had met him before and knew that he was a solid and dependable knight. Hugh de Puiset might be a churchman, but it was Guy de Mornay who ensured that Durham was a bastion against attack.

"This is an unexpected visit, my lord."

I detected the criticism in his voice and understood it for he would have to find rooms for us, "Aye, Sir Guy, it is the Scots; they have raided once more."

I needed to say no more, and his eyes told me that he had not been aware of an incursion. That was good. The question was had others, not in the castle colluded? There were knights of the palatinate who wished harm upon our family. The Warlord had fought for Empress Matilda and her son for many years. You do not do that without ruffling feathers and making enemies.

"Then I will find your chambers and arrange for a meeting with the Bishop. I fear it may not be until the morning. He is closeted with a knight who arrived this morning having landed at the port of Herterpol. Sir Walter Risingham is an important knight."

I do not think that Sir Guy meant the insult and my mind was elsewhere. If Sir Walter had landed by ship, then he had come from the lands of the Empire or France. King Henry the Younger held court there where he filled his time with tourneys and plotting. I smiled and said, "No matter, Sir Guy. We had a long ride today and I will need a night of sleep to help me gather my thoughts."

That Sir Guy was intrigued was clear. There was no sign of battle upon us for Jack and I had not worn our surcoats during the fight and our helmets were undamaged. He might satisfy his curiosity by examining our shields that hung from our saddles. I would keep my words for the Bishop. I wanted to see his reaction when I told him.

We were given a chamber in one of the towers and water and drying cloths, as well as perfumed soap, were provided.

Jack and Thomas would have to earn their bed and food by serving me at the table. As we washed, I gave them their instructions, "Not a word about the raid. You will be questioned by other squires and pages. Feign dumbness. Better to let them think you are slow-witted. I know you are not. Keep your ears open but do not let others know when you garner information which would be useful to us."

Thomas was confused, "Are we not amongst friends here, father?"

I shook my head, "When we leave our valley, town and castle then we view everyone we meet with suspicion. Your great grandfather taught me that. The knights who greet you with a smile and an open palm may well have a dagger in their other hand. Better to be cautious until you have fought alongside a man. I know this is much to ask of you. I should have had Sir William spend longer explaining your duties, but we have to deal with the situation as we find it. Can you do this?"

They both stiffened their backs and nodded. Thomas said, "You can trust me, father, for the blood of the Warlord courses through my veins."

"Good and keeping your eyes and ears open means as soon as we leave this room. Who knows when the knowledge of the corridors and chambers of Durham may come in handy?"

Sir Guy sent his page to fetch us and we headed for the Great Hall which had been laid out with a huge table and the sconces were filled with burning brands. There would be more than twenty of us dining. The Bishop, his dean, and his most elevated guests, along with Sir Guy, were in the centre. I was relegated to the end of the table where I sat with Sir Hugh Manners of Etal. I did not mind for his conversation was both pleasant and revealing. He lived close to the border not far from the fortress on the Tweed, Norham. He told me of the constant pinpricks of raids across the Tweed and was here to plead with the Bishop to be more aggressive towards what should have been a beaten foe. It confirmed to me that Bishop Puiset was being, at best, complacent and at worst, possibly treacherous. I know my thoughts were coloured by

The Perfect Knight

the opinions of my father and grandfather, but I trusted their judgements.

What I noticed, as I surreptitiously glanced to the head of the table, was that the Bishop and Sir Walter were talking, at least some of the time, about me for I saw their looks and gestures. Looking away when I saw them doing so was a sure sign that they did not wish me to know this. That was interesting and intriguing; it begged the question what was it about me they were discussing? Sir Hugh kept me entertained for his knowledge of the northern borders and the Scots who lived there was detailed. He even knew or thought he knew, the identity of the Scot who had led the raiders. "It sounds like Colin of Redesdale. His family lost lands in the treaty we made with King William. He was a bitter man and you have rid the land of an enemy of England."

I nodded towards the head of the table, "And Sir Walter, what do you know of him?"

Sir Hugh frowned, "He is a Norman, that is to say, his home is in Normandy or France, he has two. Even though I was here first as soon as he arrived, I was moved from my room and told that I would have to wait until the Bishop had more time." He gave a rueful shake of his head, "The knight is patently more important than my castle and my complaint. I daresay that your arrival will extend the time I have to wait."

"I will ask the Bishop to speak to you first."

"That is generous but, if truth be told, your meeting is the most urgent. I agree with you that the presence of the Scots so close to the Tees Valley is a greater cause for concern than the pinpricks we feel in the valley of the Tweed." He held up his goblet for his squire to refill, "I will continue to enjoy the generosity of our host."

The importance of Sir Walter became clear when he and Hugh de Puiset rose to leave the Great Hall together. It was a signal that the meal was ended, and servants appeared to clear the table. The pages and the squires could now descend upon the food we had left. I hoped that both Jack and Thomas had heeded my words and were listening more than speaking. I would be particularly interested in what the

The Perfect Knight

squire of Sir Walter had to say. The churchmen left and it was just a handful of knights who remained finishing off the last of the wine. There was a good cellar at Durham and the wine was not to be wasted. I listened to the other knights of the Palatinate who spoke, albeit guardedly, about the bishop and his reign. All of them were dependent upon his largesse. He could increase taxes on a whim and was answerable only to the king. As the king spent more time in Chinon and France than England then it was unlikely that any complaint would be made but they were unhappy about his policies which they saw as weak. Our victory over King William had given both the Bishop and England great power but it was not being exercised. Bishop Puiset was the representative of England in this part of the world. Why was he vacillating?

Jack and Thomas followed me when I drained my goblet and headed up the stairs to my tower chamber. While Jack helped me to undress, I said, "And?"

"My lord, it is harder to keep silent than to train with Gerard of Chester. It would have been all too easy to blurt out something we should not,"

I turned and looked at him, "You did not?"

"No, lord, we heeded your commands." He grinned, "Even Tom here!"

I smiled and ruffled his hair, "Well done!"

"Raymond, Sir Walter's squire, is an arrogant and unpleasant mannered youth. He thought himself superior to us all and when we went to fetch the food, he took no notice of the order and pushed ahead. The cooks and the steward seemed to have been told of the importance of his lord for they said nothing."

Thomas said, "Aye, the other squires and pages wondered at that, father, for they thought the son of the Earl of Cleveland would be accorded more honour."

I laughed, "Do not worry about that. My grandfather never did. Warriors know who deserves honour and I care not where I sit. Was there more?"

Jack nodded, "Sir Walter leaves on the morrow."

"Back to France?"

"Not directly. First, he heads south."

The Perfect Knight

Whilst south could mean Herterpol and a boat back to France it could equally mean the valley of the Tees. One knight, his squire and servants did not pose a problem but if he was there to foster trouble then it did. I spent a restless night as my mind wrestled with the myriad of possibilities. It did not make for a clear mind when I rose the next day.

The breakfast was not a seated affair. Food was laid out in the Great Hall and there was both ale and wine. Men just had their squires fill a platter and they ate. The table would be cleared after a short time so that the business of the castle could be managed from the hall. I wondered if I would be seen by the bishop in public or private. I did not see Sir Walter and as soon as my platter was brought, I sent Jack and Thomas to the stables, ostensibly to check on our horses but, in reality, to see if the Norman knight had gone. When they returned I learned that he had.

I was summoned by a cleric to the office of the Bishop of Durham. Leaving Jack and Thomas to breakfast I went to a sumptuously decorated and comfortable office. Hugh de Puiset looked after himself well; he was like the monarch of a small kingdom. After kissing the ring, the bishop's seal of office, I sat. The smile of the prelate was an empty and hollow one. I had been taught by my father and grandfather how to tell the difference between a real and false smile. I looked into the cold eyes. They were like those of a crocodile. I had seen one once, at the docks in Acre where it was being transported to Constantinopolis. I had been terrified by the armoured animal!

"Sir Samuel, it is good to see you. I hope your father is recovered from the injuries he received."

"Thank you for your concern, Bishop Puiset. He is no longer young and such injuries take longer than they once did."

"I will have prayers said for him." He paused to allow me to give the reason for my visit. The courtesies were brief!

"Fissebourne was raided by the Scots, Your Grace. Although none were killed animals were taken and buildings destroyed."

The Perfect Knight

At first, he did not look surprised and when he realised his mistake he overcompensated with an exaggerated widening of the eyes and an open mouth. It told me that he knew of the raid already and that suggested collusion. "That is a shame. I will take action immediately and send a strongly worded letter to King William! I will not have the men of the Palatinate suffer such privations. The raiders will be held to account."

He might have known of the raid but thanks to the silence of Jack and Thomas he knew not the outcome. It was my turn to give the crocodile smile, "They have already been brought to swift and sudden justice and most of their bones now lie burned to the northwest of Stanhope. The animals were recovered as well as the treasure and they will already be returned to their rightful owners."

His mask slipped and the smile disappeared briefly before returning with a gushing, "Well done, Sir Samuel. The Valley of the Tees is in safe hands. I am pleased. Was that all?"

He was trying to dismiss me, but I would not have it, "Not quite, Your Grace, for the raiders managed to penetrate deep into England. How did they do that? Are the knights and castles along the border not doing what they should? Your palace at Auckland was close to their path and yet they were not hindered." I added to make it clear why they should have been spotted. "It was a large warband."

His face hardened, "Do not presume to tell me how to do my job, sir knight. Perhaps the Warlord and your father have made enemies in Scotland; have you thought of that?"

He had shown his colours and I had won. I now knew that the Bishop of Durham was complicit in the raid. I stood, "Aye, and I am proud of that fact. It is a pity that the Palatinate is not as hated in Scotland as we are. If it were then English farms would be safer."

"Get out! Ingrate! With your foreign blood, it is no wonder that you are as you are. You are a barbarian!"

I bowed to hide the anger on my face, "Of course, Bishop de Puiset." I now knew why my father had hated the man. He must have spoken disparagingly of my mother, a Jewess.

The Perfect Knight

He had not known that she was dying but it would have made little difference to him. He was now my enemy and I would watch Durham closely from now on.

As we headed south my only regret was that Sir Hugh might receive less sympathy from an irate cleric. I waited until we were on the road to Stockton before I spoke to my squire and page. Riding with my grandfather had taught me that a good knight explained all he could to the next generation of warriors. One day Jack and Thomas would be knights. Thomas would be Earl of Cleveland and the schooling for such positions could never begin too early. I told them what I had learned and how I had done so.

Jack was thoughtful but Thomas blurted out, "Then we should tell the King!"

"And we will but not by letter. We will either have to travel to Normandy or wait until he returns to England. A letter could be intercepted. The Bishop might suspect that I know he colluded with the Scots, but he cannot know and that helps us. My greater worry is Sir Walter. I would know where he has gone. Jack, how many men did he have with him?"

"His squire boasted that they had four servants and that they were all well-armed. They had two spare sumpters with them and they carried their mail and weapons."

I turned, "The servants had mail?"

"Two of them did. I learned that when we visited the stables. The ostler had not been given a coin for watching the horses and he was scathing about the tight-fisted nature of Normans!"

The information helped but I would need to speak to my father first before I did anything! Six men would be easier to find than four but they could be anywhere. If they had taken ship for the east then I would sleep easier but if they had crossed our river or, worse, headed west then I would worry. King Henry the Younger wanted to be the sole ruler of England, Normandy and Aquitaine. To gain those titles he might even ally with the devil, Scotland, and with a Bishop of Durham who was willing to open England's back gate then we were in great danger. The Warlord was dead and his son, unwell. I suddenly felt the weight of my position. It might be down to me and I knew not if I was ready.

Chapter 3

I had been away but three days and yet I noticed a difference in my father and my mother. He looked pained although the joy on his face when he saw his son and grandson return masked the pain I could see in his eyes. "It is good that you are home, my son, for your mother may not see out the day."

Thomas gripped my arm and we looked down at my mother who looked as still as an effigy on a gravestone.

"Tell me your news and then say goodbye to your mother and grandmother."

The news seemed unimportant now but as I told him what I had learned his face darkened. "Puiset is not a good bishop. I thought it was just your mother and me who were the subject of his enmity. It seems his hatred runs deeper."

"What is it about you and mother that he hated?"

He gave me a sad look, "Can you not work it out? Your mother was a Jewess. You and your sister have Jewish blood in you. I should have realised. Beware the bishop, Samuel." I nodded, "Let us put our minds to this Norman knight. You say he was Norman, but his name suggests a small manor on the River Rede north of here. It was a Roman fort and there was a wooden motte and bailey castle there. As I recall the lord of the manor sided with King Stephen and when the Empress and her son were restored, they lost their land."

"I have never heard of the manor."

"Like many, it disappeared when the war ended. It would explain his presence. The king should know of this."

"He is in France."

My father winced and then shifted in his chair to hide the fact, "Aye, he is." Shaking his head he said, "Curse my infirmity. Time was I would have mounted my horse and led men to find this knight."

I smiled, "You have done all that you needed and besides, I have seen this knight. I will seek him."

My father might have been injured and could no longer go to war, but he had a sharp mind. "As I remember it Risingham is not far from the Redesdale Valley. The Scot you slew and the knight may be related. At the very least there is a connection there."

I shook my head, "Now I see the cords of this web of deceit. It was a trap intended to take Sir William and me, along with our men. Had we not been so keen to start then it might have succeeded."

"And where will you start your search?"

"That is easy and a short ride. I will ride to Herterpol and see if he took ship there. If he has departed, then the problem has gone away." I was thinking even as I spoke, "If there is no sign of him leaving then I will look further west."

"Not here?"

"I sent Jack to the ferry. Even if the knight managed to sneak his men through the town then Egbert would remember such a lucrative fare as six men and eight horses. When I entered the gates, I asked David of Norton who was on duty had any such men passed and he said not. Jack has been sent just to confirm the fact. I will ride to Piercebridge and see if he crossed the river there. If not, then it would be Barnard Castle and then I would be worried for that is perilously close to the Scottish border. Until we have word of him and his men then all is idle speculation. He has more than half a day start on us. I will leave on the morrow. Did Gerard and Richard return?"

"They did and with the thanks of the reeve of Fissebourne. You did well, my son."

"I did what you would have done. Now rest, father, for I will take the burden from you. My shoulders are broad enough."

"Do not neglect your wife. I neglected my first one in Ouistreham and she and my first family died as a result. I have not given your mother as much attention as I should, and I know that my father regretted not giving my mother more time than he did. We serve England and the king, but we have a duty to serve our families too." He nodded to my mother, "Speak to her. Her eyes are closed but she can hear."

I knelt and kissed her cheek. Putting my mouth close to her ear I said, "Mother, know that I love you and would give my right arm to spare you this pain. I will pray for you and know that you will always be in my thoughts." She sighed and I swear I saw her try to form a smile. I kissed her again and I could smell death upon her cold skin. My father was right, she was close to death.

I stood and Thomas knelt. He did exactly as I had done and I could not hear his words. That was as it should be. Such partings are private.

As we stood and left my father said, "You have work to do and you can do no more for your mother. If you can find these men sooner rather than later then you may save lives. Your mother's is ended and Ruth and I, along with Eleanor will be here for her."

He was right and after I had warned Gerard and Richard that we would be leaving soon, I joined my wife who was with her ladies and my sister, Ruth. They were sewing a tapestry. My sister hugged me and said, in my ear, "It is good you are back safe, brother. Your wife has missed you." She looked at my eyes, "You saw our mother?"

I nodded and we embraced; we had always been close.

That Eleanor was overjoyed to see me was clear and she hugged me and led me to the chamber off to the side of the Great Hall where we could speak, "Our son is well?"

"He is. He acquitted himself as he should and was in no danger. He will have learned from the trip. I fear I must away again."

I told her my news and she nodded. She understood treachery only too well, "I knew when I married you that with the title came great responsibility. This land needs you."

"And you need me too. I promise that when this problem has gone then I shall devote more time to you and to this valley."

"Your father is unwell and I fear that your mother's imminent death may hasten his own, Samuel. Ruth and I fear for him. His servants found blood on his sheets and although he tries to hide the pain from us, he cannot."

She was telling me that which I knew already. "When my grandfather first came to this land, I do not think he knew the responsibility that it brought."

"But the people of the valley, and especially Stockton, know what you do for them. They are happy and loyal. There are many places which are not."

There was a cry from upstairs and Eleanor and I ran. We reached my mother's bedchamber and found my father prostrate over her. Ruth was there too. Thomas entered and I put my arm around him. My mother had been taken and the shell of the man that was my father looked to be crumbling already.

That evening we picked at our food knowing that my mother's body now lay guarded in our chapel. My father seemed to be a shrunken copy of the man I had seen leading King Henry's army.

"I should delay my departure, father. It is not seemly that we leave and my mother lies unburied."

"Your mother would not wish for others to suffer as a result of her death. She loved this land and the people. Unlike the Bishop they made her welcome. We cannot escape our responsibilities, Samuel. Herterpol is not far away. I will speak with Father Michael about the burial." He smiled, "Mark the Mason is already carving our effigies and the two tombs will soon be finished. Ride and by the time you return we can make a better decision about what it is that you do. Perhaps these men have returned to France." I knew from his voice that he did not think so.

The next day I rode with Jack and Thomas to Herterpol where I was able to confirm that while Sir Walter had arrived in the port, thus far he had not left. The official, John of Herterpol, who managed the port for the bishop kept meticulous records.

"If he does return then I wish him detained. Send to Stockton."

"But he is a friend of the Bishop! He told me so!"

"Unless he has a warrant from the bishop then you are duty-bound to obey the orders from the Earl of Cleveland!" I knew I was using my father's title but officials like Brother John liked to have someone above them that they could blame. He nodded.

As Jack had also confirmed that the men had not crossed on the ferry then we knew they had travelled in a different direction.

I put that from my mind as Thomas and I went to my father to speak of the funeral. "Father Michael will bury her tomorrow. All the arrangements have been made. She would not have wished for the lords and ladies to attend. She was a simple woman and her ladies from the town and those in the town whom she helped will attend."

I was astounded at the numbers who attended. She had been a much-loved woman and the tears as she was placed inside the partly finished tomb touched me as they were genuine tears for the woman who had followed my father halfway around the world to begin a new life. Even though I was leaving early the next day we gave my mother an old fashioned, English send-off. We feasted and we drank. We each told the story which made us smile. Thomas' story was the last and was telling.

"I remember when I was but three or it may have been four. I cannot remember my age but I can recall my grandmother." He smiled at his mother, "You were unwell, mother, and father was with you. I did not know the ailment, but I feared that you would die. Grandmother Rebecca took me to the gatehouse overlooking the river and she pointed south. She said, *'Thomas, the place that I was born is so far away that a horseman would wear out four or five horses if he tried to ride there yet I can see that land now. My mother and father lie there, dead but,'* and then she tapped her chest, *'in here they live still. Your mother will not die, at least not yet, but when she does, and we all die, then when you close your eyes you shall see her. When I die then know that I will always watch over you.*' And she was right, you did not die, mother and I took comfort from Grandmother Rebecca's words." He looked down at his food strewn platter and said quietly, "I can feel her now and her love."

We were all silent and I swear that I too felt her spirit sweeping through the Great Hall. I looked at my father and saw the smile on his face. Our eyes met and he nodded. He felt it too. We retired soon after.

After just three days in Stockton, with four sumpters and two servants, my column of men headed west towards the old Roman fort of Piercebridge and the next crossing of the river. All were silent. My mother's death was too recent for the normal banter of the ride. The silence helped me to think and to plan. I left Sir William at Stockton for he now knew he needed his own familia and he would begin the process of selecting and then hiring a handful of men. My father had promised him the vacant manor of Elton. First, he would need the permission of the king but it was the start of William's knightly career.

That the men we sought could have swum at Yarum was a possibility, but it was more likely that they headed west. As we passed through Sadberge it was confirmed that six armed men had ridden west some days earlier and so we moved a little quicker towards the crossing of the Tees. We rode along Cocker Beck and saw their spoor. They had camped where they would not be seen; the remains of the fire were cold and the animal dung some days old. I knew we had to hurry if we were to catch them.

There was no lord of the manor at Piercebridge. Sir Richard lived in Gainford to the north. The crossing was a popular one for the old Roman Road from the south passed through it and so there was an inn, the Fox Covert. The landlord told us that the party had eaten in his inn and had one of their horses shoed by the smith and then crossed the river. That had been two days earlier. The loss of a horseshoe had delayed them and given us an idea of their route. The road headed south towards Richmond and

The Perfect Knight

Middleham to the west and York to the east. It was the toss of a coin to decide which one to take. I opted for Richmond, not least because we could spend the night there. The castle was now King Henry's and as such had a constable, Roald. I knew him and was guaranteed a welcome.

He kept a good watch on this royal castle. Along with Robert Fitz Ranulph's castle at Middleham, Richmond guarded the western side of the Vale of York and none passed through without the scrutiny of the lord of Middleham and the king's constable in Richmond. "Six men and horses would have been seen, Sir Samuel. They did not pass here, and my riders watch the roads west. Look to the east and there you should find a trace of them. Since your grandfather brought peace to this part of the world then there are few mailed men we do not know."

I was satisfied and the next day began the ride to York. If they had not headed west then that left York in the east. The Archbishop was Roger de Pont L'Évêque, but he was ill and said to be dying. There would be little point in seeing him. My father had told me that although King Henry had placed him there, the king did not trust him. Ranulf de Glanvill was High Sheriff but as he was Chief Justiciar for England, I doubted that he would be in York. The Constable, Sir Robert Fitz Herbert, would be the man I would see and I knew him to be both trustworthy and honourable.

York's Roman walls, now augmented by King Henry's towers and powerful gates, always made me more comfortable. With Stockton guarding the Tees and York guarding the Ouse then the land between was safe. My livery afforded us entry and we headed for Clifford's Tower, the mighty keep which dominated the city. The cathedral was a modest affair, but it was still the holiest place south of Durham and north of Lincoln. Leaving Gerard and Richard to arrange the stabling and Jack to see to our horses I went with Thomas to visit the constable.

He admitted us to his chambers immediately, "Welcome, Sir Samuel. I take it that your visit is not one of courtesy?" I liked Sir Robert for he was plain-spoken and got to the point. I told him of my quest, and he nodded. "Strange that you

The Perfect Knight

should say that for two days since six such men were seen by the Lord of Malton, Sir Roger Fitz Hugh. He sent a rider to tell me of their presence for they appeared to be attempting to move furtively across his land. They were heading east."

I nodded, for now, I had clear evidence that Sir Walter was still in England and therefore still a potential menace. I wondered what the knight was doing in that part of the land. It was far from a large port and nowhere near the border. What mischief was he planning? "Tell me, Sir Robert, you know the knights of this part of England better than I do. Which ones are less likely to be supporters of King Henry and more likely to side with his eldest son on the throne?" I saw the fear in his eyes, and he looked at Thomas. "This is my son, Thomas, and can be trusted. You know I am the king's man. All my family are and whatever you tell me shall remain with me. You have my word."

He nodded, "The lord of Wykeham, Sir Richard Fitz William, is known to be a friend of the young King Henry. He returned more than a year since to the family home from Paris where, it is said, he lived with the Young King Henry. He is the only one whose loyalty is in doubt." My eyes bored into him. Taking out his cross he kissed it, "I swear!"

"And does he have a castle?"

Shaking his head Sir Robert said, "The king's castle, which is being improved, is at Scarborough." I remembered that it had been one of King Stephen's supporters, William le Gros, who had built the original castle. "The other castles are at Helmsley and Pickering. Their lords are loyal to the king. Guarding the southern approaches to York I know that for certain."

"Then we can assume that Sir Walter will be making for Wykeham but why?"

"I know not."

I smiled, "Perhaps I should visit with this Sir Richard."

"Would you wish me to accompany you, Sir Samuel, in my position as High Sheriff?"

I shook my head, "If I am wrong then I would not wish your relations with this lord to be put in jeopardy. At the moment all I have is conjecture but everything I have learned leads me to believe that there is something going on and the more I hear the more I fear for the safety of this land. Let my men and I discover the truth and then we can act. However, it would be as well for there to be a neutral observer so that the truth can be reported accurately. Have you such a man who could come with us?"

"Brother Raymond was a Knight Hospitaller and is recently returned from the Holy Land. Not only is he a wise man he is also a doughty knight. He has chosen a life of peace copying out holy works. I know that he would be keen to ride the road again, albeit briefly. He has been within the city walls for two years!"

I knew, from my father and my time in the Holy Land, that the holy order to which Brother Raymond belonged did fine work. I also understood that a man of war finds it hard to endure a life of peace even though that path was self-chosen.

"Come, we shall see if he is willing and if not, I will find a sergeant at arms from the garrison. Brother Raymond would be the better choice."

As it turned out Brother Raymond was more than willing to accompany us, not least because he remembered my father from his time at Bella Aqua which had become a Hospitaller establishment when we had left. He had a ring of greying hair around a tonsure, but he still looked to be a fit man and I saw a warrior rather than a priest.

"I was a young sergeant at the time, but I knew your father's reputation. He is well?"

I shook my head, "My mother recently died, and he had a fall from a horse. He does not appear to be recovering from either event."

"I shall pray for him," he turned to the Sheriff, "and what is it you wish me to do, Sir Robert?"

"Sir Samuel goes to uncover a plot. As a man of God, should it come to it, your testimony might make all the difference."

"Then you will need my cross and tonsure, but should I take my sword too?"

I laughed, "You have the right of it!"

The Perfect Knight

We left the next morning and headed northeast along a well-maintained road. To the north lay the vast forest which finished not far south of the River Tees. I intended for us to stay at Pickering Castle for it would be a relatively easy twenty-five mile or so ride and I hoped to glean information from Sir Edward Thornton. The constable had assured me that he was a loyal knight and I vaguely remembered my grandfather speaking of a Thornton who had fought with him at the Battle of the Standards. As we rode, I spoke with the knight hospitaller, although now he was happy to be a humble brother spending satisfying days copying out Bibles.

"Like your father, Sir Samuel, I chose to come home for the simple reason that I could not see a victory in the land where Christ died and too many of those who were in the Holy Land were not there for the right reasons. They sought land and power. It is a rich land and the ones who are there seek to profit from it. I had done my share of both fighting and caring. The Master accepted my resignation and after an interesting two years wandering Italy, France and then England, I settled in York. It is quiet and seems free from politics and plots. I am content."

I nodded, "And yet the constable thought that you would leap at the opportunity to come with me."

He chuckled, "There you have me. I confess it was your family name which drew me."

"My family name, I do not understand?"

"I play chess with the constable. He is one of the few men who can give me a good game and I had spoken to him of my admiration not only of the Warlord but his son, William. I know that your family puts honour and the kingdom before personal gain. That is rare. I believe that is why he suggested my name so rapidly. I had often expressed regret that while your father was in the Holy Land, I did not get to serve with him and by the time I reached England the Warlord was dead. I am happy for what may prove to be a last adventure and I do not think it will end bloodily. I am just intrigued."

"It may be nothing. I may be chasing a goose and not a fox but there was something about both the Bishop and the knight which did not sit well with me. Call it a suspicious

The Perfect Knight

mind if you will or an itch that I cannot scratch. Heaven knows that I would be happier in Stockton while my father is ill, but you are right, there is something in the Warlord's blood that makes a man behave as I do. For the life of me, I cannot see what this knight is doing here. From what I have learned, apart from the Lord of Wykeham, the land seems loyal to King Henry."

The knight hospitaller nodded and patted his horse, almost absentmindedly, "Scarborough is a royal castle and although the port is small, the harbour is barely big enough for a pair of cogs and half a dozen fishing ships, yet it is a place where men could be landed. Until the King's man, Maurice the Mason, has finished his work then the castle will not be as strong as it should be. I have heard that the mason is still in Dover and it is one of his men who supervises this work." He shrugged, "I am just speculating, of course. It is like a chess game and a clever man thinks a few moves ahead. Perhaps I am giving the king's enemies too much credit."

I did not think so and his words set me thinking.

Sir Edward was delighted at our arrival. His castle had few visitors and his father had served with the Warlord. The presence of a crusader also added piquancy to our visit. I tried to be circumspect about Wykeham and its lord, but it proved unnecessary as Sir Edward had little time for Sir Richard of Wykeham. The knight, it seemed was open in his support for Young King Henry. The more Sir Edward spoke the more I realised what a foolish knight was Sir Richard. If he was supporting the young Henry for what he could get out of it, land and the like, then he did not need to oppose King Henry. Young Henry was the designated heir. He had been crowned and all that he lacked was power. Suddenly the words of Brother Raymond made sense. If Young King Henry was tired of waiting for his father to either die or simply abdicate then Sir Richard's actions and the presence of Sir Walter made sense. He was fermenting trouble far from London but close to a castle of the king. When we left the next morning, I was pleased that we had stayed with Sir Edward for I was now forearmed and knew what to expect.

Sir Edward had been scathing about the way that the knight managed his manor and some of the company he kept. I got the impression that Sir Edward had no time for an older man like Sir Richard whose values were more akin to the Warlord's than to his own!

"Have you a story, Sir Samuel, ready for Sir Richard?"

I nodded, "We are visiting Scarborough Castle to see some of the innovations which are being implemented by Maurice the Mason with a view to improving Stockton Castle."

He beamed, "And that would work. Let us see the sort of welcome he gives us."

Wykeham was halfway between Pickering and Scarborough. It lay on the main road and we passed other travellers. We were just a mile and a half from the manor when my leading scout, Ned, stopped and examined his horse's hoof. It looked innocent enough, but I knew it was the signal for danger. The rest of my men were immediately alert, and it was only Brother Raymond who was oblivious to it all.

I reined in next to Ned and patted my horse's neck. "There are men, my lord, watching from the trees. I have counted four and they are good."

"I do not think that we are threatened but let us be ready to fight if we have to," I replied.

He mounted and took the lead once more. I did not look directly at the trees but glanced and sniffed. He was right, they were good, but they were also pungent. I could smell them.

Brother Raymond smiled, "Your men are well trained, Sir Samuel. I like the secret signals."

We were just half a mile from the manor when I heard hooves clattering through the trees. My men all drew their weapons but when the hooves faded then they sheathed them.

I said, "They will know we are coming. I dare say Sir Richard will be preparing a face for us."

"A mask can tell you much about a man, Sir Samuel. We will see."

The Perfect Knight

The manor was a fortified house. There was a ditch that was too deep for mere drainage and the door was reached by a short wooden staircase. Whilst there were no crenulations, I saw that there was a walkway around the roof. It could be defended. It was also large with many other buildings hidden behind it. I reined in and two men strode from the house. Neither was Sir Walter.

"I am Sir Richard, and this is my home, the manor of Wykeham. From your livery, you must be related to the Earl of Cleveland."

I dismounted and held out my hand, "I am his son, Sir Samuel, and this is Brother Raymond who has joined us to visit Scarborough Castle."

I saw we had piqued his curiosity. That he knew me was not a surprise but by bringing the priest I had muddied the waters.

"Have you time to partake of some wine? There are water troughs behind for your mounts and my sergeant at arms will fetch ale for your men."

I saw through his ploy immediately. I guessed that Sir Walter and his men were just waiting for an opportunity to escape and by taking us all either into the hall or around the back it would disguise his exit.

As soon as we entered the manor house, I knew that there was no lady of the manor. It reeked of a male-dominated world. The tapestries which hung from the walls were all martial in nature and the furniture, though well-made was solid and masculine. Brother Raymond and I sat on the two chairs proffered by the servants and when the wine was poured, they left.

"We get few visitors here, Sir Samuel, and I would appreciate your views on the wine."

I sipped it and nodded, "A good one. Chinon?"

He beamed, "You have a good palate, Sir Samuel, it is."

"And what brings you from the busy town of Stockton to our little sleepy backwater?"

"I am anxious to see what improvements have been made by Maurice the Mason to the castle at Scarborough. My father has asked me to help improve our defence. I thought to see what good King Henry deems appropriate."

He made his first slip then. The smile was not with his eyes but with his mouth, "I have not yet visited the castle. Perhaps I should."

"Come with us. I believe that it is only nine miles hence."

"Unfortunately I have much to occupy me here and unlike you, I have no castle."

I drained my goblet, "Well, we should be heading for the castle."

Shaking his head the knight said, "Another goblet of wine and," he clapped his hands, "some food perhaps?"

That he was trying to delay us was clear, but the question was why? Was it merely to allow his confederates to escape or was it more sinister? Was there an ambush waiting for us? I chose to play along with our host. "Of course, my lord."

In the end, we were there for an hour. Sir Richard filled every silence with words. He was almost babbling as he attempted to keep us there. I caught the eye of a bemused Brother Raymond who raised an eyebrow. I shrugged. I could play a part as well as Sir Richard and I wanted him to think I had been taken in. When we rose to take our leave we were not hindered.

"You must call in when you are done with the castle and its mason. When do you expect to return?"

"That depends upon the constable. If Sir Hugh allows, we might stay for some days."

Our horses were waiting for us and we mounted. Waving, we headed down the road and I did not speak until we had passed the village and were on an empty road. I reined in and Richard son of Aelric and Gerard of Chester joined me.

"Well?"

"There had been at least thirty riders lord, for the stables were empty and yet the yard was filled with horse dung."

"Have archer scouts travel ahead of us through the trees. I would not be ambushed." While I waited for them to get a head start, I turned to Brother Raymond, "What are your views, Brother?"

The Perfect Knight

"He was buying time for Sir Walter to escape but thirty men is more than six."

"Aye, I know. Let us hope we reach Scarborough safely. My scouts should ensure that."

As the huge keep of Scarborough loomed up ahead of us, I breathed a sigh of relief. There was to be no ambush. The road led first to the small port and settlement and then wound up a cliff to the gatehouse and barbican. The castle had been well sited. An assault up the cliff was doomed to failure. However, that would be when the new defences were in place and I saw now much building work. The constable was John of Ravenscar and he was a local man. The castle teemed with workers whose cranes and scaffolding were everywhere, especially the impressive barbican and gatehouse. They were also building a wall to allow defenders to rain arrows and stones on any who managed to brave the cliffs of the headland and then try to cross the deep ditch.

The Constable bowed as we dismounted at the entrance to the mighty keep, "My lord, I am honoured that the son of the Earl of Cleveland should visit with us." Had I been south of Lincoln then I might not have been identified; in the north, the gryphon marked me as a descendant of the Warlord.

I had decided to keep the story I had told others, "I am here to see what Stockton can learn from Maurice the Mason."

He beamed. He was proud of his castle, "He is down in Dover but when the work there is finished, early next year, then he will return to ensure all is done to his satisfaction. You are welcome to stay although I will have to send to the town for more supplies."

I frowned as Jack and Thomas led off our horses, "I would have thought you well supplied, John of Ravenscar."

He shook his head, "I have but six sergeants to feed and the workers supply themselves."

I felt a chill rush down my back. I now saw the danger. The constable led us not to the Great Tower that was the keep but to a large wooden hall set against the southeast wall overlooking the south bay. It looked, from its age, to be part of the original castle. "The garrison, small though it is, sleeps in the tower while as you can see," he pointed to the tents which proliferated in the inner bailey, "the builders use the tents. I fear that you and your men will have to sleep in the half-built hall." He pointed to where men were erecting another stone building between the hall and the tower, "That will be an accommodation building but the priority is the barbican and defensive wall. King Henry was adamant that this jewel of the north should be well defended."

We entered the wooden hall where servants were fanning the flames of the fire and moving the tables and benches into position.

"Constable, I shall be open with you. I have another reason for my visit. I believe that there are enemies of our king who would attempt to do harm to the garrison and the castle."

He gave me a look that suggested that I was simple, "Who would wish such a thing?"

I leaned in close as did Brother Raymond and told him of the raid by the Scots. Gradually the doubt was replaced by belief, "It is strange that you say so for a month since I was visited by the Lord of Wykeham. He asked for a tour of the castle."

The Lord of Wykeham had lied to me. "Did he give a reason?"

Once again, I saw realisation dawn, "No, although he was quite interested in the outer defences."

The outer defence of the castle, as I had seen, was still the original wooden wall of William le Gros. Until the workers had built the stone wall to protect the ditch then the castle was vulnerable. The barbican was strong but until the eighteen feet high wall was completed, the castle was open to attack.

"Constable, why are there so few men in the castle?"

The poor man looked confused. I saw now that he was here almost as a caretaker, but someone had miscalculated. "We had two knights and forty sergeants until two months since when a message came to say that they were needed in France. Sir Geoffrey and Sir Eustace seemed happy to leave

The Perfect Knight

the dull life of the castle which was a building site. They headed south to take a ship from Dover."

"And the message came from the king?"

"Now that you mention it, no, although I did not read the document. It was delivered by a pursuivant."

"I fear treachery. Brother Raymond, what are your thoughts?"

"I think that we have arrived just in time. If these confederates of the Young King Henry have thirty men, then they could take this castle. It seems to me that the garrison was drawn away through deceit, and that deceit will be revealed soon enough. If there is to be an attempt to take the castle, then it will be soon. I wonder if our presence will have changed their plans."

Shaking my head I said, "If anything it will accelerate them. We have arrived just in time but those thirty men who fled Wykeham could already be heading this way." I turned to the constable, "Tell me what you normally do at night."

"After the labourers from the town have left then the gates are lowered and the bridge over the ditch raised. The half a dozen masons who are in the tents make their own food and I send them ale. My men and I eat in the tower."

"And you keep a night watch?"

His face told me that he did not, "I keep one of the garrison to patrol the upper floor of the keep, lord. From there they have a clear view to the town and the sea."

Brother Raymond shook his head, "And if he watches all night then I am a Musselman!"

I saw then that my arrival would have upset the plans of Sir Walter and Sir Richard Fitz William. Pointing to the sea I said, "I saw no ships in the harbour but so long as we are here then they cannot do that which they intend and steal the king's castle from him."

Brother Raymond nodded, "I must play chess with you, Sir Samuel. You have a sharp mind. I concur. It would be simple enough to take this castle. If we were asleep in the hall and while the wall from the barbican to the keep is unfinished then men could scale the wooden wall and we would be burned in our beds. The builders could be slaughtered while Sir Walter and Sir William entered the keep and took it. All that they would need to do would be to hold the castle until confederates arrived."

I saw that the constable was not convinced. "Constable, the Scottish king and many of his lords are still resentful that they were humiliated by my grandfather and had such draconian terms imposed upon them. This could be the spark they seek and with a king's castle in their hands then those who are opposed to our king could rise and join the Scots."

"Aye, if you were the young King Henry you would have to do nothing except to wait in France and be invited to take the crown." Brother Raymond convinced me that I was right.

Jack and Thomas entered the hall. The four servants had finished their work and we were alone, "Jack, find Richard son of Aelric. I want them in the tower. Maurice the Mason has built well and there the top floor affords a fine view of the defences. Thomas, fetch Gerard of Chester and my men. Constable, you and your men defend the keep."

I saw that he was uneasy about this and I wondered at his credentials. "Are you certain about this lord? It is treason for someone to try to take the King's castle."

"There are many, I believe, who would trade an older King Henry for a younger one who might return to them the lands that they believe they are owed. Have your servants cook the food but take it to the men in the hall. Have the workers sleep in the basement of the keep. That they will be unhappy I do not doubt but I would have them safe."

"And you, my lord?"

"I will occupy the barbican with my men at arms. They will have had men watching you and your routine, Constable. This way we may spring our own surprise upon them." I led them from the hall and saw that darkness was about to descend. Already the east, the side facing the sea was almost in darkness. Those who wished us harm could be in position already. The labourers had long since left and the masons had lit their fires to cook their food. All was normal.

Jack returned with Thomas and my men at arms. "Jack, fetch our arms. Thomas, you shall be with the archers. Tell Richard that they are to watch for shadows from the east."

The Perfect Knight

"I would be with you, father."

I ruffled his hair, "Aye, I know but I will be easier in my mind if I know that the thick walls of Scarborough's great tower protect you. Brother Raymond, I leave my son in your charge."

"And he will be safe." He smiled at Thomas, "Come, Master Thomas!" The Hospitaller and the constable flanked my son as they hurried through the dark to the great tower.

I saw that Gerard and my men had grabbed food and as I led them to the barbican and gatehouse Gerard gave me a loaf and a hunk of cheese, "Not hot fare, my lord, but something for your belly. We will feast when these traitors are done with."

With the bridge drawn up and the gates closed, we were safe in the gatehouse, but we would not remain there. When Jack arrived and after we had eaten, we headed to the top of the towers where, hidden by shadows, we waited. If I was wrong, then we would all lose a night of sleep and I would look foolish. If I was right, then by dawn there would be a bailey filled with the dead and dying. This would be a night that would show me if my grandfather was right and I was a leader.

Chapter 4

I did as Gerard suggested and ate although I tasted nothing. I realised that the bread ovens must still be burning as the bread was fresh and warm. The constable must have ordered them lit in anticipation of our breakfast. That was good and might allay the fears of the men who, even now, might be approaching the walls; they would see it as a sign of normality. I hoped that they would see what they hoped to see, the castle as it always was with no one in the gatehouse and none guarding the walls. One attempt had been made on my life and this would be a way of killing two birds with one stone. Having my scouts precede on the way here might have saved us from another ambush.

Gerard said, quietly, "If they come then they must outnumber us, my lord. They know our strength to the man. The Lord of Wykeham can add to those who left when we arrived, and he knows that there will be just over thirty men within these walls not to mention the builders and the servants. We have no idea how many he brings."

I nodded for he was right, and I was taking a calculated risk. I was counting on them trying to take the keep and if they had questioned the labourers, or even sent a spy inside the walls then they would know what the garrison did. I was pleased that the labourers had left before we had made under cover of darkness to the barbican, and now we waited. "Aye but I think the mind behind this is Sir Walter. His plan to ambush me in the Palatinate was well thought out and he will have planned this attack equally well."

My men were all experienced, but it was Jack who spotted the shadows as they climbed over the unfinished

The Perfect Knight

stone walls from the steep side that faced the town and the sea. They were aided by the scaffolding which was there to help the masons to build. We watched to see if we could count their numbers, but we could not. My men and I wore no helmets we just had a coif and arming cap. That helped our hearing. The attackers were confident, and we heard them speaking, albeit quietly as they negotiated the scaffolding and walls which, in the dark, would not be as easy as during the day. I nodded to Gerard who slipped down the stairs to open the gate of the barbican. Neither he nor my men at arms wore chausses and their buskins would make no sound on the cobbles. The road which wound and climbed to the keep had another unfinished wall to the right. Beyond it lay the empty tents of the masons and the hall we were given to use. If, as I now suspected their spy had told them that we were within the walls of the hall, then they would send at least one party there while another went to the keep. The gate of the keep, the great tower, was now locked and guarded. My archers would wait until they had a clear target before they loosed an arrow from the top of the huge donjon.

As I slipped out of the gatehouse, I saw that I was at the rear with just Jack behind me. He would watch my back. My men were moving like wraiths up the winding cobbles. The scaffolding and piles of stones waiting to be laid helped to disguise them and they kept to the side. We could see the attackers as they moved towards the keep and the entrance to the bailey. When the work was finished there would be another gate, but, for now, it was just a gap. I saw the enemy split into two. Numbers were impossible to ascertain and I would have to rely on my men being better than the enemy. I was confident in my own skills even against superior numbers, but I hoped that Jack would keep behind me. He was still learning, and I did not think that the two knights who led these men would think twice about despatching a squire to an early grave. The ditch before the inner bailey was still shallow and its deepening would be one of the last tasks. I saw the shadows pass over it easily. From the corner of my eye, I watched the other group as they climbed the steps to the gate of the great tower. Soon they would know

The Perfect Knight

that it was barred. I concentrated on following Gerard and my men as they spread out in a line.

The party before us split into two and a dozen men ran at the tents where they assumed the masons were to be found while the majority ran to the hall. As they passed the mason's fire some picked up brands to set fire to the tents and it was then that the alarm was given. It came from the great tower as axes rained down on the door. The constable shouted the alarm and the men before my soldiers gave a shout as they fell upon the tents and the hall.

In contrast, we were silent and as the men attacking the tents were closer, we attacked them first. We outnumbered them and I did not even have to strike a blow for they were slain by my men. Not all died silently but their shouts were hidden by the shouts and cries of the others attacking the barred keep. I heard, as we moved down the slope towards the hall, the sounds of arrows. Richard son of Aelric had his archers choosing their targets. Our luck could not last as when one of those attacking the hall turned and saw us, lit by the mason's fires, he shouted a warning. There were eighteen or more men and I recognised Sir Richard Fitz William, lord of Wykeham.

"Kill them!" Hurling their brands at the wooden hall he and his men ran up the slight slope to us. It was only a slight advantage, but we used it.

None of us was using shields and I took my dagger from my belt to face the huge brute of a man who, with bared head and wielding a war axe, ran at me screaming. I saw two others with swords in close attendance and took in that Sir Richard Fitz William was hanging back. As the axe was swung at my head, I took one step back and the axe missed me by a handspan. When the axe head had passed, I stepped forward and hacked at the right arm of the man. My sword sliced through to the bone. He screamed as he dropped the axe and tried to stem the bleeding. I moved further down the slope to close the distance between me and the two swordsmen. The axe had fallen from the stricken warrior's hands but he was brave and tried to pull a knife. I slashed across his face with my dagger ripping across his nose and one of his eyes. He would no longer be a threat.

"Stay close, Jack!"

"Aye, Sir Samuel."

Two swordsmen had been rushing to finish me off and my rapid movement down the hill had confused them. I took the two poor sword swings they used on my blades and then used my fast hands to twist both dagger and sword and strike at the two of them. Many years of training with Roger of Bath and the rest of my grandfather's men had given me hands like lightning. My sword caught one on the cheek and laid open the back of the hand of the other. I punched the hilt of my dagger into the face of the one with the slashed hand and lunged with my sword at the leg of the other. With no chausse to protect it the blade slid down through muscle before grating on the bone. I did not pause but took another three steps to reach Sir Richard. Behind me, I heard a cry as Jack finished off the man with the face smashed by my dagger.

"Traitor, surrender and I will get you a fair trial." I kept as calm as I could for I wanted him alive to tell me all that he knew.

"Fool! Old King Henry is finished and when my lord and master sails across the Mare Anglicum then you and the lickspittles like you will get the death you deserve. I shall be Lord of Stockton!"

Even as I advanced towards him, I saw the danger he and Sir Walter represented. They were a challenge to all the families like mine who had supported the crown. They were like the followers of Stephen who saw an opportunity to take without effort!

I had said nothing, but his words had distracted him so that when I swung my sword from on high, he barely managed to bring up the shield he held to protect his head. As it was, he slipped a little down the gentle slope and I advanced. He was off-balance, but he tried to gut me with a lunge of his sword. It was easily deflected by my dagger. I was aware of the clash of steel all around me and, occasionally, the thrum of a bow and the sound of an arrow.

The Perfect Knight

Even if Gerard and I failed the keep would be safe. I guessed we had killed or wounded perhaps nine or ten at least. Sir Walter would have been better to attack us in the rear rather than continuing to try to take the keep. He did not and I pressed my advantage.

Taking another step closer, which put the knight on flatter ground, I hooked my left leg around his. Neither of us was wearing spurs and there was no chance of becoming tangled. I pushed both weapons hard against his shield. He tumbled backwards!

"You have no honour! You tripped me!"

He sounded like a petulant child and I laughed, "Thus speaks the knight who comes in the night to slay masons and burn men in their beds!" For some reason, his accusation made me angry and instead of trying to disarm him, I brought my sword down towards his head. He could have raised either his sword or his shield and his life would have been saved. Once more his own words had distracted him. The end of my sword scored a huge dent in his helmet and bent the nasal. The metal forced my sword to the right and the edge bit deeply into his cheek, tearing the mail coif. He screamed and was then silent. It was only later that I realised it had been the force of the blow to the skull which had ended his life. I whirled around and saw that Jack had obeyed my command and stood guarding my back. Gerard and my men were now fighting equal numbers of the enemy and I saw that the bodies which littered the slope between the tents and the hall were those of the rebels.

"Now, Jack, a war cry and an attack. Let us end this!"

He grinned, his teeth shining in the firelight of the mason's fire, "Aye, Sir Samuel!"

"Warlord!" We both screamed and ran at the side of the man fighting Martyn Longsword. Even as the man turned, Martyn ran him through and then screaming joined the two of us as we ran at the next man. The others turned and fled. Three did not make it as my men showed no mercy and hacked at their backs.

"Now for the keep! If we can take a prisoner then so much the better."

The Perfect Knight

That their plan had failed gave me no satisfaction for there were still traitors both in England and abroad and I knew that I was duty-bound to defend the king whom my grandfather had taken under his wing to train and to mould. King Henry felt like one of the family and I would do all in my power to help him rule the kingdom.

We now had the slope against us and the lack of sleep, fighting and the slope itself slowed us as we headed up to the keep. A voice shouted, "Sauve qui peut!" It was not Sir Walter's, but the effect was the same. The attackers ran.

I shouted, "Look for Sir Walter and his men at arms!"

"Aye, my lord!"

Arrows plucked at the fleeing men although the mail of the men at arms saved them. The rest were like the men we had fought and the Frenchmen who had come to take Scarborough Castle fell. I heard the Constable shout, "After them!" It meant Brother Raymond and the garrison would be added to our numbers. Richard son of Aelric would continue to rain arrows and death upon the fleeing attackers. We had a chance to take prisoners for the enemy had to negotiate scaffolding as well as building materials. If they paused to open the gate at the barbican then we would have them.

I saw three men clamber over the scaffolding and race down towards the gate. "Egbert, take three men and secure the gate!"

"Aye, lord!"

I knew that it left me with fewer men, but I did not want Sir Walter to escape so easily. I think Sir Walter must have read my mind for seven men turned to face us. With Jack, we had eight but almost half of the men who faced us wore mail. They had their backs to the scaffolding and were in a line with Sir Walter and his squire in the middle. I knew that four of those who faced us were the men we had chased from Durham. I recognised Sir Walter and the squire but the last man, who was mailed, had the accoutrements of a knight.

I chose to give them the same chance as I had given Sir Richard, "Surrender and you will be given a fair trial."

The seventh man shouted, "Merde!" confirming not only that he was French but that they would fight. Behind me, I heard the clash of steel as the constable and Brother Raymond despatched the tardier attackers. They would join us, and we had time.

Jack appeared at my left shoulder, "I can take the squire, lord."

"Are you sure?"

He nodded, "I have insults to repay and he is dressed and armed as I am. You have taught me well, Sir Samuel, trust me."

I nodded and we advanced. Gerard had taken upon himself to fight one of the two mailed men and I would deal with Sir Walter. None of these men had shields and so it would be an equal fight. They suddenly rushed at us and one of my men, Ralph, was taken by surprise. He was hacked across the neck by the Frenchman and slumped to the ground. Gerard's right side was exposed but even as the mailed man slashed at Gerard, Brother Raymond's sword met it and sparks flashed in the dark.

I had my own battle to fight and I balanced myself as Sir Walter swung his sword at me. The blow was filled with venom and I had to use both my sword and dagger to slow down the blow. I used the flat of my sword so as not to take the edge off. He had put so much force into the blow that he had been unable to use his dagger. As he lifted his sword he lunged with his dagger and I countered with my own, stepping closer to him as I did so.

We were face to face and he spat his words at me, "It was your family that cost mine its home and now I will avenge that loss. Your father's injuries can be laid at my door!" He laughed, "When you die the line will die! The Warlord's work will have been for naught."

He did not know about Thomas and I would not enlighten him. I now had even more reason to kill him, but I put that from my head. My grandfather had taught me to fight cold, like hardened steel. Even as I brought my sword over to bring it down onto his mailed head, I realised that the first raid, the one which had drawn my father north, had been the initial attempt to end our line!

The Perfect Knight

Sir Walter blocked my blow, which had been delivered with the flat of the blade. I wanted him a prisoner. His blade shivered and I saw that a tiny piece had been shaved from his blade. He was fighting with passion whereas I was thinking out each blow. All around us I heard the clash of steel. I prayed that Jack was enduring his combat and hoped that Richard and his archers would soon join us. We were too far from the keep and it was too dark for them to be of any use. We needed their numbers.

Sir Walter's dagger almost caught me out and had I not been wearing mail backed mittens I might have lost my hand. As it was the dagger scraped along the back of the mitten and across the mail links at my side. The weaponsmith at Stockton would have work to do! I used my right shoulder to push against him and he fell back against the wooden scaffolding, his weight breaking it. A large piece fell down from above and, as luck would have it, came between us. The Frenchman fighting Brother Raymond was caught by the end of the lump of timber and Brother Raymond's hand darted out and drove his blade into the links of the man's mail. The Hospitaller twisted the weapon and I heard a grunt of pain.

Sir Walter tried to make his escape. The falling lumber had made a bridge and he and one of his servants began to climb up. Martyn Longsword swashed at the servant's legs. The man jumped and, in doing so, lost his balance and tumbled over to fall onto the cobbles. I did not wish to risk such an end and so I ran along the wall for the enemy were broken. As I passed him, I saw Jack bring his sword down to smash into the helmet of Sir Walter's squire. The ring was deafening and the dent so deep that I knew the squire would not rise. Martyn Longsword joined me as we ran up the side of the building works and, when we neared the castle, headed towards the wall that the enemy had used to enter. I saw Sir Walter silhouetted on the top of the far wall but even as I ran, he lost his balance and fell screaming. I ran down the cobbles towards the gatehouse. We passed the man who had fallen, his skull was crushed, and his legs lay at an unnatural angle. He had died.

The Perfect Knight

Egbert had secured the gate and the bodies of the men who had fled that way lay on the ground along with Tod Tallman, one of my men. He shook his head, "He died well, lord, but we made these pay the price." I saw that the four bodies we saw had been butchered and mutilated. My men had been angry to lose one of their own. Ralph had been wounded but he would recover.

I nodded, "Open the gate to allow Martyn and I to track down the ones who jumped from the wall. Let none other leave!"

When we left the gatehouse we turned right, and I saw the body of Sir Walter. I thought that he was dead, but I saw a movement. We hurried to him, keeping our swords at the ready. He lay on his back and the movement I had seen was the sword falling from his unfeeling fingers. His eyes were open, "You won you bastard, but not fairly!"

The words came out slowly as though he was learning to speak for the first time.

Martyn said, "He has broken his back, lord. He is as good as dead already."

I nodded, "Would you like a warrior's death?"

"From you, I want nothing save that our positions were reversed, and you were lying here. Then, when our French allies come, I would let them see your head on a pike!"

The effort was too much for him and, with a sigh and a tendril of blood from his mouth, he died. I took his sword and rose. "Have his body recovered. We will bury him. You shall have his mail for it was your blow which led to his death."

"Thank you, lord."

"Then have two of our archers ride to Pickering. I need men here. The rider can go to York as well. The traitor gave us an event but not a time. It could be that the ships are due here today!"

I joined Brother Raymond and the Constable. They were questioning the surviving Frenchman. Brother Raymond stood, "The man has been gutted but refuses to give us any information. He declined to give us his name, but I recognise his livery. The red with the yellow diagonal and three gold stars is distinctive. He is Guy d'Aumale and I believe related to the man who held this castle until King Henry took it forty years ago, William le Gros."

The dying Frenchman hurled a look of absolute disgust and hatred at the Hospitaller. I nodded, "No matter, I had a full confession from Sir Walter before he died. A French fleet is approaching, and I have put in place a plan to thwart the attack."

"Curse you Englishman! Had you not been here then the castle would be ours and in the hands of its rightful owner! One more day was all that we needed."

He had given me, unwittingly, the timetable. They were coming tomorrow. I took the Constable by the arm, "Then we have time. They will not be arriving today but tomorrow. I need you to rouse the townsfolk. We need the harbour blocking off with fishing boats and men need to watch the beaches. Have timber driven into the sands to stop ships landing."

"I will!" He shook his head, "Who is behind this treachery?"

"I would guess Young King Henry, but I know not the truth. With those involved dead then the son of King Henry can deny all."

He nodded and left.

By the time dawn came, the bodies had been stripped of their mail and weapons and burned. Sir Richard, Sir Walter, Tod, and Sir Guy, who finally succumbed to his wounds, were buried in the graveyard close to the Chapel of Our Lady. Sir Edward arrived later that day with fifty men. Not all were warriors, but they were armed and were ready to fight for King Henry; that was good enough for me. Better ten patriots than a hundred mercenaries. I told him what I knew and we both decided that we would not wait in the castle but meet the ships at the quayside before they could disgorge their men. We made certain that not only the banner of King Henry fluttered from the battlements but also those of Sir Edward and me. It was early evening when Sir Robert Fitz Herbert rode in at the head of a hundred mounted men from York.

"Another one hundred are marching and will be here during the night. Tell me all."

When I had done so he said, "Perhaps I should have listened a little more closely to your words. I thought it fanciful that half a dozen men could pose a threat to this land. I was wrong."

"I do not think I believed it myself until I saw them climbing over the wall. Perhaps we can thwart this attempt to suborn the crown!"

"I pray so."

By the sixth hour of the next day another hundred men had joined us from Malton. The beaches bristled with spears and half-buried logs. The harbour entrance had a double line of boats preventing ships from sailing into the harbour and their decks were lined with archers. The two breakwaters were similarly covered with archers and men at arms. It was noon when we spotted the strange sails. Four cogs, all of them French-built from their lines, appeared on the horizon and made directly for the harbour. When they were less than a mile away they reefed their sails. They could now see us, and the four ships closed with each other. Brother Raymond began to sing the Te Deum and we all joined in. The women and children of Scarborough had gathered too and almost six hundred voices joined in the singing. Perhaps the French might have given up their attempt anyway, but I like to think that God was on our side.

Sir Edward had taken charge and he kept a watch there all night. Some fishing ships left the next day and returned with the news that there was neither sail nor ship to be seen. They had not sailed north or south and we assumed that they had given up their attempt. We had stopped them.

Sir Robert Fitz Herbert clasped my arm as my men and I prepared to head back to Stockton. "I will write to King Henry and tell him of the service you have done. God knows your family has been doing it for more than half a century. England shall never forget you and your family's service."

I was not sure about that, but I left to return to my home knowing that I had done what my father and grandfather would have wished!

The Perfect Knight

Brother Raymond took the opportunity to speak to me before we headed north. "Thank you for giving me this chance for one last adventure. It is out of my system now and I can face the future content. I have slain my last man. That he did not die immediately gives me some comfort, but I think that when I return to York, I will seek a place in the hospital. Copying books that will only be seen by the rich does not sit well with me. There is a hospital run by the brothers close to the river. Only the poor go there; the hours are long and the food is just enough for a man to live on but it will suit me and I will serve my days there. I can see that your family has given service to this land and that you will continue to do so. I will try to make my own life as fulfilling." We bade farewell and I never saw him again but he was often in my thoughts. The threads which bound lives were hard to explain. He had known my father and that made him come with us. Had he not been there we would never have discovered that French ships were sailing to Scarborough and although we had parted there was a bond between two men who had fought together.

As we headed north, I thought about the idea of service. I suppose he was right. I had spent much time with my grandfather in London. He had been struck down and I helped to tend him. He told me then about his life. He told me how he had been a spoiled arrogant noble who viewed life in England and in Norton in particular, as a punishment. That he had changed to become the Warlord who saved England was as miraculous as St Paul's conversion on the road to Damascus. It was Sir Alfred who had set the family on this course of service. I was merely continuing the tradition. I looked at Thomas, would he be the same?

Chapter 5

Stockton 1182

My father was closer to death by the time I returned from Scarborough. I had not been away long but he had deteriorated dramatically. The physicians were as baffled as I was at the decline. I got to speak to him and later, that brought me comfort. Had I dallied on the road home then I might have missed the words we exchanged. As was the way with our family his first concern was the safety of the realm and was relieved when I told him of our success.

"Good." His head rolled back, and he closed his eyes. Ruth came in and put her arm around me. There was pain etched all over my father's face. He opened his eyes and said, "It is good that you have come, Ruth. A man could not have had two better children. Watch over each other and do not be like the king's sons. I have brought you up better than that!"

Ruth leaned over to kiss our father, "You have been the best of fathers and you were the best of husbands,"

"I have tried. Now, Samuel, watch this land and watch your family. As I discovered one son is not enough. Sire more. This is good land. It took an adventure to the Holy Land to discover just how good but I found your mother there and so it was fate. Your grandfather believed in Fate." I could not help the tears which formed in my eyes for he was too young to die. His thin hand reached up to wipe away the tear. "No tears for I am content. I leave this land in good hands and I shall see your mother. Who knows, perhaps there will be the men alongside whom I fought in the heaven

I hope to find. Surely my time as a crusader has earned me that right."

He was almost pleading with me and I held his hands in mine, "You are, like your father, a hero of England. You never did one dishonourable thing in your life and I am proud that you are my father. I can only hope that I will be half as good a father as you have been to me."

He nodded, "You will be for your grandfather saw in you the future. Our family does not go in for sentiment, but you know that…"

"Aye, I know and each time we visit the chapel we shall say prayers for you, mother, grandfather and grandmother. The chapel will be our place of pilgrimage."

Ruth shook her head and held our father's head to her bosom, "I am of this family but not afraid to say what I said to our mother. I love you father and I always will."

"I know and I am content." He yawned, "Samuel, Ruth, I am tired. Let me sleep awhile and when I am awake, we can talk more. We did not talk enough when we could and now I regret that."

I nodded, "As do I. I will await the tales you never told me about fighting the Ayyubid." The words were wasted for he was asleep.

He died in his sleep. Ruth and I held his hands until he slipped away. He was buried in the small chapel within the castle walls. It was where I had held my vigil before I became a knight. Then there had just been the tomb of my grandmother. Now she and the Warlord lay between beautifully carved effigies of them. The funeral interrupted the work of the mason who was still carving my mother's effigy. Now he would carve the image of my father with sword and shield as well as crossed ankles. All would be done well and I had meant what I had said, the chapel would be a place of pilgrimage for our family where we could honour our sires and grandsires and their ladies.

I had written to the king to tell him of my father's death and to add my portion of the tale of treachery in the north. He had not replied but that suited me for I was able to give my attention to my manor. I was now the Earl of Cleveland.

The Perfect Knight

There were few earls in the north. As the senior knight, I was often consulted by others who sought my advice. That I was not as old as some did not seem to bother them. I also had a squire and a page to train. Jack had acquitted himself well at Scarborough and he and Thomas were close. It made it easier for me. I was able to let Gerard of Chester work with them. As a reward for his conduct on the road I had Alf, my weaponsmith, make Jack a hauberk. I would have two mailed men to follow me although the prospect of war seemed remote.

I thought my life would continue in the same fashion, but Fate intervened once more or perhaps King Henry had decided I had rested upon my laurels too long. Many months after my father had died and been buried my sentries reported ten riders waiting at the ferry. They were cloaked in red and mailed. The lack of banner was suspicious and so the captain of the guard summoned men to the walls and the river gate was manned, although ten riders did not seem a real threat. However, it was a visitor and the spurs told me that they were knights although their cowls hid their identity. I descended with my squire and page. Eleanor and Ruth busied themselves preparing a welcome. I had enjoyed the hospitality of many halls and now it was my turn.

As the riders walked up the cobbles from the ferry to the castle, I saw a familiar gait and when the cowl was lifted, I saw that it was King Henry. I dropped to my knee, "King Henry, I was not expecting you!"

He raised me to my feet, "Let us go within. My visit is, perforce, a secret one. Let us go from men's gaze." As we hurried into the outer bailey and headed for the Great Hall he suddenly said, "This takes me back to the time of your grandfather. This became like a home for me and those memories are precious, for I saw a happy lord with his family."

I did not point out that it had not always been so, and it had taken the death of my father's first family in Normandy to make it so.

Eleanor was flustered and fell to her knees when she recognised the king, "My lord, we were not…"

The Perfect Knight

He raised her up, "I am here as an old friend of the castle and the family. Treat me like one. I shall be away by morning. My ship is sailing up the coast from Scarborough. I come to speak to your husband, my most loyal Earl of Cleveland."

That sounded ominous and I knew that my time of peace was almost over.

It was only when he took off his coif that I saw how much he had aged. He was an old man and as his son, Young King Henry, was not yet twenty-seven, that came as a surprise. My father had not looked as old just before he died. My steward took the king's cloak and riding gauntlets as we headed to the fire.

Servants were already flying through my castle making sure that the table was laid and that there were chairs. The fire was stoked up. We were used to the cold in the north, but King Henry had been in France; he would notice the change. I heard my wife chivvying the cooks and servants to make sure that all was in order.

"Jack, take the King's men to the warrior hall."

The oldest looking warrior gave a questioning look to the King who waved an airy hand, "Go, if I am not safe in the Warlord's haven then I should let my son have the throne now."

I was left alone with the king and my son. I asked, "Should my son leave?"

"No, for he is your heir and needs to know the faith your liege lord has in you." He waited until the servants had fetched food and wine before he spoke. "I come here in need of a new Warlord. I need the Earl of Cleveland."

"I am not my grandfather, King Henry."

"No, but as you showed at the Tower when I was kept in France you have your grandfather's skill for your grandfather held my city for me. You are your grandfather's heir!" I nodded and tried to keep the glumness from my face. "It is Henry. I gave him the crown but that was not good enough. I gave him Normandy and still, he was dissatisfied. He asked for the homage of Geoffrey and Richard. It was not speedy enough in coming and so now he raises an army in

The Perfect Knight

Brittany to threaten Poitou. I need you to join me. I sail tomorrow and I would have you leave within the week so put your affairs in order. I am old now and I need your sharp young mind to aid me. We have to win, and time is not on our side. Richard is already raising an army, but the gryphon banner will strike fear into men's hearts and you can inspire our men. Richard looks up to you already and knows that thanks to your work at Scarborough, Henry fears you. I spoke to the constable there and he heaped praise upon your head."

"Tell me, my lord, how was it that the garrison was withdrawn?"

"Treachery! I trusted Sir John d'Alençon and he used his position to send a letter in my name. He fled to join my son, Henry. But for your arrival, I might have had to fight a French army in England and that would be unthinkable."

"And how many men would you wish me to bring?"

"It is you I need, Sir Samuel. Even if you took just those men who saved my castle at Scarborough along with Sir William then it would be enough. You showed, when you defended London, that you have a mind like your grandfather's. It is not a skill that can be taught. I tried but I am a pale shadow of the man your grandfather intended me to be. Even your father, God rest his soul, was not the military magician that your grandfather was but you are. Men told me how you were able to see solutions to problems even before they occurred and that is a rare gift. Prince Richard is the bravest warrior I know, and I hope that your presence will help him to become a better general. You will come." His voice was pleading rather than commanding.

I nodded for I had no choice and yet I was not happy as it meant I would be leaving my wife and my home. At least the valley would be defended by the other knights. Poor Sir William had no sooner been given a manor and gained men at arms and archers before he would be whisked off to war. I glanced at Thomas' face and saw the joy and excitement upon it. I was the same the first time I had ridden to war with the Warlord.

The Perfect Knight

We discussed the role of the Bishop of Durham in the attempt to cause mischief in the north, "You have direct evidence that he was involved, Sir Samuel?"

"Direct? No, but in my gut, I feel that he was behind it. How else do you explain the ease with which the Scottish warband managed to reach Fissebourne undetected?"

"You may be right, but I do not wish to push the Bishop into the Scottish camp. I will write a letter to the Bishop reminding him of his responsibilities. If you have a scribe, I will dictate it before we eat. We have time?"

"We have time."

That evening I invited my sister to join us and sit on the king's right hand, the place of honour. Since her husband's death, she had been somewhat reclusive. Thomas was the one bright part of her life and when he was around, she was a different person. I sat her next to Thomas. Both he and Jack were given a night off serving at the table to sit in the elevated company of King Henry and his household knights. I had fought alongside most of them and knew that I had their respect. The feast was a success. King Henry flattered my wife, the food, the furnishings, and all. He was a ladies man! Ruth took it all in but spent most of the evening speaking with Thomas. Knowing that he was going to war and across the sea made her make the most of every moment.

The ship docked during the night. It was not an easy river to navigate at night and the fact that the king's ship had made the voyage in such a short time told me that it was shallow drafted and had a skilled captain. I would be leaving from Herterpol. It might take the king more than two days to reach the sea if the tides and the wind were against him. I rose before dawn and breakfasted with the king. "You are to meet me at La Rochelle. I am gathering my army at La Roche-sur-Yon." He dropped a purse of coins upon the table. "You will need to pay for a ship. I know that this service is outside England and, as such, I cannot force a noble to serve. This should pay for the passage but if, as I believe, you are your grandfather re-incarnated, then you and your men will profit from the campaign and we will defeat my rebellious son."

The Perfect Knight

I had learned, the previous night, that the king's favourite son, John, was the Lord Lieutenant of Ireland. I did not like the petulant boy and was glad that he would not be part of this campaign. That Geoffrey, another son and the Duke of Brittany, had joined his brother surprised me and my discussion with King Henry had told me that King Philip Augustus of France was, in all likelihood, behind this conspiracy. It was his way to win back France by using the gullible and pampered princes.

"Fare ye well, Sir Samuel, and tell Lady Eleanor I thank her for her hospitality." Without a backward glance, he stepped aboard his ship and they cast off. I felt sorry for the crew who would be exhausted already. Perhaps the haste with which the king headed north explained his haunted and gaunt appearance. His sons had not helped that was for certain.

I had no time for idle thoughts. I sent Jack to Sir William to explain what was needed. Richard son of Aelric sent two of his archers to procure a ship from Herterpol. I hoped that the Bishop would not put any hindrance in my way. I had sent the king's letter with another rider to Durham. I was not confident that it would have an effect but there was little that I could do about it. I leaned heavily on Ruth. My wife and I had still failed to conceive a second child and it had made Eleanor tearful and often in low spirits. While I was away then Ruth would be the rock that kept Stockton whole. The folk of the town liked her for she had always been of a charitable disposition and she had used the wealth left to her by her husband for good. I doubted that she would ever marry. Like me, she had married for love. My grandfather had been the same. Adela had been the only woman he had ever loved.

Gerard and I began the planning while Jack rode the relatively short way to Sir William's manor. This would be William's chance to see his new men at arms and archers in action. "We will need spares of everything, Gerard, and do not forget that we may well need tents. With less than a week to prepare it will be hard."

"I know that there are sword blanks in the armoury. It will not take long to have them prepared. The long spears you favour will just need their heads fitting and then they will be the equal of any lance. It is the surcoats which are the problem. We have no spares and combat is hard on such garments."

"I will see my sister, Lady Ruth, the ladies can sew surcoats instead of tapestries."

Gerard nodded, "Would you like me to choose a man at arms to carry your banner, my lord?"

I smiled, "I think that Thomas can do that, eh, Thomas?"

"Aye, father!" He grew a whole foot.

"Then he shall need better protection than he has, my lord. I will have Alf make a mail coif."

I shook my head, "There is no need. I have one I wore when I followed the Warlord. It will do but he needs a short sword. I know he cannot use one well yet." I turned to him, "You have a week to improve rapidly. Jack will be watching my back and cannot worry about you."

"I know, father and I will work so long as the sun shines."

"And a horse, my lord?"

Thomas had grown but he had some growing to do. A pony would be too small. He needed a young horse, perhaps a yearling but most of those were unschooled. "We shall have to find one. If we cannot then it will be a pony." I saw my son's face fall. I softened the blow with a promise, "I will ask the horse master."

Our horse master, Will, bred horses for us to the north of Stockton, close to Thorpe. I rarely got to visit him, but Gerard had become a good friend for Gerard loved to be around horses. When he had come to us, from Chester, he had needed a horse and he and Gerard had got on well.

The list of tasks seemed never-ending, but I knew that the best way to diminish it was to begin early. We started that day and by the time William and his men joined us, two days later, we had the swords all ready as well as the spears. Gerard had six sumpters to carry the spare weapons and arrows which we would need. The archers had fletched

The Perfect Knight

shafts, but the heads were unattached. They might only fit them the day we needed them; bodkins for mail and war arrows for the rest. While all this was going on, I sat in my father's solar. The Warlord had kept maps there and while most were of England and the borders, there were some of the Loire. My grandfather had been given manors along the river and one of them now belonged to his former squire. I began to copy out the maps onto one piece of vellum. I would not risk the maps, some of which were more than forty years old, on a sea voyage but I would make one map which might be of more use and easier to carry.

As well as the sumpters, Gerard also brought unexpectedly good news; there was a yearling palfrey, Skuld, at the horse farm. The horse master had bought a mare that had yet to be foaled at the Northallerton market. The breeder had been of Danish blood and the mare was called Sif. He had sold the mare at a fair price with the proviso that any offspring be named Skuld. Will had learned that this was a spirit who foretold the future. Will had used his stallion whose line had begun with the Warlord's warhorse to mount the mare. The resulting foal was born healthy and proved to be perfect for it took to the schooling as though it had learned in the mare's womb. I let Gerard take Thomas to the farm to pick it up and the sumpters and to see the foal. We had already bought more horse furniture from the tanners at the east end of the town. I would not rely on buying in Poitou. If the land was at war, then that might be impossible.

We had not replaced Tod and so we had one fewer man at arms to take with us. That was made up for by the eight men William brought. He had four archers and four spearmen. The four men who brought a shield, helmet, short sword, and spear might become men at arms but that took time and training. For now, they were the raw clay that Sir William would mould into warriors. They had padded gambesons and simple pale blue surcoats. They were the ones we had in store awaiting the gryphon to be sewn upon them. We also discovered that there was a ship which was bound for Aquitaine, but the bad news was that it left a day earlier than

The Perfect Knight

I wished. That might suit the king but neither my men nor I wanted to leave a day early. It hastened the preparations but the night before we were due to embark, we feasted in my hall. We hired musicians and had the best of food, wine, and ale. Aquitaine was renowned for its wine, but my men preferred ale and as Gerard said, "French ale is perfect for healing wounds!" The feast was reflective rather than merry. This would be the first time we had left England's shores as a company and who knew when or even if we would return.

My sister's arm was around my wife's shoulders as they waved to us in the first light of dawn. We left by the town gate and people had gathered to bid us farewell. We were close to the townsfolk and word had got out that, once more, the earl was leaving Stockton to defend the king. They had been doing this since the time of the Warlord and was a tradition. The children and grandchildren of the men who had followed the Warlord, now men and women grown, were there and it was yet another link to the past. Martyn Longsword was descended from Roger of Lincoln and his long sword had been carried when Roger of Lincoln had gone to war with my grandfather.

Once we had left the town we rode hard towards the coast. The hamlets and villages through which we passed consisted of a handful of houses. Stockton was the stronghold that they used in times of danger. Thanks to our vigilance that had not been for some time, but the enemy had been at the gates before now and we were cheered as we rode towards the port. The fluttering gonfanon and banner, proudly carried by Thomas, told them that we were going to war.

The ship, **'*White Swan*'**, was tied up to the quay. The tide was on the way in and so it meant that we descended the gangplank to the deck. We had timed our arrival to make it so. The horses would have to endure a voyage without any cover. The ship had been chosen because it often carried horses and there were metal cleats along the gunwale where the mounts could be tethered. We had taken our own oats, but the captain had provided straw. He wanted as little mess on his deck as he could. The saddles and my men's

The Perfect Knight

equipment were placed below decks. Sir William and I, along with our squires and Thomas, would share a small cabin but the men would have to share the deck with the horses. Most would be on the forecastle deck and the lucky ones, the aft castle.

The captain, Roger of Newcastle, was a man who seemed as round as he was tall. His mahogany-coloured face bespoke many years at sea. He greeted me as I boarded, "My lord, I hope that we can load quickly for I would leave on this rising tide, There are savage rocks just south of here!"

I nodded and pointed to my men who had already loaded half of the mounts, "My men know their business. How long will the voyage take?"

He waved a hand at the scudding clouds above us, "That depends upon the winds, my lord. If the Good Lord is kind and sends us favourable winds, then we could make it in eight days. If he does not feel inclined to do so, then it could take two weeks. Do not fear for my ship is sound and we are used to transporting horses. You are fortunate that I was heading for France. I have a hold full of arrows sent by the Bishop of Durham bound for Anjou."

I looked at him curiously, "And to whom will they be delivered?"

He shifted uncomfortably, "They are to be landed at Vannes. I shall drop you and your horses first and then sail back north."

I nodded. He was being practical. His hold would pay for the voyage and we were the bonus. However, Vannes was not in King Henry's control. I guessed that the arrows were bound for young King Henry or, perhaps, the Duke of Brittany, his brother, Geoffrey. This would be news to deliver to the king who might now realise that the Bishop of Durham was no friend to King Henry!

I rejoined Sir William and our squires, "Our bags are stowed away?"

Jack nodded and Thomas said, "It is a black hole father! There are no beds!"

I laughed, "At sea you have a sack suspended between two hooks. You will sleep comfortably for we will hug the coast down to Dover and it is only when we near Brittany that we will risk more violent seas. By then you should have legs and a stomach which are used to the sea."

The captain beamed when the last horse was fastened, and the tide was almost full. We headed through the breakwater of the harbour and he set a course south by east. We were able to stand on the starboard side and see first the sands where the seals basked and then the entrance to our river. As the tide was high there were ships already heading for Stockton. It was not necessarily to deliver goods to us but the iron that was mined to the south of us was a valuable cargo and many ships sailed to Stockton for that cargo. We used much of it but there was a demand, especially in times of war and iron was something best carried by ship and not carried on wagons. It made the winding voyage worthwhile. By the time we passed Hwitebi, it was almost noon and I was pleased with the progress. It would have taken more than a day of hard riding to reach the port and, an hour or so later we passed Scarborough. All my men lined the side for there lay Tod and we all remembered him. The great tower looked even more spectacular viewed from the sea as it seemed to reach to the clouds themselves, situated as it was on the high cliff. It was an illusion, but I now saw why the plan had been hatched. Dover was too strong to take but a castle which was unfinished was a mighty prize and with a French army ensconced would have been hard to retake.

Nine days later we reached our destination. Thomas, Jack, and Geoffrey, Sir William's squire had all been sick for two days but after that, they had recovered. For my men and our squires, it was a leisurely voyage. With horses on the deck, there would be no training as the sound of clashing steel might upset them not to mention the fact that there was little room in any case. The routine of feeding and watering the horses and then depositing their dung over the side gave a structure to the day. As the coast was just a grey smudge men either carved wood or bone or, in some cases, gambled. We played chess with a crudely carved set the captain had aboard. We only had rain twice, which was a miracle. The

The Perfect Knight

men used their oiled capes as tents while we huddled in our cabin with the door ajar. Thomas did not like to be shut in!

When we saw the towers of La Rochelle and Vauclair Castle, we knew that our life of leisure was ended. King Henry's standard fluttered from both the towers which flanked the narrow entrance. The chain between them had been lowered to allow us entry. I wondered about reporting the destination of **'White Swan'** but decided against it. Roger of Newcastle was just doing his job and earning a living. As the last horse was disembarked, I said, quietly, "Choose your sides wisely, Captain. I serve the true King of England. Make this your last voyage to deliver to his rebellious sons."

He looked unhappy and nodded, "It does not sit well with me, my lord, but it was the Bishop of Durham who hired me, and I have a crew to pay!"

"Think about what I have said, my friend!" I might have stopped the delivery but I knew that the king's sons had few archers and the best ones were with us. I liked the captain and did not wish to deprive him of an income.

The Perfect Knight

Chapter 6

The king was not in La Rochelle and that suited me for after a voyage across the sea our horses would need some time to recover. The army was camped close to the town walls and we walked our horses to a suitable site for the tents. We had been economic with them. I shared one with Sir William and our squires and page while the archers had a second and the men at arms a third. Some of them preferred to build a hovel. So long as there was not a heavy rainstorm they would be as comfortable as in a tent. Leaving the others to set up the tent I stretched my legs to seek someone in authority. I headed back to the town and found that the Duke of Aquitaine, Prince Richard, was in the castle.

My father and grandfather had known the king's sons better than I. They were all younger than me but, unlike their father, none had spent long in England. Richard, however, proved to be a man who wore his heart on his sleeve. It seemed that he had admired my grandfather and as soon as I was admitted he came down the dais to embrace me as though we were long lost friends.

"At last a real warrior to fight alongside us! When my father told me that you were coming to join us, I knew that our fortunes were on the rise. My two treacherous brothers will rue the day they raised their weapons against us." He put his arm around my shoulder and said, "This is the grandson and heir of the Warlord! This is the Earl of Cleveland!" There were genuine cheers, but I know that many who shouted loudly were flatterers attempting to ingratiate themselves in the duke's favour. "You shall have a chamber here in the castle." He turned to a liveried servant. "Have Sir Jocelyn's room prepared for Sir Samuel!"

I shook my head, "I am camped with my men. Do not trouble yourself on my account."

"Nonsense, the hero who saved London for my father shall not sleep in a tent!"

I learned that Prince Richard was not a man to be gainsaid. When he wished something then it happened. Having said that I found him to be good company, but others had a different opinion. He could be a great friend but a deadly enemy. I always remained on good terms with him and his familia who were cut from the same cloth as he.

His servant hurried off and I was led by the duke to the table where his household knights were seated. As wine was poured, he said, "Thanks to my brothers we will be outnumbered when we fight. You have been in such a situation many times and your advice will be key."

I nodded. Walking around the camp and town I had heard men speaking of the duke's brother, "I have heard that your brother, Henry," I did not give him his title for fighting his father showed that he was not the king, "attacks monasteries and robs them."

Duke Richard looked confused, "Aye, that is what men do when they make a chevauchée."

"A chevauchée is what you do to an enemy's lands. Raiding monasteries in the land of your own family is something barbarians do. Even the Seljuk Turks do not raid monasteries. We use that, my lord, express outrage that your brother makes war on God!"

Realisation dawned and Richard beamed, "Did I not tell you that the minds of the Warlord's family are weapons to be used? Aye, you are right, Sir Samuel, but how do we fight them on the battlefield?"

"The way we fought the Scots along the border. Use your castles to base your men and when the enemy makes a raid then trap them."

One of the knights with Duke Richard, Sir Simon de Lusignan said, "But the people will have been attacked by then."

"And when we return their animals and treasure we will be seen as their saviours and feelings will turn against Henry. My lord, I doubt that we have the men to keep the border completely manned. The land from which the attacks are made is the land of your mother. It is only your brother who has chosen to make war against his own people. So long as we do not attack his lands which rightly belong to your parents then we will be seen as being in the right. We do not raid monasteries and we have God on our side."

I saw now, all too clearly, what we had to do. This was the border fighting with which I was familiar. The difference was that my men were unfamiliar with the terrain. We needed local knowledge. La Flèche was the answer. Sir Leofric had been my grandfather's squire and whilst the castle and manor were in Anjou and the land of King Henry the Younger, I knew that he would not fight against his rightful lord. The problem was that La Flèche lay eighty miles to the north.

"Where are we, my lord, with the muster?"

"You have made the swiftest of passages. My father has not yet returned, and he will be bringing loyal knights and lords from England. We have a month. Why?"

I was careful with my words. I did not wish to put Sir Leofric or his family in danger. "I would ride to the border to assess the potential routes an enemy might take."

He frowned, "That is dangerous. What if you met my brother and his men? I would not have you taken for ransom before we have the opportunity to use your mind."

"Trust me, my lord. It is what my men and I do. The danger will come the closer we get to the Loire, but we are adept at hiding and we need to help our horses recover from the sea voyage. We would be away no more than a week, perhaps ten days."

He stroked his beard reflectively and then nodded, "I will accompany you as far as Poitiers. You are right, we should use our castles and Poitiers is a better place for the army to gather. When my father arrives then this town and castle will fill up."

The Perfect Knight

I knew that might add half a day of riding for it took us out of our way, but it could not be helped. "Excellent plan, my lord, and you are wise to use Poitiers. It is a strong town and well placed for you to intercept any warriors heading into Poitou to raid."

It took longer to reach Poitiers than I would have liked. I preferred leading my own men who were all mounted. Many of the men who followed Duke Richard were on foot and there were wagons carrying tents and supplies. Sumpters made for a faster journey. Once there I wasted no time in bidding Duke Richard farewell. Until King Henry arrived, I doubted that there would be much fighting. The present state of affairs was that the Young King Henry's knights led raids to juicy targets south of the Loire. Duke Richard would now be in a better place to discourage such raids. The two castles of Chinon and Saumur were fortresses that protected the northern border of Poitou but there were many fords where horsemen could make a raid across the Loire.

We rode hard and reached the fortress that was Chinon. It was one of Queen Eleanor's favourite castles. Now imprisoned by the King in England, she was far from Chinon. The Constable had a castle he could defend but not the resources nor the horsemen he needed to stop the attacks from the men led by the Young King Henry. I had to tell the same story to him that I had to the Duke, that I was scouting. He appeared relieved.

"Any information you can discover will be invaluable to us, my lord." I smiled for now that I was an earl, men like the constable deferred to me. It was strange because I did not think I had changed.

"And Saumur?"

"The Constable there has the same problem I do. Not enough horsemen to deter the attackers."

"And do we know where they cross the river?"

"They now hold the land close to Tours and could cross there, but as many of the raids have been south of Saumur, I am guessing they must be crossing either downstream from Saumur or between us."

"Then that is where I will start."

The Perfect Knight

It was not really a lie as La Flèche lay in that direction and Sir Leofric might be able to give me valuable information as well, I hoped, as assistance.

We were heading into land which belonged to the Young King Henry and his brother the Duke of Brittany. The surcoats we wore would identify us quite clearly as the King's men. Even without the pursuit of Sir Walter and the victory at Scarborough our enemies would be well aware of my loyalty. We did not know the land, but I had good scouts and they wore no surcoats. Richard son of Aelric had his archers spread out as we headed north to the Loire. The crossing at Chouzé-sur-Loire was in our hands but as it was just a detachment from Chinon under the command of a sergeant at arms it was hardly a secure place. I knew that such men could be suborned. Sir Richard Fitz William had been a knight but he had been seduced by the lure of a young king promising much. The man seemed loyal enough as we passed and even warned us of Angevin patrols. We left the bridge and found ourselves in Anjou. We had thirty-two miles to travel but half of it would be through the forest. The constable and the sergeant at arms had confirmed what I suspected already, there were no castles for us to worry about but as we had to pass through villages such as Vernantes and Mouliherne our enemies would know I was in their land and while we might reach the castle of La Flèche relatively easily, getting back might be more of a problem.

I voiced my concerns to Sir William as we rode beneath the eaves of the forest just a few miles north of the Loire, "I fear that I may be putting Sir Leofric in jeopardy for he is a knight of Anjou. He owes allegiance to the Duke of Brittany. I hope for a scout from him, but it may well be that I just make the enemy suspicious of him."

Sir William was clever and had a quick mind, "Sir Samuel, until we enter the castle of La Flèche then there would be no suspicion."

"Aye, but there is a town through which we have to pass."

"Then let us not enter the town." He pointed to the sky, we had just crossed a clearing, probably made by charcoal burners and we could see the sun. "It may well be almost dark when we reach it. If you remove your surcoat and your spurs, you, your squire and page could simply walk across and ask for shelter in the castle. We could spend a night in the forest."

"That might work. A good plan."

Thomas had been listening, "Unless, of course, Sir Leofric has changed since the time of the Warlord and now supports Young King Henry."

I whirled, "Why would he do that? He was the Warlord's squire!"

Jack said, in defence of Thomas for my words had been harsher in tone than I had meant, "Your son could be right, lord, for as far as I know from what you have said, you have never visited him. Did your father?"

I realised that they were right, "Not for many years but I know that he was loyal." I rode in silence as I wrestled with the doubts which had been rightly raised. "I have cast the die and if I am betrayed then it is meant to be." I smiled as I patted Thomas' horse, Skuld, "Let us pray that you are not the harbinger of bad news, eh?"

"I pray so too, father but I had to speak for the thoughts just came into my head."

"And I was wrong to use such a tone with you. Always say that which is in your heart, Thomas. That is ever the right thing to do."

We watered our horses at each village through which we passed. To do other would have aroused suspicion and as we saw no riding horses then I hoped that word would not get out yet, but others used the road and the sergeant at the Loire had said that the Angevins and Bretons were using mounted patrols. Sir William was right, and we saw the smoke from the houses of La Flèche in the distance. We entered the forest, and I took off my surcoat as did Jack and Thomas. We also left our shields. "From now on we speak Norman!"

Jack said, "I know few words, lord."

Thomas smiled, "Luckily I know many. I shall chatter like a magpie eh, Jack!" My son was showing a completely new side to him on this campaign. No matter what the

The Perfect Knight

outcome I would know him better and that could only be for the good! "Sir William, I leave the men under your command. If aught happens to me then return to the Duke."

"I will, my lord."

Richard had two of his archers follow us, using the woods so that if I was taken then the others would know. I knew from the maps I had copied that there was a river that acted as a sort of moat to the south of the town. It meant the town had layers of defence. Since the time of my grandfather, Sir Leofric had added a bridge to the southern bank of the river and we walked our horses towards it and the gatehouse that protected it. Riders would arouse more suspicion. The gatehouse on the bridge which crossed the Loir, a tributary of the Loire was made of stone and had two small towers. I saw that it could be defended by the outer walls of the town just north of us. A pair of sentries stopped us from crossing the bridge, "What is your name and what is your business here?"

I took on the identity of Brother Raymond. It was a lie and went against my nature, but Thomas' words had planted the seeds of doubt in my head, "I am Sir Raymond, and I was a knight hospitaller. I am heading north for a life of peace."

"You do not have the skin of a crusader nor do your servants."

I smiled, "These were hired when I reached Italy and I left the Holy Land three years since."

The smile seemed to work, and we were allowed to cross the bridge. The sun would soon set, and I knew that the gates to the town would then be barred. We passed through the town whose street and square were now emptying as people hurried home for their evening meal. When we reached the castle, I knew that I had to be truthful. There were two spearmen wearing the livery of the lord and their spears crossed before the bridge which spanned the water-filled ditch.

"I am Sir Samuel, Earl of Stockton here to speak with the lord of the manor."

One of them turned and said, "Send for Sir Alfraed."

The Perfect Knight

Those four words filled me with dread. What had happened to Sir Leofric and what relation was Sir Alfraed to the knight who had held the castle for my family? The name had been my grandfather's but that could be a coincidence. The knight who came to greet me was my age and he smiled, "Earl," he gave a short bow, "it is an honour to have you in my castle."

I nodded and smiled back, "And I am here in secret for I know that your land and that of my king are at war."

He gestured for us to enter, "You are right. Come." As we crossed the bridge into the triangular castle he said to the sentries, "Raise the bridge and close the gate early."

"Yes, my lord."

Our horses clattered over the cobbles under the arched gateway and we entered a small castle. I already knew it was triangular from the maps I had copied. He waved over a servant, "Take these horses and see that they are well looked after."

"Yes, my lord."

Sir Alfraed had presence and knew how to command but I did not know his relationship to Sir Leofric. I should have asked him at the gate and now I could not bring myself to ask the question. As we entered the keep, he stopped and answered the unspoken question, "My father is not well. You should know that before you see him, Earl Samuel. He has not left his bedchamber for a month and each day he grows weaker."

"He was wounded?"

Shaking his head the knight said, "I wish that was the case for we have physicians who can tend to wounds. It is something inside which eats at him. He will be glad to see you for he will have many questions and I hope it lifts his spirits. Since my mother died, he has been low." He turned to Jack and Thomas, "If you two wait here I will take Sir Samuel to see my father. It is right that they should be alone."

I ascended the stone stairs to the first floor and passed through the great hall and then up a wooden flight of stairs. A priest and a physician were just emerging from the room and neither looked happy. Sir Alfraed merely nodded at them and led me into the bedchamber where a servant was straightening the bed. The man in the bed looked grey and old. My grandfather had looked better before he had died. Sir Leofric's eyes were closed, and his hands folded together almost as though he was at prayer. Sir Alfraed took a chair and placed it next to the bed.

"The doctors have said that sleep will help him, but I am not sure. Henri, wait without. Sir Samuel will summon you if you are needed." He smiled at me as I sat, "I am glad that you have come."

He did not know the reason but suddenly that did not seem to matter.

The shutters were closed, and the room was lit by candles. The flickering light seemed to dance around the walls, and I watched the world-weary face of the former squire of the Warlord. He had not been my grandfather's first squire, that had been Sir Harold, but I knew that the Warlord had thought highly of Sir Leofric who had been as a rock here in Anjou. The manor still belonged to my family but there was no thought in my mind to attempt to reclaim it. Part of that was that I would, if I did claim the manor, have to pay homage to an enemy of my king.

Sir Leofric's eyes flashed open, almost as though he had heard my thoughts. His rheumy eyes squinted as he saw me, "Do I know you?"

I smiled, "No, Sir Leofric, but you knew my father and grandfather. I am Sir Samuel of Stockton, grandson of the Warlord and the new Earl of Cleveland."

His face cracked into a smile, "My lord." Then he shook his head, "That you are the earl tells me that your father has died." I nodded, "Soon I will be joining him, but I am glad that you have come to visit me." He held out his hand and I took the veined, bony claw in my two. The hands seemed as cold as ice. "Yet I do not think you came just to see me, did you?"

"No, Sir Leofric. I am in Poitou with King Henry and this is a scouting expedition. My men hide in the forest to the south of here."

He closed his eyes briefly and when he opened them shook his head, "The king is not as lucky as I am and as the Warlord was. His sons are not loyal. My boys, Alfraed and Richard, are but I fear they may be asked to fight the rightful king. I can do nothing, and I shall not leave this bed."

"They have been summoned?"

"I know not. They worry about my health and would not wish to add woes to burden me. I was the one who swore an oath to King Henry and I have not sworn a new one for the new duke. When I die all that will change. Now that you have come, Sir Samuel, I have more reason to live." He looked around, "Where is Henri?"

"He waits without."

"Summon him. I would have wine and perhaps some food."

He appeared less grey and I spent an hour with him. While he ate, I told him of the end of the Warlord in London. He had heard the story, but I had been there, and he wanted the details. I spoke of my father and then the attack on Scarborough. When Sir Alfraed came to fetch me to dine in the chamber below Sir Leofric was ready for sleep. He took my hand, "Thank you, Sir Samuel. I have reason to live once more."

As I descended Sir Alfraed said, "It is hard to see him each day growing closer to death. He looked better just now than I have seen him for some time. I thank you."

I felt guilty for I had not come to bring him succour but to seek help from the family and, in doing so, I might put them in jeopardy. I decided to wait to speak to Sir Alfraed about the matter at hand. His brother Richard was much younger than Alfraed and he bowed when he saw me. "We are honoured to have one of the Warlord's family once more under our roof. I grew up with tales from my father about the Warlord and Empress Matilda."

Sir Alfraed held out his hand for a beautiful and heavily pregnant woman, "This is my wife, Lady Isabelle."

"I thank you for your hospitality and apologise for the unwarranted intrusion."

She smiled, "Like Richard, I have heard the stories and found that I regretted never meeting the great man. Meeting his grandson is an honour."

I shook my head, "I am not even a shadow of the Warlord. We shall never see his like again."

The Great Hall was a slight misnomer for it was not large, but the meal was a cosy affair. We spoke of domestic issues and ignored the strife and dissension in the land. It was only when Lady Isabelle retired that the matter of the civil war was broached. Our squires and Thomas had joined us, and we sat before a roaring fire.

"You did not come here just to see our father, Earl Samuel, and I thank you for not bringing up the real subject of your visit while my wife was present, but I think I know what it is."

"You do?"

"You wish us to join you and fight for King Henry."

I shook my head, "No, for that would put you and your families in great danger. I know Young King Henry and he is a petulant and vengeful prince. No, you need not raise your hands against your neighbours, but you are right I did come here seeking help, but it is not the help of an army. I need someone who knows the land to act as a scout for me. Do you have such a man?"

They both looked relieved and Alfraed rubbed his chin and nodded, "Aye, I think we can help you there. One of the archers who came to live here with my father, Griff of Gwent settled here. He had a farm. When he died his son, Mordaf, sold the farm and moved into the town where he makes arrows, he is a fletcher. He is unmarried and he knows the land. His father trained him to be an archer, but he lost two fingers. That is why he makes arrows."

"And what makes you think that he would help us?"

"He lost his two fingers not by accident but by design. He was serving with the Lord of La Lude when he was captured by a French knight, Henri de Verneuil. As he was an archer, the Frenchman ordered him to lose his fingers. Mordaf hates the French. I will send for him on the morrow."

The Perfect Knight

I was relieved not least because of the connection to my grandfather. We then chatted about other matters. "Your father says you have not been asked to swear an oath to the Duke and his brother."

"No, and I would find it hard to do so yet what choice would we have? This manor is our life. We have no other income." Sir Alfraed looked at me intently, "I am aware, my lord, that it is your family which owns La Flèche and we are the guardians of it. When you came, I thought it was to claim the income."

I laughed, "Fear not, Stockton is a richer manor than this and none in my family would take this from you. When your father dies, Sir Alfraed, and you inherit you will be asked to swear an oath. I beg you to do so. I would hate to think of a vengeful prince taking away that which your family has worked so hard to build."

"But that might mean fighting against you and the rightful king."

"Believe me I know that, but this is your home and you are Angevin now. Your father was English but no longer."

The sobering thought made us reflective and silent. I broke the mood by saying, "So, Richard, when shall you be knighted?"

He looked sad, "My father said that he would give me my spurs, but he has not left his bed for some months."

I banged the table, "We can remedy that. I am Earl of Stockton and tomorrow I shall dub you. It is the least I can do."

We stayed up later than I intended but I know that it did Thomas and Jack good to see the two brothers.

The next day, while we waited for Mordaf to arrive, we had a simple ceremony in the Great Hall and Richard was knighted. When I had risen the three of us had gone to tell Sir Leofric what we planned and, like my visit the night before, it seemed to perk up his spirits. When he was informed of my plan to use Mordaf he was delighted, "Griff of Gwent would be happy to know that his son was serving King Henry. He married a local girl else he might have returned to England."

The Perfect Knight

When Mordaf arrived I could not help but look at his maimed right hand. He had a haunted look about him. I wondered at his existence in this Angevin town for only the archers who served Sir Leofric would need his arrows. I wondered why he stayed.

"Mordaf, son of Griff, this is the Earl of Cleveland." When Sir Alfraed said my name Mordaf brightened. "He comes with an offer for you. He would hire you as a scout. You would be serving Richard, Duke of Aquitaine, and King Henry of England. How does that suit?"

He did not ask how much he would be paid but said without pause, "Aye, my lord, for I know that the French are behind this mischief and I would pay them back for this!" He held up his hand.

I nodded, "There may be an opportunity for revenge, Mordaf, but my primary concern is to use you to gain an advantage over King Henry's enemies. You understand that?"

"Yes, my lord, and I am cold now. You can trust me. All that I will say is that if you wish any Frenchmen to be killed then I am your man. I was a good archer and I have learned to use my right hand to wield a knife."

Inwardly I shuddered for in taking his fingers the French knight had made a killer. I nodded, "Then you are my man. We leave immediately."

"I need a horse, my lord."

Sir Alfraed said, "Then I will give you one, Mordaf, and we will watch over your home for you."

He shook his head, "That is kind, my lord, but I am not sure I will return. My father always wished to return to England and, if I survive, this might be my opportunity." He looked at me.

"Of course, you shall have a place in Stockton."

"Good."

While he went to fetch his war gear and Jack and Thomas fetched our horses I went with Richard and Alfraed to take my leave of Sir Leofric. His last words to us showed that the Warlord's presence was still all around us, "My lord, I confirm now that La Flèche will always be your family's manor and we are custodians only. My sons will be here to serve you at any time should you ask." He looked at his sons, "I know that you will do this, but I would have you swear."

They both took their swords and kissing the hilt said, "We so swear!"

Sir Leofric smiled, "Now I can die content. Fare ye well, Earl Samuel."

As we left the keep, I said, "I shall not ask you to compromise your lives unless it is the direst of circumstances."

Sir Alfraed nodded, "We know the debt of honour we owe. We shall be here!"

Chapter 7

I do not know what the guards at the bridge gate thought as we headed south but as Sir Alfraed and Sir Richard accompanied us they could say little. There would be speculation and my identity had been revealed but I doubted that any harm would come of it. Sir Leofric could take any suspicion and blame for he was so close to death that he cared not. I thought it a shame that both he and my father had endured such lingering deaths. At least a death in battle was swift. That was how I wished to go, fighting with sword in hand and not rotting my life away in inches.

The two knights were impressed when my archers ghosted from the forest and my men were happy to see us safe and sound. "If you are questioned about my visit then use the semblance of the truth, that I came to see an old friend of my grandfather's."

"It should not come to that. I pray you success."

"Thank you, Sir Alfraed."

Sir Richard beamed, "And once more I am in your debt. I thank you for the spurs!"

"I do not doubt that your father would have done so had he been able."

The two men turned and headed back to their castle. As we rode south, I was pleased that I had made the visit. I was sad to see Sir Leofric's condition but happy that he had two such fine sons.

I turned to Mordaf, "Welcome to my company. Richard son of Aelric is my captain of archers and I am sure that your scouting apart, they will appreciate having a fletcher with

The Perfect Knight

us." He grinned and I could see that he was happy. Is there anything we should know before we head south?"

He nodded, "If you managed to ride this road without meeting a patrol then you were lucky. There are trails in the forest and as we are all mounted they should be almost as easy to negotiate as this road with less chance of us meeting enemies."

Sir William nodded his agreement, "We made a large camp, my lord, and there was both fire and smoke. While those in La Flèche might not be concerned, the wind was from the north and may have drifted to some of the towns."

I waved my arm to show I agreed and Mordaf led us into the trees. It was a more nerve-wracking experience for we could not see too far ahead. Had we been on the road then we would have seen any enemies. Here we relied on Mordaf's skill and my archers' noses.

It was getting on towards evening when the line of archers stopped and Richard son of Aelric rode back, "My lord, there are men ahead on the road. Mordaf says they are Breton horsemen and that they look to be ready for an ambush. He thinks that they are waiting for us."

They were aware we were in the area and they were waiting for us. "Can we get by them without being seen?"

He shook his head, "The forest ends just short of them. They are not watching the trees but any movement we make will result in them seeing us. We either speak to them or fight them, my lord." I looked at the sky and wondered if we could wait until dark. By my estimate, we were eight miles from Saumur. If we waited until dark, then we would have to camp in the forest. If we eliminated the threat, we could use the road and be behind Saumur's walls by dark. That made my decision for me. "Richard, have your archers dismount and tether their horses. Mordaf, our squires and Thomas can watch them." I turned to Sir William. We use swords and walk our horses as close as we can then our archers can thin their ranks." By the time I had donned my helmet and our archers had tied up their horses then we were ready to ride, "Richard, you know what to do."

The Perfect Knight

"Aye lord. Come lads, let us get as close to them as we can."

They disappeared into the forest and I drew my sword. I hefted my shield onto my shoulder and allowed it to hang there from the long strap. My left hand was free to use the reins. I raised my sword and we moved towards the road. The wind helped neither side, but I knew that there would come a point where the Breton horses would sense ours and whinny. That would be the point at which we would charge. I hoped, by then, that my archers would be in position to attack. The sun was setting behind us and I saw, to my right, the open, farmed fields. Richard had been right; we would have been seen. By leading and walking our horses rather than trotting we made little noise and ahead, I heard the murmur of conversation. The Bretons would have a dilemma. If they had received word about a column of men heading north and then been ordered to ambush them on their return, they would now have to decide either to camp or return whence they came. If they returned to their home, which I presumed was in the west, then they risked running into us. Waiting to ambush was stressful.

A last flaring of the sun in the west lit up the helmets of the Bretons. I saw at least two of them wore mail and that suggested knights. The sun would take half an hour or so to set and by then we would either have won or our bodies would be in Breton hands. I could neither see nor hear my archers as they closed with the road, but I knew that they were stealthy. The Bretons had more chance of seeing us for our horses and our mail made us bigger targets. We grew ever closer and I knew that soon we would be seen.

"Knights!" The Breton voice told me that we had been seen and I spurred my horse.

I heard the thrum of arrows and the first cry as one blossomed from the chest of a Breton light horseman. We had caught them unawares. They had been spread out on both sides of the road and had been facing north. Our appearance from the west had confused them. The sun was setting behind us and while it lit us up it was also in their eyes. I saw an arrow smack into the mailed shoulder of a

The Perfect Knight

Breton man at arms. He still came on at us but he would be weakened in combat. I made for the leading knight. My archers would be forced to pick targets to the side. We were not in a solid line, the thinning trees prevented that but we were in a rough arrow formation with Sir William just on my right shoulder.

Holding my sword slightly behind me I swung at the right side of the Breton knight. He had a long spear which he poked at me. This was not the flat of a tilting yard and the wavering spearhead did not strike true. It hit me but it was more of a glancing blow to the side. It tore through the surcoat and caught on mail rings. The spearhead was stronger than the mail and the rings were torn but by then my sword was sweeping across his chest and he was unable to bring his shield around. The edge of my sword ripped through his surcoat and mail. Unlike his strike which had just torn my mail my sword ripped into flesh. His cantle held him in position and as I passed him the spear fell and my sword came away bloody. A Breton light horseman was behind him and I had to react quickly. I jerked my reins to pull my horse to the shield side of the Breton and as his spear struck fresh air I brought down my sword to hack across his shoulder.

A Breton voice told me that we had won, "Back! Reform!" As they turned, arrows slammed into their backs. I saw the Breton knight, supported by his squire and with mailed men around him, leading the flight. Many of the mailed horsemen had arrows protruding from their shields, cantles and mail. They would rue the day they attempted to ambush English archers.

I reined in at the road and turned to see that all our men were intact. One of Sir William's new men, a spearman unused to fighting on horseback, had blood flowing freely from his arm. Already Gerard was reaching for his bag to tend to it.

Cupping my arms I shouted, "Bring the horses!" The four I had left to watch them would only have two or three horses each to lead and soon we would be mounted and able to head down the road.

The Perfect Knight

Martyn Longsword returned from checking the Breton dead and to ensure that any wounded were tended to. He led two horses. "There were just four of them dead, lord. I found their horses wandering. We lost none."

"Thank you." Seeing that my archers had mounted I sheathed my sword, "Mordaf, lead off, down the road this time."

"Aye lord." He was grinning, "We showed them. A pity they were not French, eh?"

I had the weaponsmith at Saumur repair my mail and Sir William's spearman had his wound stitched. We spent four days riding along the river to identify possible crossing places the two rebellious sons might use. We found too many and as we headed back to Poitiers I was in low spirits. Although men on foot might find it hard to cross the Loire, horsemen could do so easily and they could raid with impunity. Mordaf had proved to be invaluable and we had saved time so that we were able to report back to the duke and his father, the king.

Leaving Sir William to see to the men I reported directly to King Henry. Once more I was struck by the way he had aged so suddenly. I knew that I was lucky that I had but the one son and he showed no signs of the rebellious nature of the king's brood. "I fear, my lord, that your sons can cross the river at will. Neither Chinon nor Saumur are in a position to stop them from doing so."

The king frowned, "Is there nothing we can do?"

"You could base large numbers of horsemen in each castle but that would tie them down." I hesitated for I was about to suggest a strategy to the king, "I believe that we have the beating of your sons, my lord. You and Duke Richard are better generals and warriors. Let us meet them head-on. Make it one battle to see who wins."

I saw Duke Richard grin for the idea appealed to him. The lack of confidence was apparent, however, on the face of King Henry, "I like your enthusiasm, Sir Samuel, but you are not the Warlord."

I could have been hurt by the King's words, but I was not for he was right, yet he had come all the way north to

The Perfect Knight

Stockton just to seek my help, "No, my lord, but he trained the two of us. That will be enough."

He nodded, "Then you need to find where they are."

I turned to Duke Richard, "Which were the monasteries he raided last, my lord?"

"Le Dorat and Tersannes, to the east of us."

"Then that is where we look."

"And I will come with you while you, my father, prepare the army to follow us when we have them cornered."

As soon as I knew what we were about I summoned Sir William, Mordaf, Gerard and Richard son of Aelric, "We are to find the enemy and bring them to battle." I had my map, and I jabbed my finger to the east of us, "We seek them there."

Mordaf nodded, "There are forests there, but it is more generally well farmed and tended land. There are castles, my lord." His words were a warning for castles housed horsemen.

"We will not be alone. Duke Richard and his men will be with us. Your task will be to find them and mine will be to advise the Duke."

Sir William smiled, "Much as the Warlord did with King Henry when he was younger."

"You are right but I do not think that I can fill my grandfather's boots, but it is good that you remind me. I shall keep the image of the Warlord with me. He stopped me from making mistakes."

Thomas had been listening and he said, "I wish that I could have seen him. When kings and princes speak of him the way they do then I know he was a great man."

"And you, my son, have his blood in your veins as do I. Our task is to mould you into a warrior first."

Sir William nodded, "And watch your father for he has great skills when it comes to battle. He does not waste men's lives."

Anxious to move on I said, "Go and prepare. If any of the horses show signs of weakness, then have them replaced. We cannot afford to be on foot. How is your man, William?"

"He can ride but he is not yet ready to fight."

The Perfect Knight

"He can join the squires, pages and Mordaf as horse holders. I can see that our archers will be needed more than ever." The brief battle with the Bretons had shown me what they could do. All the warriors who had died were struck by arrows.

As a scouting force, we were strong. There were more than two hundred and fifty of us. More than half were knights; they were eager to follow the Duke of Aquitaine. The only archers we had were mine and Sir William's. There were other archers at Poitiers, but they were not mounted. My grandfather had been prescient and when he had started to use mounted archers it was a revolutionary move. My father had furthered the idea when he had returned from the crusades. He saw how effective a fastmoving force of mounted archers could be. Sadly the war bow was not the weapon to use on horseback, but we had adapted the technique and now my archers were confident riders, and they could, if they had to, fight with swords and bucklers from the backs of horses.

I rode with Duke Richard and allowed William to ride ahead with my archers and men at arms. I knew he would not be foolish and both Gerard and Richard son of Aelric would offer sage advice if it was needed. I used the time to begin my training of the duke. The first thing I had to do was to focus his attention for he was obsessed with the idea of war and fighting. I was trying to teach him strategy.

"Duke Richard, if we come upon the enemy then charging at them with knights may not be the most effective way to war."

He looked puzzled, "None can stand against mounted and mailed horsemen!"

"Really? How about a wall of spears backed by crossbows and archers? I have seen horses ride at men and not charge home because of the barrier of men."

He laughed, "My horse is a warhorse, and he would trample any who was before me."

"And every knight and man at arms who follows you has the same steed?" I saw doubt flicker across his face and pushed home my advantage, "What if the enemy has horses?

They can flee or they can charge. If it is the former, then your mounts could not charge home or you could be led into a trap. Better that you pin and hold the enemy so that they cannot flee. I would urge you to hire, as I do, mounted archers."

"You sound like my brother, Henry. He has hired mercenaries to do his fighting for him. He has crossbowmen from Genoa and swordsmen from Swabia. He has hired Magyar light horsemen as well as many knights who flock to his banner in the hope of reaping the reward of pillaging a rich England." He shook his head, "He cares nothing for England. Where we ride is the land he wishes and, of course, Aquitaine. He shall have that over my dead body!"

Knowing that we fought mercenaries helped me for the Scots often hired Irish Gallowglasses and whilst they were fierce, wild fighters, they fought for pay and when the paymaster was taken then they tended to flee. My archers were not worried about Genoese crossbowmen; they hated the crossbow. We saw none for the first two days and then, when we made a stop to water and feed our horses, John Longbow rode in, "Sir Samuel, we have found the trail of horsemen in the south leading from La Souterraine to Limoges. They had wheeled vehicles with them too."

"Ride back and have Sir William find them and threaten their rearguard. We will follow." He whipped his horse's head around and headed for the scouts. Duke Richard had some local knights amongst his men. "My lord, is there a road which leads south so that we can cut off these raiders?"

He did not know but he waved forward a knight, "Sir Jean, is there another road we can take to Limoges?"

"Yes, my liege, there is a small road which leads through Châteauponsac. As we are all mounted, we may make good time that way."

I nodded, "Then lead on and keep up a good pace. We have, Duke Richard, a God-given opportunity. With our men closing with their rearguard then their attention will not be at their fore. They may turn like a bull to deal with a couple of terriers biting at its heels."

He showed then that he was decisive. He shouted, "Arm for war! When we spy the enemy then we attack!"

He had no idea of numbers, but he was fearless. My task would be to keep him alive. Sir Jean did as I had asked, and we passed through the sleepy village of Châteauponsac and the knight took us due east towards the Limoges road. It was all that I could do to keep Duke Richard from galloping ahead. All that I was able to do was to keep my horse neck and neck with him and close to the rump of Sir Jean. Our line of knights and mounted men at arms spread out behind us. We caught up with their advance guards at the village of Razès. It was a crossroads although the road we met was larger than ours. The advanced guard had stopped to water their horses and Duke Richard did not hesitate.

Drawing his sword he spurred his warhorse and shouted, "Charge!"

In hindsight, it was reckless to the point of foolishness but as with much that Richard did the gods of war smiled upon him and we caught the Bretons dismounted and without helmets. The forty men who had kept up with the Duke simply swept through the sixty or so light horsemen. We were mailed and had weapons in our hands. We slashed, stabbed, and chopped. Their horses fled and I heard horns from up the road. The main body of men appeared and spying us rode to meet us. The rest of our column had caught up with us and so the odds were slightly better than otherwise. Even so, I estimated that the main body had five hundred or so men. That I could not see men on foot meant that they would be with the rearguard and I could rely on Sir William to deal with those.

"Duke Richard, have your men make a wedge with you and me as the point!" I was giving orders to a man who would not even take orders from his father but something in my voice, or perhaps my name made him obey.

He nodded, "Form a wedge on me!"

We headed up the road leaving the Bretons who had survived to take their horses and flee. The road was wide enough for nine horsemen and I rode on the right-hand side of the Duke of Aquitaine. Sir Jean had bravely taken the left

The Perfect Knight

side of the rear of Duke Richard's horse. We headed up the road towards a hotch-potch of knights and men at arms. There were Normans and Bretons, but I also saw Italian Normans and Lombards. They were mercenaries. When we crashed into them Duke Richard showed that he had been right about his horse. It snapped and bit at man and horse. His mighty sword smashed through the helmet and skull of the Lombard who was foolish enough to face him. I tried to keep up with him to guard his right side. A spear was thrust from a Pugliese knight and my sword hacked it in two before sweeping the blade sideways. It barely missed the knight's horse and it caught him in the chest. His cantle did not save him for he fell sideways and as he fell his body dragged his mount to the ground making the knights behind him swerve.

 Duke Richard was an unstoppable force as he seemed oblivious to danger and his confidence was such that, miraculously, none of the spears and lances thrust at him seemed to harm him. Of course, he was fighting mercenaries. I have never liked the idea of mercenaries as I believe a warrior has to believe in something other than money. The fact that I paid my men at arms and archers well did not make them mercenaries. The first wave of knights and men at arms, their lances and spears shattered, drew swords but by then the rest of us were amongst them. I had no squire to watch my back but the men who followed Duke Richard were the best at what they did and the odd lance and spear which scraped my surcoat, helmet, and mail, did no harm. I was protecting the right side of their leader and Duke Richard's knights would do all in their power to ensure that I came to no harm.

 The breakthrough came when a Breton lord faced up to Duke Richard. He was not a mercenary and was surrounded by his oathsworn. When their two swords came together it was like a clap of thunder and the sparks added to the image. I had to swing my shield around to my chest to prevent the metal headed spear from skewering me. The Breton could not bring his shield around fast enough and I smashed my sword against his chest. I tore a long gash in his surcoat, and he reeled. I pulled back and swung again. Practice in

Stockton's outer bailey meant I could hit the same place repeatedly. When I struck again, I was rewarded by blood on the blade and I had hurt him.

"Yield or die!"

He nodded and dropping his spear, slid from his saddle. A squire appeared to help to tend to him. He took off his helmet, "Your name, my lord?"

"Sir Samuel of Stockton!"

That was all I had time for as Duke Richard had not wasted any time in knocking the Breton lord from his saddle. The Breton had surrendered, and we moved on to the next band of men at arms and knights. Duke Richard's fearless attack meant that he drew two or three men to him. They would not risk fighting him alone. He unhorsed one and I galloped at a second who had a war axe ready to strike at the head of the rampant knight. My sword slashed across his left arm. I had a powerful right arm and it was bred from many hours at the pel. I did not break the mail but I broke his arm. The axe fell and he wheeled his horse away to escape me. The last of the three fighting Duke Richard also turned and fled. Not only were these not as ready to face the fearsome Duke Richard and his knights, but they were also assailed from the rear by arrows. It had to be my men. The dual attack broke them, and they fled. The open fields made it easy for them to do so and we were left with a few dozen dead bodies and ten or so captured knights. None of those we captured was a mercenary.

Duke Richard took off his helmet and stood in his stirrups to peer around the captured men and the bodies on the battlefield, "Where is my brother? Could he not face me?"

The knight who had surrendered to me stood and said, "He is in Limoges, my lord. The last I heard he was unwell."

Duke Richard snorted, "Unwell? What is the disease, cowardice?" He turned and said to no one in particular, "Send for my father and the rest of our men! We have the pup cornered now!"

A voice shouted, "Yes Duke Richard!" and I heard hooves galloping off.

The Perfect Knight

"Thank you, Sir Samuel! Your strategy was sound and your courage beyond compare. It is an honour to ride with you."

I nodded, "If I might go to see to my men, my lord?"

He smiled, "And you were right about the archers! I shall begin to hire them."

I saw a fire burning and my men waved cheerily as I rode up and then dismounted. I was relieved to see Sir William, my son, and the rest of the men were whole. They had captured the baggage train. My former squire looked exultant, "We took their rearguard before they knew it and slaughtered their crossbowmen. Some fled but enough died to know that our archers are their superiors."

I nodded, "Thank you for watching over my son."

Sir William smiled, "He is a sound little warrior, Sir Samuel. He obeys orders and is as calm as any."

It was too late to continue on and so we camped at Razès. Duke Richard was in a fine mood and I noticed that he treated all the captured men well. Their squires would be sent, the next day, to fetch ransom. Thomas and Jack were happy to be back with me and I left the Duke's fire as soon as it was politic to do so. Our first real battle had gone well. My men were happy for the men they had slain, the rearguard's crossbowmen and spearmen had been mercenaries and had full purses. Some pack animals had died in the attack and they ate well on the butchered animals. As most of the wagons contained looted treasures, they would not benefit from their recapture but knowing that the church would have its treasures returned could not harm a man. All my men were aware that death could be around the corner and an unshriven man needed all the sympathy that God might give. As I rolled into my cloak I, too, was happy. The Duke was a brave leader and he listened. We had won and lost none. Perhaps this campaign might prove to be a successful one. I began to dream that I might do the Warlord's name justice.

The next day I spoke to the Breton knight, Sir Alan de Baud, whom I had captured. He smiled ruefully as we arranged the ransom. I did not ask for an exorbitant amount but a paltry one would have left the Breton insulted. "You are a true gentleman, my lord. It was vanity that made me seek you out. I knew the reputation of your family and more, I had heard how you had recently held off two attacks in your own land. I thought to see if I had your mettle. It seems I was wrong, and I must return to my home and improve."

"I work every day as does my squire and my page. My grandfather was a great leader, the Earl Marshal of England and yet he practised every day. The day a knight does not practise is the day he should hang up his sword."

"You may be right." He glanced around in the way men do when they know not who might overhear them, "My lord, may I have a word in private?"

We were not in the company of just my men and there were other knights who had captured warriors discussing ransom. I nodded and led him away from the other knights. "Speak."

"I heard of your success from a relative of Guy d' Aumale, the knight you slew. He has sworn vengeance upon you for Sir Guy borrowed money to hire the men he took, and it meant the family was impoverished as a result."

I shook my head, "Even had I not killed him they would still have lost the money. How can I be the one who caused the impoverishment?"

"You are right, my lord, but Geoffrey d'Aumale is not only young but reckless. He does not see it that way. The family was promised the castle and manor of Scarborough if they had succeeded and Sir Guy was promised ennoblement to the rank of earl."

"And where is he now?" I looked around, "If he sought my head then all he had to do was to find me on the battlefield."

"He is young and reckless, but he is also cunning. He rode with Young King Henry. He and the six knights he leads were part of the escort of Young King Henry."

"Then when I find the rebellious son, I shall find this man and I will give him the opportunity of a combat with me."

"You have cost his family dear and he was forced to sell their castle to pay off the debts. The money that was left he used to buy swords for hire. He did not buy the best, he bought killers. That is why they were not with this battle of men. They ride with their lord. Beware them for they have no honour."

Sir Alan was a true knight. There were some men who were given their spurs and never deserved them. He truly did. I now had another reason to seek the son of King Henry.

Chapter 8

Aquitaine 1183

The king and the army he had gathered joined us before we reached Limoges. Ours was a mustered army and that took longer to collect than a mercenary one. When mercenaries are offered payment for their swords, crossbows, spears and axes they are like rats descending upon a fallen sack of grain. Young Henry had tried to take a shortcut to victory and he had paid the price. His men had not been good enough and his hiring of such men as d'Aumale was evidence of that. I had not mentioned that my enemy was with his brother to Duke Richard for it was my problem, but it highlighted an issue with his elder brother. Why had neither he nor his brother, the Duke of Brittany, led the army? In my eyes that was a mistake. King Henry might be unwell but he rode at the head of his army and he was a happy man as he rode at the fore of the column of loyal men to the mighty city of Limoges. There was a castle with walls, twelve paces high and a walled city. I did not relish a siege to take it. I rode with the King and his son to the gates of the city. To my great surprise, the gates were opened and the burghers within abased themselves before King Henry. The King of England, too, seemed surprised by their action.

"Where is my rebellious son, Henry? Is he within the castle?"

The Mayor rose and said, "No, King Henry, he is at Martel for he was taken ill. Men say he is close to death and he sent a message for you to go to his side and be with him in his hour of judgement. I beg you to restrain your warriors for we offer no resistance and," the nervous mayor glanced

The Perfect Knight

up at Duke Richard, "would not risk the wrath of the Duke of Aquitaine."

Richard was delighted with the compliment and beamed. King Henry was a wiser man, "Then all will swear loyalty to their lord and master, Richard, Duke of Aquitaine and send a man to have the gates of the castle opened."

The mayor nodded and gave his orders. I saw the man created by my grandfather. King Henry was often called wily and cunning, but I preferred wise and quick. His decision was the right one for this way he did not risk losing face demanding that the garrison of the castle surrender. Who knew what hotheads might remain within? The king turned to us and said, quietly, "We have it seems, won. Sir Samuel, take your men and ride to Martel. I need to know the veracity of this report."

Duke Richard said, "You do not believe it?"

"Let us say that it could be a trap for my son could be luring me to a place where I could be ambushed. Martel, as far as I can recollect is more than sixty miles from here. I would not risk an army to discover if the men of Limoges are still colluding with my son."

King Henry could also be ruthless. He was risking a small part of his army and that part would be led not by his son but the head of the family which had ensured that he attained the crown. It was a compliment that he thought we could manage what he asked but our journey was not without risk.

I nodded, "Very well, King Henry. I had best leave now."

"Aye, but take care. I send you for I know that you and your men will be vigilant and not swayed by the blood of success which courses through the veins of others. If my son, Henry, is not close to death and this is a trick, then I would have you fetch him back to face my judgement." He took a ring from his finger, "If he is close to death then take this ring and give it to my son as a sign of my forgiveness."

I nodded knowing that if it was a trick then the rebellious son would have far more men than I did, but I knew the risks and I would act accordingly. I had a personal interest in this. From what the Breton knight had told me, d'Aumale would

The Perfect Knight

be with the king. I told Sir William, Richard, son of Aelric and Gerard what I had heard. Forewarned was forearmed.

The land through which we rode was not forested. It had been farmed for many hundreds of years and was rich and ordered. The folk who lived there wanted no war and even more importantly, there were no castles on the journey. Limoges had a great citadel that could control an area fifty miles from its centre. I could see no reason why the mayor would risk the wrath of the king and his fiery son, Duke Richard.

I was still vigilant and Mordaf rode ahead with my archers. We had supplies taken from the French column and my men had full purses. It was good to be away from the main army where the only orders came from me. We rode in our normal formation that meant we could react quickly to any danger. We spoke to each other as we rode but our eyes and ears were constantly seeking signs of danger.

"Does this mean we go home soon, Sir Samuel?"

"I am not sure, Jack. Even if the news is true there is still Duke Geoffrey although as this revolt was begun by Young Henry, I think his demise means that it will end. We shall see. Why, do you want to go home?" He hesitated and I added, "Come now, speak truly for you know that it is my way."

"I would do more than hold horses for the archers, my lord. I am sorry but I wish to ride at your back as Sir William did when he was a squire."

I understood what he was saying. How many times had I begged to be allowed to wield my sword in battle? "Perhaps you are right. Next time we ride to war we should bring horse holders with us."

Sir William nodded, "Servants, perhaps?"

"I was thinking more of old soldiers who might yearn for the life on a campaign and yet cannot fight. There must be many of them in Stockton. One legacy of the Warlord is that the many soldiers who fought for him and survived stayed close to Stockton. Not all are married and not all wish to spend days in the taverns talking of battles past."

The Perfect Knight

That seemed to brighten up both Jack and, unsurprisingly, Thomas. Of course, the corollary to that was we would have to be back in Stockton to find them and so far as I could see the campaign was not yet over.

We reached the monastery to which Young Henry had been taken just two days after leaving Limoges. We travelled much faster than the army did and when we reached it discovered that Henry was still alive. We were greeted by his friend, William Marshal. My grandfather and he had been friends although I doubted that the Warlord would have approved of the support given to a rebellious son.

"I fear, Sir Samuel, that King Henry is close to death."

I shook my head, "When he rebelled against his father, he lost all rights to that title."

"Nonetheless, it was given and until I am told other he will be accorded that way. Come, we should hurry for his life is measured in hours and not days."

I restrained him, "Before we enter, I need to know if there is a knight with you. He is called Geoffrey d'Aumale."

The look on his face told me his opinion of d'Aumale, "He was but the air is cleaner now that he and his bandits have fled. When we heard of your approach he and his men fled, taking with them some treasure from the monastery. I knew not why they were taken on as protectors for there was not an ounce of nobility in them as their flight shows, but the king seemed to like them and until he was struck down was ever in conference with them. Why do you ask?"

I smiled, "This knight has sworn vengeance upon my head. I would have expected it in battle but when I heard he protected your lord I was wary."

"You need not fear the rest of us, Sir Samuel. We are all honourable knights."

I nodded, "That is what I had heard. Then lead on for, as you say, time is not a commodity we can squander."

I left my men with Sir William and hurried to the candle-lit chamber. There was the stench of death in the room. The heir to England was dying, "Is that my father who has come to see me?"

I neared him and took his hand, "No my lord, it is Sir Samuel of Stockton, but I come to you from your father. He feared the news we had was a trick."

He closed his eyes and shook his head, "No trick, I am marked to die. I did not see the Holy Land but my friend, Sir William here, has promised to take, when I am dead, my cloak and cross to Jerusalem."

I took out the ring. "Your father sent this ring as a token of his forgiveness,"

He greedily grasped and kissed the ring before slipping it onto his finger and sighing, "Now at the end, I wonder at my vanity. Had I waited I would have been king but coming on the campaign has cost me dear." He looked up at Sir William, "I should not have raided the houses of God and he would not have punished me thus." Sir William's silence was eloquent, and I guessed that the knight had advised the would-be king against such action.

A physician loomed closer, "My lords, we must see to the king. Whilst his end is nigh, we must make him as comfortable as we can. I pray that you leave us."

Nodding the two of us left. Once out in the fresh air, I said to Sir William Marshal, "You will go on a crusade?"

"I will if only to obey his last command, but my heart will not be in it. I would return to England. Sir Samuel, you are close to the king. I beg you to ask him to forgive me too."

"I will." I knew that the heart of William Marshal was true.

It was the 11th of June when Young King Henry finally died. In the last days before the young king's death, Sir William told me that he and the young king had fallen out the previous year and they had been estranged. But for his reconciliation with Young King Henry, he would have had no need to seek King Henry's forgiveness. As it was, he was charged with a trip to Jerusalem and then a trip to the court of King Henry. He was a true knight and when he made an oath, he was faithful to it. There were a dozen household knights with the young king and, after parting from William

Marshal and with the entrails from Young King Henry's body in a jar, we set off for Limoges.

I had sent a rider with news of the death of his son already but when we reached Limoges, I was touched by the remorse shown by the king, "He cost me much, but I wish he had lived to cost me more." He turned to the knights who had fetched his son's body. Sir William Marshal was not with them having left to perform his own particular crusade, "Your penance is to take the body to Rouen Cathedral where it shall be buried. His entrails you will take to the monastery at Charroux. Do this and your crime of rebellion will be forgiven."

When they were gone, he held a meeting with Duke Richard and me. I wondered at my inclusion at first for the king spoke of inheritance. "Richard, you are now my heir." He turned to me, "Until I have this ratified in Rouen it is your duty, Earl, to see that my wishes are carried out."

"Of course, my lord."

Father and son clasped hands and Henry then said, "And as you are now the future King of England, I think it only right that John is made Duke of Aquitaine."

Richard's reaction surprised his father but not me, "John, Duke of Aquitaine? He cannot even control the barbarians of Ireland. He has lost control of that land and you would reward him with Aquitaine? Father, have you lost your senses?"

The row went on for the rest of the day although it was in private. That evening the two were back on speaking terms but that was all and there was a chilly atmosphere as we ate. King Henry looked, to me, to be unwell and he backed away from the argument. "Tomorrow I will leave for Rouen and you, Sir Samuel, shall be part of my escort."

The look on the face of Duke Richard told me that he felt he had been punished by his father. His face reddened and he stormed out.

King Henry shook his head, "Children! I have but three children and yet two of them still conspire to make my life a misery. I blame their mother. She was always a wilful woman."

The Perfect Knight

By the time we reached Rouen, King Henry was most definitely unwell. It seemed to me nothing more serious than a summer chill that often occurred in France. Whatever the reason when I asked, he granted his permission for me to return to England, but the question of succession was still hanging in the air. My men were pleased to be going home but I felt uneasy. There was unfinished work in France and my family responsibilities hung heavily about my shoulders. D'Aumale and his knights were still abroad. We had heard, as we headed for Rouen, that he had been heading north too. Was he going to Paris to seek employment with the cunning King Philip?

My sour humour was alleviated to some extent by Jack and Thomas. Thanks to the attack on the rearguard they had coins burning a hole in their purses and they spent them, not on frivolities but on weapons. They both bought fine Spanish daggers and Thomas had enough for a better sword. Jack had the coins for a short mail vest that would fit below his surcoat. He knew that one day I would buy him a hauberk but until then he would be as a man at arms. Many of my men made similar purchases. Rouen was a fine trading centre and goods came not only from France but also further afield. We left in September and I looked forward to being with my wife but, even as we left France, my thoughts were with a bickering father and sons.

Mordaf did not stay with the king but, instead, returned to England with us. He had explained it this way, "I seek revenge on de Verneuil, but I cannot achieve that alone. At least not do so and live. You are the only lord who offers me the opportunity to have revenge. I have waited this time and I can wait a little longer." When I had said I might not be returning to France he had laughed and told me that this brotherly dispute would carry on for years to come. He was proved right.

England had a king, but he was absent and there was unrest in the land. The civil war was still a raw wound and the rebellion of the king's sons had not helped. We took the first ship we could which landed on the south coast of England. We would have a long ride home but with horses and ponies captured in the short campaign, we would be able to ride them hard. We made the journey back to Stockton in ten days and arrived back after most of the harvest had been collected and the land was preparing for winter. The long journey north had been a reminder to me that we were a backwater and Aquitaine was many miles hence. Any news which reached us would be out of date by the time it arrived.

The news which finally reached us was not good. King Henry and Richard had fallen out again and the king had ordered Geoffrey and John to make war on their brother. That he did not summon me was a relief for I saw no end to this sibling squabbling; especially as it was fostered by their father. I did not think that the two brothers would stand much chance against Richard who had shown me that he was a good leader and men liked to follow him. We had seen no sign of Geoffrey in the brief rebellion and John had been a disaster in Ireland. That all changed when a visitor from France, delivering my ransom from Sir Alan de Baud, told us that King Philip Augustus of France and King Henry had formed an alliance against Richard. Even Duke Richard might struggle against such an alliance. I was not summoned and so I spent the time making my wife happy and training my son.

The latter was easier than the former. My wife felt that she had let me down in not producing more children. We tried constantly but four stillborn children did nothing to make her happy nor to give up on the attempt. I tried to make her see that we had been blessed by a son and that he was loved by all. That seemed to aggravate her mood for she worried even more then about his dying in battle. When the first King Henry had left a land without an heir then the country had been plunged into civil war. My sister Ruth did her best to lighten her mood, but it was hard. In the spring we took her to York where she prayed at the Minster. It seemed to help her, that and the many merchants of that busy city who allowed her to spend the money I had accrued. We had some months of smiles and I was happy.

Thomas was growing and developing skills. He and Jack were still unhappy about their lack of combat but what they

The Perfect Knight

had seen helped to show them the way to become better warriors. Both realised that skills in horsemanship were as important as those of swordsmanship. Skuld proved a willing accomplice for my son and the two of them improved so much that even Will the Horse Master was impressed.

"Lord, it is as though the two of them were sired by the same father. They think and move as one."

He was right. Thomas did not even need to use his hands which was a great advantage in combat. It allowed him to use his shield offensively, as he did when fighting on foot. I was pleased but I felt sorry for Jack, the page was a better horseman than the squire. It was nothing to do with Jack's diligence, he worked harder than any, it was simply the horseflesh and the bond between rider and mount.

Summer saw my wife pregnant again and Ruth and I ensured that her life was as trouble free as possible. The servants did all that they could to make her life easy and we prayed that it would result in a healthy baby. In that we were disappointed for in November the midwives and physicians pronounced the babe dead. It was the worst of news and even when we heard that King Henry and Duke Richard had made peace, thanks to the intervention of Richard's mother, it did nothing to make us smile. I saw then, in that week of such contrasting news that my family was more important than any bickering noble. I had been summoned to the meeting of reconciliation in London, but I did not attend, sending Sir William in my place. It seemed that both duke and king wanted me to arbitrate as I had the respect of both men. My reasons for not attending were personal but I was glad that I was spared the ordeal for whatever decision I made would have upset one of them. The king showed his cunning when he summoned his wife to Normandy where he forced her to order Richard to hand over his ducal castles to him. It ended the war but not the rift. If anything it made Richard angrier than ever.

I had thought that I was free from the strife, tucked away in my own corner of England but I was wrong.

As part of Jack and Thomas' training, we would ride, once a week, to a different manor. All lay within twenty miles of Stockton and we could get there and back in a day. Sometimes, like that fateful day, we had planned a two-day ride with a camp made at night time. We would ride with my men at arms and my archers would lie in ambush somewhere along the route. It could be before we reached the manor or afterwards. Gretham lay close to Herterpol. It had no lord of the manor living there for he had gone on crusade and a new one had yet to be appointed. That was the work of the Bishop of Durham. He would be waiting for one he could appoint who would serve his purposes. We planned on visiting Gretham where my archers would ambush me and then head to Fissebourne. There we would show our presence in case there were others who sought to steal the produce of hard-working farmers.

Positioned, as it was, close to the estuary of the Tees, Gretham was a place which had, on occasions, been raided by pirates. It was not like the time of my great grandfather, Ridley, when Vikings would come in large numbers to steal but it still happened. Frisians, Danes, and Norse would still come from their poorer countries to take animals. It had been some time since we had ridden there, and it struck me as an opportunity to show my son a different side of our land. These were not the wooded lands where men could hide behind trees nor the fields lined with brambles, hawthorns, blackthorn and elder. This was boggy treacherous ground with saltmarsh bogs waiting to drag the unwary down. The best land was close to the houses of Gretham village and they farmed the land as best they could. The beef and the mutton they produced was much sought after as it was fed on salty grass. As the land turned from farmland to sand then the people either fished or lit fires to render seawater into salt. Others hunted the seals which basked on the mudflats. Even the road from Gretham to Herterpol turned into a track for half a mile or so. It was as different from Stockton as it was possible to be.

As we headed towards the village of Cowpon, Jack asked the question which was also, no doubt, on Thomas' mind, "Lord, I understood when we rode towards Wolviston, Hartburn and Elton for they are close to Stockton and the land is like that in Norton but this is unique." He waved a hand at the bleak and empty horizon. There were just a few tendrils of smoke from those making salt and the handful of houses that made up Gretham. "We are unlikely to find such land in England."

"You think so? There is land exactly like this in Lincolnshire and Norfolk and what if we went to the Holy Land, as well we might? I was young when we left but I know from talking to Masood that he felt most at home in this bleak landscape. It was far colder than his home but the people who live here must eke out a living and that is like the land from whence he came. Let us see, eh?"

I confessed that I knew not where my archers would spring forth and I was interested to see myself where they had secreted themselves. Thus far I had managed to detect their presence. Jack and Thomas were getting better and had learned to spot the signs but had only managed to spy out the archers once.

The ground rose and fell. We twisted and turned around boggy hollows of stagnant water lined by weeds of all description some of which were almost as high as a man. Here there were no roads, but tracks made by the locals who knew the land. As such, they were narrow and forced us to ride in twos. Jack and Thomas were before us and studied the ground intently. I confess that I had not seen the archers but, as we neared the hollow before the dunes Skuld snorted and baulked. I was as proud as a man could be as Thomas shouted, "Ambush! Draw weapons!"

I saw Jack look around, mystified for there was nothing to be seen. I shouted, "Obey my son!" and drew my weapon. The headless arrows sailed from behind the dunes to our right. None would hurt for they had no heads, just a lump of mud fashioned around the end to make the arrow fly true.

Richard son of Aelric and my archers rose, grinning, from behind the dunes, "Well done Master Thomas although I think it was your horse and its nose which sensed us."

Thomas leaned forward to pat the neck of his mount, "The wind, Richard son of Aelric, is from behind us but it was Skuld who knew you were there. My horse is well named."

I dismounted and said, "Water your horses and then we shall head back."

I took out the skin of water I had brought for my horse and handed it to Jack who opened the stopper. Mordaf and Richard came over to me. Their faces were serious, "Lord, Mordaf has spied something which alarms him."

I looked at the scout who said, "It may be nothing, my lord, but when we were looking for a place to ambush you, I found tracks of horses and their dung. They were shod."

I nodded, "How many?"

"Thirty or more. They were heading south and west along the edge of the estuary and the mudflats."

I looked south, "Go and see if you can determine where they went. We will follow."

Gerard had joined us and heard the latter part of the conversation, "It could be just men from Herterpol, lord. Perhaps the Bishop has sent a new lord of the manor and, like you, he rides the land."

"You could be right, Gerard and that is the answer I hope for but bearing in mind what we learned in Aquitaine I would err on the side of caution. We have perilously few men now in this part of the world. The days of the Warlord and large warbands are gone."

My garrison of just forty men was the largest south of Durham and north of York. Even Barnard Castle had just thirty men. My lords of the manor, most of whom did not even have a castle, had fewer than ten men. If they were called upon to supply warriors for war they would have to dig into their purses to hire them or to arm their farmers. The victory against the Scots and my grandfather's legacy meant that the twenty odd men I led were the only real deterrent against bandits and warbands. The warriors I had left at the castle were the older warriors and their employment was more in the nature of a pension than anything else. Stockton Castle's walls and the townsfolk would be the real defenders if we were attacked.

The Perfect Knight

We mounted and followed Mordaf. We had now left the trails and climbed our horses over marram covered dunes. Mordaf awaited us by the river. He shook his head, "The tide has come in and covered the tracks." He turned to Richard, "I know not this land and have yet to ride it. What does the river do?"

Richard son of Aelric said, "It twists and turns before reaching Stockton. The only settlements of any size twixt here and Stockton are Billingham and Norton. If the horsemen followed the river and found the mud then they could avoid both by heading just north of the river. Mordaf, how old were the tracks?"

"The dung was warm. They were no more than an hour ahead of us."

I made the decision, "Their movements are suspicious enough to warrant investigation. Richard let us head for the Portrack lakes. The river meanders much down to Mandale and we might be able to get ahead of these strangers in our land."

We turned our horses' heads around and headed away from the dunes to return to the road that passed through Cowpon. I knew that these horsemen could be innocent but there were just too many horses to ignore. I turned in my saddle, "Martyn Longsword, ride back to Herterpol and ask if any horsemen left the port and headed south. Meet us at Portrack."

"Aye my lord." He turned his horse and rode hard towards the nearby port.

As we passed through Cowpon and then Billingham I warned the people to be watchful for a strange band of horsemen. The raids by the Scots were close enough in the memory to ensure that the people knew how to defend themselves.

I knew that I should have sent a rider back to Stockton as soon as Mordaf reported his find. I think my mind was too preoccupied with Thomas' success. I put my son from my mind and, as we clattered along the stone road towards Billingham ran through all the different outcomes this event might bring. The more I thought about it the more sinister it appeared. It was the middle of the afternoon when we reached the marshes around Portrack. The river was at its most meandering at this point and if you followed it then you would have a long journey. As, however, there were few people living there and only ships which might see you then it was the perfect way to approach my town unseen. If I was an intruder, then I would be able to hide from the ships which used the river as I would see their masts and the reeds gave a perfect opportunity to hide. We dismounted on the slightly higher ground above the reeds where there was grass and allowed the horses to graze on it. The twists and turns in the river, the trees which lined it, in parts, and the reeds meant we would only see a column of horsemen when they were close. The road we had followed and only recently left led to my town and we could be there in less than half an hour. If we had to wait until dark, it would not be a problem.

Mordaf had tethered his horse and made his way, along with Tam the Hawker's son, down to the river. It was not an easy passage for this was late summer and the brambles were rampant. They would be able to keep a better watch for this mysterious party of horsemen.

As we swatted away the swarms of flies which tried to feast upon us, Jack asked, "But what mischief could they cause, my lord?"

"Our castle is strong, but we are not at war. If these are enemies then they might choose to take the castle by ruse or cunning. We do not keep a strong watch on those who come through the town. Our best warriors are here."

"Then, my lord, why not simply ride back and man the walls?"

"A good plan, Jack, if we were sure that they would try to take Stockton." I waved a hand around, "The rest of the manors have even fewer warriors. We warned Billingham but there are too many for us to visit. If they follow the river then this would be a good place for them to rest their horses and, if they plan to attack any of our manors, prepare for the attack."

We turned and had hands on our weapons as a horse clattered up behind us. It was Martyn Longsword, "Sir

The Perfect Knight

Samuel, the horsemen were landed from a pair of French ships in the middle of the night, four nights since and housed in an empty warehouse. There were four knights, and the rest were armed warriors. There were thirty-nine of them."

"The Bishop's steward told you this?"

Martyn shook his head, "No, lord, he said no horsemen had arrived, but I stopped at '*The Blacksmith's Arms*' in Stranton." '*The Blacksmith's Arms*' was next to the village smithy. I knew that the blacksmith's wife had an alehouse next to the smithy. He shrugged, "Alf was a friend of my father's and he has a water trough. As I watered my mount, he told me the true story. He knew it from one of those who drink in his wife's alehouse. He was told that no word of the arrival should leak out." He shook his head, "Such a thing is impossible."

"Then the Bishop is playing a dangerous game once more. King Henry should have dealt with him when he could. I can see that I shall have to do so but that must wait until we have dealt with this problem."

My grandfather had been wrong and I was far from perfect. I did make mistakes and this one risked being fatal for my family. Almost forty well-armed horsemen could easily dispose of the old men I had left guarding my home. The horses had rested, and we rode as though the devil was behind us. If this was the enemy I suspected then he was ahead of us! I cursed myself for my complacency. The ransom I had received from the French ship was stored in my castle and all knew of it. In addition, I had the pay we had been given by King Henry. My men also stored their coins in my castle. It was safe enough unless there was a knight with a grudge who felt that I was responsible for his financial losses. I knew that this was Geoffrey d'Aumale. Enough time had elapsed for him to concoct a plan and gather mercenaries willing to fight with him for a share of Cleveland's coin. Many might well have been the men we chased away north of Limoges.

The road to Stockton passed what we called Portrack Lake. It was a misnomer for it only flooded in the winter and the rest of the time was just a boggy overflow for the river.

The Perfect Knight

We could have risked riding across it but that might have delayed us and so we thundered down the road towards the east gate of the town. The gates were only closed after dark and rarely guarded. As we galloped through, I saw some of the tanners who worked at that end of the town, close to the cattle market, having their wounds tended. There was little point in stopping and so, drawing my sword I galloped through my town. I saw others receiving attention. I prayed that the gates to my castle had been closed but, as we neared the gates, I heard the clash of steel. There was fighting in my outer bailey.

There was no order to us, and we galloped through the town gate and into a one-sided battle. I saw five of my men, warriors who had fought with my grandfather and father lying dead. The French, for it was indeed the men we had followed, were butchering the old men left to defend my castle. I was relieved to see that the door to the keep was barred but there were half a dozen men with axes trying to break it down. A couple of arrows were sent from the fighting platform of the keep but they had little effect. I had no archers in my garrison save for the ones with me.

"Richard, clear the door. Gerard, let us rid my castle of this vermin!" I knew that there would be anger amongst my men for the bodies we had seen were friends of theirs. It would take but moments for my archers to dismount, string their bows and then begin to slay these invaders.

I swung my sword at the back of the dismounted man at arms who had an axe raised to end the life of Garth of the Well. Even though the mercenary wore a mail hauberk my blow, delivered from on high and with all the anger my body possessed, broke not only the mail but, I suspect his back. He lay writhing on the ground and I urged my horse to the next man.

A French voice shouted, "We are undone! Make for the river!"

That made no sense to me for they would be trapped there and I wondered why they would trap themselves against the river. They could reach the river as there was a gate from the outer bailey that led to the chapel and then the river gate. It would be unguarded, and some might escape. I did not want that.

I wheeled my horse to the left to cut them off. Storm Bringer was part of me and understood what I wished to do even before I had thought it. I heard Jack shout, "We are with you, Sir Samuel."

It was comforting and, at the same time a worry. Thomas was not yet ready to face swords for hire. The French who were already horsed were now galloping towards the open gate. The rest were trying to mount their horses and flee, I saw one rider plucked from his horse by an arrow as he stood with a foot in the stirrup. I could leave Richard and his bowmen to finish those off, but the majority were now hurtling towards the gate. I was the first to reach them and I saw that we had cut off eight of the horsemen. Gerard and my men at arms were racing to our aid but until they reached us it would be the three of us who would have to hold them up. I backhanded my sword across the chest of the leading horseman and, as he lacked a shield, hit his chest and knocked him from his saddle. Jack and Thomas combined to attack the second man from two sides. Jack was the one who killed him and as the rest of my men caught up with the others, I turned my horse and headed for the gaping river gate. To my horror, I saw the masts of two ships! It all became clear. The two ships had landed the horsemen and then continued down the river to Stockton. The French ship bringing the ransom had set a precedent and no one would wonder at two ships arriving. Had they come with horsemen then the gates would have been barred. It was a clever plan and had come within a whisker of success. Even as I reached out to slash at the back of the last horseman in the line, I saw two horses being led aboard. The horseman I chased whipped around his courser's head as he tried to bring his sword around from his right side. I had to get to the ships and quickly. I lunged with my sword and found his eye. Driving through the orb and into the brain rendered him dead but, as he fell, his dying hands dragged his horse with him and my horse had to swerve to avoid the obstacle. I saw that five men had boarded but the two ships would take no more and they began to pull away from the shore. The fact that it was a slow departure did not help for the tide was high and we could not swim.

The four men who had not managed to escape saw the ferry tied up to the quay and they raced aboard. I reached it just as they left the bank. Had my horse been fresh I might have risked a jump, but we had ridden too far to take the chance. The men thought that they had escaped when a flurry of arrows came from my castle walls and all four aboard the ferry were slain. The current would take their horses to the other shore and I saw the ferrymen there react and they launched the small boat they used. The horses and dead men would be recovered but the knights had escaped. I had recognised the livery of Geoffrey d'Aumale and knew that I had been right. As I dismounted and led my horse back to the castle that was cold comfort to me for the raid had cost me men.

Chapter 9

Stockton 1185

Nine of the men left to guard my castle had died and another four were wounded. My sister had been the one who had closed the gate to the keep but for her it might have fallen as the attack had been swiftly carried out. When we questioned the last survivor, we discovered the full extent of the treachery. The man had a bad wound and begged us to tend to it. I agreed but only if he gave us the full story. Sir Geoffrey d'Aumale, when he had fled Limoges had approached King Philip and told him of his plan to rob the castle of the Warlord. It was the French King who financed the attack. It was cleverly conceived. He infiltrated an English mercenary into Stockton. He pretended to be a trader in hides, but his purpose was to learn our routines. He had waited until he had learned that we planned a two-night exercise and rode to Herterpol to tell Sir Geoffrey. Knowing that I would be absent and the age of the garrison they had planned on reaching my town, as they did, at dusk. Their plan was to ride into the castle, empty the treasury and armoury and then, after firing the castle, escape by sea. Mordaf's sharp eyes and the vigilance of my sister had thwarted the attempt, but it had cost us dear.

Eleanor was badly affected by the attack and made her spirits even lower than they had been. The attack had made her faint and, in her condition, that was not good. Leaving Gerard to make good the damage caused and remove the bodies, my sister and I took my wife to our chamber. I sent for the doctor and when he examined her, he found blood.

The Perfect Knight

"My lord this does not look good. Lady Ruth and I will make an examination, but I fear the worst."

I stalked the corridors until Ruth emerged, "Brother, you have lost another child and this one was a girl. I would say that Eleanor can recover and have more children, but this is not the first time she has lost a child. You will need to be strong and," she looked at me meaningfully, "here. Your family comes first and not the king and his sons."

"You are right, but I have some unfinished business with Sir Geoffrey d'Aumale. When my wife is well, and the world has returned to normal then I will hunt him down. He may try to hide but there is nowhere dark enough or deep enough for him to escape me."

I had no chance to speak to my men. Gerard, Jack, and Richard took over the running of the castle and I stayed in my chamber with a broken wife. This time it was not an act of God it was a willful act by a degenerate knight. The Bishop of Durham and the King of France were also culpable. That night I began, as I held my sleeping wife's hand, to plan my revenge. I knew that d'Aumale would flee to France for he was on French ships using the French king's coin. That Philip Augustus had financed the scheme did not surprise me. Young King Henry had been gullible to form an alliance with him. Philip wanted the whole of France and the best way to get it was to cause confusion and dissent in Aquitaine and in England. I knew that the temporary alliance of King Philip and King Henry was just a political act by both kings and would not last the year. The French king must have gambled that his involvement would remain a secret. Robbing Stockton would have sent shock waves through England and given hope to the Scots. The problem closer to home was Bishop Puiset, what was he doing? More importantly, how could I stop him? By the time I woke sleep had helped to form the plan and it would just need the time my wife took to recover to put them in place.

My first act was to spend some of the money I had accrued. After we had buried our own dead and burned the bodies of the dead mercenaries I met with Jack, Thomas, Gerard, and Richard. My wife was resting and Ruth sat with

The Perfect Knight

her. We had decided that Ruth would watch her during the day, and I would tend to her at night. I would not be leaving Stockton any time soon.

"We need men. I will not leave Stockton so unguarded and vulnerable again. The mercenaries came for our coins. I intend to spend them now so that they will not be tempted. Richard and Gerard, take a man with you and seek warriors to serve us. We have, thanks to the attackers, spare horses, and weapons, we just lack the men to ride them. I would double our numbers. Hire the best!"

"And do you care whence they come?"

"What do you mean, Gerard?"

"The Welsh have good archers and the pay in Wales is lower than in England. We can hire men there who are hungry for better pay. The same would be true of Welsh spearmen. If you wished men to stand on your walls, they would be perfect. It would mean that Richard and I could travel together and save time."

"The Welsh eh?" I had not thought of that but it was a good idea. The Welsh were hardy fighters. I would not contemplate Scots for we were too close to their homeland and the Irish were fine fighters but unpredictable. The more I thought about it the better the idea sounded. The civil war had stripped the land between Oxford and London of the best warriors and Gerard's idea had merit. "I like the idea. You can take as long as you like but return with men. Then we need to look at our defences. We have become too lax. When the enemy warriors were at the gates in the time of my grandfather Stockton was vigilant. I will call a meeting this week with the mayor and his council. We need a night watch to be organised."

Jack's father lived just outside the town walls but still knew the townsfolk well. Jack often spoke with him, "That may not be as easy as you think, Sir Samuel. I know that my father has ceased to drink in the alehouses of Stockton because he does not like the attitude of some of the townsfolk. The fact that a stranger was allowed to infiltrate into the town, and we were not told tells you much." He paused, "I am sorry if my words cause offence, my lord."

The Perfect Knight

"Continue to speak as you do. I want us to be open and honest with one another. You may be right, but the fault lies with me. I have not looked at my town for some time and I know that my father was distracted too. The Warlord made it a safe and secure place to live and we must continue that tradition." I stood and waved over Ralph, my steward, "Ralph, come with me to the treasury. We need to begin to spend!"

"Aye, lord."

The chests were brought up to my Great Hall so that I could see the fortune I had accrued. We counted out two fat purses of coins for my two captains and they left. I counted out another large purse, "This is for Will, the horse master. I need another ten coursers to be bred. We plan for the future." The last two purses I counted out were for altogether different purposes. "This one is to provide comfort to those families who lost men in the attack and this last one to build a tower on each of the three town gates. I want local men to be hired to do the work, Ralph. We do not hire those who live far away." He nodded. "And I would have the chapel enlarged. The masons have finished the effigies of my mother and father. The Warlord and my grandmother are interred there. I need a place for Lady Eleanor and for me."

Thomas' head whipped around, and I saw the horror on his face, "But father you are young! You cannot prepare to die!"

I lowered my voice, "Thomas, your mother is still ill, and I have enemies. I pray that God will allow me to see you grow into a man and become the Earl of Cleveland, but I cannot guarantee that. It gives me comfort to know that when I die, I shall lie in the chapel with my forebears and that each time you visit the church that you will think of me. I am not being morbid but practical."

I saw him nod but also saw realisation dawn that what we did was dangerous, and we could die. That evening my wife rose from her bed to eat with Ruth and me. I told them of my plans, but I did not tell my wife that the plans for the enlargement of the chapel were for our tomb. "The chapel is too small. I remember when I wed there we could barely fit just a handful of people within. Now we have two large tombs within it we need a bigger church; it will be a larger monument which will do justice to the Warlord." I had already spoken to Ruth and she smiled at my words.

"Husband, are we safe within these walls? When those men burst in, I thought we were doomed."

I patted the back of my wife's hand, "Until Gerard and Richard return with more men then the warriors I have trained and employed will stay within the castle. Trust me none can best them. You should not worry about that but just concentrate on getting well."

"Yes sister, and we shall need your nimble fingers if we are to make surcoats for these new warriors." Ruth and I had already decided that occupation was the best medicine for Eleanor. If she was busy, then she could not brood about our dead child. I had already decided that we would not risk another birth. Thomas would be our only child.

I sent Jack that night on a little scouting expedition and he reported to me before I retired for the night, he confirmed what I already suspected.

I sat Thomas next to me at the head of the table on the day we invited the council and the Mayor to our Great Hall. My wife, sister and their ladies were in the corner sewing and that was deliberate on my part. I wanted the council to see that even our ladies were making our town stronger. The Mayor was Harold Egbertson, the grandson of the first ferryman, Ethelred. The family had done well for Stockton and had begun to build ships. Harold employed a lot of men and his election had been unanimous. The other council members were also prominent men from the town. John the Tanner was there as well as Alfred the Weaponsmith. Both were very supportive of me as they profited from the castle and its garrison. Similarly, Walter the innkeeper from the tavern, the *'Warlord's Sword'* benefitted from visitors passing through the town and the garrison who used his alehouse and doxies. It was the other two who had less reason to support me. Wilfred the Merchant was unhappy about the taxes the town charged when ships docked. He was reluctant to pay any taxes believing that he had a right to keep all his coins. He had the largest house inside the town walls and was also annoyed that he could not enlarge it because of other properties. The last man on the council was Henry Wolsingham who owned the workshop which made tiles and pots. He had moved south from Wolsingham some years earlier, while the Warlord was still alive, and his business had prospered but he resented paying what he considered taxes which were too high for a small town like Stockton. There was something about him I did not like and I wondered at his wealth. I was ready for all. I had servants wait on us for Jack was training with my men. I had realised that he needed his spurs, and his training would need to be accelerated.

"Gentlemen, welcome." They all bowed but I noticed that Henry Wolsingham's was a cursory one. I was not precious about such things, but it was a warning of his attitude. "Sit and eat while we talk for I have much to say." I waited until goblets were filled and the members of the council had all taken some food. "Firstly, I need to apologise for the attack which caused some families distress. Ralph the Steward shall make all necessary recompense. The fault lies with me." I saw a smug smile fill Henry Wolsingham's face. "I have been remiss and allowed the town's defences to be neglected but I shall remedy that straight away. Ralph the Steward will hire local men to build a stone tower at each of the three town gates."

The words had barely left my mouth when Henry Wolsingham pounced, "And who shall pay for that, Sir Samuel? You cannot expect us to bear the cost for we pay too much in taxes in any case!"

Harold turned angrily to Henry, "That is not the way we speak to the lord of the manor! Moderate your tone. The Earl does not need to improve the defences of the town. They are there to protect us."

I held up my hands, palms outward, "Peace! Yes, Henry Wolsingham, I will pay for the workmen and the materials, but Harold is quite right I do not need to. The men of Stockton need to look to their own defences. The town ditch has become filled with rubbish and no longer constitutes a defence. It needs to be cleared. That will be the duty of every man in the town." I looked pointedly at Henry, "Every man." I did not raise my voice but there was power in it. They all nodded, "Then there is the matter of the town watch. Those raiders simply entered your town. There was no attempt to stop them. I asked my squire to walk the walls the other night. There was no night watch. The gates were closed but with a ditch filled with rubbish and none to keep a lookout then any enemy could have gained entry, opened the gates and then the town might have suffered even greater privations."

Wilfred the Merchant snorted, "You cannot expect us to be the night watch! Surely that is the duty of the lord of the manor!"

I said nothing and waited. It was Alfred the Weaponsmith who answered for me, "When Sir Samuel calls us to arms then we are duty-bound to go. I know not about the rest of you, but I cannot remember the last time either Sir Samuel or Sir William, his father did so. When the Scots raided it was Sir Samuel who led his men to hunt them down. The least we can do is to keep watch on our own walls. There are one hundred men, at least, who live within the walls of Stockton. If we have four men each night doing four hours and another four to replace them then it will be a duty we have to perform once every eight or nine days. The loss of a bare four hours of sleep a week seems a small price to pay."

All but Wilfred and Henry nodded.

I seized the opportunity to bring up my next point, "And that is another matter. Sunday morning used to be the time when all men practised arms by the well. It has stopped and for that, I take the blame. It will return beginning this Sunday. Alfred is quite right. I have not summoned the fyrd but I want to know that if I do then the men I lead can fight."

They all nodded.

The last matter I have to bring up is, perhaps, the one of most concern to me." I paused to watch their faces, "The spy who entered our town lived amongst us for some days and yet none mentioned it or reported it to the castle." I looked directly at Walter although I already knew who had harboured the man.

Walter shook his head and spread his hands, "He did not stay at my inn."

I nodded, "I know. He stayed with you, Henry of Wolsingham, did he not?"

He reddened and said, defensively, "And why should I not offer shelter to someone who brought business into the town? He said he wished to buy pots and tiles from me for he had heard mine were of the highest quality."

Harold snorted. He knew that to be a lie as did the rest of the council. Henry of Wolsingham only sold the pots and tiles that he did because the nearest other supplier was twenty miles away. It was laziness amongst the townsfolk which brought him business.

Glaring at Harold he continued, "I have a right to entertain whom I please. The Bishop of Durham is a friend and knows me well!"

If he thought that would intimidate me, he was wrong, "I care not if you are the friend of the Archbishop of Canterbury. You had a duty to question your guest closely unless, of course, you were colluding with him?"

He heard the threat in my voice, and he changed his tone, "Of course not, Sir Samuel, and I will do as you ask. We all will." He was clever and by using the word, *we*, was including the others in what I now suspected to be treachery. He had known the purpose of the spy and his association with the Bishop of Durham, far from vindicating him merely made him look even more guilty.

I allowed silence to fill my hall. Only the sound of thread being pulled through cloth could be heard. When it became almost too unbearable, I smiled, "You are the town council and the requests I have made need to be voted upon. What say you?"

As I expected there were only two who, from their faces, dissented, but they all voted in favour of my suggestions. To do otherwise would have suggested that they were in league with the attackers. I did not have to use my vote and that pleased me. Harold and Alfred hung back after the others left, "We should have kept a better watch, my lord, I am sorry."

"No, Harold, I was remiss but let us use this as a warning. The civil war might be over, and the threat of the Scots diminished but there are other threats to our realm, and we must be vigilant."

When they had gone Ruth rose and came over to me, "That was masterly, brother, but why did you not arrest Henry of Wolsingham?"

"I believe he is the bishop's man. Wolsingham is close to Durham and I think that the Bishop sent him here to act as a spy. Now that we know he is the spy we can watch him. When my wife is better, I shall ride to Durham and speak with de Puiset. He cannot deny that armed horsemen landed at his port and raided English lands. I will be interested in his explanation."

Ruth turned and shook her head, "I fear it will be some time before you can leave your wife alone for she is fragile."

"Then I will write to King Henry and tell him of the attack. I will keep to myself my suspicions about the bishop for that is not something one puts in a letter. That will be for the king's ears. We have time."

My men were away for a month but the eighteen men they brought back were of the best quality. My two captains were apologetic that they had not managed to hire more but many Welshmen had taken coin to sail to Ireland to fight for Prince John there. We set the ones they had brought to work immediately; good as they were we had high standards and my captains set about making them Stockton men. Jack and Thomas had both improved dramatically. Soon I would be able to knight Jack and elevate Thomas to squire, but the time was not yet right. When, in autumn, the letter came from King Henry it reassured me that my actions had been justified and he would watch out for d'Aumale. He also wrote that Queen Eleanor had forced her son to hand over the ducal castles in Aquitaine, which was still her land, to Henry. I had heard that was what had happened, but it was good to hear it confirmed by the king himself and told me I

The Perfect Knight

still had his confidence. The war was over and it allowed me to look north at Durham.

The summer had seen an improvement in Eleanor and, indeed, she told me that she was ready to try for another child. I was adamant we would not try and told her that she was too fragile. I used the word Ruth had used for it was true. She was like the glass in Durham Cathedral, beautiful to look at but not to touch. She seemed to accept my decision but her parting words, as she returned to her women, was like an arrow to my heart, "I am your wife and one day we shall lie together, and I will conceive another child. I know that the time now may not be right, but I love you, Samuel, and I will have another child by you, even if it means my death!"

A week later I went with just Thomas and Jack to Durham. The Bishop had been in London for a month and I knew that he had just returned to the north. This seemed like a good opportunity, before winter set in, to clear the air and let him know my thoughts. Gerard insisted upon an escort as far as the Wear. I would not allow them in the castle itself as that might make me look as though I was afraid of the bishop and I was not. They waited at Stancliffe Grange. The lord of the manor there, Sir Roger Stancliffe was a good knight and a doughty fighter. He had little time for politics and my men were welcomed.

We crossed the bridge into the town and followed the winding cobbles to the castle's main gate. We were not hindered as we rode, and we dismounted in the outer bailey. "You two stay with the horses and keep your ears and eyes open."

"Sir Samuel, do you not wish a witness?"

I smiled, "No, Jack, that is the last thing I want. I need to speak with the bishop alone so that I may speak truthfully. He may not reciprocate but that does not matter so long as he knows my mind." I turned to Thomas, "You will learn, Thomas, that direct action is often the only answer to some problems."

I was taken to the Bishop's chamber which was guarded by a man at arms. The fact that I was admitted so quickly made me suspicious. Often the prelate had left us kicking our heels to show his power; this time he did not.

"I pray you to take a seat, Earl Samuel." He was according me my title which was another rarity. A cleric sat with a wax tablet and a scribe.

"I beg you to send your man hence for what I say is for your ears only. If you choose to divulge it to another when I have left then that is up to you." I carefully chose my words so that he would think he might learn something to his advantage.

"Canon James, you may leave us and tell my sentry to stretch his legs. I do not think that I am in any danger from the Earl of Cleveland." When Canon James had gone Hugh de Puiset poured us two generous goblets of wine, "Now then what is this secret you wish to divulge to me?"

I smiled but it was with my mouth and not my eyes, "You already know the secret Bishop Puiset. The purpose of my visit is to tell you that I know it now." I saw fear in his eyes. He had sent his guard hence otherwise I am sure that he would have called him back.

"What secret?"

"That you are a traitor who plots with the King's enemies. You are in league with the King of France and you actively supported Young King Henry in his war against his father. You have turned a blind eye to raiders in this land and actively supported men who were sent to kill me. I know all about Henry of Wolsingham." My last barb struck home. He thought I had him as a prisoner and that he had told me all. He quickly gulped down half of the goblet of wine, a sure sign that I had spoken the truth. "No denial, Bishop? Your honesty both surprises and impresses me."

"Of course I deny it. The idea is so preposterous as to be above a reply. Where is your evidence?"

"Bishop, I came here today to tell you that I know you are behind these plots and treacherous acts and that I will be watching you. You have sent a spy into my castle. Two can play this game. You will need to scrutinise every man who comes to serve you for who knows which will be my spy. I still have the ear of the king and while you plot with his enemies, I will tell him precisely what I believe you have done."

"He will not believe you!"

"That is what you hope but know that I have enough evidence to make him question your loyalty. If I had the testimony of Geoffrey d'Aumale then you would be in chains now and I would throw you in my dungeon. I seek the knight and when I find him then you will be revealed."

He stood, "I have heard enough! Leave! Guards!" This time my smile was genuine for I had him reeling. He was spluttering red-tinged spittle as he babbled on. "I shall take action. I will write to the king! I will appeal to the Archbishop of York!" His voice rose as he lost control.

The door opened and the guard stood there looking confused. He knew my reputation and I did not think he would lay hands on me. I stepped into the doorway and turned, "Write to whomsoever you will and speak to any bishop you like. I will stand in any court with my witnesses and my evidence. I will even offer trial by combat. Would you relish that, Prince Bishop?" He looked down and I knew that I had won. He would do nothing. "I thought not, farewell, Bishop," I looked at the sentry, "and you, warrior, should choose a more honourable master for the one you have is little more than a wizened, corrupt snake!"

I strode out. The raised voices had been heard and I was stared at all the way to my squire and page. I mounted and gave a flourish, saying for the benefit of the Bishop, "You know where I will be if you need me!"

We galloped out of the gate. I said nothing until we reached Stancliffe Hall. After bidding farewell to Sir Roger we headed to Stockton, I told Gerald, Jack, and Thomas what I had said.

Gerard looked over his shoulder, "My lord was this wise? I agree he is treacherous, and I have seen the evidence of that treachery but suppose he sends men after us?"

"That is the last thing he will do and, in any case, do you fear any men hired by the Bishop of Durham?"

He smiled, "You are right on both counts, but we will need to watch our backs from now on."

"I think, Gerard, that we would have to do that in any case. This way the air is cleared and there are doubts no more. We and the Bishop of Durham are now enemies. We were enemies before but only we two knew it. However, when we return to Stockton, I want Mordaf to watch Henry of Wolsingham. I need to know who comes to tell him to run!"

It was two days later when Mordaf reported that a merchant and his servant arrived at Henry of Wolsingham's home just before the gates were closed for the night. I rose early and was waiting by the north gate when the three of them, Henry and his two visitors, along with sumpters carrying a heavy load appeared at the gate.

"And where are you going, Henry?"

Richard and my archers were on the town walls with nocked arrows.

"We have business in Durham."

"Yet in two months your taxes will be due. Will you be absent when my reeve comes to collect them?"

He gave a nervous laugh, "Of course not! I shall be gone but a few days and then I will return."

"Ah, and so the horses carry your pots and tiles, do they?"

"Er no, I ..."

"Jack, open one of the bags."

"My lord, I protest!"

"If they are pots and tiles then my men will repack them for you. In any case, the gate will not open until I say so." Jack undid the straps and lifted the flap on the satchel. He took out a sack of coins. I nodded, "The rest, Jack."

The bishop's man shook his head, "There is no need my lord. It is all the money I have made in Stockton. I intend to invest it."

"That is a great deal of money from the sale of second-rate pots and tiles. I take it your accounts are here too?" His eyes made the mistake of glancing down at the satchel hanging from his saddle. "Thomas, the satchel."

Thomas unfastened the strap and brought the satchel to me. He handed it to me, and I unrolled it. Inside were the parchments marking the sales of the pots, "So these are the accounts. I will have my reeve and Father Michael examine them to see how much tax we are owed. Until then the coins and the accounts stay here."

"I can go?"

"Open the gates! Of course, you can, as you say you will not be gone long and the money to which you are entitled will be here waiting for you when you return. It may take a week or so for us to examine every entry but I am a patient man."

The archers with nocked arrows prevented him from simply grabbing the reins. He must have known that if he stayed I would find evidence of wrongdoing. I saw him sweating and looking around nervously for some means of escaping with what I knew were ill-gotten gains. I had been suspicious before and all that I had seen confirmed his guilt.

Dropping the reins he snarled, "I will report this to the Bishop of Durham. You are robbing me!"

"As all will attest, I am merely confiscating the coins until I can verify the true owners of the money."

He and the two men left.

Gerard asked, "Was that wise, lord? We will not see him again."

"The fact that I let him go means that when he reaches the Bishop his loyalty will be in doubt. Why did the Earl of Cleveland let a known spy leave? Has he been turned? I am playing games with the bishop. If there is evidence, then my reeve and Father Michael will uncover it."

The two men were rigorous in their work and after counting the coins examined every entry. The coins were proved to be too much to have been earned legally. The accounts for the sales of the pots and the tiles showed that the man had been charging too much and making an excessive profit but that did not account for the money. When we found a larger than the usual number of French coins then it became clear that he had been paid from France. The priest and Jonathan, the reeve, asked me what they should do with the coins.

The Perfect Knight

"They belong to Henry of Wolsingham. We take the taxes that he owes and the pay due to his workers. The rest we seal and store in my treasury. It shall rest there until he returns to claim it."

Father Michael was a clever man, "And he will then be questioned about the French coins and tried in court."

"If he returns then aye and if not then after five years we shall distribute the coins to the people of Stockton. It is clear that he has overcharged them for many years."

Jonathan asked, "And the workshop, lord? There are six whom Henry of Wolsingham employed, what of them?"

"A good point and I know not the answer. Come with me and we shall see them."

The master potter was a grey beard called Egbert. The rest were all young men who had been employed by Henry of Wolsingham when he had come to Stockton. It was a rare occurrence when the lord of the manor came to call and they bowed and scraped before me.

"Enough of that. Your master has fled and I am not sure that he will return. I am here with my reeve and Father Michael to make a decision about the future of this workshop."

The younger ones looked worried but Egbert the Potter just nodded, "He will not return. He had little interest in pots except how much money it would make him."

"And that begs the question why he began the business in the first place." I had often wondered what had made the man from the Weardale valley come so far south to Stockton.

"The clay, my lord. Stockton clay is good clay."

"Yet the pots and the tiles you make are expensive and not the best quality."

Egbert was not afraid to speak the truth, "And that was Henry of Wolsingham's decision. He saved money on the charcoal we used to fire the ovens and did not allow long enough for them to bake."

An idea formed in my mind. "And if you ran the factory, Egbert, would you make better wares?"

The Perfect Knight

"Of course, but I know nothing of the selling of them. I am just a master potter and one who is close to the end of his life."

I looked at Jonathan and Father Michael, "I see an answer here. We let these men continue to be employed. Jonathan, you shall see to their pay and do the accounts." I saw him sigh, "Until we can find someone to take over the accounts."

Father Michael said, "I can ask the Prior of the monastery at Blackwell for help. Often young men seek the life of a monk and find it not for them. Such men are unsuited to normal work but able to scribe. There may be such a man."

"Good, and as for the sale of your wares I think that you will find that when people see that they pay a fair price for a serviceable pot then you will not have to sell, they will sell themselves. But you, Egbert, must make these young men your apprentices. They shall become indentured to you."

"That was what I asked Henry of Wolsingham, but he did not wish the commitment nor the expense."

I smiled, "The expense is not a problem. Your former master has left enough money for us to use."

As we left I said, to the priest and my reeve, "You had better go to his home and see what remains there."

"And then, Sir Samuel?"

"You have badgered me to build an almshouse for the poor and I have been remiss. We shall send a letter informing Henry of Wolsingham that we intend to use his home as an almshouse until he returns. What say you to that?"

He brightened, "I say that I can see God's hand in this!"

The letter was writ and sent but no reply came. Two months after he fled us, he was discovered in Herterpol, close to the quayside with his throat cut. His murderer was never apprehended. I suspected his former employers had little time for him and one or the other had deemed him surplus to requirements. When we had searched his home, we had also found a connection to Scotland for there was a letter from the Laird of Redesdale thanking him for his assistance. He was a spy with many masters!

The Perfect Knight

Chapter 10

Stockton 1186

Duke Geoffrey of Brittany and the next heir, after Richard, to the English throne, died in Paris. He was killed accidentally at a tournament but his death ended once and for all the threat he posed to his father. At the time I felt relief, but it was like the rolling of a single stone that precipitates an avalanche. In the late spring, I received a letter from King Henry summoning me to Normandy. He needed me once more. I knew that Duke Richard was in Toulouse, fighting Raymond, Count of that County. Why did King Henry need me? I guessed he needed a warlord. I did not truly understand nor did I wish to go but a command had been issued and as it was delivered by a pursuivant I could not ignore it.

Eleanor was less fragile than she had been, but I still worried about leaving her. I spoke to Ruth about the matter. My sister and I were close and had grown ever closer since the death of our parents and Eleanor's condition. She had chosen the life of a widow rather than that of a nun following her husband's death, but she had an appetite for life. In many respects, she was the lady of the manor. She had taken over the almshouse Father Michael and I had created and made it a place of joy for the poor. Many had their lives changed by the work my sister did.

"I do not think that you should go. Our father and grandfather were much used by this king and his mother. Our grandmother died of the plague because the Warlord was absent. This family has done enough for the

Plantagenets." The firmness in her voice often reminded me of my grandfather.

I smiled for Ruth always spoke her mind, "I know but our father and grandfather would have obeyed the missive, would they not? Besides, I think that this is a summons to war and soon the whole of the valley may be needed" She nodded. "Then the question I ask concerns my wife. How will she take it?"

Ruth was thoughtful, perceptive, and clever. She knew my wife and me as well as we knew ourselves. She took my hand in hers, "Your wife is a good woman, probably too good for she puts the lives of others above her own. She feels guilt that she has borne you but one child. I know that there is a danger she might not be able to produce another child, for she is older but you have not lain with her since…" I shook my head. "You should do so. She will cope with your absence better if you do so. She feels that you shun her." Before I could protest, she held up her hand, "I know that you do not but she is a woman. I miss my dear departed husband, but I know he cannot share my bed. A woman needs that sort of tenderness."

"I do not want to put her through the torture she endured the last time."

"The last time our town was attacked, that caused the loss, and, since then you have made your home safer. Consider my words."

I did and two nights later I told my wife that I had been ordered to leave for Normandy. We were in bed and she was in my arms. She rolled on top of me and kissed me passionately, "Then before you go lie with me one more time I beg of you. I am stronger now than I was and I have prayed to God each night to forgive me for whatever sin I committed. I know I have done something wrong to be punished."

"You have done no wrong, my love."

"It feels that way to me. Let us be husband and wife once more." The urgency in her voice and the passion meant I could not refuse, and we lay together.

The Perfect Knight

The next morning it was as though she had been reborn. There was a joy about her that made her voice sound as though she was singing. Ruth beamed and said quietly to me, "You have done the right thing, brother. This is the Eleanor who gave birth to Thomas. Whatever happens, you have shown that you are not only a perfect knight but a good husband too."

I wondered at that, but my procrastination meant that I was forced to hasten our departure. The valley knights had not been requested and that pleased me for it meant I could ask Sir William to keep a watch on my castle and town. The new men were now Stockton men and I was confident that they would watch my walls. I should have knighted Jack before now, but I now had two squires for Thomas had become as proficient as Jack and I was confident in the men I led, and I just hoped that my service to the king could be brief. I also had recently acquired a page. Robin son of Alf was an orphan and had seen ten summers. His father had died fighting for my father and his mother had died of the winter chills at the same time my wife had been ill. He had been taken in and looked after in my castle for my people were ever thoughtful. Ruth had been teaching him to read and Martyn Longsword had a special affection for him and took him under his wing, showing him how to use weapons. He had pleaded with Martyn to be taken with him and Martyn asked me to consider it. Martyn had been a shield brother of Alf and I acceded. He would be safe for I would leave him, when there was danger, with the baggage and the horses. It took a month to find a ship but that helped us ensure that all the war gear we took was sound.

We headed for Herterpol and the ship that awaited us. As we entered the south gate to the town, I found myself viewing everyone with suspicion. The men who had come to do my family harm had come from Herterpol. There had been complicity, not necessarily from the townsfolk, but the officials had chosen to look the other way. I was curt to the point of rudeness and wasted no time in boarding the ship which was a large cog and easily accommodated my men. This would be an identical journey to the one we had made the last time the king had needed us. The difference this time was that my squires were more prepared and the rest of us had fought together enough times to be of one mind. That always helped. For Robin it would all be one great adventure and his eyes were as wide as a full moon. The other difference would be that I would not be seeing Sir Leofric. His son Sir Alfraed had written to say that his father had died. Another of the warriors who had saved England for King Henry was dead. I doubted that the king would have even remembered the young man who rode at the Warlord's side. At least Sir Alfraed would not have to worry about choosing sides. Geoffrey, Duke of Brittany was dead, and it was his widow, Constance, who ruled the land. She would be swayed by King Henry. The voyage was a longer one than normal thanks to perverse winds.

We reached Rouen in September during the late afternoon and I wondered about the timing of our summons. The campaigning season was almost over so why had we been summoned? There was a great deal of activity in the city and men were being mobilised. It was not just my ship that disgorged men. There were other ships from Southampton and Dover. Perhaps there was war although there had been no news of it in the north of England. Rouen was a walled city and the camp which had been prepared for us was outside the city walls. While Gerard and Richard led my men to the camp I went with my squires and page to the castle and King Henry.

Once more, when I met him, I was struck by how much he had aged. He had lost two sons and I knew there was a conflict with his eldest and heir. His senior knights and lords, most of them Norman, were in the Great Hall. I was greeted and dismissed almost in the same breath, "Ah, Sir Samuel, it is good that you have arrived, we need your sage advice. When we have made our initial dispositions then we will speak alone. For the meanwhile help yourself to wine and food."

A table lay laden with wine, cheese, bread, and ham. We headed over and I looked at the milling lords. It was infuriating to have been summoned so hastily and then left to

The Perfect Knight

cool our heels. In a way, I understood for there appeared to be an urgency about the way King Henry commanded but I did not even know who the enemy was. I did not have to wait too long for it was almost time to clear the Great Hall and prepare it for the evening feast.

King Henry came directly to me and put his arm around me. It was a rare gesture of familiarity and I saw some of the Norman lords start. "Sir Samuel, each time you come to me you grow more like the Warlord in stature. It gives me both comfort and hope." A servant came over when the king waved to him, "Have your squires take your bags to your rooms, Jacques here will show them." I nodded and Jack, Robin, and Thomas hurried after the liveried servant. "Come, you and I will go to my solar." He said no more but his hurried, slightly lopsided gait told me the urgency. Once in the cosy room, he waved me to a seat. He sat wearily and poured two goblets of wine. That a servant had not done so was a surprise. Perhaps King Henry did view me as he had my grandfather.

The hustle and bustle of the rest of the castle seemed to be far away for it was silent and the late September sun shone through the glazed window. "A pleasant room, King Henry, and away from the noise of the castle."

"Aye, I remember the one in Stockton where your grandfather would teach me to be king. I have not always heeded his teachings and that I regret." He drank and shook his head as though to rid himself of doubts, "King Philip Augustus has made unreasonable demands of me. He wishes to have custody of Geoffrey's children and Brittany itself. More, he wishes the return of the Vexin to the French crown. The demands are unacceptable, and he only does so because he sees me as weak. He has an army gathered on the borders with Berry. He has also demanded that my son, Duke Richard, cease besieging his uncle, Raymond Count of Toulouse. This young king thinks that this old lion is ready to retire. With you at my side, we will prove him wrong. I have set my lords to begin to move my army south to counter the threat of Philip. The lords of Anjou and Normandy have been summoned and together, heir to the

The Perfect Knight

Warlord, we shall show this young cub that we still have teeth and claws."

I nodded, sipped my wine, and asked, "And Duke Richard, what of him?"

His eyes suddenly looked fearful. He shook his head and leaned forward, "It is sad, Sir Samuel, that I cannot trust my eldest. I would hope that he would stand by my side but the fact that I am uncertain about his loyalty means I cannot take the risk." He stopped and stared at me, "You are my man are you not? I can trust you to be loyal?"

I sighed, "King Henry, when has my family been anything less than loyal. It has cost us dear but I swear that my family will never betray you."

His smile made him look younger, "That is all that I needed to know. The problem is one of my own creation. When Alys, Countess of the Vexin and Richard were engaged she was given the province of Berry. I kept her close to me to enable the wedding to take place whenever Richard agreed." He suddenly looked at me, "Richard does like women does he not? Alys is comely and witty."

I shrugged, "I know not, my lord. I have fought alongside him but…"

He nodded, "My son has dallied and procrastinated so much that King Philip is now demanding that the wedding takes place soon. It is why he has his army close to Berry. If he does not like my answer, then it will be war. I wish you to take command of the vanguard. Your men may be few, but they are amongst the elite of my army. We gather at Blois." He smiled, "Ironical really, as that was the home of the man who denied my mother and me the crown for so many years. Your grandfather bested him though and I hope that the sight of your gryphon will inspire fear in our enemies and hope in our friends."

A servant knocked on the door and then opened it. The king frowned. "My lord, the papal emissary still awaits you."

He nodded and rose, "Aye, the Pope, it seems, has news for me. You shall sit on my right hand this night. Until then, farewell."

The Perfect Knight

Thomas was waiting down the corridor, "I have our rooms, father, and Jack and Robin are stabling our horses."

"I fear that we shall be here but one night and our horses will need to be seasoned on the road. When you have shown me to the chamber then go to Gerard and tell him that we leave first thing in the morning. We are to be the vanguard and we go to war."

The chamber was well apportioned and showed me my elevated status. Such things did not worry me, but I knew that other lords, who may not have known me, would take note. After unpacking my bags Thomas scurried off and I first washed and then sat on the cushioned chair to gather my thoughts. I would need to write to Ruth and tell her of my future whereabouts. I would not worry my wife, but my sister would need to know. We had brought parchment, goose feathers, and ink for just such an occasion. I sat and wrote giving only the information that she would need. It was unlikely that travelling on an English ship back to England it would be intercepted, but I just said that we would be in Blois. I sealed it and when Jack returned, I gave it to him and a coin for the captain of the ship which had brought us. He headed to the river and I felt happier knowing that those in England would know where I was. Before I had left, I had told my knights, Sir William and the others that I anticipated a call to them from King Henry or Duke Richard. My summons had been a warning, a precursor of what might be.

That evening my over-worked squires and new page had to wait at table. I had kept them both occupied right until the feast. The last food they had enjoyed was the cold fare of a ship's breakfast and their only repast this night would be what we left!

The papal emissary, a cardinal I did not recognise, was seated to the left of the king. I was seated between the Archbishop of Rouen and the king. Walter de Coutances had only been the archbishop for a year. Before then he had been the Bishop of Lincoln. He was King Henry's man and I saw why I had been seated where I had. It was to hear the conversation between the two men. Normally I would not have enjoyed such a position, but this proved to be informative.

"Archbishop, you must impress upon the French King that Brittany is part of my domain and my son's children are not to be used as hostages. If he attempts to take them then he risks war. Let him know that you are his only chance of peace. I hope that Cardinal Carnelli will support us when he arbitrates on behalf of the Pope. The Pope would rather have the French and we fighting Saladin in the Holy Land."

"From what I understand, my liege, King Philip Augustus is not averse to a war."

I could tell that he was masking his true words and King Henry spotted the deception, "Speak plainly, Walter, he sees me as a weak old man who was badgered and bullied by three disobedient whelps." The archbishop hung his head. "Tell him that I have the grandson of the Warlord to lead my armies. I have the man who thwarted his attempts to take Scarborough Castle and to rob Stockton."

Now I knew why I was the vanguard. I was a target. King Henry was letting the French king know where I would be, at the head of his armies and he was making it easier to draw the French to the place he wished to fight them. He was clever but the risk would be to my men and to me.

The archbishop said, "This will encourage the French, Sir Samuel, to defeat you! Yours would be a banner they would wish to hang in Saint-Denis."

I smiled and it was not arrogance that made me do so but the knowledge that my family had rarely suffered a defeat. "The Scots and the French have been trying to do that since my great grandfather returned from Constantinopolis. I trust in English men at arms and archers. Do not worry about me, Archbishop." I turned to the king, "And which men will I be leading?"

In answer, the king waved a hand around the room, "You may choose the best from this hall. I trust you enough to know that you will not leave me with the dregs. It is the main guard which will have to fight the battle; under your guidance of course."

The Perfect Knight

I looked around the room but saw few nobles that I knew. I understood the reason. The best young nobles would all be fighting at Toulouse under the banner of Duke Richard of Aquitaine. The lords who had followed the Warlord were now too old to fight and would be in their manors. The ones who would serve King Henry were, largely, Normans. There were few Bretons as the war between England and Brittany would have soured relations. I would have to ride to war with men I did not know, and I now began to understand why my grandfather had spent so much money building up a large force of his own. They were always the core of men on whom he could rely. I had less than twenty to do the same. I looked and saw younger warriors, most of whom were about my age. There was one older warrior and although he was seated next to others, he looked to be alone and I wondered at his story. The others were plain to see. They were young lords looking for coin and advancement.

As the conversation flowed, not about the coming campaign, but a future crusade, I wondered what it would entail for me. My father had gone to the Holy Land to atone for the death of his first wife. I had been to that land and had no desire to visit it again. Would I be left, as my grandfather was, to protect England? Perhaps that was my fate.

The next morning I was awake well before dawn and went to the Great Hall to breakfast; the tables had been laid out with bread, ham, cheese, and small beer. There were no benches for with the army about to move then the lords who had been accommodated in the castle would have to eat and then quickly leave. Jack, Robin, and Thomas grabbed some food and then went to prepare our horses. I wanted to catch the nobles as they ate so that I could ask the questions which would determine if they were the men I needed for the vanguard. They needed to have men who were all mounted and enough of them to get the job done. I needed a mix of mailed men and light horsemen or archers. I was not hopeful about mounted archers. The Normans preferred crossbows and none, so far as I knew, had mounted crossbowmen. I needed to speak with them as I also needed men who would obey orders while retaining the ability to think for themselves. This was where I missed the knights of the valley. I knew them. I wished that Sir William was with me, but he was guarding my home.

Sir Rolf d'Avranches was the first to enter. I had noticed the young Norman the night before and saw that he listened more than he spoke. That appeared to be a good sign, but it could simply signify nervousness and a lack of experience. He recognised me and bowed, "My lord, you rise early!"

I waved a hand at the food, "That way I have the choice of the freshest food!"

He laughed and shook his head, "I think not, my lord. You lead the van and I suspect that you will be away before half of the lords have risen!"

"And you, Sir Rolf, why are you so early?"

"I did not drink as heavily as some of the others and, to be truthful, I wish to be about this business sooner rather than later. My wife is with child and it is our first. I would return to be there when my son is born."

"Or daughter, eh?"

"No, my lord, it will be a boy. I am of Norman stock and we are descended from the Norsemen. There are still women who have the ability to see the future; they are called volvas. One of my wife's women, Agnetha, is one such and she told me that I would have a son."

"That sounds to be suspiciously like witchcraft."

He shrugged, "A witch to me sounds like something evil. A volva can heal, and they understand birth in a way that a doctor cannot. I am happy to have them living amongst us."

That he was not afraid to argue with me made me feel well disposed towards him. "And how many men do you lead?"

"Not as many as I would wish and yet the ones I have are the best, or so I believe. I lead four knights and their squires. We bring fifteen men at arms. Five light horsemen and I have five bowmen who are mounted."

I looked at him in surprise, "Mounted archers?"

He smiled, "I told you that the blood of the Norsemen runs strong in my town. Vikings were always good archers. I

The Perfect Knight

know they are not the equal of the men you lead but they are better than any we have met so far."

That decided me. He was just what I needed, "Then I would have you with me in the van!"

He beamed, "I confess, my lord that the other reason I rose early was to make myself available. I hope that does not offend."

I laughed, "No for we shall need men with such foresight and if the blood of the Norseman runs in your veins then who knows, we may need your second sight."

The next lords who came in were still suffering from the night before and that did not bode well for the campaign. The third one, however, was known to Sir Rolf who said, "This is a neighbour of mine, Sir Ferry d'Herouville."

The man was a little older than Sir Rolf and had an ugly scar running down his right cheek. It was close enough to his eye to make me think he had almost been blinded. "Sir Samuel, I am pleased that I have met you. I understand that you are to lead the van and I beg the opportunity to ride with you."

He seemed eager and that made me suspicious but before I could question him Sir Rolf said, "Sir Ferry has good reason to wish to fight alongside you, my lord. His father fought alongside your father, Sir William when he had the manor of Ouistreham."

I nodded for it was an understandable reason but would not necessarily guarantee him a place, "And who do you lead?"

"I lead a conroi of two knights, twelve mailed men at arms and twelve light horsemen. We are all well mounted, my lord and fought against the Bretons when the king's sons rebelled."

Sir Rolf said, "My lord, I can vouch for his men and, like mine they can also trace their grandsires back to Duke Rollo. They are tough warriors."

I nodded for I had looked into Sir Ferry's eyes and knew that he was a man of his word. "Then ride to the camp and join my men."

The Perfect Knight

Fate brought me the last of my men. I had spoken to another two lords and found them lacking the skills and, to be honest, the attitude that I needed. The greybeard walked in and as the last man I had spoken to deliberately shunned him it made me warm to him. I was in a hurry and could if I needed, use just the two Normans I had spoken to. Something made me speak to him.

"I am Sir Samuel of Stockton, the Earl of Cleveland. Your name, my lord?"

"Sir Louis de Barfleur."

He was a Norman from the Cotentin Peninsula. "I seek men to be in the van of King Henry's army."

"Then you had better look elsewhere, Sir Samuel."

"Why? Do you not wish to fight?"

He shook his head and gave me a lopsided smile, "I wish to fight more than anything, but I fear that I will be left to guard the baggage."

"And why is that, my lord?" I was intrigued.

"My younger brother fought alongside the Young King Henry and when the young king died, tried to rob the corpse as they brought it back for burial. He fled and his horse tripped, breaking his neck. It saved him from a dishonourable end."

I did not think so but I ignored the comment. "You are not your brother. Tell me how many men you lead?"

"I have one knight, my youngest brother as well as fifteen men at arms and ten mounted archers."

"Then you have been sent to me for a purpose. If you would then I will have you with my vanguard."

"But the others…"

"I care not about the opinion of others. Gather your war gear and meet me at the camp."

I had my vanguard.

Chapter 11

Aquitaine 1187

We left Rouen by late morning. It was a good sign for many companies would have taken a whole day to pack up their camp but the ones I was leading were as efficient as my men. There was no real urgency as the main part of the army would not leave for a day or two but I wanted to be on the road so that we could thoroughly scout ahead. We would be riding close to the border with France and secrecy was impossible. Just as we knew that the French were mustered on the border with Berry so they would know that King Henry was marching south to meet them. We had to find any of their scouts before they found us. Our route was almost due south but once we had passed Évreux we would have to swing a little west for Chartres lay on the main road and was held by the French. They controlled the land for ten miles to the west. We were not there to fight battles. After that, we had to pass Dreux which was an oft fought over border town and that might be our first test.

Mordaf led followed by Richard whom I had given command of the mounted archers. The fifteen Normans we had acquired would make a big difference. I noticed that Richard had my archers riding next to the Normans in a column of twos so that they could begin the training of these new men. Mine had it down to a fine art and their knowledge would make us a more effective fighting force.

I rode with the three knights. Sir Rolf and Sir Ferry had made Sir Louis welcome and we rode four abreast. Whilst letting them know what we had to do and the importance of our role I also picked their brains about the land and the

The Perfect Knight

enemies we might meet. The Count of Évreux, Amaury, was a supporter of King Henry but he was not, it appeared, an active one. I knew the type. My grandfather had told me of nobles who ostensibly supported Empress Matilda but were quite happy to change sides if events went against them. We would be welcomed in Évreux but there would be few knights in our army who came from the city. Part of our task was to let the nobles know that the king would be following us. There would have to be preparations made for him while we would just take what was available.

Count Amaury was pleasant to us and he gave slick and smooth answers to my questions. He had known about the French movements but had not, it appeared, done anything about following them or discovering their intentions. He had been the one who had speculated that they were heading to threaten Berry. He was a political noble. Nothing he had told us and by implication the king could be deemed as treacherous if the French were successful. It was Robin, Jack and Thomas who discovered more pertinent intelligence. When they joined me in our chamber, they told me that they had picked up from gossip amongst Count Amaury's knights' squires that Châteaudun, which lay to the south of us, was held by Sir Henri de Châteaudun and he was a loyal Frenchman. Orléans lay close to his castle and that was a vital French fortress. It was rumoured that Sir Henri de Châteaudun might challenge our passage. I knew, from the maps I had studied, that north of the town was a large forest and the small town of Brou lay just at the edge of it. I doubted that this French knight would have enough men to hurt King Henry, but any attack might demoralise what was, in essence, an inexperienced army.

We had to wait for King Henry at Évreux in any case. He and his leaders would occupy the chambers we had vacated. When we saw their banners, I started my column of men down the road towards our next halt while I rode with my squires and Robin to apprise the king, before he entered the castle, of the new information. He shifted uncomfortably in his saddle as we rode the last mile to the town together. He was getting too old for such campaigns. He gave me a sad smile, "You have, I take it, news?"

I nodded, "I did not receive this knowledge from the count."

"I know that Count Amaury is very adept at ensuring that whatever the outcome of this confrontation he will emerge unscathed. Your grandfather taught me well and I am not a fool."

I had been gently chastised. "I believe that the castle of Châteaudun may try to hurt us as we pass through the forest north of their town."

"And we have to pass through it."

"We do. I plan to ride further ahead than you might normally expect and if there is one, trip the trap."

"Do not put your head too far out, Sir Samuel. I do not need you to be hurt fighting insects! We have a wolf who seeks to devour our lands."

"Do not worry, King Henry, I have no intention of being hurt. We will use speed. It is fifty-two miles to Châteaudun, and your army will take three days to reach it. We will be there by tomorrow night while you are still on the road south. I intend to make Brou secure for us. I care not if Sir Henri squats like a toad in his castle just so long as he does not damage the ability of this army to fight. I may be wrong and there might be no ambush, but it will not be time wasted."

He smiled, "I am glad to have you with me. Your advice is sage. Keep me informed."

I gestured to Jack and Thomas, "Know that any message from me shall come from one of these two. Any other word is from the enemy!"

We turned and galloped our horses after my men. I had been pleased with the opportunity to speak to the king for I knew that we did not need to have our leader in the dark, but it had also given me the chance to let my three Normans lead for a while. It could only do them good. We managed to make the castle of Senonche although it was a hard ride. Our horses were weary, and I knew that the next days would be as challenging.

The Perfect Knight

The knight who ruled the manor was Sir Geoffrey de Senonche. I had not met him, but I knew from the three Normans who rode with me that he had a certain reputation. He was his own man who like to be left alone. His father had kept out of the war between his rightful lord, King Stephen, or, as my grandfather had always referred to him, Stephen the usurper, and Empress Matilda. I wondered at our reception. In the end, he was courteous and although our men had to rough it in the outer bailey, we knights had chambers and were feted.

I liked Sir Geoffrey who looked to be old enough to be my father. He was open, bluff and honest, "I know what men say about me, Sir Samuel, but know this, my family has seen lords like Stephen of Blois and even your king, Henry Curtmantle, use the people and the lords around here as pawns in their giant chess game. We are discarded as soon as our usefulness is finished. I admired your grandfather but he, too, was used. I never understood why he stayed so long at the side of the Empress. Your king would not be king but for him."

"Is that why we were welcomed?"

He laughed, "Aye, for I have heard only good things of you and your father. He went on a crusade for the right reasons and not for gain. Oh, I shall welcome your king and bow for he is the ruler of this land now but I shall not send men to fight against the King of France. It is not cowardice, it is practicality!"

We left as dawn broke and rode through the forest which surrounded Senonche. Mordaf rode with Tam the Hawker and they ranged half a mile ahead of the archers. Whilst the knights and men at arms rode along the road the archers spread out in a long skirmish line and travelled through the woods. They were looking for signs of horses. It was a task that needed to be done although if they found nothing then it would be good news for it would mean that we would not be ambushed. We had a clear sight of the archers nearest to the road and we kept a tight formation. We rode, largely in silence although I did not discourage conversation from the other knights. Sir Louis kept his own counsel, but I knew he was listening.

"The lord of Châteaudun does not have enough men to hurt the main army, Sir Samuel, so why the concern?"

"Easy to answer that question, Sir Ferry. Firstly, this is good practice and that, like training at the pel is never wasted. Secondly, if we are spotted by the Lord of Châteaudun it will make him wary of us in future and that is not a bad thing but the main reason is morale. If he attacked the king and the leaders of our army it would make the others, the spearmen, men at arms, crossbowmen, and archers, less confident and I am here to tell you that confidence is one of the key factors in determining who wins a battle or a war. My grandfather was often outnumbered but he trusted in himself and in his men. He did not lose."

Sir Louis suddenly piped up, "And did I not hear, my lord, how you, as a young knight, held the Tower of London against great odds?"

"I did but my grandfather was there."

"And dying."

The memory of his death was still painful to me and I felt his loss each time it was mentioned. The word barely made it past my lips, "Aye."

We were close to Brou when I heard hooves on the road, and I drew my sword and then sheathed it I as Mordaf and Tam reined in, "Lord there are men ahead finishing off making hides for what looks like an ambush. They have felled trees and are disguising them with ivy and other climbing plants."

"You have done well." I circled my arm, "We will rest here, Tam, fetch our archers."

Sir Rolf said, "Should we not attack them?"

I smiled, "Aye we could but there is another way. We wait until dark and then I send my archers to eliminate their sentries. It is my belief that the Lord of Châteaudun will man them before dawn. Imagine his surprise if we are there. With luck, the sentries will have lit fires and be cooking food. That also saves us a task."

The Perfect Knight

I saw Jack and Thomas grinning at the lesson I was giving the Normans while Robin was staring open-mouthed. He would become used to my ways.

Richard son of Aelric came over and Mordaf joined us, "Mordaf, how many sentries would you estimate?"

"There were fifty men building the hides but the fires they had lit were just for a dozen men or so." That told me there would just be sentries watching the ambush.

"Richard, take our men and eliminate the sentries. When the sentries have been taken then send for me."

"Aye, lord." He waved over my archers and they led their horses through the trees following Mordaf and Tam.

The confidence of my men was in direct contrast to the doubt in the Normans' eyes. I dismounted and let my coif drop down over my back. Thomas brought me the ale skin and I drank deeply. Sir Ferry asked, "What if they leave more than a dozen men to watch their hides, my lord?"

"Unless they have left the whole fifty then Richard will deal with them."

"You are that sure, my lord?"

"Yes, Sir Louis, for they are all archers who know how to be both silent and deadly. They will try to take prisoners, but their bows guarantee that they will succeed."

We heard nothing while we waited. When I heard hooves thundering up the road I mounted. Tam the Hawker jerked his reins to stop his horse, "We have the hides, lord. Two men resisted but the rest are bound." I nodded, "They have two deer cooking on the fires!"

"Excellent, we eat well this night." We headed down the road. The men building the hides and left as sentries would have had more attention on the treat of their lord's venison than on an attack. We were supposed to be still in Évreux and that was more than fifty miles away. The last thing that they would have expected would be an attack so soon. The ten men were well bound, and Richard had tied them together so that no individual could escape. I saw two freshly piled mounds of earth. The would-be heroes were already buried.

The Perfect Knight

The smell of the venison made me realise how hungry I was, but I still had plans to make before we could eat. "Tether the horses to the north of the camp. Gerard, when they have eaten, I want four men to watch them and another three to be guards for our prisoners. Richard, when you and your men have eaten, I want the archers in a line two hundred paces from the hides to the south."

Sir Louis asked, "Do we put up tents, my lord?"

"No, tonight we use the hides or hovels. One night of discomfort will not hurt us."

I made sure that we were well away from the prisoners when we ate as I wished to tell the knights, Gerard and Richard my plan. I knew that Gerard and Richard would explain it in their own way to their men. The Normans who they led would have a lesson in brevity.

"When they come tomorrow it will be at dawn, perhaps before. I cannot be certain as I do not know the mind of this lord. I will have the prisoners bound and gagged and seated around the fires. In the half-light of dawn he will just see men bowed around a fire and that is what their lord will expect to see. Richard, you and the archers will be behind the hides; that way you can cover the prisoners and the camp. Sir Louis you and your men at arms will be behind the hides and your task is to protect the archers and our horses. Sir Rolf, you and your knights will be with me and half of the rest of the men at arms. We will be secreted in the woods to the east of the road. Sir Ferry, you, your knights, and Gerard of Chester will have the remainder of the men at arms to the west of the road. The Lord of Châteaudun or whoever leads his men will travel up the road. When they have passed us then we will attack them in the rear."

Sir Ferry asked, "Is that honourable?"

I laughed, "Sir Ferry, there is little enough honour at a tournament and none at all in war. When you fight in battle then you do all you can to win. A knight who fights just to take a prisoner and collect a ransom is a dead man walking. If you fight a crossbowman or man at arms he will stick you with a knife just as soon as he can. Is that not right Gerard?"

The Perfect Knight

Gerard had an evil grin, "Without missing a heartbeat, Sir Samuel. Knights always carry full purses!" I saw Sir Ferry and Sir Rolf's hand go, involuntarily, to their purses. It proved my point.

"Now eat. I want men watching all night. Two men from each conroi will walk the perimeter. I do not think that any will come in the night, but I would be a fool if I did not plan for such an eventuality. I will take the second shift with Thomas. Jack, you, and Martyn Longsword can have the first shift. Wake me when I have slept for two hours!" My words were intended for the ears of the Normans and I was telling them that I expected the knights to do as much watching as the men at arms.

Robin asked, "And me, my lord?"

"We will wait awhile before you have to endure a night watch."

Jack knew better than to let me sleep too long and roused me while some of the men were still eating. "Come, Thomas, we will see how alert our archers are." I saw that Sir Ferry was one of the sentries with his squire. I waved to him and headed through the trees.

This was a lesson for Thomas. I wanted to see if he could move silently in the short mail hauberk he now wore. I had boots over my chausse, and I chose a path that was free of both leaves and twigs. I was pleased that Tom only crunched one leaf. It still sounded loud, but I knew it was not. I used my nose to identify my archer sentries and I stopped. I could not see them, but I knew where they were. Thomas started when Richard rose like a wraith just ten paces from where we stood.

"Very good, my lord. You got to within fifty paces of us before I heard the leaf." I saw Tom's head drop.

"Anything?"

"No, my lord, and while we were waiting for you, I asked our prisoners a few questions. I think their only two heroes died and Mordaf's scarred hand scared them. They could not wait to tell us what we wished to know. These are castle soldiers. Their lord, Sir Henri, hopes to be here just after dawn. He knows that King Henry will have to pass this way

The Perfect Knight

and he hopes to bloody the king's nose. The twelve men who were sentries would walk back to Châteaudun while the ones who come to ambush will all be mounted, even the crossbowmen. He hopes that a sudden attack on our vanguard or even the king and his bodyguards would shock us so much that we would not pursue him as he races back to his castle which is just a few miles away and he will garner the glory of a victory."

That was useful information and told me much about this French knight, "Aye, well I shall relieve you in an hour or so and you and your men can grab an hour or two of sleep before you pose the prisoners around the fire. Tell them that they will not be harmed if they do not try to alert their lord. If they do try to alert him then they will die!"

"Do not worry, Sir Samuel, they will be as quiet as mice."

I did not speak as we headed back to the camp but when we reached the camp Thomas said, "Is my task to stay with the horses?"

"Not this time, Robin can do that. We will not bother with helmets, but we will take shields and spears. You will watch my left and Jack, my right but you shall be behind me."

I saw that Sir Ferry had rolled into his cloak and one of his men now took his place. He had shown me that he had done a longer shift than I had asked Jack to do. I took out my whetstone and sat sharpening my sword and dagger before the fire. I saw one of the prisoners open an eye at the sound. Even though his hands were bound he made the sign of the cross. Richard was right. These were garrison troops. When I judged dawn to be an hour away, I went around to wake first Gerard and then the knights.

"It is time. When we are to attack, I will have Jack sound the horn twice. Remember we want Châteaudun eliminated as a threat. I intend to give the castle to the king. It may prove to be a good bargaining tool with the French King!"

Gerard had already divided the men and as they gathered their weapons, I fitted my coif over my arming cap. It was not as good as a helmet but in the half-light of dawn, I would

The Perfect Knight

have better control of my senses. I did not tell the others to emulate me, but I saw that my squires and men at arms did as did Sir Louis, but the other Normans retained their helmets. That was their choice. With so many men moving through the trees silence was impossible and by the time we reached them my archers were on their feet and were ready to be relieved. Words were unnecessary and Richard and I merely nodded as we passed. I pointed towards the road and led my men. I had just over twenty with me and this was a worrying time for me. I was relying upon surprise to win the day, but the Normans with me were an unknown force. How would they fight? I knew the quality of my men, but they were less than half the ones I led. We reached the road just half a mile from the camp. I circled my arm and men found themselves somewhere that they could hide. Our surcoats would be easy to pick out if the French came in full daylight, but I counted on them being focussed on the road ahead and not the trees. Even so, we were all more than thirty paces from the road and, so far as I could see, none could be seen from the road. I drew my sword and there was a hiss from both sides as my men did the same. We were ready.

It was still not quite the first light when I heard the jingle of mail and horse furniture. I also heard the murmur of conversation. We all shrank behind the foliage. There was a convenient beech branch just before me and the leaves broke up my outline. By keeping my head still I would be invisible. The lord and his six knights led the column, their coifs hung about their shoulders, their helmets and shields dangling from their cantles. He had not bothered to use scouts and that showed his confidence. He still expected us late in the day at the earliest or, perhaps, even the next day. Behind the knights came the mounted men at arms and there were just twelve of those. Behind them came the forty mounted crossbowmen riding sumpters. Finally, the squires led the other sumpters carrying the supplies that they would eat. It seemed to take an age for the almost one hundred men to pass us. I realised then that Lord Henri was overconfident. The crossbows, released from behind a hide, would be accurate but they took an age to reload and the twelve men at

The Perfect Knight

arms, with their spears, would not have been enough to protect them. It told me much about the lord.

When the squires had passed us, I waited until they were thirty paces from us and then waved my men forward, through the trees. Martyn Longsword extended the line to our right and I stayed on the left. When we sprang our own trap then any who fled would head down the road and it would be up to the knights to stop them!

From ahead I heard a shout as the leading French knight approached the camp. I turned to Jack and nodded to him to ready the horn. He spat and put the mouthpiece to his lips. I guessed, for the sun was just rising above the trees to our right, that the camp was clearly in sight of the French lord and he might wonder why his men were not standing. Timing was all for the leading horsemen had to be close enough to guarantee that my archers could send a bodkin into mail. I had already told my Norman allies that I cared not for ransom. My archers would send their arrows to kill. It was the only way to ensure success. When there was a second shout I said, "Now, Jack!"

The horn sounded and I knew that it would be disconcerting for the French, especially the squires, as it would be coming from behind them. We hurried forward and I heard the cries of alarm and pain as the French were showered with arrows from my hidden archers. The squires turned to look for danger and, by then, Sir Rolf, Gerard and I were within ten paces of them. They had reined in and seeing us were torn between flight and fight. As they drew their swords, we ran at them and they were pulled unceremoniously from their saddles.

Sir Rolf, have your squires guard them and their horses. Disarm them and bind them to discourage flight!"

"Aye, Sir Samuel! Guy, you know what to do!"

"Aye, Sir Rolf!"

Some of the squires had been hurt when they had fallen and with a sword at your throat, a man is less inclined to be belligerent. We hurried further up the road. The crossbowmen had also halted, and some had begun to dismount. The men at arms and the knights who had

The Perfect Knight

survived the attack were now trying to get down the road, but it was blocked by their own crossbowmen and some chose to try the trees. That was a mistake for Martyn and my men were waiting for them and stepping out from behind trees hacked into the heads of their horses and their legs.

A crossbowman had almost managed to pull back his string when I reached him. I swung my sword across his middle. The crossbow was shattered, and the edge of the sword sliced through his brigandine. He dropped his useless weapon and begged for mercy. I saw Thomas and Jack lunge with their swords to wound two other crossbowmen. Robin was safe with the horses. Sir Rolf and Sir Ferry had slain their men.

I shouted, "Drop your weapons and fall to your knees and you shall live!"

The shock of so many men appearing from behind them had driven every ounce of courage from them and they did as they were ordered. It was then that Sir Henri chose to lead his handful of knights and men at arms who remained, to charge us. They cared not that their own crossbowmen were in the road and with swords drawn they galloped down the road. The crossbowmen hurled themselves into the trees where our men at arms restrained them. There were just five of us in the centre of the road; myself, Sir Rolf, Sir Ferry, Gerard and Sir Hugh, one of Sir Rolf's knights. Behind us stood just Jack and Thomas. The rest of the squires were guarding prisoners. I let my shield hang from my left shoulder by its long strap and held my sword in two hands. This was all about who would blink first.

The Lord of Châteaudun rode directly for me. I was in the centre of the road and, perhaps, he recognised my livery. I saw riders behind him as arrows slammed into their backs. Richard son of Aelric would do all that he could to protect me. That the Lord of Châteaudun would reach me first was clear and he rode at me so that my shield offered no protection. Sir Rolf was on my right with Sir Hugh and I hoped that they would stand. The horse might try to avoid hitting me but if there were two men there, he might be forced to stop. The swing I used was from left to right. I was

The Perfect Knight

gambling on the fact that his horse would be distracted, and the knight could not be certain that he would ride in a straight line. The knight's blow would be aimed at my head and, without a helmet, then any hit would kill me. It would be a quick death! I saw the muzzle of the horse turn to my right as I swung my sword. I had to commit to the strike and I waited for the blow which might end my life. My swing bit into the thigh of the knight. His mail chausse slowed down the strike but it hacked through mail and into his leg. His blow was a good one but the movement of his horse's head meant it caught me a glancing blow to my right shoulder. He did not break links as it was with the flat of the blade, but it hurt and I knew that I would ache the next day. The horse's head continued to swing and that, allied to my blow made the horse and rider begin to tumble to the ground. As the horse's head smashed into the bole of a tree, killing it instantly, the rider crashed to the ground.

Pointing my sword at the other Frenchmen I shouted, "Surrender or die! There are archers behind you who will kill you where you stand!"

Swords clattered to the ground and we had won.

Chapter 12

Châteaudun 1187

I was forced to return to Châteaudun with Lord Henri for the cut he had suffered was a deep one and whilst we had saved his life, he needed the medical treatment his doctor could give him. The gates were open when we arrived, and we simply rode in. We captured the castle intact for he had brought his warriors with him for the ambush. His wife rushed to him, hurling murderous glances at us.

I said for the benefit of all but particularly the lady, "This castle is now under the control of King Henry of England. All within its walls will be safe so long as they cooperate with us." I saw the lady of the manor rise and prepare to spit insults in my direction. "King Henry will decide what happens to this castle but until then, my lady, it is I who will make all the necessary decisions. Think on that before you say something that might result in incarceration for you!"

A priest hurried over and whispered in her ear. She nodded and followed her husband and the physician into the keep.

"Secure the walls and disarm the guards. Thomas, Robin, take some men and make sure that the food which is being cooked is not tampered with."

Nodding my son and my page grabbed two of our men at arms and hurried down to the kitchen. I had sent Jack directly to King Henry so that he could now head straight for the castle and avoid the forest. He would have a quicker ride as a result; he needed to be in the saddle as little as possible. It was the middle of the afternoon before I had time to eat or drink anything. I had almost forgotten about the town which

The Perfect Knight

also needed to be secured but Gerard had made it safe. With the gates manned, none could enter or leave without our say so.

Thomas and Robin brought food and wine for my knights and me. Thomas had already arranged for the men at arms and archers to be fed. He could now replace Jack and I began to think of knighthood more seriously for my senior squire. Robin was still young but he had shown that he could obey orders and was malleable.

The Norman knights, even the dour Sir Louis, were ebullient. Sir Rolf shook his head, "If you had said before we left Rouen that we could take a castle without losing a single man I would have laughed, my lord."

I sipped the wine which was excellent, "We were lucky, Sir Rolf. If the lord of this manor had not tried to gain a little glory for himself then he would not be wounded and twenty of his men would still be alive. Who knows, they might have managed to get back to this castle, secure the gates and we would be outside instead of eating and drinking in comfort. If you take risks as he did then you have to live with the consequences."

Sir Louis asked, "What will the king do with it, Sir Samuel?"

"I do not know for certain, but I would have thought that holding it as a bargaining piece might be the best."

I slept the sleep of the dead that night. My men had managed to rest a little during the day and it was Thomas who arranged the night watch. He had taken to heart his new role as a squire. King Henry and his bodyguards arrived at noon the next day. Jack was with them and the king was in a fine mood. He took me to one side and clapped me about the shoulders, "This is most unexpected and gives us the chance to make King Philip Augustus reconsider his threats." He looked at me with his piercing eyes. I know that it intimidated some men but not me. "You did not promise the lord of the manor anything did you?"

"No, my lord. I said that this castle was now yours and you would make any decision."

"Has he paid you ransom yet?"

"Not yet but the others have. We found the treasury when we arrived, and it is a full one."

"Then he can afford a generous ransom. I will speak with him. Get some rest for I would have you return to the fore tomorrow. The difference will be that I shall be closer to you."

Something in his words made me suspicious, "King Henry, did you know that there would be an ambush?"

He never faltered, "I was told that men might attack us in the forest. It seemed prudent to let you disturb the game. I knew that you would come to no harm!" He turned and left.

I seethed within. It was not just my life that had been risked but my son and my men not to mention the Normans who had so blindly followed me. I chose not to say anything to my squires as there was little point. We would now be closer to the main army. I would stay within hailing distance of the main battle. I sought out my two captains and my knights. "We leave tomorrow and this time we will ride just ahead of the king. Be sure that you secure the ransoms from the knights we captured."

"Aye, lord. We have them already. It was fortunate that we took their castle as they could not make the excuse that their coins were not close to hand." Sir Louis seemed to me to be an eminently practical man.

Sir Rolf had not enjoyed such success before, "And their horses, mail, and weapons were unexpected. It is a shame that Sir Henri's horse died."

I shrugged, "As I said before we fought, I never fight for ransom. If some coins come my way, then so be it."

In the event, I received a huge ransom from the lord of the manor. I do not know what the king said but it seemed to satisfy the lord and lady. I packed my coins in bags which we hung from our spare sumpters.

The last part of the journey was simpler than the first part. We were joined by reinforcements from Le Mans and Alençon, swelling our ranks, and we reached Blois without incident. The French were just south of us and were close to Châteauroux, sixty miles away. They had gathered their army and with our reinforcements and the capture of

Châteaudun, King Henry felt confident enough to take on the French without the aid of his son.

This time we were so close to King Henry that I was able to ride closer to him and speak. He waved away his bodyguards so that he could speak plainly. By now Jack and Tom knew when to make themselves scarce and they took young Robin with them. "My son wishes me to fail, you know. He would have me lose to King Philip so that he can take him on and defeat him."

"Are we going to fight him?"

He smiled, "You have seen through my ploy. Of course not. If we fought, then we would lose men who would be ransomed or killed and that would weaken both of our countries. The Archbishop of Rouen is busy with the papal emissary to negotiate a truce and a peace plan which will allow us all to leave this conflict with some dignity. With that done I can address the problem of my sons." We stayed for a month in Blois as we gathered more men for this confrontation with the French.

We reached the town of Châteauroux and faced each other. Our armies were evenly matched. The French had more crossbows, but we had more archers, and I knew which I would prefer. The French knights were older but that did not make them any better than the young bloods who had accompanied King Henry. Heralds and pursuivants were sent to arrange the place we would fight. King Henry wanted me and my men on his right, the place of honour. Even as we prepared, we were surprised when King Henry's son Richard appeared with a small contingent of men. It was not enough to alter the prospect of battle but his presence, as Duke of Aquitaine, added a third party to the discussions.

When Cardinal Carnelli and the Archbishop of Rouen arrived then the whole situation changed. A tent was erected and the two kings, along with Duke Richard, were summoned. The two armies knew that there would be no battle, yet both faced each other. It was as I viewed them that I saw the standard of d'Aumale. My enemy was still alive and in the bosom of the French army. If there was no peace, then I might be able to face him in battle and end his life.

The Perfect Knight

When the two kings walked together from the tent then I knew there would be no battle and that, with luck, the war would end, and I could return home. Surprisingly the party headed towards our lines and more than that, they seemed to make for me. They stopped before me and I bowed to the two kings and the future King of England. What did they want with me?

It was King Philip Augustus who spoke, and he addressed me, "I have often wondered what you looked like, Earl Samuel. Your name has come up many times at my court as did that of your grandfather. You do not look like a mighty warrior who has a mind as sharp as any fox. Duke Richard does but not you."

I was being complimented and insulted in the same sentence. I was lost for words and it was Duke Richard who defended me, "Do not underestimate Sir Samuel, King Philip. I have learned that he has those qualities you seem to attribute to me."

"And would you serve me, Sir Samuel? I would give you a fine manor."

I was being played with and used as a tool. He must have known I would say no and I wondered why the deception. "A man can only serve one king my lord and I made an oath to serve King Henry of England. I am flattered but I must decline."

He nodded and said, "I only make the offer once and as you have spurned it then you must bear the consequences." I had made him an implacable enemy. I watched his gaze turn to Duke Richard, "And you Prince Richard, would you follow my banner and fight against your father?"

Before he could answer, King Henry spoke and I saw, in his eyes, that he was angry but the smile he masked it with hid it from the French king, "Answer him, Richard. Your brothers chose the route to treason and God punished them both." I saw the Archbishop and the Cardinal make the sign of the cross.

Duke Richard was enjoying the attention and he grinned, "I thank you, King Philip, but I must, for the present, decline your offer."

His words were a warning to his father to accede to future demands or risk the consequences. Almost as though he was calming the troubled waters the Archbishop said, "And do not forget, my lords, that Cardinal Carnelli has brought a request that England and France make a joint crusade to retake Jerusalem from Saladin!"

The Cardinal nodded, "There is peace here and you should both begin preparations for a crusade. Use that as the mortar to bind your houses together."

Although all nodded King Philip said, "And when Duke Richard and my sister Alys are wed then the familial bonds will hold us tighter together."

Silence fell and I wondered that Richard had procrastinated over the marriage. I knew that it was a problem from conversations with King Henry and the question was why?

King Henry broke the silence, "For my part, I will take the cross and I shall return to England and begin to raise the money needed for a holy crusade."

Duke Richard's face broke into a grin which made him look almost like a child being given his first pony, "And I will join you, father! I will take Jerusalem for the Pope and rid the land of this Saladin and his Seljuk Turks."

All eyes swivelled to King Philip who nodded, "And France will join. However, this must, perforce, follow the wedding!"

The grin went from Duke Richard's face, but he recovered quickly and turned to me, "And you Sir Samuel, will you take the cross?"

King Henry said, "Aye, for it was your father who took the cross and with England at peace then we need your sword and your sage advice."

All eyes were on me and I did not like the attention. I did the only thing I could do, I spoke the truth, "My lords, I have a wife who is with child and until she gives birth, I cannot commit to leaving England."

King Henry shook his head, "It will take a year, at least, to raise the money and the army we need. You have time."

The Perfect Knight

I nodded but I did not want to go on a crusade and in my head, I said no. I should have said no out loud for all believed I had agreed to go on the crusade.

The war was over, and we went our separate ways. King Philip headed back to Paris. Duke Richard returned to Aquitaine where he intended to punish some lords who had chosen not to follow him to war and I went with the king. Our progress was much slower than I would have liked. After four weeks of travel when we reached Rouen King Henry announced that he would be staying there for a month. The reason for the length of the journey was King Henry's illness and he needed a month to recover. I was given permission to leave and I found a ship leaving for Southampton. It would mean a long ride through England, but it was the first ship that was leaving and I was anxious to get back to Eleanor.

It was as I went to speak to the king that the steward hurried over, "My lord, this arrived a month ago and I had almost forgotten it." He handed me a letter bearing the seal of Stockton which I had left with my sister. The writing was hers, it was distinctive. She liked to use a large first letter of each line, much as the monks did. She was very artistic.

Brother, there is no easy way to give you the dire news which I must impart. I had hoped that you would have returned home by now and I have delayed some days before sending this missive. Sometimes God acts in a way we do not understand. When my dear husband was taken from me then I fell into deep despair and it was only your family who brought me back into the light. Eleanor died giving premature birth to your daughter who was born dead. She was happy during the pregnancy and she did not seem as distressed as in the other pregnancies but despite all the efforts of the midwife, Father Michael, and Doctor Atticus we could not save her. She is interred in the chapel. The masons await your return for the completion of the effigy. I pray you to return with all speed.

The Perfect Knight

Know that I will always be here in England watching your castle and your town for you. Whatever you need from me is yours. You are a true knight and, as our grandfather said, a perfect knight.

Your sister,

Ruth

I felt as though some assassin had stabbed me in the back. I re-read the letter three times in the hope that I had made a mistake, but I had not. Thomas saw my face and said, "Father! What is amiss?"

I put my arm around him and said, "It is your mother, Tom, she is dead!"

He threw his arms around me and we both wept. I cared not that men stared at us. A man cannot lose his wife and not shed a tear, not a real man. I doubted that King Henry would have shed a tear, but kings were different to mere men. Jack and Robin stood protectively to shield us from the gaze of men.

"I must go and tell the king I return to England. Have the men take our gear to the ship. It is good that there is a ship to take us to England for I need Pegasus' wings to get me back to Stockton."

The king was sympathetic when I told him, but he also reminded me that he still had a call upon my services. "Go back to Stockton and spend the winter putting things in order. Come the spring I shall have need of you."

I bowed, turned on my heels and left. He might summon me but I was not sure that I would go. We boarded the ship and spent the night on board as we waited for the tide to be right. My men were all wary of me and gave both Thomas and me the space we needed. We did not speak for I was alone with my thoughts. I had been needed by the king, but my wife had needed me more. I had not been there to hold her hand and, who knows, perhaps my very presence might have saved her life. Once that seed was planted in my mind it grew. I had not been there for my wife when she had

The Perfect Knight

needed me. This was not like my father whose first family had died of the pestilence. Had he been there then he would have died too and I would not have been born. That my wife had been happy for me to serve the king was of little comfort to me. I did not sleep that night although I wrapped myself in my cloak and fur, for each time I thought to slip into the black void of sleep the thought would enter my head that I was the one responsible for the death of my wife. I heard the crew beginning to release us from the land even though it was still black night, and I went on deck. As I moved, I realised that Thomas was not in the cabin with me. The crew were busily releasing hawsers and ropes while others scurried up the ratlines to release the sail. I saw Thomas at the prow, close to the bow castle. There he was out of the way and almost as alone as it was possible to be on a packed ship.

"You could not sleep either, son?"

He shook his head, "I never told her I loved her, at least not enough and I cannot remember my last words to her! That is terrible. I was a bad son."

I put my arm around him. He almost had a man's body but part of him was still a child and he mourned a parent. "No, you were not. We both obeyed a command and did not question it. Perhaps we should question these commands a little more in future."

"Cast off!"

The ship lurched a little to larboard as we were released from the land and the wind tugged at the topsails.

"There is nothing for us in Stockton now, father. Perhaps we should go on the crusade!" I was silent. Maybe he was right and then I thought of not only my sister but also the men and women in my castle who were part of my family. It would be wrong to abandon Ruth and my people. I had decisions with which to wrestle on the long journey home.

Dawn broke behind us, but it was hard to tell for the sky was filled with the darkness of storm clouds. They pushed us along at an alarming speed, but it was like riding an unbroken horse. It was hard to know which direction the wind would take us. The journey to the sea took us ten hours and Thomas and I never left the deck as we stood beneath our oiled cloaks willing the land to be behind us so that we could reach the sea and then the voyage home. I was grateful that it was the next high tide when we left the estuary of the Seine for the waves were as high as the ship and we were still close to the land. Once we reached the open sea then we would be in for a tumultuous trip.

One of the crew came to us, "My lord, the captain begs you to go to your cabin as he fears you will be swept overboard!"

I contemplated tempting God and staying on the open deck. Would he punish me by sweeping me over the side? Then I realised that if he did it would not be a punishment for I would be with Eleanor once more. "Come, my son, let us obey the captain."

Although we were drier in the cabin we shared with Jack and Robin, we were not more comfortable. The ship rose and fell and without the sight of the horizon seemed even more frightening. We were knocked from side to side and the descents into the troughs felt like a drop down a huge cliff. The storm lasted all that day and although our voyage was hastened I would have preferred a longer but safer voyage. The ship looked as though it had been in a battle with pirates when we docked at Southampton. The captain shook his head as we parted, "I fear I shall not be hurrying back to Rouen, my lord. We have a week of work at the least here. If any others wish to return to England, they will need to find another ship." He waved a hand around the harbour. It was full. "Most of these will just make short voyages to London, Harwich and the like. The sea twixt here and France is as treacherous as an inn full of Frenchmen!"

I smiled for I knew that Frenchmen would use the same phrase about Englishmen. Enmity ran deep between the two nations.

The horses had suffered on the voyage and there was no possibility of making a journey north for a day or two. We found an inn on the outskirts of the town, *'The Buck'* and my men used the time to spend the coins they had collected from the men who had tried to ambush us. Southampton was

The Perfect Knight

a busy port and the merchants had all kinds of items they could not get in Stockton. Some of the men had wives or sweethearts and the rest had mothers and sisters. Gerard of Chester was different. As yet he had not found a woman to court and he stayed with my squires and me.

"I am sorry for your loss, Sir Samuel, Master Thomas. Lady Eleanor was just that, a true lady. The Countess of Chester and Lady Ruth are ladies too and from my travels, it is rare to meet three such paragons."

I nodded for he was right. I had come across other ladies who were as cruel and vindictive as any bandit or robber baron. "It is good of you to say so and I know that my wife thought well of you and all of my men. She knew the value of loyal warriors."

He nodded, "I just wanted you to know that all the men feel the same. They asked me to tell of their regret."

I knew that I was lucky to have such loyal men.

When the horses were ready, I did not ride towards London. I still had bad memories of the civil war there. Instead, I took the more direct route through Oxford to meet up with the north road at Leicester. It was a quieter road and that suited all our moods. To be truthful I was avoiding any who might know me. If word reached my friends that I was travelling back to Stockton they would expect me to use the places along the Great North Road. They would expect me to stay at the Tower and thence places like Northampton. This way I would avoid having to explain myself.

England in late autumn is filled with unpredictable weather. I knew that it could be pouring with a deluge of rain in Stockton and yet Hartburn, just a mile up the road could be enjoying the sunshine. So it was as we headed for Oxford. Rain lashed down and then suddenly disappeared four miles along the Roman road. The wind would whip up from nowhere finding gaps in cloak and surcoat. In many ways it helped for the puddled roads made us concentrate on our riding and stopped us thinking about Eleanor. That she was on all our minds was clear. The conversation was about the road, the weather, the state of the horses and Stockton was never brought up for to do so risked bringing up Eleanor.

The Perfect Knight

The pain and the remorse were too great a risk and we stayed on safer, though wetter ground.

We stopped at Abingdon, just six miles from Oxford. The rain had relented, and the water trough was sheltered from the wind by the smithy who was shoeing Martyn Longsword's horse. The heat from the forge was welcoming and the wife of the smith brought her ale for us to drink. I overpaid. She was one of the first women we had seen on the road and somehow, I knew not why, I felt guilty that we might be robbing this woman, this mother, this wife. Besides, gold was the last thing I needed to worry about. The ransoms and the coins taken from the dead meant that my treasury would soon be filled with my coin and that of my men.

As we drank Gerard pointed his beaker up the road, "Did I not hear a story, my lord, about the Warlord and the Empress escaping Oxford in the middle of winter wearing white clothes and crossing a frozen moat?"

My men leaned in to hear our words and I nodded, "Aye, the usurper would have had the Empress but for that. From what my grandfather told me Empress Matilda was a force to be reckoned with. He was very fond of her and spoke well of her right up to the end. He became like a foster father to King Henry during that time."

Remembering the Warlord made me feel both sad and hopeful at the same time. Sad because he was no longer with us but hopeful because there had been times when he and the Empress seemed alone and the prospect of reclaiming the crown impossibly remote yet he had succeeded. He had even overcome the death of his wife, my grandmother Adele. The Warlord's blood meant that I had the same chance to recover from what seemed like a mortal blow. He had found solace in helping Matilda and her son recover their lands. Should I not now commit myself to do the same for King Henry? That he had enemies was clear and was it my fate to help him make his crown safe?

It took more than a week to reach Lincoln but at least that meant we had less than a third of our journey to reach home. Lincoln always felt like the north was close and that we were

The Perfect Knight

leaving the south. This was the King's castle, and we were welcomed within its walls. It was peaceful in England and the garrison was small enough so that my men enjoyed the comfort of a bed and not the stables. The constable, Sir John Lytton, was also a good host and keen to know about the events in France. We had been amongst the first of the English to leave and as I had been close to the king he knew he would hear the truth from me.

"We had visitors a week since. A party of knights travelling north came from London and they told us that there was little fighting between the two kings and that peace was made. Is that true?"

I nodded, "Aye, there is an uneasy peace, but I do not expect it to be permanent and the kings said that they would go on a crusade."

"Is that not a good thing, my lord? Surely that means the peace will last."

I smiled, "Sir John, which of them will lead? The two greatest kings travel together, and one will wish to take command. Who will that be?"

"Why, King Henry of course!"

I shook my head. I could not reveal that King Philip had tried to make Duke Richard change sides, but I knew that King Philip would never yield to King Henry. "I have met this French king and I do not think he sees himself inferior to our king. If anything he thinks that he is superior and that the Norman lands King Henry rules means that he should pay homage to him."

Sir John laughed, "That is ridiculous! King Henry and Duke Richard control more land in France than the King of France."

"Aye but King Philip does not see it that way!"

It was a pleasant evening for Sir John was a good host but as we headed north on the Roman Road, travelling the last hundred or so miles to Stockton, there was something nagging in my mind. It was not what Sir John had actually said which niggled in my head but the implications and yet, for the life of me I could not bring those thoughts to mind.

The Perfect Knight

York was but two days from home and although we had the time, for there was still light, there was little point in heading further north. The next beds were at Easingwold and York offered my men the chance of a bed once more. Lincoln and Oxford had been the only places on the ride north that they had enjoyed a bed. They also had the chance to drink in the alehouses along the river. York folk had Viking blood coursing through their veins and they not only brewed good ale, they knew how to enjoy themselves. While my squires and I enjoyed the Archbishop's table, they caroused in York.

The next day, as we headed towards our last stop, East Harlsey, the men had thick heads and sheltered beneath the cowls of their cloaks as a biting east wind coming all the way from Norway flecked the first flakes of snow into their faces.

Jack asked, "East Harlsey has no lord of the manor does it, Sir Samuel?"

I had told Jack that I hoped to knight him soon and I smiled, "Why, do you wish it as your manor when you become a knight?"

He shook his head, "No, Sir Samuel. As much as I wish to be a knight, I am not sure that I am yet ready to be one. I have seen the way men look to you when we go into battle. You make decisions that are always right, and I do not have that ability. I think I need a few more battles."

"You are wise, Jack, and it is a shame that there are not other knights who would think as you do."

He nodded, "I just wondered where the lord of East Harlsey went?"

"He and his son died in battle fighting for the Warlord and King Henry. My father never got around to appointing another. I would have given it to William, but he favoured the smaller manor of Elton. The reeve at East Harlsey was a former man at arms, Wilson of Bristol was a good warrior and a better man. He married a local girl from the nearby village of Ingleby Arncliffe. I think my father felt that as there was no knight who needed a manor, he would leave it in the hands of a most reliable and trustworthy man at arms.

The Perfect Knight

He lives in the manor house. Our men will have to endure a stable for their last night before we reach Stockton but we will enjoy a fine chamber and a roaring fire." I waved my arm at the tiny flecks of snow that swirled around us. "This has yet to lie but come the morrow we may find that we have to pick our way home."

When we stopped at Easingwold to tighten our girths and water our horses the innkeeper brought out mulled ale for us. This was land where my livery was well known. "A bitter day to be travelling, Sir Samuel! Still, it brings coins to my establishment!" It was a subtle way of reminding me that the ale was not free. Many lords would have expected to be given the ale but I was not one. I flipped him a coin and he grinned, "Thank you, my lord, you can always rely on an English knight to be generous. Not like those French knights who came through five days ago."

Suddenly, all thoughts of home evaporated, "French knights?"

"Aye, my lord. A week since six of them passed through. Miserable and mean they were. In fact, they followed a couple of parties who passed through a day or so earlier and they were just as tight-fisted and unpleasant. I guessed that they were swords for hire heading for Scotland or, perhaps, the Palatinate."

"How many?"

"In each party?"

"Altogether."

He rubbed his chin, "I would say about thirty altogether. Some had crossbows but most were spearmen riding the poorest nags I have ever seen. I am guessing that your ferryman would have made coins from them, eh my lord? You have to pay to cross the Tees."

"They were heading for Stockton?"

"Aye, they asked for the quickest road to Stockton and I told them through East Harlsey. It is funny that for they asked had you passed through on your way from France."

"Who asked?"

"Why the knights, my lord."

The Perfect Knight

Gerard had been listening and he stepped forward, "I shall give up drinking, my lord, for it has come to me that I heard of mercenaries passing through York and heading north. Had I not had so much drink then I might have made the connection for why would mercenaries be heading north?"

I shook my head, "No, Gerard the death of my wife has muddled my mind too. When we were in Lincoln the constable spoke of knights passing through who told him of events in France."

Thomas said, "I do not understand, father. How is that significant?"

"We were the first of the English contingent who left France. The French left before we did and the crossing from Calais to Dover is shorter. The Constable said that they came from France and that means they were enemies. I fear that those who seek to do us harm await us on the road to Stockton."

Chapter 13

Knowing that there were enemies lying in wait and thwarting them were two entirely different things. We spent almost an hour at the inn while we discussed what we might do. We decided that we would continue north and try to trap the ambushers. The delay in starting meant we would be unlikely to reach the manor much before dusk. The weather which had seemed merely annoying now seemed sinister as though it was conspiring with our enemies. The sleety snow made it hard to see and, as we left the village to ride the last miles to East Harlsey, we rode as though for war! This was not Mordaf's land and so he stayed with the spare horses at the rear. Richard and his men strung their bows and hung them from their saddles. They spread out in a line both across the road and to the side. The land rose and fell, passing through shallow valleys. Mercifully there were no forests for this land was tilled. Towards Osmotherley, to our right, the hills were forested and rose threateningly, but they were too far from us to pose a real danger.

Gerard rode next to me, "Lord, I think this is d'Aumale and his men. One of the men who spoke to me in York said that one of the knights, mercenaries, he called them, wore red with the yellow diagonal and three gold stars. That is the livery of d'Aumale." He shook his head. "We are in England and the French knight was not in my head."

"I am as culpable."

He shook his head, "This makes it clearer and easier to understand, my lord, and we are in a better position to predict d'Aumale's plans. This man sought you. The questions about the road home were pointed. We know he

The Perfect Knight

will attack us twixt here and Stockton but even with this weather it is unlikely that crossbowmen will be able to attack. All the places they could use are too far from us." He waved a hand around and I saw that he was right.

There were few places where they could hide close to the road and Richard and my archers checked those well before we reached them. "You are right, but they must have a plan." It came to me, "East Harlsey! The landlord in Easingwold had said to head there. Even if we did not stay in the manor, we would stop and be unsuspecting. The village is small and Wilson of Bristol has just the men from the farm to defend it. These are mercenaries and knights. It would be like the attack on Stockton all over again."

"The man is driven by hate, my lord!"

"No, Jack, I think it is more financial. I agree that he bears me enmity, but he could not afford to hire mercenaries, not a second time. He is being funded and I think it is by the French King. He also bears me ill will for I have spoiled his plans and I refused his service."

I reined in and whistled for Richard. He rode back, "Yes, my lord?"

"I believe that the danger lies at East Harlsey. Send two men to scout it out but I do not want them seen."

"Then I will go with Tam the Hawker. And if I find danger?"

"Then send Tam back with word and you watch the hall!"

Once the two men rode off, I felt easier about the rest of the journey. I had convinced myself that the danger lay just four miles up the road and although we were vigilant, I did not have to endure the stiff neck of anticipating an attack and having to constantly turn my head. It was not yet dusk but already the dark skies made it feel so and, as we passed the Priory, I wondered about seeking shelter there. I dismissed the thought immediately for I would be putting those in the Priory in danger and the threat to not only me, but my town would remain. I knew that there would be a trap and I had to face it and end this.

Tam rode back across the fields which already had a faint covering of white. His hoofprints stood dark against the white. His face was grim. "They are there, my lord. We saw no sign of your reeve nor any other of the farmworkers, but we saw the men at arms. The village is under their control. They have men who have attempted to hide at both ends. We saw them and heard them. There are five men at each end of the road and the rest appear to be guarding the hall. Richard is waiting at the far end of the village."

Our slow and cautious approach meant we would reach the village in darkness and that would detract from the efficiency of my archers but that could not be helped. It seemed clear to me that they did not know we were here, and I would use that to my advantage.

"We need to act quickly, Tam, take the rest of the archers and rejoin Richard. Eliminate the guards at the far end of the village and rouse the villagers. I am loath to use them, but we need all the help we can get and if there is no sign of Wilson then I fear the worst."

Thomas said, "Perhaps they are held prisoner, father."

"And that is the hope which burns in my heart, but I am prepared for the worst. We will walk the last half mile from the bridge over the burn and Mordaf and Robin can watch our horses while we approach on foot."

Gerard said, "Will there be a signal, lord? Shall you use the horn?"

"Not this time for I do not want Geoffrey d'Aumale to escape. He will end his life here in England."

I saw the shock and horror on the face of my son, but he was learning the reality of his future as a knight.

We rode until we could smell the woodsmoke from the handful of houses that made up the tiny village. We crossed the narrow bridge and dismounted. There was a gap in the hedgerow close to the bridge and we entered the field that had a flock of sheep sheltering against a stone wall on the far side. We tethered our horses to the blackthorn and hawthorn hedge. Not a word was spoken as I drew my sword and dagger. I would not wear my helmet and I would not carry a shield. We stepped back into the road and I saw that the snow had lain there and there were no footprints. The ambushers were waiting for us to pass through. They would have no way of knowing when we would pass through just that our passage was inevitable and as the manor was part of my estate I would probably stop. The snow was getting deep enough to crunch a little and, when we found another gap in the hedge to the right, I waved Martyn Longsword and four of my men through. I was left with my squires, Gerard of Chester, and the rest of my men to continue to walk up the road to the village.

We heard the mercenaries before we saw them. From the smell of the woodsmoke, they had a brazier burning and were cooking food. It was carelessness on their part. The point of being a sentry was to be invisible and to spot intruders. Perhaps they were relying on hearing the hooves of our horses or, more likely, as darkness had now fallen, they had assumed we would not be arriving this night. We moved even more slowly but I was confident that if they had a brazier then their night vision would be impaired. We turned a corner and I saw their huddled shapes. Two had their backs to us and I saw the faces of the other three beneath the cowls of their cloaks. They were just ten steps from us, and I knew that my men would act instantly. I ran towards the sentries. Of course, the movement and the sound of my boots on the snow alerted them but none appeared to be holding a weapon. I saw shock, and then realisation as they recognised the danger. It was then that they stood and reached for weapons. I saw one begin to open his mouth but by then I had reached them, and I stabbed him in the throat with my sword. The shock was so great that none appeared to think to give the alarm but to be fair to them they were fighting for their lives and my men were not in a merciful mood. The other four died quickly, one of them falling on the brazier. Thomas had the wit to pull the body from the fire. Burning hair and flesh would alarm the rest just as quickly as a shout.

My other men led by Martyn appeared through a gap in the hedge. There was a single farmhouse down a small track, and I waved for Martyn and his men to check it. They would be careful but I hoped it was villagers we could arm and they might aid us. We headed towards the dark shape that was the manor. Its only defence was a ditch around it with a removable bridge near to the door. The roof had a fighting platform for the hall had a slate roof. If the enemy kept a watch there then they might see us but it was a chance I had to take. As we neared the hall, I heard a cry from the northern end of the village. Richard and his men had either been spotted or one of the sentries had managed to give the alarm. It did not matter for we were close enough to the hall now and I ran towards the door.

Suddenly light flooded the courtyard as the door was opened and I saw a knight standing there. He looked north and did not appear to see me even though I was just twenty paces from him. He cupped his hands and shouted, "Eustace! What is it?"

There was no reply and he stepped from the doorway to look south. It was then that he saw me, but I quickly closed the distance between us and even as he shouted a warning, I rammed my sword into his middle and threw his body from my blade into the courtyard where his blood began to stain the snow.

Holding in the entrails which threatened to spill out of his guts the knight shouted, "Arm yourselves, we are under attack!" His head fell to the side and he was dead.

The knight I had slain had managed, in his dying, to warn the ones within. The hall had a narrow entrance that was designed to slow down an enemy. I ran down it and bundled into a man at arms who stepped from the room I knew to be the main hall. It was too small for the term grand hall, but ten people could dine there. I knew for I had been there with my father. The man was mailed and had a sword which he instinctively slashed at me. I blocked with my bloody sword and pinned the weapon to the wall. Bringing up my dagger I drove it under his armpit. He had mail but the narrow tip pierced it and went into his flesh. The nerves severed, the sword fell and as I tore out the dagger, I caught an artery and bright blood spurted. I pushed the dying man back into the hall and stepped in.

There I saw Geoffrey d'Aumale and the other four knights. They had armed themselves and seeing me they

The Perfect Knight

came directly at me. I moved close to them for that way Gerard and the others could follow. I made directly for Geoffrey d'Aumale despite the fact that two of his knights tried to step between us. My move surprised them, and I pushed them out of the way. Behind me, I heard Jack shout, "Protect Sir Samuel's back!"

My sword and dagger blocked the late strikes from the two and although a dagger tore through my surcoat and across my mail hauberk no harm was done and I found myself face to face with the man who had tried to hurt my family already. The low ceiling meant that neither of us could bring our swords from on high but the foolish knight must have forgotten that as he tried to smash his blade into my helmet. It caught on a beam and I lunged with my sword. He wore good mail and although I penetrated and tore through a couple of mail links, it held. I tried to bring my dagger up into his throat as he pulled his sword from the ceiling. He blocked it with his own sword and we were face to face.

He spat at me and said, "You have the luck of the devil, Englishman, but tonight your luck will run out. I bring knights to this fight and you bring pathetically inadequate squires."

I brought my head back and headbutted him. It was a well-timed blow and I broke his nose, "Keep talking for the sound of your voice makes me want to end your life even quicker."

Behind me, I heard the cry of someone who had been hurt. Steel clashed and men cursed. The room intended to hold ten was now packed as my men and Sir Geoffrey's fought to the death. This was not a place for skill but for survival.

Sir Geoffrey's eyes were streaming as blood poured from his nose. I pulled back my dagger and stabbed it again. It was not exactly blindly but I could not be certain where it would strike. When he cried out then I knew that I had hit flesh. He took a step back, towards the fire and I lunged at his neck. He tried to avoid the blow, but his streaming eyes impaired his judgement. I caught his coif, but the edge of my

The Perfect Knight

sword scored a line along his throat. It was not a mortal blow, but I watched in the firelight blood begin to drip down his neck. He swung his sword across his body, and I blocked it with both sword and dagger. It almost proved to be a mistake for he rammed his dagger at my face. I turned and his dagger scored a long wound along my cheekbone. He seemed to think that he had won, and I saw, as his eyes cleared, the look of joy on his face as he pulled back his dagger to finish the job. My hands were quicker, and my sword deflected the dagger upwards as I pushed my own dagger into his side. He had good mail, but an earlier blow had damaged the links and the luck Sir Geoffrey said I had, came to my aid again and the tip found not mail but his gambeson. It ripped through and into his right side. I felt it grate off a rib and he screamed. I kept pushing until my mittened hand reached the gambeson and then I twisted and pulled. His sword and dagger fell to the ground and his dying hands tried to clutch at me. I shook him off and his body fell into the open fire.

I was aware that the hall was now silent save for the odd moan from a dying warrior. I turned with a smile on my face, but that smile left me when I saw my squire lying in a pool of blood. Gerard and Thomas were trying to staunch the bleeding, but the pool told me that it was a fruitless exercise and that Jack had been mortally wounded. I dropped my weapons and knelt next to him. I slipped off the mittens and held his hand.

"Jack!"

He opened his eyes and, as he spoke to me, blood trickled from his mouth, "I killed a knight, my lord. Perhaps I am ready to be knighted after all."

"And I shall knight you, just as soon as you are healed."

He shook his head, "No, Sir Samuel, for I am dying. I should have liked to go to the Holy Land with you but…"

His eyes glazed over and Jack, son of John of Oxbridge died. He had been protecting my back and it had cost him his own life. I closed my eyes and said a prayer, "Lord, take this boy and give him a place in heaven for he deserves it. He died well protecting his lord and I shall remember him to my dying day."

I heard my men and Thomas say, "Amen."

I did not rise immediately for I was wondering how I might have saved the young man who had such potential and would have made, like Sir William, a worthy knight of the valley. How would I tell his mother and father that he had died?

"My lord." Gerard's voice made me rise. "We have found Wilson of Bristol's body along with his son and the other men. The women were bound in the barn."

I turned sharply, "Were they…"

"No, my lord."

I looked around at the dead. "Are any left alive?"

Gerard shook his head, "Two of our archers, Peter and James, died. Walter was wounded and our men had not an ounce of mercy in them. Martyn found Wilson's body and our hearts were hardened. Did we do wrong, my lord?"

I looked down at the body of Jack and shook my head, "No. Be gentle with our dead. We shall take them home to bury in Stockton. Take the mail from the enemy and fetch me Sir Geoffrey's ring. I know whence I shall return it! Burn their bodies but do it so that the wind takes the smell well away from here. The people have suffered enough." Turning to Robin who had arrived with Mordaf and the horses, I said, "Now you may be regretting your request to come on crusade with us, Robin son of Alf. You can return to Stockton if you wish and none shall think badly of you."

He shook his head, "No, Sir Samuel, it has merely hardened my resolve to be a squire in Jack's memory. He was kind to me."

It was late by the time all was done. My men all chose to sleep in the barn and guard the dead bodies of our men. I was in no mood for sleep and I needed to speak with Agnes, Wilson's widow. "As soon as the men appeared, my lord, Wilson knew it was trouble, but they gave neither him nor my son a chance. Crossbows slew them and John of Osmotherley who was with them. They took the women and had us guarded in the barn so that the men of the village would not try to help you."

"You knew what they intended?"

"The men who guarded us were English and they spoke of how clever they were. How they had travelled up here so quickly that they knew they would be here before you and that you would stay here. One had served at Barnard Castle and he boasted of how he knew Stockton Castle well." She shook her head, "My lord, they planned to sack your home!" She began to weep.

"Peace." She dabbed at her eyes and nodded. "And what of you, Agnes? What now?"

She looked around at the hall, "This is my home. I was born just a couple of miles from here. Where else would I go? I would stay here and continue the work my husband did. He was a good reeve and the village all looked up to him. I know I am a woman but…"

I held up my hand, "I am more than happy for you to stay on as reeve, but do you need anything from me? Men perhaps?"

"I think, my lord, that this has been a lesson for the village. The men will be more vigilant. The Sunday practice will be rigorous, and we will watch our own homes."

After she had gone to bed and Thomas and I were alone to sleep in the hall I wondered at that. I had been the reason they had been attacked. I should have ended the threat from d'Aumale sooner. The King of France had much to answer for and the ring I returned to him would tell him that he had failed and that I knew he had been behind the attack. I had much to occupy my troubled mind.

We crossed the river with the bodies slung over the saddles of their horses. I had them laid in the chapel and sent riders to fetch the families of the dead. I saw the tomb that the masons were making. It was unfinished, of course, and I put my hand upon the stone before I left to speak with Ruth. She held her arms wide for Thomas and me to embrace her and the three of us hugged in silence. What words were there for that moment? I knew what my sister and son were thinking.

The Perfect Knight

When we stood back, she said, "The bodies you brought back tell me that you were attacked."

I nodded, "The same ones who attacked my town, but they will do it no longer."

She was suddenly aware that there were just two of us, "Not Jack?"

I nodded, "Aye, it will be hard for his father to bear."

Tom said, quietly, "Aunt Ruth, he would have made a great knight. He and I protected our father's back, and it was he who slew the knight who would have stabbed my father in the back. I killed the man at arms who stabbed him, but it gives me little comfort. My blade was a heartbeat too late."

"My son, you did well." I slipped off my cloak, "I had better prepare to meet the families of the dead. What do I say, Ruth?"

"The words will come. Just speak the truth and they will understand."

She was right. John of Oxbridge arrived first, with his wife, Maud. John was a warrior and he helped me, "Did my son die well, my lord?"

"He was protecting my back and he killed a knight. I would have knighted him when we came back to Stockton for he was ready."

John nodded, "I had three sons, lord, as you know. Jack was like me and the other two are more like their mother. Jack wanted to be a warrior and we all know the risks a warrior takes." He looked at Thomas, "And now you will wear the mantle, Master Thomas. I pray that you have more luck than my son." My son gave a bow, and I knew that the reason he did not speak was that he might unman himself. "My lord, we would like to bury our son at our farm. I will speak with Father Michael for him to say the right words and to bless the ground, but we have spoken of this and having our son close to our home will be a comfort. We can tend his grave each day."

"Of course. Your son has mail, weapons and a sack of coins, John. I know they will not compensate for your loss, but he would have wanted his family to reap some benefit from his death."

"Aye, he would. He was always a thoughtful boy." John put his arm around Maud who was weeping, "Thank you, Sir Samuel. Knowing he died well gives us some comfort and knowing that his killers lie dead also helps. Now, with your permission, we shall take our boy home and begin to mourn."

That Christmas was a grim one in my town. My lady had been taken and the men who had died, especially Jack, were popular. Their deaths were like spectres hanging over the tables as we celebrated the birth of Christ. It was not joyless for all of us were glad to be alive, but the laughter did not ring around my hall as it had when Eleanor and Jack had been amongst us. Our lives had changed.

Chapter 14

Stockton 1188

The year saw a change, especially in Thomas. It was as though he was trying to be Jack and himself. Now with a mail hauberk taken from one of the French knights he and Skuld worked every day to become as one. It was as though he was trying to be the perfect squire. He took seriously the training of Robin as he tried to mould him into a squire. Tom was his own biggest critic and he needed no one to tell him when he had made a mistake or not done what he intended. Ruth also changed. She had no children of her own and I saw that with Eleanor gone she became a foster mother to her nephew. It was good for them both. And me? I changed too. I worked with the masons so that the chapel, which had now been enlarged, was a shrine to the dead. The Warlord and his wife, my mother and father and now Eleanor all lay beneath effigies which were so lifelike that when Eleanor's was revealed it took away my breath. The mason knew my lady and he told me that it was an honour to carve her. I also changed for I looked inward and not outward. The valley was all that concerned me. The squabbles of the king, his sons and the King of France were unimportant.

Each day I went to the chapel to watch the work and sit, quietly, and contemplate death. A knight knows that he is unlikely to reach old age but the women in our family seemed fated to die young. I prayed that Ruth would not be another who died too young. One chilly March morning as I left the chapel with an icy wind coming from the east, I wrapped my cloak tighter about my shoulders and saw that

Thomas was waiting. He looked pained. "What is amiss my son?"

He shook his head as we headed towards the inner bailey, "I wake in the night with a pain." He tapped his chest, "Here. I miss my mother. Is that not strange for over the last few years I have seen far less of her?"

I sighed for his words echoed my thoughts, "I have the same pain and the same blackness. Each night, since she has died, she haunts my dreams. She appears and I try to speak with her but cannot. Every day since we returned, I see the evidence of her hands throughout the castle. The cushions she sewed for the chairs in my solar. The tapestries she and the ladies made for the Great Hall. When I lie in my bed, I can smell her. I roll over and there is emptiness there which reflects what I feel in my heart." We had reached the keep and I stopped, "Tom, I put on a face each day to greet my men and my people, but it is just that. It is a mask to hide the pain and the ache I feel within. Knowing I shall never touch her hand or hear her voice makes me want to rail against the fates which conspired to take her from me. My only comfort is that I shall be with her, one day. Being the lord of the manor does not protect a man from such pain. He has no choice but to endure it. I now understand the emptiness in my father's eyes after my mother died and I wish that he had spoken to me more. That is why I speak to you now. When you wed then make sure you spend as much time with your wife as you can. Life is too short for sport and hunting. As lords, we have to go to war. Our king commands and we go but for the rest," I waved my arm around the inner bailey, "this is more important. Your wife and your children are all. Do not forget that."

He nodded and I saw tears welling up in his eyes as he saw the pain in mine, "I will and I thank you, father, for being so open. I shall bear the pain easier now knowing that you share it too."

We entered my keep and, somehow, the shared loss made us both closer and life a little easier. That day saw us both begin to get on with our lives and although I visited the

The Perfect Knight

chapel every day the darkness was not as all-enveloping as it had been.

That spring I held a tournament for the knights of the valley. I used the captured gold to have worthy trophies made and we held the tournament, on Mayday, by St John's well. I gave the town a holiday and hired men to entertain them. They had suffered because of me and this was their reward. I should have done it sooner, but my mind had been in a dark place. Despite Ruth urging me to do so I did not participate but watched from the stands we had erected. My sister was next to me as the Lady of the Day and it was she who gave out the prizes. Breaking with tradition I held a squire's competition, and it was no surprise to me when Thomas won not only the lance tournament but also the sword and buckler one. The feast we held was a celebration of warrior skills and a feast in honour of my wife. Enough time had elapsed for Tom and me to be able to don a face to smile at people. The hurt was held inside.

Sir William of Elton had won the lance tournament while Sir Richard of Hartburn had won the sword. Sir Roger of Norton and Sir Ralph of Thornaby had been the runners up and it was good that the knights to whom I was closest should have shown that they were the best.

Sir William was gracious in victory, "Of course, if Sir Samuel and Storm Bringer had been in the tournament there would have been but one winner!"

Sir Richard laughed, "Perhaps it was as well that he just watched for I would not have liked to risk my sword against his."

Shaking my head I said, "I am no tournament knight, Sir Richard."

Sir Ralph nodded, "No, Sir Samuel, for you are a warrior, like your father and grandfather. I hear that the Pope has asked for a crusade. Will you be going?"

The food had almost all been consumed when Pandora's Box was opened. I had hoped that none would speak of this. We knew that there was still an uneasy peace between France and England and the new crusade tax told all of King Henry's intent. I had my own thoughts and had wanted

The Perfect Knight

longer to think about a crusade. For myself, I was happy to go on a crusade as, like my father, it would atone for the death of my wife, but I knew that if I went then my knights would go and I would be risking Thomas.

Silence descended upon my hall. I smiled at the expectant faces along the table. Sir Ralph's question had made them all look at me. I drank some of my wine, "The King will expect us to go but as he still dallies in France, it seems to me that there is no urgency." The silence continued and I sighed, "Aye, I will be going but I do not expect any other of the knights of the valley to follow me."

Sir Roger laughed, "Of course, we shall. Our sons are now our squires and they have been badgering us to take the cross ever since the tithes were collected to pay for the crusade. I, for one, would like to go. I have a yearning to see where Christ was crucified, and the Pope has said that all sins are forgiven for crusaders."

I laughed, "And what sins have you committed that need a journey halfway across the world?"

He shrugged, "With the Scots cowed and the French at peace what else is there for a knight to do? We were all trained to be warriors and a sword which sleeps in its scabbard might as well be beaten into a ploughshare."

It was as though the box, now opened, affected all the knights. The squires who had been fetching and carrying food and drink now sat at the benches vacated by the ladies and there was a buzz of anticipation as the conversation about a journey to the Holy Land flowed. It was not just a box we had opened but a dam we had burst. I sat back and Ruth leaned over, "Brother, I know your thoughts. You wish to go alone for you do not think you will return."

I turned and stared at her, "You have been with the women who spin and sew."

She laughed, "I know you brother. I was the same when my husband was killed, and I thought to enter a nunnery. It was your Eleanor's need for a friend and now Thomas' need for a mother which has given me a purpose in life. Know that if you go, I will watch your town as though I was the Earl of Cleveland."

The Perfect Knight

I nodded, "I know but it pains me to think of taking so many of the protectors of the valley away."

"God will watch over this valley and when you return it will be to a verdant and happy land."

Nothing happened for some time. King Henry did not summon us, and I wondered if we should just go on crusade ourselves. I had enough in my treasury to pay for our passage. The idea appealed as it would mean I would be in command of my men and not following King Henry. As summer drew to a close, I sat with Ruth and Thomas in my solar enjoying a wine sent by Sir Alfraed of La Flèche. I decided to broach the subject which had been on my mind since the tournament.

"Thomas, I think I shall knight you come the summer solstice. You acquitted yourself more than well at the tournament and I deem that you are ready."

I saw Ruth smile and nod but Thomas shook his head, "No, father, I am not nor am I ready to cease to be your squire. The fight at East Harlsey showed me that you need a squire at your back and there is none that is ready to take my place." He smiled, "I can see through you, father. Your motives are for the best, I grant you but I know what you are about."

I shook my head, "You are ready for knighthood."

"You think to make up for the fact that you did not knight Jack but there is more. You knight me and then ask me to stay behind in England while you go on the crusade."

I started for he was right. That had been in my mind.

Ruth said, "And is that a bad thing, Thomas? You could learn to be the lord of the manor while your father followed the cross."

"Aunt Ruth, I am touched that you both care so much for me that you try to use honeyed words to trap me. I will be on the crusade with my father and I will be his squire. That is the end of it." He smiled, "Besides Robin is not yet ready to take on the mantle of squire. He has grown and he has improved but he is not yet ready. When we are both improved, I will accept the spurs."

"And if I choose not to take you?"

The Perfect Knight

He laughed and I saw that the boy was almost a man, "Thanks to the coins we have earned and taken I would pay for myself to take a ship and follow you! You cannot gainsay me, father."

Ruth laughed and patted Thomas' hand, "He is your son, Samuel. Admit defeat."

I nodded for she was right.

The parchment which arrived by ship was our summons to the crusade, but it did not come from King Henry rather his son, Richard. The letter said that he tired of his father's vacillations and would go on the crusade as Duke of Aquitaine. He begged me to accompany him. His words in the letter were telling, *'so that true Englishmen can fulfil the wishes of the church even though their king thinks only of himself.'* The two were falling out and it left me in a difficult position. I showed the letter to Ruth and Thomas.

Ruth nodded, "If you do not go then Duke Richard will take offence and one day, he will be king of England."

Thomas sighed, "And yet if you do then King Henry will take offence and take it that you are siding with his son."

"Then I am damned if I do and damned if I don't. Perhaps there is a third way." They both stared at me as though I had gone mad. "Suppose I take my men and persuade King Henry to do as he promised and go on the crusade. The people of this land have given him the money. Perhaps he needs me to be the one to nudge him to make the right decision. My grandfather would have told him and my father would have persuaded him. I am neither my father nor my grandfather but mayhap my appearance and name might stir memories of his youth and he might heed my words."

Once the words were out then events began to unfold. I told my knights that I would go with my familia and Thomas to speak to King Henry, and that they should prepare themselves for my message asking them to join me when I had persuaded King Henry to keep his promise. Speed was vital and I took only those men who had been at East Harlsey with me. We were two archers down and Walter's wounds had not healed sufficiently to take him. The night before we left Thomas and I ate with Ruth. We had already arranged

The Perfect Knight

for her to rule in my absence. I knew that the Bishop of Durham would not sanction the action, but I cared not. Ruth was a strong woman. We did not speak of the manor on our last night in Stockton but of Eleanor and our parents. She rarely spoke of her dead husband as the thought of her loss brought tears, but our parents and Eleanor were safer ground. Thomas was also able to talk with fond memories of all of them. Throughout the whole night, the spirit of my grandfather hung over the hall he had built. He seemed to inhabit every part of it. When I was in his solar, he seemed to have his ghostly hand upon my shoulder. Even the goblet I used was his. We never once mentioned his name, but he was there, and it was comforting.

I was mindful of the fact that I had not said a proper goodbye to Eleanor. The death of my wife had shown me how parlous life was and so I hugged my sister tighter than I normally did and whispered in her ear, "Know that I love you sister, and that I know Stockton is safely held in your care."

She pulled away and said, "None of that, Samuel! You will return and bring my nephew back with you. I will watch your castle until the return of the knight. Then we shall give Thomas his spurs and he can find a wife and sire more offspring with the blood of the Warlord coursing through them. Now go and look after yourselves." The warmth and love in her words overwhelmed me and I merely nodded.

The eminently practical Ruth waved us off from the town gate as we headed towards Herterpol and our waiting ship.

Chapter 15

Normandy 1189

By the time we reached Normandy, it was November and King Henry and his son had fallen out once more. I had been in Stockton when the relationship had broken down. King Henry, Duke Richard and King Philip had met to discuss the marriage of Alys to Richard. During the discussions, Richard had demanded to be named as King Henry's heir. The king had remained silent. That had made the reckless Richard change his allegiance to King Philip and swear homage to him.

When I met the king in Rouen the king was a man almost broken both physically and mentally. He had developed an ailment that caused him to vomit blood and weakened him. He was like a pale wraith. When I arrived, he was pleasantly surprised but wary. "Why have you come, Sir Samuel? I did not summon you."

I decided that the truth was the best way forward, "Your son asked me to fulfil the promise we made to Cardinal Carnelli to take the cross. I came here to persuade you to do so also."

He dabbed away a fleck of blood, "And you think that I am fit enough to do so? I can barely ride through my city. I will take the cross when I am well, and this problem is resolved." He looked around and saw that we were alone, "I think to disinherit my treacherous son and announce that John will be my heir."

I shook my head, "That would be a mistake, my lord."

"Why?"

"We both know that Duke Richard is impulsive but he would be a better king than John. Let me speak with him for he seems to value my opinion and I will try to persuade him."

The king shook his head, "I should not need to persuade my son to pay me homage. John will be my heir!"

I could not persuade him, and it was with some relief that the Pope intervened and arranged a meeting between Richard, King Philip, and King Henry at La Ferté-Bernard. The castle there was, effectively, the border between the domains of England and France. My men and I travelled with the king. I knew that there might be conflict. I had sent d'Aumale's signet ring to the King of France which would annoy for it would show the contempt I felt for him and a king cannot be having knights insult him. I also knew that Duke Richard would not be happy that, instead of riding to join him, I had joined his father. Now that he had joined the French camp then that made us enemies. I was prepared for I was a knight who had sworn an oath to King Henry. As my grandfather showed, a true knight does not break his oath merely because others do so. I would face them at the peace talks. Although these were peace talks King Henry took his army with him. It would not do to appear weak. However, the army that came with the king was a shadow of the one which had defeated Young King Henry. When we arrived at the meeting place, we were dwarfed by both Duke Richard's and King Philip's army.

As we approached the town I spoke to the King, "Let us send for more men, King Henry. This does not bode well."

"There is a truce while there are peace talks. If the talks fail then we head back to Normandy and muster an army that will sweep our foes from this land. Fear not, Earl Samuel, I know what I am doing." It was at that point that he began to vomit more blood. Hitherto we had hidden the fact from the ordinary knights and warriors, but all saw it and it was a bad omen. King Henry was housed in his castle and he asked for me to join his senior leaders in the Great Hall. I spoke to his physician while the king lay down to recover from his latest attack.

"What causes this, doctor?"

"He has something wrong in his stomach. When he drinks ale or wine it exacerbates the problem. The drinking of milk seems to give him some relief." He shrugged, "When we are alone, he can drink milk but a king who drinks milk in front of his knights and warriors would be seen as weak."

"Surely it can be cured?" The doctor shook his head. "But the king cannot die. He is barely fifty-six years of age."

"It is in God's hands, but I will say this. Riding on a campaign does nothing but aggravate the illness as does the heating of the blood. He needs to be calm as much as possible. When this is over, he needs to go to a town and rest where he does not need to ride."

The next day we met with a clutch of clerics in the huge tent erected between the two armies. There were bishops, archbishops, and a couple of papal emissaries. It became clear, once the talks began, why there was such a heavy church presence. The Pope wanted us to fulfil our oaths and fight Saladin. We arrived first and that was calculated. King Henry wanted to be seated when King Philip and Duke Richard appeared. It would disguise his illness. I stood behind him along with Sir Walter Tremaine, another loyal knight. When the French King and Duke Richard arrived, they each had two advisers. It was a chilly moment. The three men merely nodded to each other. There were no words of greeting. Prayers were said and then one of the papal emissaries spoke.

"His Holiness is disturbed that two such great Christian nations should be fighting each other when all those in this place have sworn to fight the Turks who have taken the Holy City of Jerusalem. Pope Clement begs you to put aside your differences and to make peace for the sake of Jerusalem."

I had no idea what King Henry would say but when he did speak it both surprised and dismayed me. "I believe I have a solution, King Philip, that will end this conflict." I saw a frown appear on the face of King Philip. With Duke Richard as his ally, he now believed he had the upper hand. "You have, for some time, demanded that the marriage between your sister and my son Richard takes place. It is not of my doing that this has not taken place. However, my solution is that she marries my younger son, John."

Richard leapt to his feet, "I see now what you plan, you treacherous wolf! You would make John your heir!"

King Henry remained calm, but I saw his fingers gripping the edge of the table. "I have not said that."

"But it is in your mind. I cannot accept such an arrangement."

King Philip shook his head, "Nor can I. These talks are over!"

I wondered at the brevity of the meeting and I deduced that no matter what King Henry had said King Philip would have ended them but King Henry had been foolish and said the one thing which would infuriate Richard. Was King Henry trying to create a war in which he would be the innocent victim having made what sounded like a reasonable suggestion? The two of them glared at us and then stormed out of the tent. King Henry tried to rise but began to vomit blood. I said to Sir Walter, "Stay with the King and I will fetch his physician."

I ran out of the tent back towards the house we were using. Thomas was waiting for me and he ran with me. I said, "Fetch our men and bring them to the peace tent!"

The physician and his servants seemed to be ready and waiting. As I burst in, he said, "The King?" I nodded, "I knew that conflict would irritate the condition."

When the physician and I returned the king was more irritated than anything and tried to wave us away. I was firm, "King Henry, let the doctors deal with the problem. My men and I will stand guard to ensure that no harm comes to you." Before he could say anything, I said, "Thomas and Robin stay with him and I will ensure that the sentries are set."

My men had surrounded the tent and I said to Richard and my archers who were at the rear, "Let no one enter without my permission." I walked around to the front and saw that Gerard and my men at arms were there already. However, Duke Richard, along with some of his men, was approaching the entrance and I sensed trouble. I reached

The Perfect Knight

Gerard at the same time as the Duke. I placed myself between them.

Duke Richard's face darkened, "What means this?"

"The King, your father, is unwell and my men and I are giving the physician the chance to tend to him, in private."

The Duke tried to push his way through, but Gerard and I stood firm. "I am his son!"

"You gave up those rights, Duke Richard, when you swore an oath to King Philip." His hand went to his sword as did those men who were close to him. I shook my head and said, calmly, "These are peace talks. They have not gone well but if you draw your swords then blood will be spilt. I know you are a puissant warrior, Duke Richard, but you have seen my men and know their worth. Are you willing to risk your life and your men's?"

"I shall not forget this, Earl." His hand slipped his sword back into its scabbard. "I gave you the chance to join me on the crusade and you have spurned my hand of friendship. That is a bitter pill to swallow!"

"There are many things which have happened lately that I wish I could forget but I cannot, and I find it sad that three of his sons should turn on their father. Two died. Does that not tell you something, Duke Richard?"

"When my father dies then I shall be king."

"Perhaps but I swore an oath to the King of England and while he lives, I am his man. When there is another, whoever that king shall be, I will swear an oath to him."

He grinned, "Even my brother, John Lackland?"

"If that is King Henry's choice then aye."

Out of the corner of my eye, I saw King Philip approach. He too had men with him and I wondered if my men and I would be called upon to fight.

"So, Sir Samuel, you are determined to fight us, I see."

I shook my head, "No King Philip, I rarely choose to fight but if someone tries to murder me and my family then I will fight back and I will be suspicious of all those who seek my death."

"It was not I who sent those killers to attack you."

The Perfect Knight

"And you will swear to that, King Philip? There are bishops aplenty. I am sure we can find one and some religious relic." He glowered at me but did not answer. When a sufficient silence had given his answer I said, "I thought not."

Just then the tent flap behind me opened and King Henry stood there, supported by my son, Thomas. He smiled, "The thing about tent walls is that they are thin, and I have heard every word you have said. If the peace talks were not ended before then they are now! Sir Samuel is a true knight. He was protecting his king. I find it sad, Richard, that he did so yet not my son. Perhaps he is right, perhaps God did punish my other sons. King Philip, you are treacherous and that is all that I will say to you. You have suborned two of my sons. Thank God at least my earls are loyal. Come, Sir Samuel. It is time we vacated this place for the air is pestilential."

As we left to begin to pack for our journey west, I could not help but compare myself with the Warlord. When all the rest of the nobles had sided with Stephen the Usurper, he had stayed loyal to a dead king and Empress Matilda. You cannot change your blood.

We left the next day. My men and I stayed close to the king as he rode. Our army had not grown, and we were vastly outnumbered by our enemies, but I did not believe that they would attack, as we headed for Le Mans. I do not think any of the other lords with us did so either but we were vigilant nonetheless. I believe that King Philip and Duke Richard saw an opportunity to attack a king who appeared to be close to death anyway or perhaps they had always planned to attack us when there was an apparent truce. King Henry had not yet announced that his son John was to succeed him and the two men who brought their army to cut off our escape to Le Mans and then Normandy planned on forcing the King to announce that Richard would be his heir.

Richard, along with Mordaf and my archers, was riding ahead of us and they managed to give us a warning that we were about to be attacked. At the same time, a rider rode up to the king to tell him that his castle at La Ferté-Bernard had fallen. War had begun! Mordaf galloped in, "My lord, King

The Perfect Knight

Henry, there is a huge army blocking our way to Le Mans. They have more than four hundred knights."

Despite the king's illness he still had enough wit to realise that we had no chance of defeating the enemy and so he gave the only order he could, "We ride for our castle at Le Mans. Sauve qui peut!"

I turned to Sir Walter Tremaine, "I will guard the king. Take command of the rest of the army and try to delay them." He nodded, "Do not waste men!"

"I will not. Guard him well, Sir Samuel." He shouted for the rest of the army to follow him and headed for the main body of Frenchmen arrayed in a solid line across the Le Mans road and in the fields besides.

I shouted, "Martyn Longsword, Thomas, flank the king and guard him with your bodies. Mordaf, fetch our archers, we head west. Gerard, I want a sword point to cleave our way through. Robin, watch yourself and do not take risks!"

King Henry turned in his saddle, "But Le Mans lies to the south and west of us!"

"And there are men waiting there. Sir Walter will bloody their noses. My sole aim is to save your life!"

It was a dishonourable attack by the two leaders of France and Aquitaine, but they had made a mistake. They had been so keen to stop us that they had not waited for all their men to be gathered. They had more men than we did but they were spread out thinner than they would have liked. Knowing that the king was guarded not only by his household knights but one of my best men at arms and my son meant I could concentrate on forcing our way through the thinnest part of their line that I could. They would want King Henry their prisoner and that would give me an advantage.

Richard led my archers to filter in behind us. They would not be able to use their bows, but they were bodies and could use swords, besides which they were my men. I spied a couple of dozen French knights and their squires blocking the road. They were backed up by what looked like ten light horsemen and they were astride a side road to the west. I did not know where the road led but that did not matter as we could, if we had to, cross country once we had passed the barrier of knights. We had to pop the cork on this bottle and the best way to do that was with decisive sword strokes. As I slipped my shield over my shoulder, I drew my sword and pointing at the enemy to signal a charge, spurred my horse. This was where our common experience of so many years came to our aid. While King Henry's household knights might have been tardy my men at arms and archers would know my signals and commands and obey instantly.

 That we had taken them by surprise was clear for, as we closed the gap to them, they seemed to look at each other for one to give orders. By the time they had realised what we were about and had drawn weapons and spurred horses we were riding faster and about to hit them. Horses are sensitive to the mood of their riders. They sense a lack of confidence and act accordingly. Storm Bringer, in contrast, was, like me, eager and ready to fight. The French horses baulked and tried to turn as my sword point of horsemen barrelled down the road towards them. With my shield held close to my chin and my sword before me, Storm Bringer swept between the first two French horses. Gerard was almost level with me and John Wulfstun close to Storm Bringer's rump. One French knight managed to hit my shield with his sword but having to swing over his own shield weakened the blow. I used my own stroke, not to swing but to ride with levelled sword and strike, in the throat, the French knight to my right. His horse was already trying to move to its left and as the knight fell from the horse his dying hand dragged the unfortunate animal to crash into the hedgerow to the side. The French horses following saw the gap and headed towards it rather than risk the wall of steel and horseflesh that lay before them. Taking advantage of the confusion I swung my sword sideways at the French knight who was trying to control his horse. His sword flapped at me and when my blade rang against his helmet, he was stunned and involuntarily dropped his sword.

 The thin line of knights had been undone by their animals and the speed of our attack. All that lay before us now were the light horsemen and this was where Richard son of Aelric and my archers would have a chance to show their sword skills. The light horsemen had the advantage of spears, but I wore mail and the two spears that were thrust at me tore just my surcoat and were stopped by my mail. They had no such protection and my sword almost severed the arm of one light horseman. Gerard slew the horseman to my right, and, behind me, I could hear the death cries of the men slain by King Henry's familia. They were not in the mood for mercy having been ambushed. As the last eight light horsemen turned tail and fled, I saw the open road before us. Sheathing my sword and reining in a little to allow my horse a breather, I risked a look behind and saw that Thomas, Robin and the King were still there.

Shouting, "Mordaf!" I spurred Storm Bringer to get my horse to canter.

"Aye, my lord?"

I saw that Mordaf's brigandine was blood-spattered. My scout hated the French and had taken advantage of the attack to satisfy his need for vengeance for the loss of his fingers.

"Find us a road to Le Mans! We avoid any further fighting!"

"Aye, my lord!"

As we began to ride, I slipped my coif from my head and I heard the sounds of battle fading behind us. Sir Walter was obeying my orders. The question was, would Le Mans still be in friendly hands? This was treachery of the highest order and if Le Mans was held by those loyal to Duke Richard then our fight and flight might be in vain!

Chapter 16

We reached Savigné-l'Évêque, which lay just six miles from Le Mans and found a party of men at arms sent by the seneschal to patrol the road. They were known to the king and were loyal. They told us that Le Mans still lay in loyal hands and we pushed on to the castle. The king's physician had been lost somewhere on the road and when we reached the castle, and after passing through the outer suburbs to reach the town wall, I ordered the castle doctor to tend to King Henry. The blood down his front was not from a wound but his ailment. As his doctor had said, riding and stress were a bad combination.

The seneschal, Guy de Le Mans, was a good, if unimaginative soldier. I was blunt when I spoke to him, "We need to be prepared for a siege. The King of France and the king's son will sweep our men before them. Any who make it here will be in a poor condition. Send a rider to Alençon to ask the seneschal there to muster an army. We shall need it."

Sir Guy shook his head, "I fear there will be too few to counter the army you describe. Perhaps we should sue for peace."

I shook my head, "That time may come but not yet. The king's enemies hold the advantage here and we need to improve our chances."

"I will do as you ask, Sir Samuel." He smiled, "I knew your grandfather and I see him and hear him in your words and voice. It gives me hope."

I saw little hope for I had counted on Norman knights from Alençon being there to give us a fighting chance. I went to the gatehouse as a pair of riders left the castle to

The Perfect Knight

head north. I saw the first of those who had been with Sir Walter Tremaine as they made their way towards the castle. They would give us our only chance of survival. Thomas, Robin, and Gerard joined me.

"Father, the king asks for you."

I nodded but did not move, "I want the three of you to stay here and watch for the French and Duke Richard's men. Send to me if I am needed. The gates must be closed before they can force them. We need as many men within the walls as we can but let us take no chances. Have Richard and the archers man this gatehouse. I do not doubt that the crossbowmen will give a good account of themselves, but my archers' bodkins will deter Duke Richard quicker. He knows that if they aim at him, he is a dead man!"

"Aye father."

The personal knights of King Henry were like a flock of clucking hens outside the king's chamber. It irritated me, "You can do nothing here except to make my head hurt! Go to the walls for soon our enemy will be here and you can do the king more good there."

My voice was angry, and they all obeyed. Perhaps, like the seneschal they saw and heard the Warlord and not his grandson who was trying to do his best to save a king. I did not think I would succeed. All that I could hope for was his end to be peaceful. The doctor had gone, and his squires and servants were there. That so many of them had survived was down to our attack on the road. Had we tried to head south then many of them might now be prisoners or lying dead!

The king was on a bed and he waved his hand, "Leave us!" They obeyed and he gestured for me to sit on the chair next to the bed. He gave me a wan smile, "I was born here, you know? Fifty-six years ago and then I had no kingdom. My mother and I were in the hands of your grandfather and here am I, at the end of my life, in the hands of his grandson. Give me advice, Sir Samuel. You are young but I know that you have the Warlord's mind."

I had to be honest with him. The Warlord had told me that kings and empresses needed such honesty. "King Henry, things look bleak. That this attack was premeditated seems obvious to me and your enemies have many more men than we do. They planned the attack before the truce talks and all else was for show. The garrison here and the men who survive the battle are all that we can hope for. Alençon offers you the chance to send for an army from England and to use the knights of Normandy. The other choice is to head to Chinon."

He nodded, "As you say, Sir Samuel, I have limited choices and God, it seems, has sent this vile ailment to hamper me." He looked to heaven as he clutched the cross which hung about his neck, "What sins have I committed, lord?"

I knew from my grandfather that the king had made not only many mistakes but committed many sins. I said nothing.

"How many men survived the encounter?"

"That I do not yet know. I have my men watching the gate and I came here to ensure that you were recovered. I shall return as soon as you no longer have need of me."

"I think, Sir Samuel, that this is as well as I am likely to be. I must ensure that John becomes king and not that ingrate and traitor, Richard."

I said not a word for I doubted that, at the moment, either was the king that England needed. We had been lucky with King Henry but his sons…

I headed back to the gatehouse and saw the first arrivals. As I had expected they were the ones who bore injuries and wounds. Sir Walter was not with them. It was dark by the time he arrived with a horse bearing the scars of war and with half of his familia gone. I descended to meet him in the outer bailey. He patted his horse on the neck and kissed its muzzle, "But for this brave warhorse I would have perished, and I fear that he will need rest for some time before I ride him to war again."

"You held them, then?"

"Aye, but it cost us." He laughed, "Duke Richard is the warrior. King Philip and his bodyguards just followed in his wake, like a flock of seagulls behind a fishing ship, hoping

The Perfect Knight

to pick up titbits." I nodded for I had the measure of Philip Augustus. "Is there hope, Earl Samuel?"

You do not lie to brothers in arms and I shook my head, "The garrison is small, and I fear that there will be more men come to swell the enemy numbers. There is little that we can do but fight on. If we are able, I would take the king from here. The choices are Chinon and Alençon."

"I would choose Alençon but then I am Norman."

"It makes sense to me for Chinon is too close to Duke Richard's lands. He has enemies but not enough to aid us."

"All are weary. Let us have a night to rest and see what numbers are available and we will make a better decision in the morning."

We had but two hundred knights left to us. The garrison was half that number but at least we had the benefit of their bows and crossbows. The seneschal also brought in those from the suburbs to swell our numbers so that we could man the town walls with more than five hundred men. We would force Richard and Philip Augustus to build siege engines. That would buy us time.

Our tiny numbers were apparent when we dined. Of the two hundred knights who had come with Sir Walter forty of them bore wounds. Conversation was perforce, limited. King Henry spent the whole feast speaking of the mistakes he had made and how he might have made better decisions. I kept silent for I knew that it was his nature and that of his wife, Queen Eleanor, that had led to this disaster. The Warlord had almost lost his son, my father, but he had taken him back and they had become closer. That was the difference. King Henry had allowed his sons to drift away; indeed, he had encouraged conflict between them. Had not the Empress died then she might have had an influence. Her death had changed both my grandfather and the king. In my grandfather's case, it had merely made him sadder but in the king's case, it was as though he was an untrained horse and given too much rein.

"I have decided, Sir Samuel, we will try, if we can, to ride to Alençon. I will send ships for men and we will await our foes in Rouen. That mighty citadel will not fall. I will send for John and have him crowned before I die."

None of us gainsaid him for we could see that the King of England did not have long left to live.

I asked to be woken not long after midnight for I wished to see what the king's enemies were up to. The captain of the guard shook his head as I approached. "My lord, I fear that they are using the suburbs to get closer. Soon they will be able to send arrows and bolts at our men watching the walls."

I nodded, "And in which direction is the wind?"

"Why, my lord, from behind us!"

I smiled, "Good!" The walls had a couple of small stone-throwers. They had a limited range and were notoriously inaccurate, but they would serve my purpose. "Captain, fetch kindling, oil and fire. We will set alight the suburbs. With luck, we will not only deny them shelter but mayhap we might even hurt them!"

Just doing something positive put a smile on the face of the garrison. No one likes to feel helpless. The odds were that we would still lose but at least we would not be giving in without a fight. Sir Walter joined me as did the senior knight from King Henry's retinue. Sir Hugh de Bourg was an experienced knight and we had mutual respect.

"King Henry asks what you plan, my lord?"

I pointed, "The enemy draws closer and they seek to use the suburbs for shelter. We will fire this side of the town. The wind is blowing towards them and we should be safe."

"I will go to tell him."

Setting up stone throwers is never quick and the last thing we needed was to begin a fire in the castle. We were already taking a risk using fire over the buildings before us. The outer wall of Le Mans had a wooden palisade and if that was set on fire then we might be in trouble. The engineer in command of the two stone throwers was a careful man and that pleased me. I approved of his caution and, until day dawned, there was no need for haste. It was, indeed, almost dawn before he was ready, and he looked to me as King Henry emerged from the gate tower. The burning kindling

The Perfect Knight

was sent high into the air, the machine making a loud crack that sounded louder in the silence of dawn. The engineer waited until he saw it land. It was well beyond the outer palisade and struck in the centre of the suburbs. They were small mean houses that were packed closely together. The kindling smashed onto a straw roof and burst into flames. The second fireball was sent soon after and then the engineer had his throwers release their deadly fire at regular intervals until a section of the suburbs, one hundred paces wide by forty paces deep was on fire."

The faces of the defenders showed their glee and when we heard screams, we knew that some men had been trapped by the flames and perished. The king was happy too. He came over to me, "I thought we might have to ride today. I am pleased that I have another day to recover."

I thought that if he had a week to recover it would still make little difference, but I said nothing. The plan was a good one but as the fire took hold and more buildings were set alight, I felt a breeze. The wind was turning and worse, it was increasing in speed. I saw the flames and smoke as they began to burn closer to the walls. I turned to the engineer who would know such things, "Tell me, will the wind turn back to blow as it did before dawn or is it likely to continue to turn in this direction?"

His drawn face told me the answer before his voice, "I fear the wind will take hold of the fire and burn our own walls."

"Thank you for your honesty." Turning to Sir Walter I said, "Have our men and the king mounted. We need to leave, now!"

Thomas and Robin had already raced off and I knew that Storm Bringer and Skuld, not to mention all our gear would be ready and there would be no delay from me. The king was another matter. The doctor who had attended him shook his head as the king was led from his sleeping chamber, "I fear this will do the king's health no good at all, my lord!"

The king shook his head and said, "If I am to die then let me die in action and not sleeping like some dotard who has outlived his usefulness. Besides, it does not do to die in the same place as you were born! Come, Sir Samuel, one gamble failed. Can you get us to Alençon?"

I smiled, "We can try, and we shall not give up without a fight. We have one hope; the fire is on the eastern side and has not yet spread to the north. This fire might destroy the houses of Le Mans, but it might also prevent pursuit."

The king nodded, "Sir Guy, when we have gone you may surrender the city and the castle with honour, and I thank you for trying to shelter me in my time of need."

We were mounted, as were the king's familia and my men before half of the Norman knights who followed the king had even reached the stables. We could not afford a wait and as soon as we reached the gate, I ordered it open and we galloped, coughing and spluttering through clouds of smoke. It did little to improve the state of the king's health. We had a little over thirty miles to travel and I had high hopes of reaching the fortress of Alençon. Within ten miles of leaving the smoke wreathed Le Mans, it became clear to me that this would not be a swift journey. I rode next to the king and saw his pained expression. He was hurting. It did not help that this was high summer, and it was a hot day. The smoke through which we had ridden had made us all cough, but it seemed to aggravate the king's condition. Ten miles from Alençon we stopped, and the king dismounted. I could see that Sir Walter and the Norman knights were keen to press on, but the king was not.

We had just crossed the ancient bridge over the Sarthe in a tiny hamlet whose name I did not know. There was a church and Sir Walter and I took the king within to shelter from the sun. A priest hurried in and recognising the spurs and the king's livery asked, "King Henry, what can I do for you?"

"A little wine, father, and your blessing."

"Of course."

He turned to leave but before he did the king asked, "And what is the name of this church?"

"Église Saint-Julien."

The king nodded and waved him out. "A simple church, eh gentlemen? I like things to be simple. A man should have

The Perfect Knight

a son and be able to bequeath him his goods and lands. That is simple. See how the altar is unadorned and plain. A church does not need to be gilded with gold and dressed like a doxy!"

The priest frowned as he entered. He had heard the word doxy! The king nodded his thanks and sipped the wine. He waved away the food. "Father, I need your blessing for I fear I am close to death."

"Will you confess?" He looked pointedly at Sir Walter and me.

"I would."

"We will wait without."

As we stepped into the sun Sir Walter said, "This delay will cost us dear."

I shook my head, "It matters not for he is dying and wishes to make his peace with God. I can understand that."

Thomas brought us both over some cooled wine. I sipped it and asked, "How is it so cool on such a day?"

He smiled, "When we arrived, I put it in the river."

Sir Walter nodded, "I wish that my squire was as clever and thoughtful."

"He is my son!"

"Then unlike the king, you are lucky."

"And I know it."

The door opened and the priest beckoned us in, "The king is in low spirits and he would speak with you. I have heard his confession and if the Good Lord takes him then he will be assured a place in heaven!"

I hoped the priest was speaking the truth.

King Henry stood and smiled, "I feel better now, Sir Samuel!"

Sir Walter beamed, "Good, then we can be within Alençon's walls within a couple of hours!"

He shook his head, "No, my lord, we shall not. I will ride south with Sir Samuel, his men and my familia. You will lead the rest of the knights to Alençon as planned."

"But King Henry…"

The king held up his hand, "You are a brave knight, and I am honoured that you serve with me but I am dying. My confession made all clear to me and this simple church has helped to focus my mind. I will return to die in Chinon. It was one of my wife's favourite castles and I fear that I have not treated her as well as I might. I shall die there and if there is to be one last battle for me it will be in Aquitaine." He shook his head, "I am determined, and my mind is made up."

I knew when Fate was taking a hand and this was one such occasion. There was no point in fighting it. I turned to Sir Walter, "We will be a small party and the last thing that they will expect is for us to turn and head towards them. Your movement north will draw then thence." He looked doubtful. "The king is of sound mind. Let us both obey him and show that we are not his sons!"

That decided him, "Aye, I shall." He clasped my arm. "You are a true knight, and it is an honour to have served with you. May God be with you!"

I knew that we could not reach Chinon before dark, indeed we would still be north of Le Mans but by crossing the Sarthe and heading for the tiny huddle of houses that was Sablé-sur-Sarthe we might lose our pursuers and, more importantly, we would avoid any castles. I sent Mordaf and Tam the Hawker to the east of us where they would spot enemy pursuers long before we would. I was confident that they would have the skill to avoid detection especially as we were in the land where he had lived, scouted and hunted. I then had a plan to head to Sir Alfraed at La Flèche. There we would be safe and, more importantly, guarded. It would enable us to cross the Loir and approach Chinon from a completely different direction. We rode hard and I allowed the king's familia to guard him. I was too busy watching for enemies and signs of danger. It was good to have my son with me. He was silent for the most part, only questioning my decisions when he could see no reason for them. We stopped briefly at Sablé-sur-Sarthe and then headed south and east for La Flèche.

It was dark as we rode down the road which ran alongside the ditch. The men on the keep had seen us and our livery. I knew that they would tell Sir Alfraed who would be already

The Perfect Knight

giving orders for chambers as well as ensuring that we had easy access to the castle. It was so efficiently done that even the sickly king was impressed. Within moments of passing from the town into the castle we were whisked off to chambers and the smell of cooking food made even me salivate. As the king was escorted to his chamber by his bodyguard I said, "Alfraed, the king is ill. Send your doctor to him. The king vomits blood and all that we can do is to make him comfortable. Have some milk warmed and sent to him."

"Milk?"

"Trust me, it is medicine to him."

He hurried off and Thomas took off my helmet, spurs, cloak, coif and arming cap. I unstrapped my sword and kissed the hilt. By kissing the cross I hoped that God would smile upon us. I handed my sword and baldric to Robin. To be truthful God already had shown us that he was aiding us and the fact that we were so relatively close to Chinon made me say a silent prayer of thanks. The milk seemed to help the king and he was just relieved that he could sleep in a bed, safe from his enemies. Sir Alfraed was, as I already knew, a very loyal knight and he insisted upon escorting us to Chinon the next day. He knew the roads to take that would avoid detection and we reached Chinon safely in the third week of June. His physician, whom we had lost on the road to Le Mans had fled there and he immediately ordered the king to bed. After sending Sir Alfraed back to his home I sent out orders, in the name of the king for loyal knights to muster at Chinon. We had avoided our enemies, but they would know where we were and come to seek us out. The king was weak, and they saw victory within their grasp.

For the first ten days that the king was bedridden, I took the news to him each day. I did not honey my words but spoke the truth and I know that, although it upset him, he appreciated my honesty and there was trust between us. King Philip and Duke Richard soon conquered Maine and then moved on to Tours. When that fortress fell, and fall it would, then we and Saumur would become the border.

I took the news to him and he asked, "And the muster?"

"We have an army."

He smiled at the paucity of my description, "But not enough, you think, to face my son and the French."

"No, my lord."

"I remember often riding alongside your grandfather and fighting odds that would have turned most men's blood to water but not the Warlord."

I shook my head, "I am not the Warlord and if you recall, my lord, when you rode with my father then knights like Sir Dick and Sir Wulfric and their men were at the heart of your army. I bring a handful of archers and men at arms. We do not have enough archers to blacken the sky and drive the enemy from the field."

"Nonetheless we will take our army and ride towards Tours. I would not let them have such an easy victory. I might as well hand the crown to King Philip and my son. I would rather have one last chance of honour; I would like to be the king your grandfather made me." He beckoned me closer, "You know that I am dying?" I nodded. "Ever since that day at Église Saint-Julien, I have confessed each day to a priest. I am as content as a dying man can be. I would like to make my peace with Eleanor, but I cannot and that is my fault. I know my faults, Samuel, better than any except, I suspect, your grandfather who seemed to know me better than a father knows his son. Certainly, I have never understood my sons. I have sent a letter to John asking him to come to my aid. He has yet to respond but it is a long way twixt here and England. Who knows, he may bring an army and we can fight a battle we might win. Summon my leaders and tomorrow we ride forth to do battle for England, Normandy, Aquitaine and France!" He smiled, "Who knows, on my deathbed I may gain the crown of France!"

"As ever, my liege, I will obey!"

I was kept busy until late. I was the one who gathered the captains and lieutenants and helped King Henry formulate a battle plan. It was not the best of plans and I could not see how it would gain us victory, but it was a plan and had a slight chance of success. We would use the king as bait and hope that the enemy would try to take him. His knights and

The Perfect Knight

my men at arms would be the armour to protect him. He hoped that King Philip and Duke Richard would not succeed, and his army would lose heart. I sat, long after the Great Hall had been cleared, with Thomas, Robin, Richard, and Gerard.

"Thomas and Robin you are to stay behind Gerard and his men. I want my banner to draw them on. Richard, Mordaf will hold your horses and you will be behind Gerard and Thomas. You are the one thing they will not expect. When they charge for us your handful of bodkins can be sent at their knights. Even if you stop just ten of them they will be hurt. You keep loosing until you see the king's banner fall, and fall it will, then you mount your horses and take my son and page back here to Chinon." I saw my son, Robin and Richard open their mouths to speak. I held up my hand, "This is no time for debate. My mind is made up. King Henry is my lord and I have sworn to protect him. I want you alive, Thomas, so that the line of the Warlord can stretch on through time." He nodded, "Gerard, I give you and my men at arms the impossible task, I want you to guard my back and fight the finest knights in Europe, the knights of Duke Richard. I want no man to throw away his life. Your task is merely to stop them from getting around me. The king's bodyguard will guard him."

"You wish to die, my lord?"

I shook my head, "Of course not! I am, however, a realist and I am making plans should the worst happen. If I fall then I want you to join Captain Richard and protect my son and my page." All three stared at me in silence. I smiled, "Take out your swords and swear!"

Their faces fell for they knew that they had to obey and then to keep their promise.

I nodded, "Now I am content. I will confess on the morrow at terces and we will ride to battle."

The army we took was loyal. There were many lords who had opposed Duke Richard and were eager for the opportunity to fight as defenders of the king rather than rebels. There were other lords who feared the growth of a greedy France. Their hearts were sound but there were too few of them. I had no real idea of the number of men we would face just that they would be brimming with confidence and have overwhelming numbers.

It was July the 3rd when our scouts reported them close to the small town of Ballans. We camped for the night and we modified our plans in light of the terrain. I spoke, for the short twenty-mile ride had taken its toll on the king.

"I suspect that Duke Richard has chosen this battlefield for it suits him well." I waved my hand to the east, "It is flat and there are no woods in which we can hide archers and crossbows. He can use his superior numbers to simply sweep us away. I have ordered ditches to be dug and stakes planted to make it more difficult for the enemy to get at us but those defences will be breached. They are there to slow down the enemy. Our aim is to make the enemy come for the king and, I suspect, me. Accordingly, we will be in the centre. The men on our flanks will be our foot soldiers and they will make a barrier of spears to make it hard for them to get at us. It is the Count of Angers and the Count of Maine who will bring us victory. I want you two to be the flanks of our army and when the enemy is drawn into our centre then launch your attacks on the flanks."

The plan was a simple one and that was born out of necessity. I would be busy in the centre defending the king and I had no chance to modify my plans. They seemed satisfied and most left in a more buoyant mood than they had entered. I had done all that I could. The king spent more time with his priests than with me and I could understand that. He was dying and, to be honest, each time a servant came to me I thought it was to tell me that he had passed. I spent the night before the battle with my men. Thomas had grown so much that he was barely recognisable as the page who had followed me to war such a few years earlier. He would acquit himself well but he was not yet ready to face the full force of Duke Richard's elite warriors. We spoke, not of war, but of home. We spoke of Eleanor and Stockton. We spoke of Ruth and the old warriors we had left guarding our walls. I took comfort from the knowledge that whatever happened they would be safe. The Treaty of Newcastle meant that the Scots could not take advantage of the problems King Henry faced in France. For Robin, this would be his first battle and I prayed that he would survive. I knew that Martyn Longsword would do all that he could for the boy.

    The king had twenty knights as his bodyguard. His standard was with Sir John Knowles beside him and the other nineteen formed a barrier before him. I was in the centre of their line directly before the king. To our left and right were spearmen and behind us were my tiny warband of warriors with Thomas holding my gryphon standard. Robin had a short spear to help guard Thomas and a round buckler. The bishops and priests blessed us and then retired to the town of Ballans. There were no preliminary talks and no discussions about a truce. Duke Richard lined up his army and it was a simple formation. He and five hundred knights made up the centre and his dismounted men and crossbows flanked him. We were outnumbered three to one. There were neither stakes nor ditches before us in the centre for we had lances and our plan was to make a last-minute charge at whoever came towards us. I knew it would be Duke Richard. King Philip Augustus had his banner well behind the front line. He would be there at the kill and not before.

    I turned to the knights with whom I would fight, "Listen for my command. We make them think we will take their charge at the halt. When I give the order then spur your horses and follow me."

    They all banged their shields for they were in good heart. When you know that you cannot win then it is easier to face death. Death comes to all men and all a knight can do is to hope for an honourable end and not one such as my father endured, being eaten from within.

    The enemy horns sounded, and Duke Richard led the charge. He began at the walk and that was to help those on foot but when they were two hundred paces from us he had his horns sound and they galloped towards us with lances ready to be levelled. The two counts who were on our flanks would have to make the decision as to the best time to charge the dismounted men. We had already done what we planned

The Perfect Knight

and drawn the venom of the enemy to us. I knew that Storm Bringer was better than any other warhorse and whenever we charged, I would reach the enemy first. I intended to fight Duke Richard.

Using the long spear I had chosen as my weapon to point I shouted, "Charge!" I spurred Storm Bringer who leapt forward as I knew he would do. Within five strides I was a horse length ahead of the next knights and we formed an arrowhead. The speed of my charge looked to have taken the enemy by surprise. I aimed my horse at Duke Richard who lowered his own lance and pulled his shield tighter. The Duke, like his dead brothers, had fought in many tournaments and he had never yet been unhorsed. Like my father and grandfather, I had rarely taken part in tournaments, but I had fought in many battles. I focussed my attention on the place I would strike. I was not aiming to kill for this might be the next King of England and so I aimed at Duke Richard's chest rather than his head. I could see from the angle of his lance that he was aiming for my face. The rest of the charge meant nothing to either of us. As we neared each other I saw that his eyes were fixed on me. This was an old-fashioned battle between champions. Storm Bringer was a clever horse and when I pulled the reins slightly to my left and then back to the right, he responded instantly. The slight movement confused Duke Richard as I knew it would and as I punched at his chest his lance merely clipped my helmet. All my anger and frustration at the inequality in numbers was in that blow and, to my great delight, the Duke tumbled from his saddle. The long spear shattered with the impact and I drew my sword.

I saw that I was almost alone. The four knights who flanked me were no longer there and Duke Richard's familia came at me. It was then that I saw the leading knight suddenly sprout an arrow from his shoulder. It buried itself up to the fletch. Such a wound would have touched bone and I saw the knight clutch at the arrow and then wheel away. As more arrows clattered against helmets, shields, mail and horses I used my sword to find gaps in my enemies' mail. I knew that my archers would not strike me but the ones

The Perfect Knight

fighting me did not. King Philip and his standard still squatted like a toad at the rear of the Gascon knights trying to get to the side of their fallen Duke. I began to believe, for a brief moment, that we might actually win. If the two counts did as they had been ordered, then the men on foot ahead of us would find themselves attacked in the flanks by horsemen. Sadly that did not happen. I did not see it for I was too busy fending off the attacks of three knights but Thomas told me later. The two battles of knights did not strike home. A forest of spears stopped them. Then the men on foot to our flanks broke as mounted horsemen fought their way through the stakes and over the ditches. I disarmed one Gascon knight who shouted, "I surrender!" I knocked the second from his horse with a mighty sideswipe. The third managed to smack his sword against my shield but my horse and I were as one, a rock and I barely budged. When I stood in my stirrups and brought my sword down on the knight's head I knew that he would either be dead or out of the battle.

    The respite allowed me to look around as more of Duke Richard's knights came at me. King Henry's bodyguards were almost all either dead or wounded and I was aware that I could only see, as Storm Bringer whirled, Gerard, Martyn, and Thomas. That did not mean the rest were dead but that we were alone. When King Henry's standard-bearer fell, and the flag hit the ground then it was all over. It had, in truth, been over for some moments. Just four of the king's knights remained and when Duke Richard, now remounted, shouted, "Sheathe your weapons! You have done all that honour demands and I would not wish to see such brave men slaughtered unnecessarily!" I dropped my head and sheathed my sword. I had failed. The Warlord had never lost a battle, but I had.

    My eyes were closed when a hand touched my shoulder, "Do not hang your head, Sir Samuel, hold it high. Had I not been a helpless invalid and if more men had fought this day then I know that we would have won. This field of Ballans is now stained with the blood of my familia and I have lived long enough!"

    I turned and saw a pale King Henry.

"Aye, my father is right, Sir Samuel. You have honour and your grandfather knew of what he spoke when he told us you were the best of knights. Keep your sword and I will see that the ransom from the men you unhorsed is delivered to you!" I nodded dully and he continued. "And you, father, will now agree to my terms."

"Aye for that is the price of defeat."

"You will make me sole heir of England and all the lands you hold in France." It was not a request but a command from the next King of England.

"I will and then, with this handful of brave men, I shall return to Chinon. I am done with this world."

Chapter 17

Chinon 1189

King Henry died on July 6th in Chinon Castle. It was not losing the battle that ended his life, it was losing the loyalty of his last son. His heart was broken when the reply finally reached him from John. The letter must have arrived even as we were heading east. John chose his brother's side over his father. King Henry had been betrayed by his favourite and it sucked the last vestiges of life from him. I did not see him the moment he died. The last time that I saw him to speak with was when he tossed the letter from John to the ground.

"My last son, an ingrate! Sir Samuel, I charge you with ensuring that England has a king in whom she can be proud. I have not been such a king and I doubt that Richard will be a great one, but at least he is a warrior. Sir Samuel I cannot go on the crusade, but I would have you be there for me." I nodded. He doubled up in pain. "Send for my priest! God is calling for me!"

I turned, "Send for the priest."

I stood apart while he made his confession. He might have been right for he had no sooner been absolved than he collapsed. He did not die immediately but lingered for another day. Along with his handful of knights, I made the decisions about his burial. He told us that he wanted to be interred at Grandmont Abbey in the Limousin, but the hot weather made transporting his body impractical and instead we buried him at the nearby Fontevraud Abbey. For such an important and powerful man the mourners hardly did his legacy justice. His knights and my men were the warriors represented there. The clergy and members of his household made up the rest. His household knights were at a loss about what to do and when we ate our last meal they made the decision to follow the wishes of the king and go on crusade. I remained silent for I was not certain that King Henry would have gone to the Holy Land. When he was fit and able to go then there had always been a reason not to leave his land. He was a political man and perhaps that was no surprise given the complicated world in which he had grown up. At the last, when he genuinely wished to go on a crusade, he was unfit.

The next day, as my handful of men and I headed north to take a ship home, I reflected on the man whom I had known my whole life. In many ways, he felt like part of the family. He had always been present when my grandfather had been alive and I think I viewed him as a sort of uncle, the one most families have. The one you love but who does strange things. I know that he and my father had been very close when they were young and perhaps that made the king closer. Like a wild and unpredictable uncle, the strange behaviour was forgiven, and he was tolerated.

We were a sombre group who rode north. Gerard and Martyn were the only two of my men at arms who had survived the Battle of Ballans. I know that it was not just the two survivors who felt the loss; the archers had been close to them. It was the way of my men. They joked, bantered and mocked each other, but they were a band of brothers and the deaths, in what turned out to be a totally unnecessary battle seemed particularly pointless. As we neared Rouen where we would take ship Richard son of Aelric asked, "Sir Samuel, what do we do now? I do not mean this day but once we have returned to Stockton and resumed our lives. Do we follow King Richard and go on a holy crusade?"

"Do you wish to go?"

"It is not my choice, Sir Samuel. I am your man and if you go on the crusade, I will follow your banner."

We passed through the gate and headed for the river, "No, Richard, and I say this to all of you, I command no man to follow me to the Holy Land. I think that I must go and that means Thomas shall come too but for the rest, you have done all that oathsworn warriors must do and any who choose," I

The Perfect Knight

emphasised the word, "***not*** to come shall be given land and coin or they can join the garrison in Stockton. You have all shed enough blood for the family of the Warlord already." I saw the doubt on their faces and I said, firmly, taking my dagger from my belt and kissing the crosspiece, "I swear that what I say I mean."

It was then that they nodded, and Richard said, "Then for myself I will ask for a post in Stockton Castle. I would train young archers."

One or two others of the archers nodded their affirmation and I smiled. I had meant what I had said, and I did not want the blood of more men upon my conscience. King Henry could have acceded to his son's demands before the battle was fought and the world would be no different to the way it was except that I had lost good men. We reached Stockton at the same time that King Richard was on his way to London to be crowned at Westminster Abbey. He had been made Duke of Normandy even as we sailed up the coast of England, home. That Thomas and I would take the cross was clear to all, but it had been as we neared Herterpol that Gerard and Martyn Longsword approached me.

"My lord, we have debated long and hard on this voyage home and Martyn and I have decided to take the cross with you. I know that you go for different reasons, but we go so that we can pray in Jerusalem for the souls of our brothers in arms."

"Jerusalem is in the hands of the Turks still."

Martyn had grinned, "Aye lord, but you have not yet arrived and soon it will be Christian again!"

I shook my head, "It may be that King Richard does not wish me to accompany him on this crusade."

Thomas asked, "Then we might not go?"

"Oh, I shall go for I was there when Cardinal Carnelli asked for an oath. And while mine was unspoken a true knight does not break an oath. Emperor Frederick Barbarossa will also be on the crusade and we will offer our swords to him should King Richard choose not to accept my offer of knights." I smiled, "If we do follow the Emperor's

The Perfect Knight

banner then it will just be we four who go! I will only take the knights of the valley if King Richard asks for me."

Ruth was pleased to see me but disturbed that I was going to the Holy Land. "Brother, this cannot end well. We were both born there, and our parents returned when they knew that the land was lost."

I nodded, "I told the king I would go and it is right for I have to atone for the death of Eleanor."

Her face became angry, "You have naught to atone for! It was not your fault that she died. You followed a king and it cost you dear. Do not follow another for the seed of Henry Plantagenet is cursed." She made the sign of the cross.

I said, gently, "Sister, we are of the blood of the Warlord. Duty is within each of us. Are you telling me that if you had been born a man that you would have done anything differently?"

Our eyes met and she could not lie to me. She shook her head, "But how can you follow men whom you know to be inferior to you?"

"For England and the land we love. Grandfather did it all the time and most times he brought the best out of men whom otherwise would not have served his Empress." I swept an arm around the hall, "Our hall, our town, our valley, they are England. It is not those self-serving folk who live in London, it is places like this and are they not worth fighting for?"

She nodded, "And dying?"

I sighed, "If that is necessary." I looked around to see that Thomas was not close. "I will not dub Thomas, that can wait for I do not want to risk him. If I should fail to return, I know that you will watch out for him."

She hugged me and I felt salt tears from her, "As though he was my own son." She pulled away, "You are the most thoughtful of men. Will Thomas be happy about the fact that he will not be knighted?"

I shook my head, "He said, when Jack died, that he was not yet ready but even if he does press me, I shall keep him as my squire. He can stay with the baggage and the horses although from what I was told of Saladin's victory at Hattin, the squires were all captured too but they were treated well. He and Robin will not be risked."

"Do you have to go?"

My eyes bored into her, "I have to go!"

She nodded, "Then I shall be here as the rock of Stockton!"

The news came that the new king had been crowned on the 3rd of September. I had not been there to swear fealty, but it was a given that I would. His preparations for the crusade were now moving at a pace and I heard from riders heading north that he would be leaving England as soon as he had put in place those who would rule in his stead. The crusade was coming. I summoned my knights and told them that I would, if I was asked, go on the crusade and the matter of their involvement was their own. I told them of the end of King Henry. All had known him and fought alongside him. King Richard and his brothers had not and I knew where their sympathy lay.

It was October when we had the surprise visit from the new king himself. He arrived unannounced from the south and I guessed he had been to York. He had with him forty of his knights. It was fortunate that first the Warlord and then my father had built warrior halls which could house them although our horses had to be taken from the castle to be tethered on the town green by the well of St John.

"This is an honour, King Richard, and I fear it will not be the sort of accommodation and food you are used to!"

He raised me from my bow and embraced me, "Sir Samuel, you know more than any what is needed on a campaign. When we are in the Holy Land it will be far worse. And who is this lovely lady?"

"This is Lady Ruth, my sister."

She curtsied but her eyes were cold as she said, "Welcome to our hall, King Richard. Your father often stayed here. He was a good man!"

Her words were a challenge and King Richard's face darkened and then it broke into a grin and he laughed, "I should have expected nothing less from the blood of the Warlord. Your brother was not afraid of offending me by

The Perfect Knight

doing the opposite of what I wished but I know, that like your brother you are loyal to the crown!"

She smiled, "England is also close to my heart. Now if you will excuse me, I have rooms to prepare and a feast to organise."

It was autumn and my archers had been hunting. There would be venison and wild boar. I knew the king's appetite, and this would appeal to him. After Ruth had gone, he waved a hand to his knights, "Until we eat entertain yourselves. I am certain that the ale here will be to your taste. I would speak with Sir Samuel." As they dispersed like a disturbed flock of magpies, he put his arm around me and said, "Let us retire to your solar. My father often said it was a place of solace and comfort to him."

The words sounded hypocritical to me, but I nodded and headed up the stairs. I nodded to Ralph, my steward. He would fetch us good wine and food.

King Richard approved of the room which had been my grandfather's favourite. The three chairs were the most comfortable in the castle and the tapestries on the wall depicted the Battle of the Standards when the Warlord had defeated the King of Scotland and chased the Prince of Cumberland all the way to the gates of Carlisle. We chatted about the depiction after which we sat for Ralph had fetched the food and the wine.

"See that we are not disturbed, Ralph. Ask Thomas to stand guard."

"Yes, my lord."

"You are an organised man Sir Samuel. I like that. I, too, am organised and I like things clear and simple. I was on my way to Durham, but I thought to stop here. You and I need honesty and I would have the air cleared."

"Of course and I agree. There should be openness between King and Earl!"

"You know I was angry when you spurned my offer?"

"I do and you know my reasons. Knowing what I do now, I would still have acted the way I did and supported your father for it was not only the right thing to do but also the only thing I could do. I had sworn an oath."

The Perfect Knight

He nodded and swallowed some of the wine to wash down the pickled herring he had eaten, "And would you swear that same oath to me?"

"Of course." I knelt.

"Not here, tonight, when we feast." He smiled, "I like things simple, Sir Samuel, and a public oath will encourage others to swear one. I know that you would keep your word. What else would the greatest knight in the land do? And will you take the cross with me?"

"I was there when the papal emissary asked us to do so. I was willing to follow your father and I will follow you."

"You know that my father would never have gone on crusade. He would have prevaricated and found reasons not to go."

"Yet we shall never know that, will we, King Richard?"

"You still believe the best of him," he shook his head, "after he used you and your family…"

"Since the time of the Warlord and the first King Henry, our families have been tied. It is not always comfortable but there is duty and all things considered we have worked well together."

He looked relieved and emptied the goblet which I refilled, "And now I will tell you my plans." I confess that the king looked more relaxed and confident than he ever had when had been the Duke of Aquitaine. He bore the mantle well. "William Longchamp will be my Chancellor and he shall handle the finances of the kingdom. He is well qualified." He grinned and leaned forward, "Reginald the Italian bid more for the post but I deemed it a better return to employ a man I trusted. I have also made Longchamp one of the two regents."

"Not your brother?"

He laughed, "That little man could not even hold on to an island filled with barbarians! I still do not see why he was my father's favourite. No, I have upset John Lackland who will, no doubt, weep tears to my mother but Longchamp is strong." He paused and looked at me, "The other regent is de Puiset, the Bishop of Durham!"

The Perfect Knight

He was looking for my reaction, but I did not give him the satisfaction of seeing me angry. I merely nodded, "You know he is a traitor and conspired with Philip Augustus. He tried to have me murdered."

"I know all for I was told so by my father on one of the rare occasions we were on friendly terms. I know that the man is dishonest, but he rules the north and I have no time to deal with him. He was at my coronation and I spoke frankly with him. I told him that I knew of his actions and I waited for him to tell me I was wrong. He did not deny it. I gave him an ultimatum, either swear, before the Archbishop of Canterbury that he regretted his past and would no longer conspire with England's enemies or I would remove him and make you regent of the Palatinate until I had the time to arrange a replacement." He laughed, "If he did not hate you before, Earl Samuel, he certainly does now! He did as I asked and as a reward, and an inducement for him to think of England's interests I made him a regent."

I still did not like it but there was little that I could do about it. "You are king, my lord, and it is good to see you acting like one. For myself, I would happily slit the throat of that snake."

He nodded, "And I believe you would. You are a good friend, but I should hate to be your enemy. Were you my enemy?"

"When you opposed my king then you were."

He laughed again, "If only all my knights were as honest but then they did not unhorse me! I was sure I would never be unhorsed. You are a mighty knight."

"Like your father, I was trained by the Warlord."

He nodded, "There is something else I have done of which you might not approve. I will be meeting the Scottish king in Durham. In return for a large payment of ten thousand crowns I have given up the rights granted to me by the Treaty of Falaise." This time I could not disguise my reaction and he smiled, "It is only the Scots, Sir Samuel." He pointed to the tapestry, "You and your family have ever had the beating of them. You are the border knights who keep them under control, not the Bishop of Durham. I do not think

The Perfect Knight

that King William will risk your wrath but when I speak with him, I will warn him of the consequences of his seeking to gain land!"

"You are the king, my lord, and I am a loyal subject."

That seemed to satisfy him, "Good. Now the lands in Normandy and Anjou will be in safe hands, I have confirmed my father's appointment of William Fitz Ralph to the post of seneschal of Normandy. Payn de Rochefort is appointed seneschal of Anjou. I have given command of my fleet to Richard de Camville and Robert de Sablé. You will be travelling in that fleet. Can I count on your knights to follow you?"

"If they choose."

"Good for your conroi is most important to us. You are to make your way to Dartmouth in April when the fleet will sail. I will meet you at Marseille." He smiled, "We travel in concert with the French. Neither of us trusts the other and we agreed that we would travel from Vézelay to Marseille and thence to Sicily together."

"Sicily, my lord?"

His face darkened, "You know that my sister Joan was married to the king, William of Sicily?" I nodded, "When her husband died Tancred of Lecce, an Apulian lord, claimed the crown and imprisoned my sister. That she is kept in comfort does not make the act any less dishonourable and as we have to pass Sicily, I thought to show this would-be king, Tancred, what it is to meet a real king!"

King Richard was his own man and I found myself admiring him. He knew what he wanted and was doing all in his power to achieve his ends. There was a knock on the door, and I said, "Come!"

Thomas peered around the edge of it, "Aunt Ruth says that the guests await, and their hunger grows."

The king patted his stomach, "And mine does too. All that we have said, Sir Samuel…"

"Is for my ears only. I understand and you can rely on me." He glanced at Thomas, "And Thomas does not listen at doors, but he is my son and one day will be Earl of Cleveland."

The Perfect Knight

"Just so. Just so."

The king was in an effusive mood that night and was both flattering and gracious to both me and my sister. Neither of us was taken in for we knew that like all kings he would use us as he chose but it was good for the servants to hear the praise heaped upon us. Thomas waited at the table and I saw from his expression that, like me when I had been a squire, keeping quiet and listening brought news and information which shed a whole new light on events.

The king left the next morning having given me another two of the Palatinate manors. He had said, conspiratorially, "It will keep the Bishop in check, eh? And you can always reward your knights with land. Have you not thought of knighting Thomas? I watched him at Ballans, and he behaved as well as any of my father's oathsworn."

"When I deem him to be ready then I will knight him. Besides, it would mean training a new squire and with less than five months until we depart, I will have him endure his present position. Robin, my page, is not yet ready."

"As you wish." He turned to Thomas who had kept an impassive face throughout despite the fact that he could hear every word, "Remember, Thomas Stockton, when you are ready to be knighted, I would be honoured to dub you."

Even now he was trying to do to me what Philip Augustus had done to him. He was tempting my son to betray me. He did not know my son and his answer was perfect, almost as though I had rehearsed him, which I had not!

"King Richard, I am both flattered and honoured by your offer and when I think I am worthy to be knighted by the King of England then I shall come and speak to you. Until then I am still learning how to be a knight. My family have long antecedents and I have much to live up to."

I did not get excited about the manors. Kings could take as well as give. I would ensure that the manors were well run before I left but I would not count on an income that might disappear the next time I offended the king.

The king's party rode through my town towards the Durham Road, cheered and applauded by my townsfolk who,

The Perfect Knight

like those in my castle, were honoured that the King of England should grace them with his presence.

Once they had gone, I had Thomas and Robin saddle our horses and we rode to each of my knights. I wanted them all to know that I did not expect them to follow the cross, but that King Richard had asked for them. They were all honoured and eagerly accepted the offer. Some would take men with them but it would be the choice of those men and I knew that married men would not join us. It would be the young men who sought adventure. For my part, I would be taking just my two men at arms who had survived Ballans, Mordaf and four archers. Even that might be too many. The archers agreed for extra pay along with Mordaf, to act as servants. That done we settled down to enjoy Christmas in Stockton knowing that the months of January and February would fly by and we would have to leave Stockton by the end of the first week of March to guarantee to be at the muster in Dartmouth for April. Devon was a long way from Stockton.

The Perfect Knight

Chapter 18

Dartmouth 1190

The hundred and twenty ships not only filled Dartmouth harbour but also the whole of the mouth of the River Dart. I saw now why this had been chosen as the muster point for the huge estuary was perfect for the gathering of such a fleet. I did not envy Richard de Camville and Robert de Sablé for they had to manage this fleet and accommodate all the knights. Some of those who had chosen to take the cross obviously thought themselves more important than others and when we arrived, we interrupted an argument between Richard de Camville and ten knights from the Welsh borders. I think that Richard de Camville was relieved to see me. I was a well-known, not to say notorious knight. I had defied kings and unhorsed King Richard. My arrival made the Welsh knights bow and forget their outrage briefly.

"Earl, the king said you would be here with your knights." He beckoned an over-worked clerk who had a wax tablet and a stylus. "How many are you, my lord? The king did not give specific numbers that you would bring."

"There are five knights and their squires, ten men at arms and ten archers and servants and of course our horses."

He beamed, "Perfect, my lord." He glared at the Welsh knights, "The cog, *'The Maid of Avalon'*, would seem to suit. Your horses would have to endure the open deck but there is a cabin that would be able to accommodate five knights. Some knights feel that such sharing is beneath them." The last comment was for the Welsh border knights' benefit.

The Perfect Knight

I smiled, "Just so long as the ship is sound, I care not for we go to save Jerusalem for Christ our lord endured far more than the problem of sharing a cabin with future knights!" I saw the Welsh knights squirm. "When do we board?"

"Not for a week yet, my lord. We are expecting almost a thousand more men from the land around Chester and North Wales. Most will be afoot. The manor house is at your disposal." He pointed, "It is at Norton, about half a mile west of Townstal. I can provide a guide if you wish, my lord."

"No, we shall stretch our legs, and while we have voices, we can ask for directions. Thank you for your courtesy, Sir Richard."

He beamed and said, as he bowed, "Would that all knights were so easy to deal with, my lord."

The manor house was comfortable and unlike the knights who had rejected Sir Richard's choice of cog, my knights and men were practical. They did not mind living cheek by jowl. In battle, we all depended upon each other and I knew, from my father and Masood, that the enemy we would fight in the Holy Land would be the hardest we had yet faced. We spent the week practising and grooming our horses which had a very long sea passage to endure. We watched as the tiny town filled up with the huge army that King Richard had summoned. I knew that when we reached Marseille our numbers would be swollen by the men King Richard would bring and our fleet would double in size as King Philip brought his crusaders.

I think that, thanks to the way I had spoken to Sir Richard, it ensured that we were amongst the first to be boarded and to set sail. The sheer numbers of ships meant that it would be a hard task to keep them together and yet that was a vital necessity. The boarding was simpler for us than others and the reason was that all of us, knights, men at arms, archers and squires, helped to coax and coerce the horses aboard. The men who would sleep on the hold deck were the ones who determined where the horses would be tethered. The hatches for the holds had been removed to make a more comfortable passage for the animals. If rough seas threatened the integrity of the vessel then the hatches could easily be replaced but so long as the weather was benign and the sun shone then the horses and the men who tended them would enjoy the fresh air. The single-masted ships did not need a large crew and if we became becalmed then it would be the passengers who would take on the role of rowers and man the oars. We all hoped for winds all the way.

It took two days for the fleet to gather just ten miles from the River Dart and then we set sail. The two knights charged with the delivery of the fleet to Marseille had an unenviable task. Some ships were faster than others and some crews less efficient. Richard de Camville and Robert de Sablé each commanded a small and nippy cog and they became sheepdogs harrying and chasing the tardier ones. Aboard ***'The Maid of Avalon'*** we enjoyed a pleasant time. I had thought to bring a chess set and it was pleasant, while the winds were gentle, to sit on the deck and play chess. The squires also entertained us. One of the skills needed by a knight was the skill to play an instrument and to sing. I had never had a good voice, but Thomas possessed a fine one as did some of the other squires and at sunset, while we would eat cold rations and drink wine they would sing songs of love and despair, knightly jousts and the slaying of dragons. The singing seemed to calm the animals. Other ships did not have the calm atmosphere of our ship and when we reached Marseille we heard of both men and horses that had suffered on the voyage. We were lucky.

Inevitably the weather changed and when it did then the fleet lost cohesion. After a rough day and night, we woke to find half the fleet had disappeared. Luckily Sir Richard and his ship were with us and after organizing us once more we set sail for the south. Portugal lay to the east and when, as we neared the mouth of the Tagus, we were approached by a strangely rigged vessel flying the new Portuguese flag we were curious rather than worried. One ship could not harm such a mighty fleet. We hove to under reefed sails. The ship was directed to Sir Richard's. After a while, the Portuguese ship headed south and east. Sir Richard signalled that he wished to speak with each ship. Using a speaking trumpet he told us that King Sancho of Portugal had been threatened by an Almohad fleet. These Berbers of North Africa had conquered large parts of the Iberian Peninsula. We had been requested to help them and Sir Richard had agreed. The details were not elaborated upon, but I guessed that our aid would be rewarded by food and water. After he had visited each part of the fleet, we set sail to follow the path taken by the Portuguese vessel.

Tam the Hawker commanded our small contingent of archers and I ordered him to man the sterncastle. We placed all the shields around the gunwale, and we armed ourselves. Although I did not think that the knights and men at arms would have to fight it was as well to be prepared. I saw when we met the Portuguese fleet, why our aid had been requested. They were fewer in number than we were. However, the two combined fleets outnumbered the galleys of the Almohads. Despite all the battles in which I had participated I had never fought at sea and I was more curious than anything although I was a little nervous too. Unlike a fight on land, a fall here would be fatal. A man in mail does not float.

Turning to Tam I said, "Do not waste arrows, Tam, and use only war arrows."

Looking at me as though I was trying to teach him to suck eggs he nodded, "Aye, my lord, we know our business."

I realised that my nerves had made me speak merely to fill a silence. I nodded and determined to say as little as possible.

The captains of our fleet had good reason to hate the Berbers. The Almohads were not only conquerors of the land but also pirates and any vessel taken would have its crews sent to row on their galleys. They were happy to close with the Almohads. Our cogs were all clinker-built. That meant they were sturdier and could endure the Atlantic. The Almohad vessels and the Portuguese were carvel-built and while that was a cheaper and quicker form of construction it also made for weaker vessels. The difference became clear once the confused battle began. Our stern and bow castles afforded the archers on our ships the advantage of height and our captains put us close enough so that arrows could be rained down upon the open galleys. While the oars on the galleys made them more manoeuvrable, the favourable winds made our cogs just as nimble. Our captain took great delight in sending our ship down the side of a galley to crush, crack and splinter the oars. From our vantage point on the sterncastle, I saw men speared by their own oars while others were wounded with shards of wood sheared from the shattered oars. Worse was to follow for the Almohad ship we had damaged. The weight of **'The Maid of Avalon'** sprang some of the strakes of the Almohad hull and as we pulled away, we saw it start to sink. We only sank one ship, but it cheered each of us. The Berbers were not Turks but they were similar warriors and not only had we met them but in our single combat we had won. By the time darkness fell the Almohads had been defeated and we had not lost a single ship. The problem we had was that the men now thought that all the enemies we would meet would be as easy to defeat as the Almohad ships. I had never fought against the Turks, but my father had and I knew that he had the utmost respect for these warriors. It would not be as easy to retake Jerusalem.

We did not set sail again until the next day having been revictualled by the Portuguese and as we neared the Pillars of Hercules we saw, ahead of us, the sails of the rest of our fleet. As we entered the Mediterranean Sea we were reunited.

The difference between the two seas was nothing short of spectacular. We left the grey Atlantic with its troughs and stormy tipped waves to a flatter, almost benign blue water. The winds were not as helpful, but the sea seemed to be warmer and we discarded our mail for it grew too hot. The cabin became a place of refuge from the hot sun which the captain assured us would only get hotter the closer we came to the Holy Land. When I had been a child growing up in Outremer, I had not noticed the sun. When you are a child it does not bother you but as I watched men's skin redden and then blister, I remembered my mother smearing lotions on our father's skin. She had not needed the lotion for she was

The Perfect Knight

olive-skinned, and we had her blood. I hoped that Thomas had inherited protection from the sun from his grandmother!

Marseille harbour was filled with ships already and we were forced to anchor in the roads a mile out to sea. The two knights charged with the delivery of the fleet went ashore to meet with King Richard. Our half of the fleet was still well-victualled thanks to our fight with the Almohads but the other half was desperate for fresh water and food. Soon local ships were sent to revictual us for the voyage to Sicily. When Sir Richard came back to see us he told us that we would be sailing along the coast of France, Savoy and Italy. King Philip had hired Genoese ships and they would guarantee that his boats were not attacked. The Genoese ruled the Mediterranean. Our king had tired of waiting and had already set off, eager as he was to rescue his sister. King Richard showed his cunning and guile. He had left us orders to fly the Genoese flag from our masts. The red cross on the white background would be a warning to any pirate who thought to take easy plunder.

We left the next day, the 7th of August for Sicily. We had one hundred and eighty ships and over thirty galleys. King Richard's haste had also been determined by the rivalry between the two kings. Both wished to be the first to reach Sicily and thence the Holy Land. It was still a competition between the two kings. Both wanted to be the unchallenged leader of the mighty crusade. When they reached the Holy Land, they would have to vie with Emperor Frederick Barbarossa for control of the largest Crusader army for over a century.

In our haste to catch King Richard, the two knights in charge of the fleet took the opportunity to sail between Sardinia and Corsica. The result was that we reached Messina ahead of the king on September 14th. I knew, from my conversation with the king at Stockton that he was coming to Sicily, not with the same intention as King Philip. King Philip would be using it to replenish supplies before the last part of the voyage. King Richard was coming to free his sister and to punish King Tancred. We were unsure of our welcome and so although we moored in the harbour, we did not attempt to land except to buy supplies. Our horses were desperate to be off the ships and their coats told us that they had suffered on the long voyage from Dartmouth. We had to wait a week before King Richard finally arrived and we were able to land. King Richard had visited places in Italy to gain more allies. He knew that such alliances could only help England. He had learned that from his father. As soon as we landed then King Tancred retreated inside his fortress.

King Richard was determined to rescue his sister and that was his priority. I just wanted our horses landed. While the fortress was surrounded by the foot soldiers brought by King Richard, the knights and mounted men led their horses to learn how to walk again and to give them grass. There was precious little of the latter to be had close to the city and I took the decision to take my men some way from the city and to camp where there was grass. I left my knights and men at arms to watch them and Thomas and I bought two poor sumpters from a local farmer to ride back to Messina. That I had left without speaking to the king displeased him.

"I expected my lieutenants to be here so that I could give commands! Why did you leave?"

"King Richard, our horses were aboard our ship for almost six weeks. I assumed that you would want them ready to be used in war when we reach the Holy Land. You do not need horsemen to scale Messina's walls and my men can assault the fortress, if that is necessary, whenever you need them. They are just an hour away."

He seemed mollified, but continued to chastise me, "This will be good practice for when we take Jerusalem's walls. Bring back your men!"

"As you wish." The king turned on his heel and I said, "Thomas, have my men return here. You and the squires can watch the horses." I saw the disappointment on his face and shook my head, "You will be missing nothing. King Tancred does not have the men to withstand a single attack. This is one king trying to show another that he does not fear him. Sicilians will die when they need not!"

The Perfect Knight

The king was right in one respect, it was a rehearsal for what we might expect in the Holy Land. The castle was surrounded, and men prepared ladders and siege engines. The Normans who had captured the island from the Arabs had improved the ancient defences so that it would not be an easy siege. King Richard was in his element for this was war and that was the whole purpose of his life. In addition, he was rescuing his sister. Most of the men had not made siege engines. The manufacture of rams was not as easy as most of us thought. It had been a long time since I had witnessed men making rams and that had been in England. I confess that I had not paid much attention to the process for I had been a young squire at the time. However, by a process of trial and error, as well as working together, we finally constructed the ladders and the rams as well as trebuchets and stone-throwers. By the 3rd of October, we were ready to assault. This was a new experience for all of us but having defended the Tower of London from rebels and enemies I had a little more understanding of what the defenders might do. I was given one ladder for my men to use. The rams we had made would attack the gates and King Richard hoped that the use of over fifty ladders, each with up to fifty men climbing them, then the defenders would not be able to resist all of them.

As we mustered in the cool of pre-dawn, I gathered my men around me. "Tam, as soon as it is light then you and our archers can clear the top of the ladder. They will hurl stones, darts, spears and, perhaps, use boiling oil. You need to give us as much protection as you can." He nodded, resolutely. "I will lead." I held up my shield, "You use your right hand to pull yourself up the rungs of the ladder and keep your shield well above your head. You use it to support you when you have to let go with your right."

"What about your sword?"

I shook my head, "Sir Ralph, until you reach the crenulations then your sword is your enemy. It can trip you and make you lose your grip. Your weapon, until you can leap over the wall, is your shield. The edges are hard and sharp. Use them. Your helmets can be used to inflict injuries and you pray that your mail will hold. If they use a mace or an axe, then they may hurt you and stop you. Keep close to me and when we are on the fighting platform, we make it safe until all have climbed the wall. It is then, Tam the Hawker, that you will fetch our archers!"

We waited in the darkness with our men at arms holding the ladder and I could feel the nervousness amongst the men. That the Normans who held the castle would be doughty fighters was clear, but I also knew that the fanatics who held Jerusalem and Acre would be a far more difficult prospect. Perhaps King Richard was right, and we did need this rehearsal.

The sun broke from behind us; the king had used the rising sun to shine into the eyes of our enemies and his horns sounded. The first blast was for the archers to begin their rain of arrows and for the stone throwers to hurl their missiles at the fighting platform. The second blast set off the rams and it was the third blast that made us run towards the walls. With my shield before me, I led my men. A few desultory crossbow bolts crashed into my shield but the attack by the archers, stone-throwers and rams had made the crossbowmen loose their weapons prematurely. It takes time to reload. I knew that the Seljuk Turks would be a more difficult prospect as they would use bows! We passed some bodies as we ran but they were not the archers of my retinue and I ran all the faster. Gerard and Martyn placed the ladder against the wall and then leaned against it as I began my climb.

"God be with you, my lord!"

Nodding to Martyn I stepped on the ladder. I had removed my spurs and my sabatons. Buskins made climbing an easier task and I climbed as fast as I could. I reached up with my right hand, the shield on my left hand protecting me and I did not let go until my right hand was level with my waist. I then used my left hand to grasp both the strap of the shield and the rung of the ladder above my head. It was not as fast progress as I might have liked but when I heard a scream from my right as a man at arms plunged to his death, I knew that it was the right thing to do. Darts smacked into

The Perfect Knight

my shield and when a huge stone was dropped, I almost lost my grip for I was holding the ladder, at that moment, with my left hand. A scream from above and a shadowy body that fell from the wall told me that one of my archers had ensured that another stone would not be dropped any time soon.

I was aware that I was almost at the top and prepared to fight for my life. Sir Ralph was right behind me, his shield had touched the back of my leg and so as soon as I saw the gap in the stones I did not hesitate. With my shield held like a dagger, I dived at the Norman spearman who held his spear to stab me. My unorthodox attack confused him, and my shield knocked the spear up and him down to the fighting platform. His helmet straps broke and I headbutted him. I sensed rather than saw the spear which was thrust at me and I rolled from the unconscious Norman as his comrade speared him rather than me. Sir Ralph had an easier approach and as he stepped onto the fighting platform, he drew his sword and stabbed the man who would have speared me. I stood and drawing my sword was back to back with Sir Ralph, as first Sir Roger and then Sir William climbed to join us.

A Norman knight ran at me and I blocked his swing. He had the battlements to his right and had to swing from on high. In contrast, my blow was a sideways sweep and my sword smashed into his shield and he lurched to his right. The arrow which struck him in the neck was from Tam the Hawker, I recognised the fletch. As Gerard and Martyn joined me, I shouted, "Let us take the gate!"

We ran down the fighting platform, but the resistance was broken. King Richard's plan had succeeded. The attack on multiple points had spread the defenders so much that by the time we reached the towers and stairs which led to the outer bailey the castle had surrendered. We had won and Messina, not to mention Sicily, was ours.

I knew that we would not leave immediately for I had already told the king that our horses needed time to recover and besides, it would soon be winter and even the Mediterranean was not a sea to be trifled with in winter. However, when Queen Eleanor arrived in the New Year I

The Perfect Knight

wondered if we would leave at all. I had thought that the Queen Mother of England had come to be with her newly released daughter, but she came with Berengaria of Navarre. I was just a knight, admittedly one who in his own lands was considered powerful, but I was not privy to the plotting and plans of kings and queens. Berengaria of Navarre was to be King Richard's wife. The marriage had been brokered by Queen Eleanor. She was still the most powerful woman in Europe. Had the news become common knowledge sooner than it did then King Philip might have left for the Holy Land immediately. He did not learn that his half-sister, Alys, had now been abandoned. Worse was to follow. A rumour was spread that the reason Richard did not marry Alys was that his father had bedded the French princess. I would not have put it past King Henry but when the news reached King Philip, he immediately ordered his men to leave Sicily. The alliance was over and the ramifications of that did not bear thinking about. We had already heard that Emperor Barbarossa had died on his way to the Holy Land and that the few Imperial troops who remained were commanded by his son Frederick. The papal plan to retake Jerusalem looked to be in tatters before we had even left Sicily.

It was not until the 10th of April that we finally left Sicily. Our fleet had been swollen now to one hundred and eighty ships and thirty-nine galleys. King Richard had taken money from the treasury of Sicily and he added it to the coins we had for the crusade. Had there been a pirate fleet big enough then we would have made a tempting prize. We set sail for the Holy Land. Arne Arneson had been one of the Warlord's men and he had been of Scandinavian descent. As a child I had listened to the stories told by the old, scarred warrior and one which stuck in my mind was of three sisters who interfered in the affairs of men to make mischief. A few days after we left Sicily a storm suddenly blew up from nowhere. Ships were scattered all over the sea and when it abated, we found ourselves alone and off the coast of Cyprus. The island was part of the Eastern Roman Empire and was ruled by Isaac Dukas Comnenus.

The Perfect Knight

Our captain decided to seek shelter in a Cypriot port for we had suffered damage to the ship. As we headed east towards Limassol, we found more of our fleet, but we also saw, beached and guarded by Imperial troops, some of our ships. Our captain recognised the one which had carried the former Queen of Sicily, the king's sister Joan. We went close enough to see that some of the men who had been on the ships had been killed and their bodies lay on the beach.

"My lord, what do we do? It seems to me that the Imperial troops have taken Queen Joan and, perhaps the treasure they carried. It means that Limassol may not be the friendly port we hoped for."

There were, perhaps, a dozen ships close by, but we were the largest and that made me the most senior knight. "We continue to sail around the island, and we will pick up other ships. We try to find King Richard but, if we cannot, then we land and try to rescue Queen Joan. It is our duty."

Relieved that someone else had made the decision the captain set sail and signalled for the others to follow us. I wondered if we were fated never to get to the Holy Land. By the time we passed Limassol harbour we had seen more ships that had been beached and were guarded. The Duke of Cyprus had taken advantage of the storm.

"Captain, turn us around and head west." He looked puzzled, "We came from the west and we have seen that on the southern coast of Cyprus there are beached ships. The rest of our fleet is more likely to be to the west or the north of the island." He nodded and obeyed. All those chess games with the Warlord were paying off for they had given me a logical mind that enabled me to eliminate unnecessary problems and come up with a solution that might offer success. We found the bulk of our fleet to the northwest of the island, in a bay called Denizli by the locals. More importantly, the king was there and had set up a camp on the beach. I landed quickly and told him what he had seen.

He nodded grimly, "Aye, we are here because we saw Imperial troops attacking the ships which had been beached. We have a war, Sir Samuel but it is not of my making. Before we can retake Jerusalem, we must rescue my sister once more and teach the duke of this island the price of piracy!"

It took some days but we gathered the other survivors and landed our horses and men. We marched across the island. Our large numbers prevented any attacks by the Imperial troops but our progress was slow because of the terrain. We reached Limassol on the 6th of May. Isaac Dukas Comnenus quickly realised his mistake and immediately apologised to King Richard and returned not only the captured women but also all the treasure. In addition, he promised King Richard five hundred Imperial troops to aid us on the crusade. King Richard saw the incident as a sign that he should not procrastinate and on the 12th of May, he and Berengaria of Navarre were married in the chapel of St George in Limassol. Any chance of a reconciliation with King Philip ended with that marriage.

Chapter 19

Acre 1191

The castle at Acre was still in Muslim hands and the Christian forces, led by Guy de Lusignan, Leopold of Austria, King Philip of France and Conrad of Montferrat had failed to dislodge them. That may have been because they themselves were besieged by Saladin's huge army. We landed close to the Christian camp on the 8th of June. As soon as he landed, King Richard insisted upon taking charge of the huge army. That King Philip and Duke Leopold objected did not worry King Richard. As ever he knew his own mind. The Christian camp, to be fair to King Richard, was in disarray. It had been a hard winter and dysentery and disease had rampaged through the camp. The deaths had not been confined to the ordinary soldiers: Frederick of Swabia, Patriarch Heraclius of Jerusalem, and Theobald V of Blois had all died. It had been Leopold of Austria who had commanded until our arrival but King Richard was not about to put his army, which he considered the biggest and the best, in the hands of a mere duke. He smiled and he asked opinions but unless the other lords agreed then their views would be ignored. There were also politics within the camp. Guy de Lusignan was King of Jerusalem through his marriage to Sibylla, but the rightful ruler was Sibylla's sister, Isabella. When Isabella was hastily married off to Conrad of Montferrat then he had a claim to the crown. When Leopold and Philip supported Conrad and his claim then it was clear to me that King Richard would side with Guy de Lusignan.

For the first days, we were acclimatising our horses to the heat. I was not surprised by it but the rest of the warriors in the English army were. We had landed in the heat of summer and it was a foretaste of the problems we would have. The reasons for the adoption of a surcoat became clear. Mail without a covering would burn bare flesh. We were camped but I had chosen a place which was far enough from other tents to afford us some relief from any disease and also allowed a free passage of air. I made sure that we had a good supply of water and it was close to the limited grazing. Thomas was now my right-hand man. The journey from England had been a long one and he had learned new skills along the way. He felt less like a squire and more like a brother knight. I liked the new relationship. This had all been helped by Robin's presence for the young lad was happy to look after horses and to do the fetching and carrying that had been Thomas' task.

King Richard ordered the building of ladders and rams. The experience of Sicily came in handy and the lessons we had learned there helped us to make them far faster than some of the other contingents. This time my knights were assigned to a ram and so we concentrated on making a ram that would keep us safe. The Turks knew how to use boiling oil, fat, and water to make life unpleasant for those attacking. I sent my archers foraging and they took a cow which was slaughtered for food and its hide used for the top of the ram. We soaked the wood with water and fastened the almost raw hide to the roof. The rams we had made at Messina had proved difficult to move and so Gerard suggested we use grease on the wheels. Finally, with our ram completed before those of Austria and France, we practised moving it. That simple act proved vital. It seemed logical to put the knights at the front and the men at arms behind but it was a case of matching men who were the same size. I found myself third from the front. It helped us to move the ram more quickly and speed was always useful. A slow approach would allow the stone-throwers on Acre's walls more time to hit the slow-moving rams. Our own trebuchet and stone throwers would be much bigger than the ones we had used at Messina for the walls of Acre were much bigger.

The Perfect Knight

Ten days after our arrival at Acre I visited King Richard to tell him of our progress. He seemed in an ebullient mood. Waving a hand at the camps which were filled with toiling men he said, "We will have this town within a month and yet our allies have wasted time and efforts. It is little wonder that Saladin holds Jerusalem. It is as though Duke Leopold was waiting for some sort of divine intervention!"

"To be fair, my lord, he did not have the men we now have!"

"You are too kind, Sir Samuel." He leaned closer to me, "I have sent a message to this Seljuk Turk, Saladin, and asked for a meeting. I would have single combat with him to settle this matter. That is the way a knight should conduct himself."

I was doubtful that the Muslim warrior would agree to such a combat. "And has he replied, my lord?"

"Not yet but I am hopeful."

It was at our meeting two days later that King Richard proffered a parchment before him, "This Saladin plays games. He tells me that kings only meet when peace had been agreed and it is not seemly for them to make war upon each other. He is a cunning man. He hopes to have us hold a truce and stop our plans to take Acre. That sort of ploy might have worked with Duke Leopold, but I am made of sterner stuff." He tossed the missive to the table. "Your ram is completed?"

"It is."

He nodded, "Most of those under our construction are but the Austrians and the French are tardy. I do not know if I should wait for them. We could take it ourselves."

"Is that wise, my lord? After all, it might make our allies more resentful and we would lose more of our men. A few more days cannot hurt."

"You may be right, but this delay prevents us from bringing the main Muslim army to battle. I had hoped that our arrival would prompt Saladin to bring his army and to fight us. It seems he does not value Acre as much as we thought and he is happy to besiege our siege lines. Perhaps when we have taken Acre we might move on to Jaffa. We

The Perfect Knight

need to take that town before we can move on to Jerusalem." He smiled at me, "As you have finished early then take your horses and scout out the road to Jaffa. I have reports from the Austrians and King Guy, but I would have your eyes give a truer report."

"Of course, my lord, although from my memory I think Jaffa will be too far but we can scout out the road and assess the problems we might face." In truth, I was happy to do so. My men would enjoy the ride in this new land and the horses needed the exercise. They had become acclimatised, but they still needed exercise to make them ready for war. Jaffa was too far away, more than fifty miles, for us to get a really close look at it but I thought we might be able to scout at least half of that distance.

I ordered the squires to check the reins, bridles, girths, and saddles. This was neither England nor Aquitaine. Any faulty equipment might result in not just a fall from a horse but death. I spoke with Mordaf and Tam the Hawker. "I know that this land is unknown to you, but I trust to our skills. As I recall the road here follows the coast. There are villages on the way, but they will not be defended. The first stronghold is the one taken by Baldwin almost ninety years ago, Caesarea Palestinae, The Turks retook it three years since and they will have strengthened it. If we can reach the port, I will be happy but as our ships can scout it out, I will not be worried if we do not reach it. The army will march down the plain and we need to see where our enemies might try to bring us to battle."

I had acquired white surcoats for my conroi as well as white cowled cloaks. King Richard had liked the red cross of the Genoese and so my men and squires sewed those on the surcoats. It was not that I did not wish to ride with my gryphon livery but that the white cloth seemed to make us cooler. My father had given me that invaluable information. Our shields still bore my livery but when we rode, with the cowls of our cloaks over our mailed heads, we all looked identical. Even the archers wore the white over their padded jerkins. Mordaf and one of Sir Ralph's archers, James, rode forty paces ahead of my archers who each carried a strung

The Perfect Knight

bow. Before we had left England, I had bought many bowstrings as I thought it prudent to do so.

We left not long after the sun rose to take advantage of the relative coolness. As we headed down the dusty Roman Road with the heat already shimmering from it, the memories of living at Aqua Bella flooded back. My former home was now in Muslim hands as was most of the Holy Land. Saladin had ruthlessly taken back all the gains made in the Second Crusade. There were, however, still those who had lived by the coast when it was ruled by Christians and not all the looks we received were aggressive. We were offered water and smiles in some places. That boded well for King Richard. Of course, some of the villages had been scoured of all vestiges of Christianity and in those places, we found barred doors. I had a wooden board and a charcoal scribe with me and I marked the map as we headed south. I also marked each place where there was water. That would determine where we would camp each night.

We stopped at a tiny fishing village, well before noon when it would be too hot for us to bear. We sheltered in the shade of the handful of houses. This was a Muslim village, and none came out to offer us either food or water. I had the squires draw water from the well. The fishing boats had yet to return, and I felt that we were safe.

Sir William shook his head, "It is hard enough to ride in this heat let alone fight. How does King Richard expect us to fight when the heat of the sun saps all our energy from us?"

"Others did so, William. This is the third such crusade and I take hope from the fact that Jerusalem was held by us and I believe it will be again."

I noticed that the men at arms and archers were taking advantage of the rest and, the sentries apart, were sleeping or lying with their eyes closed. They were the sensible ones. It was my knights and squires who, like me, could not rest who were chattering like magpies.

Martyn Longsword was on watch and it was he who came to warn me of the danger, "My lord, horsemen approach. They appear to be Muslim."

The Perfect Knight

I did not say that any horseman we saw would be an enemy. Martyn was just doing what I had asked of him, "To arms! Archers, be ready to loose arrows. Mordaf, squires, hold the horses. Let us see if they wish to dispute our occupation of their land."

When I mounted Storm Bringer, I had a much better view of the Turks and I saw that there were forty horsemen riding towards us. The sun reflected from the metal of helmets and spears. We had brought no spears, but I hefted my shield to protect my left side and slipped my sword in and out of its scabbard.

It was clear when the Turks shouted and dug their heels into the flanks of their horses that their intentions were hostile. "Tam, when you are ready!"

"Aye, lord! Archers, choose your target and be ready for my command." I knew that they would be using war arrows; the horses were not mailed.

"The rest of you form up on me and obey all my commands immediately. Squires and pages behind." I kept my voice calm despite the trepidation I felt within. I was confident fighting Norman knights because I could predict not only what they would do but the best way to defeat them. These Muslim riders were an unknown force and might have armour and weapons we might find hard to defeat. I wished that I had spoken to my father more about his battles. There had been time for such talks but other things had seemed more important at the time. I saw now that they were not as important as I had thought. What he had told me was of the ability of their horse archers to loose from the back of a horse. It was the design of the bow that allowed them to do so and it was as they came within range of my archers that I saw the advantage in such warriors. Tam and his archers must have known of the ability of men loosing from the back of a horse for they targeted the horse archers. That left the bulk of the men, the ones with spears, round shields, and curved swords to come towards us. I knew that if we simply waited for them to strike at us, they would have a better chance of winning. Our horses were larger and theirs, I suspected, nimbler.

The Perfect Knight

Drawing my sword I spurred Storm Bringer. As arrows were flying from both sets of archers it made sense for us to close with their other warriors. "Charge them and let us see what our English steel can do against them."

I saw that four of their leading warriors wore mail. I seemed to remember that they were called askari. I charged at the leading one who held a spear. I had been right, the horses, though smaller were nimbler and the askari jerked his reins to the side with his left hand whilst thrusting at me with the spear in his right. The spear struck my cloak and white surcoat. It tore them but did little harm. I felt like a fool as my sword flailed at fresh air. I was luckier with the second warrior who was not an askari but had a padded gambeson as well as helmet and spear. He was hemmed in on both sides by two of his brothers in arms and whilst he tried to move away, he was unable to do so and swinging from on high, for Storm Bringer was taller than his horse, my sword hacked deep into his neck and shoulder. It was a mortal blow. Storm Bringer then lunged at the next Muslim horse which shied and then reared as it tried to get away from the teeth of my warhorse. I stabbed with my sword and found flesh. Twisting the sword I withdrew it. The slithery ball of red snakes which emerged told me that he too was a dead man.

I was about to order my men to hold when one of the askari shouted something and the enemy turned and fled. Tam and my archers plucked another four from their saddles before they were out of range. I whirled in my saddle to view the field. One of Sir Ralph's men at arms lay speared. The awkward angle at which he lay told me he was dead. Another, Sir Roger's this time, was bandaging his arm. Our archers were whole. I saw that while we had not killed any of their askari six other warriors and four archers lay dead. I waved to Tam to have his archers search the bodies. The horses of the dead were well trained, and they had followed the survivors south.

"I think we have learned enough for King Richard, let us head home. Bring our dead with us"

As we rode, with four archers as a rearguard, their instincts would tell us if we were pursued, I spoke to the

The Perfect Knight

other knights. Sir William shook his head, "It is like trying to catch a will o'the wisp! Their horses are more agile than ours."

"But our archers had the better of their encounter." Sir Ralph turned and pointed south, "The reason they fled was that Tam hit one of the askari in the shoulder. It must have been a bodkin and they did not relish more of them."

"You are right Sir Roger, but King Richard brought mainly spearmen and knights. Had he brought three thousand Welsh archers instead of the three thousand spearmen and knights, we might have a better chance."

It was late afternoon when we reached the camp, and I went directly to King Richard's tent. Inside there was a row going on and I recognised King Philip's voice. The days of King Richard following the advice of the French King were long gone. When the Austrian voice spoke, I knew that I was hearing an argument that suggested that the alliance was in danger of breaking up. I took a chance and, nodding to the two spearmen to raise their spears I stepped inside.

"I am sorry, King Richard, I did not know you were in conference."

The three faces were all angry and they turned to face me. King Richard said, "It was not a conference, Sir Samuel. These two fools cannot see that we have no time to waste while their men take too long building the machines your men built in two days. I can now see why so little progress has been made."

Duke Leopold almost spat out his words such was his anger, "You have not even been here a month. What makes you so sure that you are right?"

King Richard smiled, "Unlike you, Duke Leopold, I have fought in wars before and I know my business. When we took Messina we attacked simultaneously around the walls and it worked. Acre is bigger but we have more men at our disposal." He shook his head as though he tired of having to explain his thoughts to men he thought to be his inferiors, "I attack the day after tomorrow whether you are ready or not. When my horn sounds three times then we will advance as

The Perfect Knight

one. When I win it will be my standard that flies from Acre's tower."

It was a deliberate spur to encourage them into action and the two men stormed out. Neither gave me a second glance. King Richard smiled. He enjoyed playing games like this where he could intimidate people. He was a supremely confident man. "Well, how did the scouting expedition turn out?"

I told him of the different attitudes we had encountered and when I spoke of the attack he leaned forward eagerly. "You are an experienced knight. What did you make of them?"

"They are very difficult to fight against. Because most of them do not wear mail and ride smaller horses then it might appear that they are weaker, but they are not. Their horses can move very quickly and as one of my knights said it was like trying to fight a ghost. He was there one minute and gone the next. It is their horse archers that I would fear. Their range is the same as our war bows, but they can fight from the backs of their horses and ride away. I did not see it, but my father said that some could loose over the backs of their horses."

"Do they have bodkin arrows?"

I shrugged, "I did not see any, but I will ask my archers. They have an eye for that sort of thing."

"You have done well. Your map and the identification of the watering places will help us. You heard my command to those two?" I nodded. "That was not bravado, I intend to do it. You will be ready." It was not a question but a command. I nodded and left.

The next morning the trebuchets and mangonels began their rain of stones upon the walls. It told them more clearly than anything that we were about to attack. The defenders close to the stone throwers prevented a sortie but Saladin and the army he had brought to relieve the siege began to attack our camp. Guy de Lusignan, the Knights Templar, and the Knights Hospitallers kept them at bay. There were two battles going on and we were in the middle!

The Perfect Knight

It was clear to the defenders of Acre what we were about for the rams which had been built were dragged into a position beyond the range of the smaller stone-throwers on the walls. Our own stone-throwers kept them busy on the walls and we were able to bring the ram close enough to the walls to give us the shortest of journeys the next morning. Buildings had already been cleared by the Austrians and other warriors who had unsuccessfully attacked the walls before our arrival. We spent the rest of the morning before it was too hot to work, clearing stones and rubble from our route to the walls. My knights and I rested and ate in the shade of the ram while we examined the walls. Talking about such matters was never wasted.

"There is a ditch we might need to cross."

Sir William stood to peer across the open ground, "It is next to the road, Sir Samuel. We should be able to use the road and attack the gate."

"You may be right, William, for I hope and believe that our ram shall be the one that will reach there first but in the unlikely possibility that we are not I would have timbers tied to the roof so that we can use them to cross the ditch if we have to."

Sir Ralph shook his head, "That will make it heavier, lord. It will be harder to push."

"Perhaps but we will have more protection from stones." I smiled, "Sir Ralph, we are damned if we do and damned if we do not. War is about taking risks, but it is also about preparing for as many eventualities as we can. I have not noticed others doing as we did and trying out the ram. We know what to expect." I waved a hand in the direction of the French camp from whence we heard the sound of hammers and saws as they tried to build their war machines as quickly as they could. "The Austrians and the French have yet to build theirs. They will only discover their problems when they move towards the walls."

Sir Richard of Hartburn laughed, "Aye, and that will be this evening when they have spent a day building them."

"And if I know the French knights, they will not be like us and they will let the labourers who built them have the

The Perfect Knight

task of moving them. We might not have enjoyed building the ram but we are all familiar with it. Do not forget that we will be one of the few rams moving forward that will be supported by archers. Tam and our bowmen will follow us."

Sir Richard nodded, "It is good, Sir Samuel, that the men of our manors fight together. Oswald the Pig is looking forward to showing Tam that he is his equal as an archer. The men of Hartburn are very competitive."

Thomas asked, "Why is he called Oswald the Pig, Sir Richard? Does he look like a pig?"

Sir Richard and his squire, William, both laughed, and his squire said, "No, Tom, his father has a pig farm close to the Oxbridge and when we train Oswald always brings meat from the farm. The men like pig meat."

Sir Roger shook his head sadly, "And I think we will get little such fare here in this land. I tire of the taste of salted meat. You lived here, Sir Samuel, what meat do the folk eat?"

"Lamb and goat are popular while fish is readily available. I think that once the killing starts then horsemeat might be our staple diet for this is a land that will take its toll on our warhorses."

By the time we returned to our camp, having left some of our archers to watch the ram, we were wreathed in sweat. I knew that when we fought, we would tire far faster than in England or France. We needed to be as quick as we could so that we would be fighting in the early hours of the day. If the fighting lasted longer than a few hours then men would die. This was not our land.

After eating we went to the priests for absolution. In a perfect world, we would be absolved just before we attacked but that would be almost impossible. Thomas and I walked back to our camp together. The sun had not been set for long but we would retire as soon as we reached the camp. King Richard had arranged for the Imperial troops who had come with us from Cyprus to guard our camp. They would not be used in the attack for King Richard wanted it to be a Plantagenet victory, untainted by others.

The Perfect Knight

"Thomas, if I should fall tomorrow then bury my bones here. I was born in this land and I will be buried here. My soul will find your mother's in heaven."

"You will not die!" He smiled and then, after a moment said, "But where will be your marker? Where can men come to pay their respects?"

I tapped my sword, "Take this back to England; bury this."

He nodded and said, "But you will not die. Remember that tomorrow the squires do not hold the horses, we push the ram from without and I shall watch your back!"

"And I hope not to die but we have been shriven and it is as well to contemplate the worst so that tomorrow evening we will enjoy the wine and the food all the more. Life is to be celebrated, Thomas. I now know that. We have no guarantee of a long life and those who plan for years ahead are deluding themselves. If I should die tomorrow, then I am ready." I grinned, "And tomorrow night our conversation will be more cheerful." He nodded, "I gestured towards Robin who seemed to think that this was all a game, "And watch out for Robin, eh, he is young and it would be good if he lived to become a warrior."

"I will do all that I can."

Chapter 20

Our sleep was cut short when we were roused by the night guards to take our positions. The noise from the camp must have alerted the defenders but there was little we could do. Moving such a large number of men was not easy. The French and Austrian rams were dragged into position and the groaning and creaking would have woken those sleeping in Jerusalem! King Richard had chosen the main gate for the English attack. It meant that the other attackers would have an easier task. The main two gates were the best defended. He saw it as a matter of honour. As we made our way to the ram the other contingents of English, Norman and Gascon attackers followed with ladders. They would have to hope that they made the walls before dawn broke. The defenders had not only bows but also the crossbows they had taken when they had captured the castle. Daylight would rain death upon the men with the ladders. We had brought buckets of seawater for the squires and pages to carry in case they were needed to douse any small fires. They would not be of much use against a direct hit on the ram, but the odd spark might be snuffed out.

It was as we stepped into the Stygian darkness of a ram wreathed in night's cloak that I smelled the fires. I did not speak aloud but I knew that they were heating something to pour upon us. It would be a fiery and painful death if they did so. I knew, from talks with my grandfather, that oil, fat and even boiling water care nothing about mail and would insinuate itself beneath surcoat, mail, and gambeson. Boiling water would be the least painful but burning oil and fat would do more than scald the skin. I put those thoughts from my head and stood behind the bar that I would be using to push the ram. Our practice enabled us to find our places quickly. I knew that I was disobeying orders by going early but I took the decision to start us moving.

"On my count let us start to move but slowly, making as little noise as we can. It is cool and we know that the next three hundred paces are clear." There was a murmur of approval.

I heard Thomas and Robin pass on my words and Tam the Hawker said, "Our bows are strung, my lord. May God be with you."

Sir Richard said, "And if he is not with us in this, his chosen land, then we are all truly doomed!"

The men said, "Amen!" They were trusting that God did, indeed, wish us to win.

"Three, two, one, push!"

We had practised this the previous day and we all pushed off with our right feet. As we had discovered it took time to get the ram moving. We had taken five steps before I thought we had managed to leave our starting point. Of course, entombed in the wooden ram there was no point of reference. There was a slight incline on the road we had cleared. We knew that. We also had seen that there was a slight dip where the road descended towards the ditch. I was counting the steps and we had taken sixty when I heard the horn sound. Sir Ralph might have been right. We might not need the extra weight of the timber we carried on our roof, but it was too late to worry and now that the horn had sounded all need for silence and stealth were gone.

I began a chant. I had heard it when I was young, and I knew not why it came to mind but it did. Perhaps the spirit of my father brought it to me. The chant helped our rhythm and as the men joined in seemed to give us heart.

Stockton men fight the fight
Through the day and all the night
The Warlord's sword is straight and true
Stockton's men will come for you
Stockton men fight the fight
Through the day and all the night

The Perfect Knight

The Warlord's sword is straight and true
Stockton's men will come for you

The verses were repeated and said little but, amazingly, the ram seemed to be easier to push or, perhaps, we were on the downhill section. Tam, the archers, and our squires were our eyes. They shouted when we deviated from the line and warned us of obstacles. We were lucky and, thanks to the fact that we had chosen our men carefully, we kept a straight line.

"Ware stone throwers! They are using fireballs!"

The fires I had smelled now made sense. The chant continued but I knew that every man was now more nervous. I was awaiting the crack of a missile and then the heat as we were set afire. From our right, I heard such a crack and then screams. One of our rams had been hit; that was an advantage of the tomb-like ram. You could not see your comrades dying. A few paces closer to the walls we were hit. The blow was not as heavy as I had expected but I braced myself for the fire.

Suddenly Thomas shouted, "Cut the ropes which bind the timbers!"

We kept moving despite the heat I could feel from above. When the ram shifted quicker than it had then I knew that the timbers were gone.

Thomas shouted, "The timbers are burning but the roof is sound! The gate is one hundred paces from us!"

I prayed that he would take shelter, but I now had the task of building up speed. The four men at the front would be in the greatest danger for if we moved too quickly then they might be smashed, along with the ram, into the gates.

"Faster!"

All the time we were approaching the gate I was running through everything we needed to do. The log which would form the actual ram would need to be freed from its restraints to allow it to move smoothly. We would have to swing it in unison, and we would have to brace ourselves for oil and fat. The last forty or so paces were fast but not fast enough. Rocks were hurled down at us. We were lucky that none fell before the wheel. Had they done so then the wheel might have broken, and the ram rendered into a useless pile of firewood. When the ram hit the gate, we were all thrown forward.

"Ralph, Roger, cut the restraints. The rest of you hold the ropes. Squires lean in to the ram and take shelter." The ram was filled with my knights and most of my men at arms. As soon as the gate was broken, the squires and pages, not to mention the archers, would be able to shelter under the ram's roof.

"Ready, my lord!"

"Three, two, one, pull!" We pulled back on our ropes. "Release!" We let go and the huge log crashed into the gate which shivered and shook. The light from the first rays of the sun allowed us to see the gate a little more clearly now and, disappointingly, there was no damage. Rocks continued to rain down as we got into the swing of the ram. Pull back, release, pull back, release. It was not until the tenth swing that we saw a crack. It gave us hope and we pulled back harder.

From outside I heard, "Ware fire!"

There was a great temptation to run but we stayed, and the ram swung once more. I heard a crash and felt a wall of heat from our right. The heated material had missed us but as we felt the side of the ram grow hotter it merely added to our fear and it helped our efforts. Three swings later the first light appeared in the gate, but it was at that moment we heard, again, "Ware fire!" This time we felt the oil or fat hit our roof.

"One more swing and then we leave!" I was taking a risk but I felt that it was worth it. This time as soon as we had pulled back and released, I shouted, "Out!" The heat was growing but the uncured hide had done its job and slowed down the burning missile. As we raced out to the shelter of our squires' shields the ram suddenly erupted in a wall of flame. The burning fireball next to the ram had added its flames to the oil poured on top. Thick black smoke billowed up and we could see nothing.

"Shield wall, on me!"

The Perfect Knight

I swung my shield around and drew my sword whilst stepping back five paces. We were still too close to the burning ram. As my men formed up on me with the squires and archers behind, I had a chance to look at the scene from hell before me. Our ram filled the gate and was burning fiercely. The defenders were now pouring seawater to try to douse the fire but as the flames bit into the tree trunk we had used for a ram I knew that it was useless. The wood of the gate was on fire. It would take time but once the fire had died down, we would be able to get into the outer wall of the city. Other rams were hitting the smaller gates. The ram which had been next to us attacking the second main gate had been struck by stones and then fire. It was twenty paces from the gate and I could smell burning flesh. That would have been our fate and I shivered at the thought of such a death. The trebuchets and mangonels continued to hurl their stones at the walls. All along the walls, men were scaling ladders. The fact that so many men had already climbed halfway up told me that King Richard's plan was working. So many attacks on the circumference of the walls had divided the defenders and we were winning although men still plunged to their deaths from the ladders and progress was slow.

King Richard had two huge, God's Own Catapult and Bad Neighbour, and they were proving to be successful and were battering at a section of the wall close to the gate. I saw masonry begin to fall and watched more rams as they were brought up to take advantage of the cracks.

Thomas said, "Father, if we were to wet the cloaks with the water we brought to douse the flames then we might be able to run through the burning gates before they can be repaired."

He was right. When I had been besieged in the Tower of London, we had men with hammers, nails and timbers ready to repair the gates. It had not come to that, but the memory remained.

"It is worth a try." As my son took off his cloak, I shook my head, "Knights and men at arms only." I shrugged, "There is not enough water for more." We placed our cloaks to soak in the pails of water. I had been right and there was barely enough for the knights and the men at arms.

The fire was still too fierce for us to try but I saw that a pair of rams had managed to dislodge some stones in the lower part of the wall. The resultant rock fall and small avalanche stopped the rams but there was now a glacis up which men could run. It was as the first men at arms and spearmen scrambled over the jumble of fallen rock that two stone-throwers, on the inner wall, began to send stones at them. It was almost impossible for the men to negotiate the unstable blocks of masonry and to defend themselves. As the men were knocked back down the slope so arrows and bolts from the second wall were sent at them. The attack was beaten back and the men at the top of the ladders were unable to gain a foothold. The defenders knew that once the battlements were taken then the whole of the first wall was as good as lost.

Sir Robert de Sablé came over to speak to me. He had a blood-stained surcoat; he had been in the thick of the fighting, "Sir Samuel, King Richard intends to lead an assault over the rubble and the breach himself. He asks that you join him."

I shook my head and I saw the look of horror on the face of Sir Robert de Sablé, "I am sure that the king can find others to join him. My men and I intend to take this gate. When the king is ready to attack then have his herald wave his standard. We will charge and that should draw their attention from the breach allowing him to charge." He looked doubtful, "Sir Richard, there are witnesses here who will attest to my words and if we fail then I will bear the consequences. Trust me, I know what we are about."

He nodded and hurried off.

I waved my knights around me, "We have to deliver that which I promised." I looked down at the breach and saw the discussion between the king and Robert de Sablé. The king looked in my direction and I think I discerned a nod but as no one came with further orders then I deemed that my advice had been taken. I said, "Martyn and Gerard, I want you behind me." I saw that Sir William who had been my squire look offended. I smiled, "William, I need two men who have fought with me long before you ceased to be my squire. I know how they move, and they know me. We will all need to be in step as we run. A pile of burnt corpses in the gateway because we tripped will not endear our descendants to the king!"

The others all smiled, and Sir Ralph said, "If you wish, Sir William, you can be with Sir Roger and me in the third rank." William nodded.

We formed up and the rest simply took their places. With me at the front our men, after Sir Ralph, Sir William and Sir Roger were a block of warriors four men wide. It was not before time for I saw the standard waved. "Thomas, sound the horn!"

Even as the horn sounded, alerting the Muslim defenders to our intention we were running using the same chant we had before.

Stockton men fight the fight
Through the day and all the night
The Warlord's sword is straight and true
Stockton's men will come for you
Stockton men fight the fight
Through the day and all the night
The Warlord's sword is straight and true
Stockton's men will come for you

The ram had burned itself out and was now a pile of charred, though still hot ash and charcoal. There were flames licking the lintels and gate posts and one of the gates was at an untidy angle. I held my shield before my face and, holding my breath, ran through what felt like a baker's oven. We could not have charged any sooner. I smelled my cloak as it was singed by the heat, but the water had done its job. I used my right hand to loosen the cloak's clasp and allow it to drop to the ground. The Muslim carpenters were already rushing to repair the gate when we fell amongst them. This was no time for charity and we cut them down before racing towards the gate in the second wall. The two attacks must have prompted the Emir of Acre to reinforce the outer walls and he had opened the gates. Seeing the white garbed crusaders rushing towards them made the reinforcements panic. They should have simply formed lines and attacked us, but they did not. They turned and tried to get back inside the second wall and the safety of the towers. We hurtled after them. King Richard and his attack must have reached the top of the glacis for I saw arrows flying from the walls towards them. They were also loosing at us but with our shields before us, they were doing little harm.

"We take the gate and hold it!"

The order was given but it was easier to say it than to do it. The defenders who had fled were crowding the second gates and impeding those who were trying to close them. I saw a warrior on the battlements shout something and then point. The men before us suddenly stopped and whirled to face us. These were not mailed men but with a coif and helmet, shield, and spear, they could have held us. I lowered my shield for the arrows and bolts had ceased and I swung my sword from behind me. The spear the Muslim thrust at my head was a long one but my speed of reaction meant that I had closed the ground to him quicker than he had anticipated. I deflected it with my shield and swung hard with my sword towards his upper arm. His hand came up, but his smaller shield and my speed meant that it barely stopped the blow and the sword's blade struck the top of his arm. The padded garment he wore took some of the edge from my blade but the steel was so hard that I must have cracked a bone for his arm and shield dropped. I pulled back and this time aimed at his neck. The blood arched to spray both me and the next Muslim. I kept running for they had almost managed to close the gates. Had the gates opened the other way then we might have failed but they were pushing the gates to close them and I simply hurled myself at the narrowing gap. They could not bring the bar down and as Gerard and Martyn threw their bodies at my back the gap widened to the width of my leg and I put my mailed leg there. The poleyn at my knee stopped the gate from closing and when the rest of my men, having killed the other defenders who had tried to slow us, then our weight burst open the gates.

The Perfect Knight

This time we faced not men fleeing but a mob of men who had been trying to close the gates. We slashed stabbed and flailed like men possessed as we tried to hold the enclave we had made. We were a tight circle of steel and when our squires and archers joined us then we had spears to poke at the gaps and arrows to send into faces and unprotected chests.

Behind me, I heard the voice of King Richard, "On! Follow the lion and we will win! See what the hero from the north has done with a handful of men. Show these Austrians and Frenchmen how an Englishman fights!"

We were almost swept from our feet as the king and his reinforcements rudely pushed our squires and archers aside to press into our backs. I believe we might have taken the city there and then but for the voice which told the king that the army of Saladin was pushing back the military orders. I know it galled him, but King Richard could not risk losing our camp. He ordered us to fall back but as we withdrew, he ordered men to render the gates useless. We marched back to our own lines passing both our dead and the mounds of Muslims who had died to stop us. We stopped where we had begun, and King Richard took command of those who had yet to attack and led them to fight Saladin. By the time darkness fell the fires had died out and all fighting had ceased. Men were simply too exhausted to carry on. We did not return to our camp but stayed close to the walls. We ate what we could forage and waited for our orders.

Surprisingly enough there was no battle the next day and no resumption of our attack. There was, instead, an argument amongst the kings, counts and dukes. Conrad of Montferrat had taken offence at King Richard's continued support for Guy of Lusignan and he left the camp with his army to head for Tyre. I suspect, in hindsight, that this was King Richard's plan for that left him largely in control of the Christian camp. It had been his men who had breached the outer gate and so he was allowed to make the decisions. Nor did we fight the next day for the defenders sent forth an embassy to sue for peace. Our attack had obviously made them aware that we would not be defeated as easily as Guy de Lusignan had

The Perfect Knight

been. King Richard rejected the offer and the next day, as dawn broke, and having had two days of rest, the attack was resumed.

The ground was deemed unsuitable for rams and so God's Own Catapult and Bad Neighbour, King Richard's war machines, began their attack once more. This time the whole allied army would attack simultaneously and once more Guy de Lusignan with his Army of Jerusalem and the military orders would defend our camp. We were allocated, along with a hundred knights led by Robert de Sablé, the section of the wall with the gate we had first taken. A second gate further along the wall had been breached by Bad Neighbour and King Richard would attack there. The French king, and Leopold of Austria, led two attacks on two further gates. The stone-throwers hurled stones all morning and as the noon sun arrived and departed we prepared to attack.

This time we attacked in daylight and our mangonels and archers were able to clear the walls. We marched in a solid phalanx of mailed men. The flimsy attempts at repair were thrown down and we entered the outer part of the city. The last time we had been here my men and I had almost managed to take the second gate but in the intervening days, it had been repaired. We did not try to assault but, instead, moved around the city to aid the others attacking their gates. The result was that by the time darkness fell we were encamped inside their outer wall.

My men had been lucky, and we had yet to lose a man. Sir Robert de Sablé had lost three of his household knights and we heard that Philip of Alsace, Count of Flanders and Vermandois, an important noble close to the French king had also died. It drew us closer together and as we camped close to the second gate we had almost taken there was an air of happiness amongst my men. We had almost taken Acre and Jerusalem seemed a tangible target. We spoke of visiting Golgotha and perhaps Bethlehem to see the site of Christ's birth. Robin was particularly excited about that. I suppose that if we had lost men then the air might have been more subdued. More joy came the next day when the Muslim defenders sued for peace. Saladin sent messengers to say that he was happy for talks to take place, but that Conrad of Montferrat had to be a party to the talks. It delayed the actual occupation of the city which took place in the middle of July. Saladin had realised the futility of continuing a fight he had lost. The garrison was taken into captivity and was to be ransomed to Saladin and four standards were hoisted on four towers, France, Jerusalem, Austria and England were all represented. King Richard was incandescent with rage when the standard of a mere duke was hoisted and he sent men to tear it down. It proved the last straw for Duke Leopold. He commanded the remnants of the Imperial Army and whilst not a huge number they were important. They all left the Holy Land immediately and were soon followed by King Philip of France although the French king left his troops to fight the Muslims. His reason was more political. Now that Philip of Alsace, Count of Flanders and Vermandois was dead without an heir, he had to return to France and arrange for a replacement. Alsace and Flanders were both vital to France. It all left King Richard in sole command and he was allowed free rein by Guy de Lusignan and Conrad of Montferrat. It was like pouring pig fat on a fire!

Chapter 21

Arsuf 1191

I had never met Saladin but I knew from speaking to the Hospitallers and Templars, that he was a very clever man. He delayed and vacillated over the ransoms. Perhaps it was a ploy. Whatever the reason we spent the first three weeks of August repairing the damage we had done and improving the defences. As far as I was concerned it did not matter that we had no ransom yet. Our horses were grazing and had been well-rested and the work on the defences was being done by our captives under our supervision. Life was good.

On the 20th of August all that changed. King Richard felt that Saladin was playing games with him and he had all two thousand seven hundred captives decapitated and their heads displayed on the recently repaired walls of Acre. Saladin responded by executing all his Christian prisoners. We were ordered to prepare to break camp and to march south to Jaffa. Even though Saladin and all his army were to the east of us, King Richard was determined to show the world that he had the beating of all enemies of Christianity.

Now that he was unfettered by his two rivals and knowing that the two feuding kings of Jerusalem would follow all his orders made King Richard even more confident. Along with his other leaders, I was summoned to the Great Hall in Acre to be told of our plans. Even though the hall was huge there were just twenty or so men in the hall. This was not the young prince I had ridden beside in France and offered advice, this was a king who knew his own mind and had a clear plan to bring victory. I was flattered that I was greeted personally and given praise.

The Perfect Knight

"Here is the model for all knights! Sir Samuel is the reason we have gained Acre so quickly for it was due to the bravery of the Earl and his men that the first gate was forced. He is now vital to my plans and his men will be at the fore of my plans!"

I saw every face turn to me. Apart from the kings and Richard de Camville who had led our fleet, there was the master of the Hospitallers, Garnier de Nablus as well as the leader of the Norman contingent, Aubrey of Château Galliard. The Master of the order of the Templars was not present and I had already been told that King Richard had decided that this friend, Robert de Sablé would command them. I was amongst elevated company and yet I saw nothing there to intimidate me. My men had been at the fore of the attack and we had succeeded. I nodded at the praise.

"We will head to Jaffa. I know that many of you fear the Ayyubids and the Seljuks who are led by Saladin. It is true that they have a large army and that they will parallel our march down the coast, but I intend for our fleet to follow us too. Men who are hurt can be taken aboard the ships. Food and water can be carried on them. Our enemy does not expect this. Our mounted men will form the left side of the column and will be protected by the men on foot. The knights will be there to deter a determined attack by their horsemen. I have been told by many of the tactics of the enemy. The pinpricks of their horse archers are intended to make us reckless and charge them as happened at Hattin. We will not do so. Our attacks, when we make them, will be considered and every knight will heed the sound of my horn. The military orders know this land and they will be both the vanguard and the rearguard. It will take many days to reach Jaffa for we will move slowly from water to water and travel only in the cool of the morning but reach it we will!"

He showed the sharpness of his mind in the detail he gave to us. By the time we left to brief our men, I was confident that his strategy might work. It was my turn to make my orders clear. "Sir Richard, you will ride to my right and Sir Roger to my left. Sir Ralph and Sir William, you will flank them." They nodded. This was not unusual, and they were comfortable with the formation. I turned to Thomas and the squires, "As the fleet will be with us then you do not need to be with the baggage. You will ride behind your knight. Tom, you will carry the banner and a spare lance for me. Robin will guard Thomas." I saw my son and Robin swell with pride. "Gerard, you will lead the men at arms and shall be behind the squires." I turned lastly to Tam. My orders to him would be hard to bear. "Tam, you and the archers will be with the foot archers. King Richard has decided that you should all be together. That makes sense to me but I would rather you were close to us for I am ever comforted knowing that your arrows will protect us."

I saw the hurt in Tam's eyes, but he would obey orders and he nodded as I continued, "Along with Hugh of Burgundy and the King we have special orders to ride along the whole of the army as we progress south. It will tire our horses, but it is a place of honour. Baldwin le Carron is charged with ensuring that the vanguard and the rearguard do not become isolated. The great standard will be in the waggon behind the English contingent. Like all our standards that must not fall into enemy hands."

The orders having been given then knights and squires drew together. This would be the first time that the squires had ridden to war so close to their knights. The attack on Acre had seen them in danger but they had not been mounted. Now that they were to carry spare lances and spears their role was even more vital. I was not worried about my son, but I sat with him and we went through what he might have to do.

"If we charge the enemy, I may break my spear. If I draw my sword then I need no spear but if I raise my right hand then you must bring Skuld to my side and hand one to me. I know that the standard will be a burden. Can you do both; carry the standard and a spare lance?"

I saw him nod and he said, "It will not be easy, but I will become used to it besides Robin has improved and grown so much that he can carry a second spear for you too."

"And you are the senior squire so you must ensure that the other squires do as you command."

The Perfect Knight

He grinned, "They are my friends and that will be easy."

"Not so, my son, it will be harder for you may have to order them to put their own lives in jeopardy. It would be better if they were not your friends." I saw realisation set in. "We have but eleven thousand men. Saladin has anything from twenty-five thousand to fifty thousand men. Each time we fight each of us must kill three men and the Turks have many Bedouin and Nubian foot soldiers. They may not be mailed but there are many of them and their spears can kill just as easily as an askari sword. This Saladin is clever and he will not waste his elite warriors. Their attacks will be to wound us much as we might wound a wild pig when hunting. They will hope to make us bleed on the road to Jaffa."

We had already ridden part of this road which helped us but our progress was so slow as to resemble that of a snail. We set off before dawn and as soon as the heat became too much we stopped and camped by water. The pattern of attacks became clear that first day. Horse archers galloped in and loosed arrow after arrow. Our archers were brought up to counter the missiles. To my surprise, we had few casualties. Some of our mailed men on foot had up to ten arrows sticking from shields and surcoats but few had wounds. Our crossbows and bows, in contrast, brought down many of the unarmoured horsemen. King Richard's strategy was vindicated. Each day the ones who had endured the attacks were moved to the seaward side and replaced by fresh units. It maintained the morale of the men at arms and spearmen who protected our flank, but the horsemen and the military orders had no such relief and the constant attacks began to take their toll. Our knights wanted to get to grips with the Muslims and fight back! I knew that the king was being wise. Hattin had been a disaster because the knights had been reckless.

It was the second camp where tragedy struck. It was not a sword that caused the death or a fall from a horse but a reptile. We were camping and Robin was clearing stones to place the tent. The snake which had used the stones for its home struck instantly. Thomas was quick-thinking enough to kill the venomous reptile, but the damage had been done. Poor Robin died without even speaking. All our men were upset but Martyn was especially distraught as it had been he who brought him to seek a place with me. We buried him there under a pile of stones and a cross fashioned from two spears. Martyn and I spoke over his grave, but it made us all realise that this was a hostile land and death could come in any shape or form. We rode silently that next day and Robin's hackney was a constant reminder of our dead page. That day was a dark day. Jack had died but it had been fighting and for a warrior that was acceptable. To be killed by a slithering reptile was not and it dampened our spirits as we headed to battle.

We nearly had an early disaster when the rearguard was crossing a defile. The military wisdom of King Richard was demonstrated for it was our turn to ride to the rear and seeing the Muslim horsemen preparing to attack the disordered knights as they crossed the ravine, I ordered an immediate charge. Though we were few in number, we had complete surprise on our side. With lances at the ready, we ploughed into the rear of the horsemen. It took two thrusts and two felled Turks for me to lose my lance and I held out my hand. Thomas replaced it so quickly that I was able to spear a third before the enemy fled. It was our first combat, and I was pleased that all had gone well. Most importantly the squires had shown that they were calm as well as well trained.

Saladin and his army reached Caesarea Palestinae before we did and from then on he and his army were ahead of us. Their attacks continued each day. We lost them briefly when we passed Mount Carmel and the Muslims had to take the longer route on the landward side but they were still ahead of us. By the end of the first week in September, we were approaching Arsuf and our journey became easier as we passed through, for the first time, a forest. We learned from our military orders that it was twelve miles long and brought respite not only from the sun but also the attacks of horsemen.

After crossing a ford and passing halfway through the forest we stopped and camped by the river we called

The Perfect Knight

Rochetaillée. We were also protected by a marsh and the biting insects were a small price to pay. We had taken many days, weeks even, to travel the short distance down the coast but we now knew that we were more than halfway to our destination. Once we passed Arsuf then it would be an easier journey.

Mordaf woke me in the middle of the night, "Sir Samuel, it was too hot to sleep and I wandered through the woods." He smiled, "It is so long since I walked in the trees at night that I had forgotten what a pleasure it was. I heard noises beyond the woods and when I explored, I found the Turks camped there, just beyond the woods and they have sentries in the woods."

"They have dogged our trail since we left Acre, Mordaf. It is to be expected." Every day had seen men of both armies dying as the Muslims attempted to make us forget our discipline and charge them.

"Lord, they have found a plain which will suit their horsemen. They are camped along our line of march."

I knew what that meant. They could be ready to attack us as soon as we began our march and after a day with no raids, we might not be as vigilant. "Thank you."

I hurried to the king's tent. My position afforded me the courtesy of the sentry waking the king. He was not angry for I think he knew I would not wake him without a good reason. "King Richard, my scout reports the Turks are waiting for us in the plain between the wooded hills and the sea. The ruins of Arsuf lie just south of us. Mordaf believes they are camped in battle order."

He rubbed his beard, "That would make sense. We will rouse the camp an hour earlier than normal. If we are forced to stop again then we can use the ruins of Arsuf for shelter. You have done well, Sir Samuel. I will have our archers and some of our crossbows guard the baggage train and use the bulk of our crossbows to defend our infantry."

It was a good plan although I thought my archers would be better used where they could loose their bodkins at the mailed askari. It would be the light horsemen and archers who would attack the baggage train.

The Perfect Knight

Most of the army was quite happy to be roused early as it meant less time marching in the heat. This time there was the prospect of a mere six miles or so before we could rest. As usual, our task was to ride to the landward side of the men at arms and spearmen. Our mail, shields and helmets afforded us good protection and the padded caparison we used on our horses made it less likely that they would be wounded. As we began to move south with the Knights Templar in the van, we heard the sounds of cymbals, drums, gongs, and horns as the Turks were roused. As we left the wood, we spied their campfires and I saw that Mordaf had a good eye, they were camped in line of battle. The horses were tethered closer to the hills and even as we began our ponderous move south, I heard hooves as some of the Turkish regiments formed up, ready to attack. The sound of the gongs, drums, cymbals, and horns did not cease when the camp was roused. They continued throughout the battle almost as though they were using it as some sort of weapon.

King Richard and his household knights met me, "Sir Samuel, I will stay close to the van. Go to the rear and make sure that the baggage train moves as quickly as it can."

Even as I led my men north the skirmishers began their attack using the woods for cover. Bedouin, Sudanese archers and the light Turkish horse archers swarmed around the men at arms on foot. Shields were turned to face the enemy and spears poked out from behind. Mindful that our task was to get to the baggage train I commanded my men to charge some of the skirmishers. Unlike our men, they did not fight in rigid and regimented lines and our solid attack of mailed horsemen swept them away. It was like swatting away flies. They moved while we were there but as we headed north towards the baggage train, they returned to harass and harry the men on foot.

As I passed Sir James d'Avesnes he pleaded with me, "For the love of God, Sir Samuel, beg the king the opportunity to charge these Turks. Does he not think we have the beating of them?"

I waved my arm, "He has a plan, my lord and it is working. Be patient and heed your orders."

The Perfect Knight

It was as I neared the baggage train that I saw that Saladin had made the force that attacked the rear the largest of his many attacks. It was a cunning plan for the men had to march backwards and they lost cohesion. Already the Hospitallers, crossbows, and archers were losing men. Saladin hoped that we would reinforce the rear and with such small numbers when we did that then inevitably, we would weaken our line somewhere else. A large swarm of horse archers and light cavalry suddenly fell upon the men of the rearguard. I spurred Storm Bringer for it was our archers who were there. I used my spear to stab into the backs and sides of men who wore no mail. Each strike was successful, and men were wounded or killed but there were so many of them and they seemed to fight with a reckless abandon that we could make little difference and then they fell amongst my archers. I could do nothing about it for they were too far away. I saw Tam the Hawker and the rest of my men use their bows as long as they could and then when the Turks were upon them, they first swung the long war bow as a pole weapon and when that was rendered useless draw their short swords to fight with that. None thought to run. They fought to the bitter end knowing that to run would not save them. Some of the Angevin crossbowmen did. It made little difference as they were hunted and slain by arrows in the back. I spurred Storm Bringer to try to save at least one of my men and I reached Tam but it was just as he was speared. The Turk who ended his life had but a moment of glory before I rammed my lance so hard into his back that it came out of the front. I held my arm out and Thomas placed a second one there. We had been too late to save our men, but they were avenged as we slaughtered their killers and bought some respite for Garnier de Nablus and his Hospitallers. I reined in my horse and looked at the bodies of the archers who had followed me to the Holy Land. At least Richard son of Aelric and the others who had chosen to stay in Stockton would live. As for the rest...

A single horn sounded from closer to the south and I had to heed it. I had no time to mourn my dead. King Richard needed me. Six clear blasts from the horn would have meant that the whole army was to attack while one meant that we were to get to his side as quickly as we could. We raced as fast as we could and I reined in next to the king, "The baggage?"

"It is safe, but we have lost many archers and crossbows."

He nodded, "So long as we have not lost knights then all is well. The enemy horses will soon tire and then it will be time to unleash our horsemen."

I did not share the king's opinion. To me, the archers and, indeed, every warrior and sergeant we had brought were as valuable as the knights but I held my tongue.

The short rest was helping us and it was as we peered along the battlefield that we saw and heard the Knights Hospitallers suddenly sounded the charge and with cries of 'St George!' the rearguard charged the Turks. The move had not been ordered, the king and I knew that, but it had to be supported. If the Hospitallers charged and were defeated, then we would lose both the baggage and our left flank.

King Richard shook his head, "Why cannot men obey orders? They were simple enough." He turned to his squire, "Sound six clear blasts on the horn. Sir Samuel, watch my flank. You, at least, will obey my commands."

"Aye, my lord!"

I knew that we, by our very position would be at the fore of the charge and that when the Turks saw our move, they would attempt to attack our right flank. We charged after the king. My men were disciplined and kept in formation. It was comforting to know, and I was able to fight more freely knowing that my right flank was protected by two of my knights and that my son was protected by my men at arms. The Ayyubid horsemen had seen the Hospitallers' charge and they counterlcharged. It meant our first blows struck the left side of the horsemen and we came not only from their flank but their rear. I could already see Saladin's leaders responding to the move and ordering their own men to charge us. The simple clear lines men speak of after battles are nothing like the reality of the interwoven mêlées that were the reality.

The Perfect Knight

I pulled back my lance and lunged at every enemy I saw. These were not mailed men with whom we fought, and the metal lancehead always found flesh and riders were thrown from their horses. We did not have it all our own way for there were simply too many of our enemies packed into too small a space. Storm Bringer was wounded by a spear meant for me. The thrust was not deep but it hurt and was bloody. It merely angered my warhorse, and my spear skewered the horseman who had tried to hurt me. A block of men turned their horses to countercharge us. I saw the Ayyubid warrior facing me pull back his spear and I did the same. Storm Bringer was snapping and biting at the smaller Turkish horse and as my lance drove into his rider's chest the Ayyubid spear came up. It still struck me and drew blood, but the wound was in the shoulder. It hurt but I could still fight. As the Turkish spear fell to the ground, I pulled back my own lance to strike at the second warrior who was trying to stab at Sir Roger. He tumbled from his horse and Sir Roger stabbed another Turk with his lance. A moment of indecision could result in death. I ignored the blood dripping down my arm as we passed through the Ayyubid horsemen who had tried to stop us and found ourselves closer to the king. We ploughed our way through the Turks to get to our place of honour by his side.

King Richard had a reputation for recklessness but that day I was proud to follow him for although he fought fiercely there was control and as we neared the Hospitallers to save what remained of the warriors of the military order he reined in. I did so too, and it was as I turned that I saw the price we had already paid. Our squires remained as did Gerard and Martyn but only four other men at arms remained alive. Along with the losses to my archers Cleveland had paid a heavy price already. I had not seen any fall. This was a bloody battle. Other northern knights had followed my banner and I felt proud that they had done so yet I was sad at the men from Stockton that I had lost.

I saw that Thomas was still with me and that he had his sword in hand, "I see that you are still there, my son."

"Aye, but I have yet to strike a blow in anger."

The Perfect Knight

I pointed to the banner, "That is a weapon that kills yet sheds no blood."

There was a sudden shout from ahead and Sir Richard said, "Sir James d'Avesnes has led his men too far! They are being slaughtered."

I watched the King as he turned his men to go to the aid of his foolish friend and I was about to order my men to follow him when Thomas shouted, "Lord! Ayyubid! It is the Sultan's bodyguard; they seek to take the king!"

I turned and saw askari and horse archers charging towards King Richard and his knights as they charged to save Sir James. I recognised the banner of Saladin's nephew, Taqi al-Din, who led the bodyguard of Saladin. If his men struck the flank of King Richard then our king might be lost and with him, I knew, the whole army would disintegrate. It would be a sacrifice, but I had to put my handful of men between the two bands of men. By slowing down their attack then the king might have a chance. Crying "King Richard, God and England!" I led my men in a last suicidal charge. This was the result of my training with my father and grandfather. There was always a right thing to do and a true knight did not evaluate the chances of survival. If he lived then God was with him.

I wheeled Storm Bringer and led my men to their doom. The line of the Warlord would end here on the plain of Arsuf, but the king might live and in him lay hope. He was not the foolish young rebel who had fought his father and my grandfather. This campaign had shown that when he commanded, he was a warrior that men could follow. Our sacrifice would give England a king they could follow.

We crashed into the Turks. Each wore a cuirass beneath their robes and a lance would do nothing against the metal plate. I aimed at the head of the first Turk and although his spear sliced into my side driving through the mail and into my flesh, my lance knocked him from his saddle. I drew my sword. Despite his wound Storm Bringer was eager for battle and he took me deep into the enemy horde. It slowed them down but meant that soon I was surrounded for I was ahead of the knights of the valley. I wondered as I raised my sword

The Perfect Knight

to strike down at a Turk if Thomas lived yet. When I felt a sharp pain in my back I knew that my protection was gone and I had been wounded. I pulled back on Storm Bringer's reins and he reared. His flailing hooves cracked into the skull of the Turkish horse and bought me a few seconds to assess my position. I watched as Sir Richard of Hartburn was speared and slid from his horse. Even as I slashed at the unhorsed askari, from the corner of my eye I saw my former squire, William, die as two askari speared him simultaneously. He had no chance. My sword smashed into the bayda, the helmet, of the askari and he died. I reared Storm Bringer again but from my left, another spear was rammed into my side and Storm Bringer was speared in his flank. My horse stumbled and my wounds meant I could not keep my saddle. I landed heavily and my shield was torn from my grasp. The last spear had driven deep into my body and I felt the blood flowing freely. I had three wounds and I knew that at least two were mortal. I used my sword to try to help me to stand but I had no strength and I fell to the ground. I lay there waiting for death when I heard a voice.

"Lie still father, I will protect you."

I looked up and saw my son plant my standard in the ground and stand astride me with his sword in hand. The blood of the Warlord would stain this part of the Holy Land for all time. All around were the screams and clash of battle. Men cursed and pleaded in death. I would not do so. I was dying and I would slip into the eternal night silently for a scream might only distract Thomas, the last of our line. I tried to slash my sword at the Turk who ran at my son, but my hand would not grip. I was helpless and I saw the Turk and an eager companion come at him with spears levelled. The dead and the dying meant they had no clear path. My son was brave and he did not deserve to die like this and it was not fair. A squire should not be in the fore of a battle. I cursed Sir James and the Hospitallers. I could not lay this at the feet of the king. His plan had been a good one. I felt my eyes dim and all I could do was offer my son words, "Fight them, my son! You are of the Warlord's blood!"

The Perfect Knight

Darkness came over me and all sounds disappeared. For a brief moment, I saw the face of my father and the Warlord and then all went black.

Epilogue

King Richard

Sir Samuel of Stockton, the Earl of Cleveland and all the men he had led lay dead. I did not know of the deaths until the enemy had fled. They had acquitted themselves well and only seventeen of Saladin's bodyguards remained alive. The earl had not slain them all but by holding them, briefly, then my knights had been able to drive them from the field. From the edge of disaster, Sir Samuel's action had brought victory. I had seen his son, still grasping the standard and another squire from Sir Samuel's conroi bravely defying the Turks. They were a symbol of what we could do. It had been a great victory; over thirty-two emirs' bodies were found, and we slew more than seven thousand Turks. Hattin was avenged and, as I rode towards the gryphon standard, I looked forward to taking Jaffa and then the city of Jerusalem. When I rode into Jerusalem, I would have the gryphon standard of Cleveland with me. England would not forget Sir Samuel.

The End

Glossary

Al-Andalus- Spain
Angevin- the people of Anjou, especially the ruling family
Battle- a formation in war (a modern battalion)
Bachelor knight- an unattached knight
Banneret- a single knight
Burn- stream (Scottish)
Butts- targets for archers
Cadge- the frame upon which hunting birds are carried (by a codger- hence the phrase old codger being the old man who carries the frame)
Caparison- a surcoat for a horse; often padded for protection
Captain- a leader of archers
Chausses - mail leggings. (They were separate- imagine lady's stockings rather than tights!)
Cheap- Anglo Saxon market- hence Cheapside
Chevauchée- a raid by mounted men
Conroi- A group of knights fighting together. The smallest unit of the period
Courser- warhorse
Demesne- estate
Destrier- warhorse
Doxy- prostitute
Fissebourne- Fishburn County Durham
Fess- a horizontal line in heraldry
Galloglass- Irish mercenaries
Gambeson- a padded tunic worn underneath mail. When worn by an archer they came to the waist. It was more of a quilted jacket, but I have used the term freely
Gonfanon- A standard used in medieval times (Also known as a Gonfalon in Italy)
Herterpol- Hartlepool (The place where the stags drink)
Hovel- a temporary shelter used by knights and men at arms on campaign
Mansio- staging houses along Roman Roads
Mare anglicum – English Channel
Mêlée- a medieval fight between knights
Mormaer- A Scottish lord and leader

The Perfect Knight

Mummer- an actor from a medieval tableau
Musselmen- Muslims
Nithing- A man without honour (Saxon)
Nomismata- a gold coin equivalent to an aureus
Outremer- the kingdoms of the Holy Land
Palfrey- a riding horse
Poitevin- the language of Aquitaine
Pyx- a box containing a holy relic (Shakespeare's Pax from Henry V)
Refuge- a safe area for squires and captives (tournaments)
Sauve qui peut – Every man for himself (French)
Sergeant-a leader of a company of men at arms
Surcoat- a tunic worn over mail or armour
Sumpter- packhorse
Ventail – a piece of mail that covered the neck and the lower face

Background to the novel

This really is the end of the series that began with English Knight. It is a work of fiction set against a historically, generally, background. For those who have read all of the books in the series, thank you for travelling this road. As you can see I have taken out the end section. It had grown too much and can now be found on my website under background to the Anarchy novels.

The major events that happened in the book, even the ridiculous ride by King Henry from Le Mans north only to turn around and retrace his steps to go to Chinon happened. The fleet which supported the Portuguese was also a historical fact. The events in Cleveland and in England are the product of my imagination.

If you have enjoyed this saga and wish to see what happens next then Thomas, Sir Samuel's son is the hero of my Border Knight series which begins with Sword for Hire.

Books used in the research:

- Chronicles of the age of chivalry- Elizabeth Hallam
- The Varangian Guard- 988-1453 Raffael D'Amato
- Saxon Viking and Norman- Terence Wise
- The Walls of Constantinople AD 324-1453-Stephen Turnbull
- Byzantine Armies- 886-1118- Ian Heath
- The Age of Charlemagne-David Nicolle
- The Normans- David Nicolle
- Norman Knight AD 950-1204- Christopher Gravett
- The Norman Conquest of the North- William A Kappelle
- The Knight in History- Francis Gies
- The Norman Achievement- Richard F Cassady
- Knights- Constance Brittain Bouchard
- Knight Templar 1120-1312 -Helen Nicholson
- Feudal England: Historical Studies on the Eleventh and Twelfth Centuries- J. H. Round

The Perfect Knight

- Armies of the Crusades- Helen Nicholson
- Knight of Outremer 1187- 1344 - David Nicholle
- Crusader Castles in the Holy Land- David Nicholle
- The Crusades- David Nicholle
- Bamburgh Castle Heritage group
- Warkworth Castle- English Heritage Guide
- The Times Atlas of World History
- Old Series Ordnance Survey Maps #93 Middlesbrough
- Old Series Ordnance Survey Maps #81 Alnwick and Morpeth
- Old Series Ordnance Survey Maps #92 Barnard Castle

For those who like authentic maps, the last two maps are part of a series now available. They are the first Government produced maps of the British Isles. Great Britain, apart from the larger conurbations, was the same as it had been 800 years earlier.

I also discovered a good website http://orbis.stanford.edu/. This allows a reader to plot any two places in the Roman world and if you input the mode of transport you wish to use and the time of year it will calculate how long it would take you to travel the route. I have used it for all of my books up to the eighteenth century as the transportation system was roughly the same. The Romans would have been quicker! I used it in this book and according to Orbis the journey from London to Rouen would have taken 2.7 days! In summer it would have been 3.1! it is an impressive resource. It explains why Henry gets to and from Normandy so quickly.

Griff Hosker
October 2021

The Perfect Knight

Other books by Griff Hosker

If you enjoyed reading this book, then why not read another one by the author?

Ancient History

The Sword of Cartimandua Series
(Germania and Britannia 50 A.D. – 128 A.D.)
Ulpius Felix- Roman Warrior (prequel)
The Sword of Cartimandua
The Horse Warriors
Invasion Caledonia
Roman Retreat
Revolt of the Red Witch
Druid's Gold
Trajan's Hunters
The Last Frontier
Hero of Rome
Roman Hawk
Roman Treachery
Roman Wall
Roman Courage

The Wolf Warrior series
(Britain in the late 6th Century)
Saxon Dawn
Saxon Revenge
Saxon England
Saxon Blood
Saxon Slayer
Saxon Slaughter
Saxon Bane
Saxon Fall: Rise of the Warlord
Saxon Throne
Saxon Sword

Medieval History

The Dragon Heart Series
Viking Slave
Viking Warrior
Viking Jarl
Viking Kingdom
Viking Wolf
Viking War
Viking Sword
Viking Wrath
Viking Raid
Viking Legend
Viking Vengeance
Viking Dragon
Viking Treasure
Viking Enemy
Viking Witch
Viking Blood
Viking Weregeld
Viking Storm
Viking Warband
Viking Shadow
Viking Legacy
Viking Clan
Viking Bravery

The Norman Genesis Series
Hrolf the Viking
Horseman
The Battle for a Home
Revenge of the Franks
The Land of the Northmen
Ragnvald Hrolfsson
Brothers in Blood
Lord of Rouen
Drekar in the Seine
Duke of Normandy
The Duke and the King

The Perfect Knight

Danelaw
(England and Denmark in the 11th Century)
Dragon Sword
Oathsword

New World Series
Blood on the Blade
Across the Seas
The Savage Wilderness
The Bear and the Wolf
Erik The Navigator

The Vengeance Trail

The Reconquista Chronicles
Castilian Knight
El Campeador
The Lord of Valencia

The Aelfraed Series
(Britain and Byzantium 1050 A.D. - 1085 A.D.)
Housecarl
Outlaw
Varangian

The Anarchy Series England 1120-1180
English Knight
Knight of the Empress
Northern Knight
Baron of the North
Earl
King Henry's Champion
The King is Dead
Warlord of the North
Enemy at the Gate
The Fallen Crown
Warlord's War

The Perfect Knight

Kingmaker
Henry II
Crusader
The Welsh Marches
Irish War
Poisonous Plots
The Princes' Revolt
Earl Marshal
The Perfect Knight

Border Knight
1182-1300
Sword for Hire
Return of the Knight
Baron's War
Magna Carta
Welsh Wars
Henry III
The Bloody Border
Baron's Crusade
Sentinel of the North
War in the West
Debt of Honour
The Blood of the Warlord (Feb 2022)

Sir John Hawkwood Series
France and Italy 1339- 1387
Crécy: The Age of the Archer
Man At Arms
The White Company

Lord Edward's Archer
Lord Edward's Archer
King in Waiting
An Archer's Crusade
Targets of Treachery
The Great Cause (April 2022)

Struggle for a Crown

The Perfect Knight

1360- 1485
Blood on the Crown
To Murder a King
The Throne
King Henry IV
The Road to Agincourt
St Crispin's Day
The Battle For France
The Last Knight
Queen's Knight

Tales from the Sword I
(Short stories from the Medieval period)

Tudor Warrior series
England and Scotland in the late 14th and early 15th century
Tudor Warrior

Conquistador
England and America in the 16th Century
Conquistador

Modern History

The Napoleonic Horseman Series
Chasseur à Cheval
Napoleon's Guard
British Light Dragoon
Soldier Spy
1808: The Road to Coruña
Talavera
The Lines of Torres Vedras
Bloody Badajoz
The Road to France
Waterloo

The Lucky Jack American Civil War series
Rebel Raiders

The Perfect Knight

Confederate Rangers
The Road to Gettysburg

The British Ace Series
1914
1915 Fokker Scourge
1916 Angels over the Somme
1917 Eagles Fall
1918 We will remember them
From Arctic Snow to Desert Sand
Wings over Persia

Combined Operations series
1940-1945
Commando
Raider
Behind Enemy Lines
Dieppe
Toehold in Europe
Sword Beach
Breakout
The Battle for Antwerp
King Tiger
Beyond the Rhine
Korea
Korean Winter

Tales from the Sword II
(Short stories from the Modern period)

Other Books
Great Granny's Ghost (Aimed at 9-14-year-old young people)

For more information on all of the books then please visit the author's website at www.griffhosker.com where there is a link to contact him or visit his Facebook page: GriffHosker at Sword Books

The Perfect Knight

Printed in Great Britain
by Amazon